Taryn Nikolic

Counting On *Forever*

A Topaz Falls Novel

COUNTING ON
Forever

A Topaz Falls Novel
Book 5 of the Series

TARYN NIKOLIC

Copyright

Copyright © 2024 by Taryn Nikolic

No part of this publication may be reproduced, distributed, or transmitted in any form or by any means, including photocopying, recording, or other electronic or mechanical methods, without the prior written permission of the publisher, except as permitted by U.S. copyright law. For permission requests, contact www.tarynnikolic.com.

First edition November 2024

The story, all names, characters, and incidents portrayed in this production are fictitious. No identification with actual persons (living or deceased), places, buildings, and products are intended or should be inferred. Any reference to media or famous people is for reference.

Book Cover by Amanda Winsor | @caffeinereadreview
Line Editing by L.A.A.
Copy Edits by Paige Kraft | paigekedits.com
Proofreading by T.J.A.

Library of Congress Control Number: 2024919726

KDP Paperback: ISBN 9798339376330
Barnes & Noble Paperback: ISBN 9798331497781
eBook ASIN: B0DH5P6LZ9
IngramSparks: ISBN 979-8-3304-8921-3

If you wish for the author to participate in a live event, please reach out via www.tarynnikolic.com

Manufactured in the United States of America
Washington State

Dedication

To anyone who suffers from scars,
Whether they are physical, mental, or emotional,
May you heal with each passing day.
~ Love to Topaz ~

Congratulations Smiley on completing your chemotherapy!
You are one of the strongest people I know.
Your family loves you.

Potential Triggers

Although this is a small-town contemporary romance, I don't want to catch any readers off guard. The following issues are discussed, which may be a trigger for some people. Please proceed with caution if these are sensitive topics for you.

Learning disabilities

Con artist ex

Burn trauma

Childhood cancer

Genetic variants

Infertility

Pregnancy after loss

Injured parent

Sugar & Spice

The following chapters have spice beyond kissing.

Chapter 17 – Page 163
Chapter 24 – Pages 220-222
Chapter 31 – Pages 274-277
Chapter 41 – Page 354-355

Playlist

Let It Burn | Shaboozey | 3:26
I Hope It All Works Out | Mark Ambor | 2:47
Girls Like Us | Zoe Wees | 3:09
Why Can't Love Be The Reason | Shaboozey | 3:09
Way Way Back | Luke Bryan | 3:19
Austin (Boots Stop Workin') | Dasha | 2:51
Anabelle | Shaboozey | 3:06
Austin | Blake Shelton | 3:50
Bad Apple | Mary Kutter | 2:56
Scarecrows | Luke Bryan | 3:36
Control | Zoe Wees | 3:50
Come A Little Closer | Dierks Bentley | 4:41
Harvest Time | Luke Bryan | 3:27
Still in Love with You | Sade | 4:24
That's My Kind Of Night | Luke Bryan | 3:10
Tall Boy | Shaboozey | 2:20
Roller Coaster | Luke Bryan | 4:19
Hold My Hand | Lady Gaga | 3:45
Hold Me Like You Used To | Zoe Wees | 3:06
Strip It Down | Luke Bryan | 4:01
Eyes On You | Chase Rice | 3:02
Lips Of An Angel | Hinder | 4:21
My Love | Shaboozey | 3:15
Let's Be Us Again | Lonestar | 3:53
Back To December | Taylor Swift | 4:54
Stay (I Missed You) | Lisa Loeb | 3:04
Gonna Love You | Parmalee | 2:58
One | Ed Sheeran | 4:12

Perfect For Me | Bradley Marshall | 3:05
A Bar Song (Tipsy) | Shaboozey | 2:51
Stay | Florida Georgia Line | 3:19
Hair Toss, Arms Crossed | Mark Ambor | 2:37
Second Chance | Shinedown | 3:42
Scars To Your Beautiful | Alessia Cara | 3:42
The Man I Want to Be | Chris Young | 3:27
Just the Way | Parmalee & Blanco Brown | 3:13
I Won't Give Up | Jason Mraz | 4:00
Whatever It Takes | Lifehouse | 3:27
Belong Together | Mark Ambor | 2:28
Make You Feel My Love | Adele | 3:32

https://www.tarynnikolic.com/playlists

Available as a playlist on Spotify

Table of Contents

POTENTIAL TRIGGERS	7
SUGAR & SPICE	7
PLAYLIST	9
TABLE OF CONTENTS	11
PROLOGUE - JULIA	13
CHAPTER 1 - JULIA	17
CHAPTER 2 - DECLAN	27
CHAPTER 3 - JULIA	37
CHAPTER 4 - DECLAN	47
CHAPTER 5 - JULIA	55
CHAPTER 6 - DECLAN	63
CHAPTER 7 - JULIA	71
CHAPTER 8 - DECLAN	83
CHAPTER 9 - JULIA	91
CHAPTER 10 - DECLAN	99
CHAPTER 11 - JULIA	109
CHAPTER 12 - DECLAN	117
CHAPTER 13 - JULIA	125
CHAPTER 14 - DECLAN	133
CHAPTER 15 - JULIA	141
CHAPTER 16 - DECLAN	149
CHAPTER 17 - DECLAN	157
CHAPTER 18 - JULIA	167
CHAPTER 19 - DECLAN	175
CHAPTER 20 - DECLAN	181
CHAPTER 21 - DECLAN	187
CHAPTER 22 - JULIA	195
CHAPTER 23 - DECLAN	203
CHAPTER 24 - JULIA	213

CHAPTER 25 - JULIA	225
CHAPTER 26 - JULIA	235
CHAPTER 27 - DECLAN	241
CHAPTER 28 - DECLAN	249
CHAPTER 29 - JULIA	257
CHAPTER 30 - DECLAN	265
CHAPTER 31 - DECLAN	271
CHAPTER 32 - JULIA	281
CHAPTER 33 - DECLAN	289
CHAPTER 34 - DECLAN	299
CHAPTER 35 - JULIA	309
CHAPTER 36 - DECLAN	315
CHAPTER 37 - JULIA	323
CHAPTER 38 - JULIA	331
CHAPTER 39 - DECLAN	337
CHAPTER 40 - DECLAN	345
CHAPTER 41 - JULIA	353
CHAPTER 42 - DECLAN	361
CHAPTER 43 - JULIA	371
EPILOGUE - ELIN	379
DECLAN'S APPLE PIZZA	387
JULIA'S APPLE GRILLED CHEESE	389
ACKNOWLEDGMENTS	390

Prologue
Julia
Thursday, May 23

The jacquard curtains of my parents' flat hang ominously around the picture window that perfectly frames the Eiffel Tower. My fingers tighten along the edges of the papers lying precariously on the edge of my knees as I run the corner of the top sheet underneath my thumbnail.

How could Chauncy do this to me? He promised me the world was at our fingertips. Now the only definitive things about me are the marks left from the fire, marring my right arm. Tugging at the cuff of my shirt sleeve, I cover up the puckered red skin, still healing with each passing day. I was lucky to survive the fire. They still aren't sure whether or not he knew I was in the office that evening.

My heart still wants to believe he didn't know and it was an accident, but the reports tell me I'm wrong. The document on my lap has the words *accélérateur, point d'origine, allumage,* and *incendie criminel*. Investigators discovered traces of an accelerant at a point of origin. If he'd accidentally left a towel too close to the stove, there wouldn't be traces of an accelerant. My soul needs to believe that he thought I was already gone. I'm not sure my heart will survive if I accept that the man I thought loved me to the *lune et retour* wanted me dead for an insurance payout.

The second document is what makes my good hand violently shake. Chauncy is gone. When investigators went to our flat, he had already packed up what he wanted and left. I was still unconscious at the hospital. He probably hopped on the first train out of Paris with enough money to start fresh. The word *escroc* jumps off the page, forcing me to close my eyes. Did I really let a con man into my life, home, and business? It would appear so.

My right side aches as thoughts of the scars trigger phantom pains that may never leave. The skin feels extra tight as a bead of sweat drips down my chest. The summer day is hot and humid, and the air conditioning unit isn't pumping enough cool air to bring the room to a comfortable temperature. I scoot to the edge of the velvet couch, awkwardly perching on the cushion. I fear I'll crumble under the weight of the information if I allow myself to feel more comfortable.

"What did the police say?" my dad asks, his voice rumbling through the quiet surrounding the room. With the windows closed, the din of traffic on the street below is white noise.

Hot shame floods my bloodstream. My parents never liked Chauncy, but they put up with him for my sake. "They can't find him. Our accounts were drained. Nothing is left. The insurance policy for the patisserie was in his name. I was so stupid to have trusted him. They wrote he was a con man, and they found accelerant in the kitchen," I reply, closing my eyes so I don't stutter with the clogged emotions tainting my vocal cords.

"How could you have known, angel? He was your fiancé. You'd been together for almost a year. Everything in your heart told you he was a good guy. He had us all fooled," Dad says, sitting in the chair across from me. He's backlit against the window, the afternoon light framing his lean frame in a halo of yellow. His salt and pepper hair reflects the light like tinsel on a Christmas tree.

"I should have listened to you when you told me you had a bad feeling about him," I mutter.

"Sweetheart, your father and I can help you open something else. Maybe we can sell this flat and move to the countryside," my mom says, approaching me slowly.

Hot tears burn at the back of my eyes. They've worked hard to get to this point in their lives where they have a gorgeous flat in the heart of the city, with a view anyone would envy. I can't ask them to upend their lives. Mom is working her dream job as a copyist at the Louvre, and Dad is a real estate agent.

"Okay, well, what about—" Mom starts to say.

I know exactly what she will say, and I don't think I can go there. Not now, not after what I did to him and to us. Holding up a hand, I plead with her to stop. A new wave of anguish engulfs me as my shoulders shake and freshly shed tears track down my cheeks.

"No, Mom. It isn't an option," I whisper as a tear burns a trail down my jaw, plunking onto the paperwork.

"Sweetheart, look at me," Mom says, grasping my shoulders gently and avoiding the most sensitive places on my upper arm. "Rita never had kids. She always told me the year you spent as a foreign exchange student, living with her your senior year, was the happiest time of her life. She left everything to you when she passed away. You know she would want you to reopen her bakery and bring your touch of French pastry arts to Topaz Falls. You had nothing but wonderful things to say about the town and the people the entire time you were there. She missed you terribly since you left and never understood why you wouldn't come for a visit. To be honest, I don't either. I remember you were smitten with the Ambarsan boy." She tries to smirk at me but knows this is a subject I keep locked down.

I was smitten with the Ambarsan boy. She's right about that, but our futures didn't align, and he deserved to have everything he dreamed of and more. I couldn't offer him that life, and although it pained me to walk away, it was the right thing to do. I don't know if I can return there, not knowing if he's married with kids and in love with someone else.

"Angel?" My dad's voice cuts through my trip down memory lane. Sniffing, I swipe my hand across my eyes. "I believe in you and your baking. I love having you here, but your happiness is more important. When you are making pastries, you are in your happy place. Please reopen the bakery with the money your aunt left you. If, after three months, you hate living in Montana, then sell the house and the bakery and move home. Her will stipulated the sale could take place after a three-month trial period."

Standing up, I set the report on the glass coffee table and pace like a caged tiger. Only three months. I could do that. Stay for ninety days, avoid the Ambarsan family, then sell and start over in Paris, using the funds to open a new and improved patisserie. It will be one that I own all on my own, with no partners or investors to screw it up.

After eight years away, it looks like I'm going back to Topaz Falls. Like a Phoenix, I will rise from the ashes and overcome all that Chauncy did to me. I only hope my heart can survive running into my first love, Declan Ambarsan.

Chapter 1
Julia
Monday, September 23

With my luggage in hand, I finally stride through the red double doors, which have been taunting me for the last fifteen minutes as I attempted to gain the courage to step out into the crisp Montana air. Air I haven't breathed in eight years. Closing my eyes to fight the wave of nausea threatening to roll my stomach into knots, I take hesitant steps toward the curb. When I left here, I had every intention of never coming back, hoping to bury all my problems in the bustle of tourism surrounding life in Paris. It did the trick until my life imploded earlier this year.

Before I forget, I shoot off a message to Mom and Dad, letting them know I arrived safely. It might be the middle of the night, but I can guarantee Mom's sleeping with the phone on her pillow awaiting my message. Tucking the phone back in my pocket, I steel myself and square my shoulders. My eyes dart around looking aimlessly for my ride. I completely forgot to ask what make and model of car Britt would be driving.

A teal Jeep skids to a stop before me, startling me out of my almost panic attack. A mop of blonde curls leaps out the driver's side door and rushes me. Wrapping her arms around me, she squeezes me tight, comically rocking me from side to side. I wince when her arm brushes against my right side. My skin has healed in the last few months, but the memories remain fresh and the delicate new skin still prickles.

"Julia? Frenchy! You look amazing!" Britt exclaims, bubbling around me and thankfully distracting my mind.

"Hey, Britt. It's good to see you too, *mon ami*," I reply, giving her two cheek kisses. A traditional *la bise*, which I properly taught her how to do in high school.

"Oh, look at you being all French on me," she taunts, placing big wet kisses on my cheeks.

Laughing, I lean back, place my hands on her shoulders, and narrow my eyes on her. "You aren't supposed to plant one on me, let alone two. Have you forgotten all the proper French etiquette I taught you in high school? The lips don't touch the skin."

Waving me off, she scoffs. "Don't worry. I remember your version, but you must admit, mine is much more fun!" She shimmies her shoulders as she reaches down to pick up one of my bags.

"Ah, yes. The American way. Always trying to make a better version," I say with a wink so she knows I'm teasing.

She looks amazing. Britt was gorgeous in high school, so I'm not sure how it's possible to have a glow-up, but somehow, she did. Heads snap in her direction and follow her every movement. She doesn't seem to notice; either oblivious to the attention or used to it. I on the other hand want to sink deeper into the shadows.

Britt takes a small step away, and her expression sobers. "Are you sure you're okay? I know you filled me in on the basics when you reached out, but it sounds like you've been through a lot this year."

Sniffing, I swallow to ward off tears threatening to spill as my throat clogs with emotion. "Yes. I will be fine. Being here will be good for me." Then, under my breath, I mutter, "I hope." I bend down to pick up the rest of my luggage, and Britt squeals.

"Who is this?" Squatting down, she peers into the small, soft-sided case in my hand.

"Britt, meet my sweet bunny, Madeleine," I say with a big grin.

"Madeline, like the French cartoon character who lived in the orphanage?" she asks, wiggling her fingers as little whiskers approach the front of the enclosure. "Did you rescue her? Save her from being an orphan?"

"No. I actually hadn't made that connection. I was thinking more like a Madeleine, which is a petite French cake I love to bake," I respond.

Clasping her hands beneath her chin, she asks, "Is she a baby bunny? How big will she get?"

"She is actually full grown. I've had her for about two years. She is a Netherland Dwarf rabbit. Isn't she adorable?"

"Do you have to quarantine her?" Britt asks, eyes going wide.

"Not at all. There is no rule for domestic bunnies coming from France. We are good to go. Can we head to my aunt's house? I really want to get settled in before I pass out from fatigue. I've hardly slept in the last two days, and my layover in Salt Lake City was barely long enough to get through customs to my gate."

We load my bags into her Jeep and climb inside. Luckily, the airport is pretty empty at arrivals this Monday evening. It feels nice not to rush. I feel like I've been running non-stop for the last seventy-two hours between packing and saying goodbye to family and friends in Paris. I spent almost fifteen hours traveling and didn't sleep a wink. I'm ready to collapse.

As we pull out of the airport, Britt glances over at me. "What did you do to your hair? I don't remember it being that color in high school."

"Well, I figured a huge life change needed a new hairstyle. I'm trying a balayage to brighten my brown hair. When I made the rash decision last week, it didn't occur to me if this would be maintainable in Topaz Falls. Hopefully, there is a good salon in the area, which can help with the upkeep."

Britt tuts. "You aren't moving to the Ozarks, sweetie. We have an awesome salon, but didn't they tell you it only needs to be touched up every three to six months?"

No, no, they did not. Shaking my head, I reply, "I know my hair is no longer a mousy brown, but your hair change is more drastic than mine!" She looks at me, confused, as she tugs at her corkscrew curl. "You had dark brown, almost black hair in high school," I reply, raising my eyebrow.

Barking out a laugh, she replies. "Oh, I totally forgot because I started bleaching it during my freshman year of college. I've been doing it for so long that I hardly remember what I looked like before. The upkeep of this hairstyle is a pain. I've been tempted to dye it back, but I'm afraid no one will recognize me, and everyone will say Axel and I look alike. I love my brother but don't want to look like him."

Britt is still the same. Her brain and mouth move a million miles per hour, and she often speaks without thinking. *Elle est très bavarde.* I smile to myself and ask, "How are your brother and sister?" I only met Axel once when he came back for a short visit. He was in the military and always on some secret assignment. Lucy was a preteen and always tried to sit in on our conversations. She was the quiet to Britt's loud.

"Lucy is in college. She's a sophomore at Brenton University, studying genetics. She'll be home for Thanksgiving. Axel is doing well. He left the military a few years back. He started working for Lachlan at the Ambarsan Equine Therapy Ranch for veterans. He provides security and fixes everything," she replies. I nod, but my mind is locked on the name Ambarsan.

"Lachlan owns a ranch?" I ask, feeling so lost.

"Yes, about five years ago, well, maybe more now, he and Ingrid opened up the therapy ranch. He's a physical therapist, and she's a speech therapist. I work for his wife. She's the town's veterinarian who moved here last year. I'm her receptionist and man the front desk. My best friend, Freya Elin, is a veterinary assistant. You'll meet her in the next few days once you're settled in and ready to mingle."

"What happened to the Ambarsan family's apple orchard?" I reply in shock, completely ignoring the rest of the information.

"Oh, Declan's basically running it. He never left. Didn't want to go to college like Lachlan and Ingrid. He's just picking apples and stuff," she says distractingly as she pulls onto the freeway.

"Did his parents already retire?" I murmur, trying hard not to fall down the rabbit hole.

"Not really. A couple weeks ago, Mr. Ambarsan was on a ladder out in the orchard and fell off it. He broke his hip, and because of the extensive rehab, he and Mrs. Ambarsan are staying in Missoula at a medical assisted living facility or something. Their house didn't have a bedroom or bathroom situation that would work for him. Declan will run the orchard for the next month or two until they can return. I think. Don't quote me on that, but it's the gist of what I heard Axel informing Mom and Dad."

Before I can stop myself, the words tumble from my mouth. "Is Declan's wife able to help?" I cringe at how obvious I'm being, so

I force my eyes out the passenger window watching the electric poles whizz past in a blur.

"You still have a thing for Declan?" she taunts. I never stopped having a thing for him, and that's the problem. Realizing I won't respond, she sighs. Her voice is soft when she replies, "He isn't married, nor has he had a girlfriend since you left, sweetie."

Something about that statement makes butterflies flutter in my stomach, but I tamp it down. I'm here for three months, then I'm heading back to Paris. The sooner I can get this place on the market, the better. If I can get the bakery up and running by October seventh, I can head home at the beginning of the new year.

Clenching my fingers against my thigh, I ward off the negative thoughts. I still have to bake, and since the fire, I haven't been able to complete a single pastry that requires the oven. If I can't pull myself out of this funk, then I'll need to hire someone to actually do the baking part. This is something future Julia will have to deal with; right now, there are more pressing issues.

Case in point, my aunt's house. We roll up to her old Victorian house, and Britt parks her car in front of the garage. Hopping out, I grab Madeleine's case and pull the set of keys from my pocket. Britt follows me with one of my large, checked bags, setting it up on the porch. Pressing the cold metal into the deadbolt, it turns with ease. Twisting the handle, I close my eyes and push the door open.

"Wow, this looks better than I expected," Britt says, brushing past me.

Pressing my lips together, I hesitantly lift my eyelids enough to take in the entryway. My eyes widen, realizing it looks exactly how I remember it when I left eight years ago. My backpack isn't hanging from the coat rack, but the place is in great shape. The wallpaper is a burgundy damask with rich brown trim and crown molding. The elegant banister is directly in front, and I plan to honor Aunt Rita this

Christmas by making a festive garland. She spent hours weaving and decorating her garland the year I was here.

"Mom said the estate was paying someone to come in once a month to fully clean both the house and the bakery until I was ready to come and fulfill the demands of Aunt Rita's will," I explain as Britt wipes a finger across an antique table against the wall of the hallway.

"It's white-glove clean. Will they continue to clean while you're here, too?" she asks. "That would be a dream come true. I've always wanted to be rich enough that I had someone to dust my top shelves for me."

Shaking my head in amusement, I stride into the living room through the large wooden archway. Her style still marks every surface. She had a thing for fairies, so paintings, figurines, and fairy motifs are sprinkled throughout the room. I'll slowly start to pack up these items because, to sell, the real estate agent will probably want a more minimalist look for photos and showings.

Britt calls from the kitchen, startling me. "I'll run to the grocery store and get you essentials while you unpack! Your cupboards and the fridge are bare!"

"Well, the house has been empty for a couple years now. I'd hope there was no food," I reply.

"Spam and Twinkies would have lasted just fine!" she shouts.

"Yeah, I'll pass on those. I can make you a quick list of food items and give you cash. Are you sure you don't mind going to the store?" I enter the kitchen through the swinging door, almost beaning Britt in the butt as she leans over to peer into the cupboard at the end of the kitchen island.

"Looking for something?" I tease as I swat the outside of her thigh with the back of my hand.

"Yeah, I was seeing if your aunt had any cooking pans here or whether I should pick you up the basics," she says, her voice muffled as she reaches.

My gut tightens, but I force a breath out between my teeth. "Aunt Rita probably has enough pans to supply the entire neighborhood with baking dishes. They are in the skinny cupboard next to the stove. She used to keep appliances she didn't use regularly on the shelf you opened."

Standing up, Britt tosses her hair over her shoulder and prances around the kitchen, opening and shutting each drawer. "Looks fully stocked," Britt says.

Forcing a smile, I reply, "Yeah, it is literally the way she left it when she passed. The estate kept it clean but didn't go through any belongings. My parents only asked that edibles be removed to keep rodents and bugs from descending upon the kitchen."

Grabbing a pad and pen from the junk drawer, I hop on a stool at the kitchen island, just like I did when I was eighteen. Often, Britt or Declan was beside me. Britt takes her usual spot to my left, leaving Declan's seat sadly empty. The memory of his voice rolls off me as I picture our last conversation sitting here. His tone was desperate as he begged me to stay the summer in Topaz Falls. To stay with him.

Blinking away the memory, I start making a list, then pull five twenty-dollar bills from my wallet. Britt gives me a saucy salute and walks out to her car. She offloads the rest of my bags, helping me carry them up the stairs. Once inside with all my luggage, I debate whether I should take my old bedroom or my aunt's main suite, which has an attached bathroom and walk-in closet.

As Britt's Jeep pulls away, I climb the stairs with Madeleine's carrier in one hand and my carry-on in the other. I'm not ready to take my aunt's room yet. I'm sure it still smells like her, and I can picture her overflowing closet, which still needs to be sorted.

I push open the oak door to my old room and gasp. It hasn't changed a bit. Everything I left is still in the same place I set it, including the promise ring Declan gave me. It sits in the center of my old dresser, a fragment of sunlight catching on the metal band. The engraving on the inside of the ring is seared into my memory. When I close my eyes, I can picture the font and letters as if he gave it to me yesterday. *DA AIME JF*

Chapter 2

Declan

Tuesday, September 24

Smacking the steering wheel once I'm seated in my truck, I growl to relieve the tension from the meeting I just had. I wasn't meant to run the orchard. I have the muscle and energy needed to be in the orchard from sun up to sun down. Filling out forms, calculating numbers, and placing orders isn't my strength.

Chucking the stack of permits in the passenger seat, I gently bang my head against the headrest. Thank goodness we don't need an alcohol license. When I gave my dad the idea for an apple harvest festival last year, he ran with it, and it was a complete success. This year, my parents aren't able to do the behind-the-scenes work, and I didn't pay attention last year to see what he and Mom did to make it run smoothly. I'm glad Dad handled the liability insurance last year, and we kept the same policy this year. One less thing I need to worry about getting wrong.

My phone rings, and I answer it with my eyes closed. The only person calling at this time is someone from my family.

"Hello," I mumble into the phone. With my eyes closed, I wait to hear who's on the other end.

"Son?" my mom's kind voice comes down the line, and a wave of comfort swims through me.

"Hey, Mom. How's Dad today?" I ask my voice tight with frustration and regret.

I should have been the one up on the damn ladder, not him. He would have been spotting me on the ladder if I'd just been out in the orchard at 8 a.m. like we'd discussed over the weekend. Time and I have never gotten along. I'm always late or struggle to remember what time I planned with people. My phone was on silent the day my dad fell, and I missed the alarm I set, which gives me a fifteen-minute warning. Now, because of me, my dad's lying in a hospital bed at a rehabilitation center three hours away with a broken hip and fractured femur. We got him immediate medical attention, but the recovery process is lengthy. Because my parents don't have a ground-level ADA bedroom and bathroom, they chose to stay at a rehabilitation center for eight weeks or until he's more mobile.

"Oh, you know. Your father hates being in the hospital bed. They have him out of bed trying to walk with a walker, and the physical therapist comes by daily. Still, he's frustrated at how slow the recovery process is for him."

"I should be up and running right now. I'm still young. Fifty-five is too young to be held back by a broken hip," my dad grumbles from beside my mom.

"I'm sorry I wasn't out in the field on time that day," I say apologetically.

"Don't be ridiculous, Deckers. This isn't your fault. If your dad had been patient and waited ten more minutes, you would've been there, but he got cocky and thought he could do it alone," Mom says reprimanding my dad, who probably has a pout on his face. I know she's trying to make me feel better, but it isn't helping. I still feel guilty as hell.

"How is the wound healing?" I ask.

"Well, the entire outside of his leg from the hip to the mid-thigh is almost black; the bruising is so severe. They said the wound was healing nicely. With the walker, he's making good progress each day. Standing up and sitting down is the hardest for him to do right now. But enough about us. We wanted to find out how your meeting went with the County today," Mom states, redirecting the conversation.

"Oh, well. It went okay. They gave me a bunch of follow-up forms to fill out. Would you mind video calling me later to ensure I complete everything correctly since you filled out the original forms?" I mumble.

"Of course, Deckers. Don't forget to do inventory and put in the order with vendors. They'll need it by the last day of the month," Mom reminds me.

"How's the fire blight in the northeastern field? Is it spreading? Have you trimmed the infected branches off yet?" Dad asks over the line.

"Not yet. I sprayed the organic copper-based fungicide you told me to order. I'll get out there in the next few days and prune the infected branches."

Dad clears his throat and fights back a sigh. "Don't forget to dip the shears in alcohol between cuts to prevent contamination."

"Got it," I reply. The weight of the world feels like it's on my shoulders, or at least the future of the orchard and my parents' livelihood. I've been thrown into the overwhelming situation of running our apple orchard while preparing for a harvest festival. To make matters worse, the northeastern field is contaminated with fire blight, and the last time our orchard got it, I was too young to remember. We have a crew at the orchard, but they want my marching orders—orders I'm not sure I know how to give.

Turning over the ignition, I back out of the parking space to head back to the orchard. Mom says goodbye, and lights catch in my peripheral as I hang up the phone. Cutting my eyes to the right, I suck in a sharp breath. The lights of Hop Along Bakery are shining brightly. The bakery is alight for the first time since Rita Boulanger passed away. Are there new owners?

I slow my truck down to crawl past the windows. A brunette ponytail pops up from behind the counter, and my breath catches. It can't be. I feel like I'm seeing a ghost. A ghost from my past that was meant to stay locked away.

The woman spins, and I squeeze my eyes closed as a montage of still frames from the happiest time in my life rushes through my mind.

Suddenly, catching sight of my truck, her gaze finds mine. Time stands still for a brief moment when our eyes meet. Her eyes widen in shock before she points out the window and screams. I quickly look back at the road and see I've angled my truck toward the sidewalk. Attempting to slam the brake, my boot comes down hard on the gas. My truck jolts forward, lurching over the curb toward the cement planter in front of Frida's yarn shop next to the bakery.

I smash the ball of my foot against the brake, lurching to a stop just as my grill connects with the planter box. It's not enough impact to trigger the airbags, but my head scrapes against my watch as my hands grip the steering wheel. A sharp sting comes from my forehead, forcing a groan from my throat.

Dang it.

I do not need a broken truck right now. I have too much to do and not enough hours in the day or brain cells in my head to get everything done. I was already about this close to praying to God to make time stop so I could catch up with a world set on leaving me in the dust.

My driver's door flings open, and when I rotate my head, a small figure is backlit by the morning sun, surrounding her body in a golden aura.

"Julia," I murmur on an exhale.

"Declan," she gasps. "Oh my goodness, Declan. Are you okay?"

I slowly blink, trying to make sense of her presence in my small town. A town she swore she'd never step foot in again. "Julia," I mumble nonsensically. "You came back."

Her golden-brown hair is tied up in a high ponytail, accentuating her high cheekbones and sweetheart face. Her large grey eyes blink at me through thick eyelashes as she tries to make sense of the situation. A smear of grime is streaked across the porcelain skin of her forehead where she must have pushed her hair from her face. Her gentle touch clasps around my forearm, gripping my shirt as she shakes me.

Blinking, I sit up but wince when I feel something wet trickle down to my eyebrow.

"Here, let me help you out. My aunt's first aid kit is in the bakery. Let me get you cleaned up," she says, the melodic lilt of her voice sounding the same as I remembered it from eight years ago. Reaching down, I turn off the ignition, and quiet befalls us.

Rotating in my seat, I jump out and brace one hand against the door. Her small hands latch onto my hips, attempting to steady me. Considering she's a foot shorter than my 6'3" frame, she wouldn't be able to catch me if she tried. Instead, I wrap my arms around her, pulling her against my chest into a tight embrace. I've dreamt of this moment for years, always hoping she'd change her mind and return to Topaz Falls—return to me.

She smells different but the same. My Julia. Her soft hair catches against my stubble as I bury my face into the top of her head.

"We need to get you inside, Declan. You're bleeding," she mumbles against my chest.

Groaning into her hair, I rub my hands against her upper back. I can't believe she's here, and she isn't some figment of my imagination or a hallucination from stress and lack of sleep.

I silently follow her as she tugs me into the bakery.

"Your accent is stronger," I mutter.

She grins over her shoulder at me. "Well, I've lived and worked in France for the last eight years."

I grunt in acknowledgment, knowing exactly how far away she's been for almost a decade. When I cringe at the sting on my forehead from the tug of my furrowed brow, she grips my hand tighter and nods toward the door. "Come on, *Mon autre*," she murmurs, her nickname for me taking hold of my heart and squeezing it like a fucking defibrillator.

When we step through the glass door to the bakery, I expect to be surrounded by scents of vanilla and cinnamon. I stop, surprised to find only the potent stench of disinfectant. The place smells like a sterile hospital room, not a bakery.

"Have a seat." She motions to the small café table where we spent many afternoons sharing one of her aunt's pastries and doing our homework while I stole glances of her from under my hat.

After Julia left Topaz Falls, I couldn't stomach coming in here. When her aunt passed, I was angry at myself for not coming here every day to keep the memory of Julia and me alive and in the forefront of my mind. I'd like to think I was trying to move on, but everyone I've dated knows they were simply a placeholder or distraction. I made it clear in every relationship that it wouldn't be long-term. Many women tried to convince me otherwise, but those relationships ended the next day.

Julia strides confidently from the kitchen, clutching a sizeable yellow case. Setting it on the bistro table, she clicks it open, revealing a well-stocked first aid kit. She thumbs through the supplies, gathering an alcohol wipe, antibiotic cream, and a bandage.

Pulling up a chair, she places her knees between mine, leaning toward my body. Deftly, she extracts the alcohol wipe and murmurs, "This might sting, *Mon autre*." I close my eyes not to brace against the sting but to relish her nickname for me on her lips. Maybe I hit my head harder than I thought. Am I hallucinating all of this? Will Sherrif Edwin show up any minute and declare me unconscious?

She quickly fixes my cut. "It's not deep. Did your forehead bounce off the steering wheel?" Her touch kindles a fire deep in my stomach, leaving a sensation like wildfire spreading over my skin.

Pinching the bridge of my nose, I reply, "Thank you for helping me. I'm honestly not sure. I remember seeing you, thinking you were a figment of my imagination. Suddenly, you screamed, pointing out the window, and I slammed on my brakes before I took out Frida's potted plant."

"Who's Frida?" she asks, and I fight a smirk at the hint of jealousy I hear in her tone.

"Ingrid's best friend. She owns the yarn shop next to your bakery. She was in college when you were here, so you never met her. You'll love her, though." I reply, reaching out and grabbing her hand. She doesn't pull it back or flinch at my touch.

"I see. Well, I need to get back to work. I have a lot to do before opening day," she says, standing up and brushing off her apron. She looks adorable in a pair of overalls, with the pant legs rolled up, showing off her small ankles, and a cute pair of clogs. A soft, knee-length buttercream sweater hangs open, revealing the cream and navy striped apron tied around her waist. It's covered in smudges of dirt and grime, but she looks more beautiful than I remember. Her face has matured since high school into a confident beauty. She's exactly how I'd picture her to be—perfect.

"When do you open?" I ask, clearing my throat and looking around.

"Monday, October seventh," she replies, following my gaze. "The estate cleans this place each month, but I still have a lot of deep cleaning to do to meet the health department standards. I also need to come up with decorations and a menu." She sighs, stepping away from me.

"If you need help, let me know. I'm prepping for our harvest festival at the orchard. Still, I can be here at a moment's notice," I reply, tentatively stepping back into her space.

Sniffing, she stuffs her hands in her apron pockets. "How are your parents?"

Tugging at the back of my neck, I stare down at my boots. "Dad fell off a ladder and broke his hip. He and Mom are staying at a rehabilitation place until he's more mobile. They don't have an ADA bathroom at home, and the house has too many stairs. Mom is fit, but she can't lift Dad. Their size difference is the same as you and me."

Nodding, her gaze travels up my body, heating every nerve ending. "You look good, Declan."

"Not as good as you, blossom," I murmur, using the nickname I called her in high school.

Her eyes flash with heat, hopefully remembering all the times I used to call her my apple blossom. Schooling her features, she bites her lip and looks away.

"I'm glad you're back," I whisper.

Clearing her throat, her gaze cuts to mine. "For three months. Aunt Rita's will stipulates I have to open and run the bakery for three months before I'm allowed to sell it. In January, I'll place the bakery up for sale, along with her house, so I can open Fournier Pâtisserie in Paris. I'll be returning to France after Christmas."

Just like that—ice water courses through my veins. "You aren't leaving me this time," I whisper under my breath.

Without waiting for a response, I pivot on my heel and push through the front door. I need to regroup. Return to the farm and create a plan. I've lost Julia once; I'm not losing her again. She will see the value of Topaz Fall and how good we can be. We are older, and I'm wiser. I know what we had is the once-in-a-lifetime love my parents have, and I'm not giving up easily this time around. If she wants me to fight for us, I will. If the only option is to follow her back to France, then this time around, I won't hesitate. I love the orchard and my family, but no one else will ever complete me like she does. Now, I have to figure out how to make her understand that.

Chapter 3
Julia
Wednesday, September 25

My nose itches as the disinfectant I sprayed all over the walk-in freezer wafts around me. I'm thankful a cleaning company came monthly these last two years, but the freezer and ovens are not up to my standards. The layout of this bakery is so much like the one Chauncy and I owned before it burned down. I remember when we initially toured the unit with our real estate agent, I fell in love with it because it was so similar to Aunt Rita's bakery.

Coming out of the freezer, I flinch when my gaze travels to the small office. It's in the same place as my office was in the Paris bakery. At the same location, firefighters struggled to get to me when they realized I was trapped. It's the reason I have severe burns on the right side of my body. The one positive thing I need to keep reminding myself of is there is a window in my aunt's office. Because her bakery is on the corner, the office looks out on the side street, and it's big enough to climb through if I stand on top of the desk.

Next week, I'll rearrange the office furniture, so the desk is directly below the window. Formulating an escape route will hopefully help settle my nerves and set my mind at ease. The exit out the back and to the front of the store are both on the inside wall of the bakery. With the window in the office, it doesn't matter where I am in the bakery; I can get out safely and quickly if there is a fire.

It takes me a moment to realize my breathing is shallow and my vision is tunneling. With clammy palms and a racing heart rate, I know I need to sit down and center myself before a panic attack threatens to overtake me. Since the fire, I've had six panic attacks. I didn't realize what was happening the first time. I thought maybe I was having a heart attack. I even suggested to the nurse at the clinic I went to that I might have adult-onset asthma. She quickly listened to my lungs, informing me my lungs were clear.

In June, I went to see a therapist for six weeks. He walked me through breathing techniques and visualization techniques. What seems to work the best for me is simply sitting down and putting my head between my knees. Not very conducive for going out in public, as this isn't something I can do at a restaurant or store and not look a little off my rocker, but so far, the panic attacks have only occurred when I'm alone, which is scary in and of itself.

When my heart rate stabilizes, I stand up on shaky legs, hating how it affects me. A loud pounding on the front door has my breath hitch. Please don't let it be Declan. I don't want him to see me like this—not yet, and if I can make it three months without him seeing me flustered, that would be even better.

He looked so good yesterday. His dark brown hair is longer than it was in high school. He used to wear it buzzed short on the sides and longer on top, but now he has a shaggy, fresh-out-of-bed look with wavy hair that curls over his eyebrow. It's criminal for a man to have such a thick head of hair, especially when I know he has no idea how amazing it is. After bandaging his head, I ached to run my fingers through his waves and pull the errant strand away from his eyebrow. I want to know if it's as soft as I remember it. Any longer, it will block the view of his green apple eyes framed by chocolate brown eyelashes.

His square jaw is angular, and no baby fat is left to round it out. Oh, and his voice. Lordy, his timbre was warm and deep, sparking heat to spread through every inch of my body. It was better than I remember, which doesn't seem possible, because his voice always felt like home. I sighed in relief when I saw no wedding ring. I berated myself after he left for even looking after Britt told me he wasn't married. But I could never quite trust her gossip in high school. This was something I needed to confirm for myself.

I walk to the front, patting my hair and smoothing down my duster cardigan. I narrow my eyes in surprise, as Declan isn't standing at the glass. This is a good thing, I remind myself. In three months, I'm going back to Paris, so getting involved with Declan Ambarsan would be a stupid thing for me to do, no matter how my body is drawn to him like a hand to a warm tray of cookies fresh out of the oven. Just like a hot cookie, I'm bound to burn us when I leave him, again.

A couple stands on the other side of the door. The man has thick ginger hair cropped close to his head, and the woman stands barely above five feet tall with a mane of hair that looks like spun gold in the bright sunlight. She waves and plasters a huge smile on her face.

Offering her a small smile in return, I twist the key in the deadbolt and open the door. "Can I help you?" I ask cautiously.

"Hi. My name is Oliver, and this is my wife, Daniella. We wanted to welcome you to town and ask a quick question about the bakery," he says, placing his hand on the small of her back. Leaning into him, she grins up at him, and I fight the urge to be jealous of what they have.

"Welcome to Hop Along Bakery. My aunt opened this place about twenty years ago, but she passed away two years ago from—" I clear my throat and look away. "She passed away, leaving me the bakery in her will. I plan to open the second Monday in October."

Daniella and Oliver offer me their hand, and I fight the urge to offer them *la bise.* This is a small, tight-knit town, but I am not in France.

"I was wondering if I could put in a small request. Well, maybe not small since I don't know your background, but I figured I would try," Daniella says. Nodding for her to continue, I dig my hands into my cardigan pockets, struggling not to fidget with something. "I have a lot of food allergies, and I was wondering if there was a chance you could make a small pastry gluten-free and vegan." Her voice trails off at the end as her eyes move to her shoes.

When I look at Oliver, his eyes are pleading with me, and I'm unsure how to respond. My baking thrives off butter, eggs, and wheat. I'm not sure how I'd even alter a recipe to make these additions. Only, I stop myself from explaining this because the curl of her shoulders and the softness in his eyes tell me this is important. Maybe not important to me, but essential for them.

Clearing my throat, I rock back on my heels. I open my mouth to respond, then close it. The wheels in my head start to spin as creativity takes the reins. "Do you want the same thing every week, or were you hoping I'd change it frequently?"

"Oh," Daniella looks bewildered. "I'd happily pay for a batch every Monday on my way to work of whatever you felt like making. If it's the same thing every week or you want to be creative, I won't complain. I'm just not a very good baker, and when I make things with the all-purpose gluten-free flour, it comes out tasting chalky. When we visited a small town on the Washington state coast, the bakery there had some muffins to die for. It would just be nice to have some more options," she whispers.

"If you need us to shop or order the ingredients because they can't be bought in bulk or it doesn't make sense economically, just let us know. We will accommodate you in any way we can," Oliver offers.

Nodding, I figure, why not? Maybe this will give me the creative outlet to pull me from the baking funk I've been in since the fire. My menu isn't set in stone yet, so maybe adding a gluten-free, vegan option on the menu will sell.

"It's not a problem. *Ça ira*," I reply, pretending to dust my hands. "I will make a weekly item for the bakery case for others to enjoy as well. Maybe if it doesn't sell, we can look into making a small batch solely for you. I'd like to help."

Daniella steps up and offers me a small hug before dropping her head and stepping away. Oliver grins broadly, mouthing, "Thank you."

I dip my head at him in acknowledgment and watch them stroll down the street. Chauncy and I were supposed to be married this month. We should be walking down the street like them, infatuated with each other. But, with each passing month since he ran away after setting our business on fire and stealing the insurance money, he's become more of a shadow figure in my mind. The worst part of this daydream of us walking hand-in-hand down the sidewalk is that it isn't Chauncy holding my hand. It's Declan.

Sighing, I lock the door and return to my chores in the kitchen. Opening one of the ovens, I flinch at the sight of the interior. Not because it's hopelessly dirty but because that's where the fire started. Without even having to close my eyes, I can still see the flames erupting from it as firefighters rushed me out of the building. It looked like the entrance to hell as flames licked up the side, dancing toward the ceiling.

What am I going to do if I can't overcome these fears? Rationally, I know a fireball won't fly from my aunt's old oven, but my body reacts like a live wire.

Taking a deep breath and finding my resolve that this has to happen if I'm ever going to open in time, I drop to my knees and grab my cleaning supplies off the counter in front of me. Another knock startles me, causing me to drop the bottle of oven cleaner. It rolls under the steel island in the center of the kitchen before I can reach it. Darn it.

Standing up, I stride to the front door and see a small woman with long black hair and curves to die for. She's in a beautiful royal blue sweater dress with an intricate cable design accentuating her natural waist and hips.

Curiously, I open the door and lean my head against the doorframe. "Hello?"

Grinning from ear to ear, she sticks out her hand toward me. "Hi, I'm Frida. I own the yarn store next door. I wanted to introduce myself since I'll probably be your best customer." She wiggles her eyebrows, and I realize this is who Declan spoke about yesterday.

Gasping, I reply, "You're Ingrid's friend!"

With wide eyes, she pushes her lips out. "You know Ingrid?"

Wincing, I give a resigned smile. "I went to high school with Declan, so I knew of Ingrid. He told me you were Ingrid's friend when I saw him the other day. We never met because you were in college at the time. I was only in Topaz Falls my senior year as a foreign exchange student. It's a pleasure to meet you. My name is Julia."

Realization of some kind dawns on her as her beaming smile broadens. She rocks up on the balls of her feet, clasping her hands beneath her chin. "Oh, we're going to be good friends," she whispers, nodding enthusiastically.

I think she and Britt must get along well. They both act like they're overdosing on Pop-Tarts. I remember the sugar rush those would give me back in high school. Declan was slightly obsessed with them, so if I ever forgot a snack, I knew his locker would have an assortment to choose from in dire times.

Mentally shaking my head, Frida stares at me with a goofy grin. "Oh, I remember you," she murmurs, biting her lip. Shocked, I clear my throat, unsure if that is a good or bad thing. Stepping up, she wraps me in an embrace. "Well, it's wonderful to meet you. If you ever need anything, I'm right next door and happy to help." Waving goodbye, she heads back to the yarn shop.

All these huggers. I completely forgot about that Montana trait. Maybe it's countrywide, but since I've only ever visited Topaz Falls, Montana, I'm going to assume it's a local thing to hug random strangers after speaking to them for two minutes.

Locking the door, I head back into the kitchen, mentally ready to attack the ovens. I can do this. It is cold. There is no fire or heat. Just get down and clean it, Julia. Quit being *poule mouillée* because you are not a chicken. You are a phoenix who will rise from the ashes and become better than before.

Sucking in a deep breath, I drop to my knees, groaning when I realize my cleaner is under the kitchen island. Dropping to my stomach, I see it right in the center and reach my hand under, but I'm an inch or two away still. Looking on the low shelf above my head, I find a rolling pin. Jabbing it under the table, I connect it with the cleaner, rolling it to the other side. Pulling myself up, I stand, and before I can walk to pick up, there's another knock on the door.

"Do I have an 'Open' sign on the door that I'm unaware of? I think I'm busier now than I will be on opening day," I grumble into the silence.

Stomping back to the front, I stop when I see Britt waving wildly with a beautiful blonde woman beside her. Britt's friend has a long braid twisted down the front of her body, hanging effortlessly down one side. Gorgeous green eyes blink at me curiously as a cheerful smile fills her face.

I unlock the door and greet Britt with *la bise*, laughing when she overtly kisses my cheeks in return. Shaking my head, I extend a hand to her companion. "*Bonjour*, my name is Julia."

"I've heard so many wonderful things about you, Julia. Welcome back to Topaz Falls. My name is Freya Elin, but I go by Freya. I work with Britt at the veterinary clinic. I grew up in Kalispell, so this is a small hop, skip, and jump from my childhood home. Sorry, I'm rambling," she says, quickly shutting her mouth.

"Pleasure to meet you, too. Britt had lots of nice things to say about you, too. She was excited for us to meet when she picked me up from the airport on Monday. I just met my next-door neighbor, Frida. It will be a struggle to keep your two names straight." I wince and shake my head. "Sorry."

"No, it is no problem. I didn't grow up in Topaz Falls like Frida. You can call me Elin. My grandmother's name was Freya, too, so I went by Elin as a child. I knew many members of the town when I was little, so they all call me Elin. I swear half the town calls me Elin and the other half calls me Freya. I respond to either." She wrinkles her nose as she stares off into space.

Britt claps her hands, startling us both. "Leave it to me. You shall be officially rebranded as Elin. I will spread the word. I'll put this mouth to good use."

Looking skeptically from Britt to Elin, I open and close my mouth trying to think of what to say. "Are you sure? Elin and Freya are both beautiful." Britt nods enthusiastically as Elin shrugs in indifference. I try to quickly change the subject. "Were you in school the same year as us? Would I have seen you at sporting events?" I ask, trying to remember if I knew someone named Freya Elin. That name is so unique, I think it would have stood out to me in my memory.

She shakes her head and replies, "That is the most flattering thing I've been told in a long time. No, I'm thirty-six, so I was out of college before you got to Topaz Falls, and I only moved here a few years ago."

Swallowing my embarrassment, I fight not to look closer. It was an honest mistake because she's stunning, with perfect bow lips and naturally rosy cheeks. As I analyze her features, I can make out a few freckles dotting her nose and a couple of fine lines near her eyes. Her long blonde hair doesn't show any gray, unlike my dark hair where, when I start getting gray, it will stand out like a shining beacon. She does not look thirty-six, or if this is what women look like at thirty-six, then sign me up.

"Should we go get some coffee? I bet you could use the break. My treat," Britt says, tugging on my arm.

I feel like I've hardly finished anything on my task list. I can't refuse an offer like that, so I quickly lock up and follow Elin and Britt down the street. When we walk through the doors of Sleepy Mountain Roasters, I take a deep breath of the coffee aroma. It smells heavenly. A strikingly handsome man stands behind the counter with two other people.

"Who's that?" I whisper to Britt, but Elin responds with a small growl.

"That man is Anders. He is a super-rich jerk who owns a ton of buildings and businesses in the area. Before we know it, he will own half the town, and we will be at his mercy for renting and leasing space. I'd stay away from him because he's a jackass," she says with a huff.

Britt frowns at Elin. "He is really nice, Elin. Let Julia find out for herself. You just have to get to know him."

"Oh, trust me, Britt. I know him better than anyone in town," she says coldly. "I'm just trying to protect Julia before he sinks his claws into her."

"Did you guys date or something? You've never told me why you hate each other so much when everyone in town loves you both," Britt whispers.

"Goodness no. Are you joking? I wouldn't date him even if every unicorn in this imaginary situation vouched for him. If he was the last man on Earth, I'd take a raft and paddle to Antarctica. There'd have to—"

"We get it," Britt hisses. "Just don't piss him off so he won't give me coffee because Sleepy Mountain Roasters makes the best cup of coffee in town."

Waving Britt off, Elin rolls her eyes. "Yeah, yeah. I like their coffee, too. I'd just prefer if he stayed at the Kalispell location and hired a nice manager to run this location."

"Welcome to Sleepy Mountain Roasters, ladies. What can we make for you?" Anders' voice rumbles, and I shiver at the deep timbre. He is looking at Britt and me, completely ignoring Elin's existence. I guess there is bad blood between them, and now I'm curious.

Chapter 4

Declan
Thursday, September 26

These numbers aren't adding up. They never do. This is why I stay in the fields. The clipboard in front of me makes zero sense. I've added these two columns multiple times, and the number changes each time. Closing my eyes, I drop my head back and groan. The vendors need the final numbers by Monday. I'd ask Cameron, who's worked here for years, to do this, but I'll still have to sign off on it. To sign off on it, I'd have to double-check the work or simply trust he's less of an idiot than I am.

Dropping down on an empty set of crates, a cloud of dust and debris shoots up around me. I pinch the bridge of my nose and lean heavily on my knees, hoping the answer to my problems will walk through the door. Who could I ask? I don't want it getting back to Mom and Dad that I'm not capable of running the orchard. If all goes as planned, I hope to take over the orchard in a decade. Therefore, Ingrid and Lachlan are out. I'm sure they'd help, but then they'd call Mom and let her know I'm struggling to do this alone. I've shadowed my dad for years, learning the ins and outs of apple trees. It looks like I'll need to pay closer attention to what my mom does from now on, too. This is embarrassing and feels like high school algebra all over again.

Mira knocks on the partially opened door. She's a few years older than me, and her long black hair cascades down the side of her face as she peeks inside. "Declan, you in—" Mira starts to say. She freezes when she sees me, curious brown eyes assessing my somber demeanor. Stepping out of the light streaming through the open doorway, she strides into the shadows toward me.

"What can I do for you, Mira?" I ask, trying to stifle my terseness.

"Someone woke up on the wrong side of the truck bed," she mutters. Pressing her lips together, she stuffs her hands in the back pockets of her jeans and rocks back on the heels of her boots. "Cameron and I were wondering what day you wanted us to set up the tents for the bake-off competition and the tents for the various booths we have coming for the festival."

Scrubbing my hand down my cheek, I reply, "The first round of the bake-off is on October thirteenth, which is—" I pause to count it out. "Eighteen days away. We can probably wait until the Friday before on the bake-off tent, and the other tents don't need to be set up until the last weekend of the month. We have time."

Sniffing, she murmurs, "That's actually seventeen days away. Today's the twenty-sixth, and there are only thirty days in—" She glances down at me and sighs. "You know what, never mind. I'll let Cameron know."

Fighting a groan, I pull up the calendar on my phone and realize she's right. "I'll call my contact with the show today to see what they want us to do. There's a chance they will be bringing everything with them."

Nodding, she crosses her arms over her chest. "Cameron also told me to tell you we should prune the blight early next week. The copper fungicide is doing well, but we'll want to remove it soon."

I nod, glance down at my sheet, look at the jumble of numbers, and sigh. "Anything else? I'm doing some inventory before making the final request with vendors."

Swallowing thickly, she whispers, "Did you need help with the inventory?"

I think the staff assume I'm dumb. They know I didn't attend college like my siblings, who both got specialized degrees. Still, it's because I wanted to help immediately with the orchard, not because I wasn't smart enough to attend college. I could have gotten into Montana State if I'd applied.

"No, I'm good. Thanks, though," I reply, smiling tightly.

She lifts her chin and turns to leave. "It's okay to ask for help, Declan," she mumbles before leaving me in the storage barn.

Tapping the pencil against my lip, I think about her words. I don't want my coworkers to think less of me, but I really do need some help. Who could I ask?

Pulling out my phone, I pull up Anders in my contact list. The phone rings twice before he picks up. "Hey, Declan. We missed you at poker night last night. Axel has the new clubhouse up and running. It's like a man cave on steroids. You better show up in two weeks for the next one. Plus, Aislinn made cookies again."

Grinning, I stand up and set the clipboard on the crate before pacing up and down the fifteen-foot aisleway. "Yeah. I'll be there. I had something come up yesterday and couldn't make it." This included looking over the truck after jumping the curb on Monday and then writing down a list of everything I needed to do between now and mid-October. The list was fucking long and left me feeling a little light-headed. "I was actually calling for a favor."

I can tell I've startled him because I don't think I've ever asked him for a favor. He needs help at the roastery. I'm there. He needs help with a fence at his house. I'm there. But I've never taken him up on his offer to return the favor.

"What's up? Are you okay?" Anders asks. I hear a door shut and realize he must've closed the office door at his coffee shop.

Chuckling sardonically, I reply, "No, not really. As you know, my parents are at a rehabilitation facility for my dad's broken hip. Well, I'm getting the orchard ready for the Apple Harvest Festival and feeling overwhelmed."

"What do you need?" Anders asks without hesitation. He's older than Lachlan but has never treated me like the stupid younger brother.

Scratching my head, I lay it all out. "I need help with inventory and vendor ordering. My mom always does this, and I don't have a clue what I'm doing. It's due on Monday, the first."

Clearing his throat, he replies, "Of course. Tuesday is actually the first, but don't worry. I have Saturday morning free. How about I come over after breakfast to go over everything together?"

I blow out a deep breath, tension leaving my shoulders. "That would be awesome, man. I'd owe you big time. I know I'll get the hang of this. My mom just didn't get a chance to really show me what to do before the shit hit the fan. Now, everything's piling up like a truck of manure."

Softly laughing, he responds, "Man, you won't owe me anything. You've helped me more times than I can count on both hands. I'm glad I've finally got a skill to repay you for every time you've dropped what you were doing and helped me."

"Okay, how about we call it even. But, if my parents aren't back this time next month and I'm still struggling with it, you'll be on call."

"You got it. Topaz Falls is a small community. We work together and stick together," he states before saying goodbye and hanging up.

Stretching my hands above my head, I groan as the tension in my shoulders and back slowly eases. Flipping to the next sheet of paper on my clipboard, I find the to-do list for the Apple Harvest Festival. I need to call the representative for the Baking Network hosting the Great Harvest Bake-Off. I got a hold of them last year to add another layer to the Apple Harvest Festival. People from all over will also come to watch the finals. Each episode will be televised. It will bring lots of tourism to Topaz Falls this October. I keep hoping we'll get a brewery here that would want to do an Octoberfest or Brew Festival. This is a long-term goal, but I hope the orchard can pair up with them one day and make it a month-long event.

Typing in the number for my contact, the phone rings once before a woman with a deep Southern accent answers, "Baking Network, this is Dorine Metcalf. How can I help you?"

"Hi, Dorine. This is Declan Ambarsan with Ambarsan Apple Orchard calling regarding the Great Harvest Bake-Off in Topaz Falls, Montana, next month. I was calling to see where we're at with that and what you'll need from my team here at the orchard."

"Nice to hear from you, Declan. Everything is pulling together smoothly. We will arrive the Saturday before the first day of the competition to set up the seven baking stations and a large tent. Please ensure no vehicles are parked in the area we discussed for the competition," she requests.

"I can do that. The three judges will arrive Saturday evening and stay at the bed and breakfast, correct?"

"Yes, we have Pauline Denning, Renea Truman, and Jeff Alderman judging the event. The host will be Brian Ulmer. We have our own generator, so we won't need access to any power sources on the property."

"How exactly will the bake-off work?" I ask, forgetting the exact details.

"There will be three rounds of competition on the last three Sundays of October. We are starting with seven couples. The two with the lowest score are removed from the competition in each round. I'm not sure if you've watched the show before, but this competition will focus on apple recipes. We will do three bakes per day. First, contestants will create a breakfast favorite chosen by them. The second challenge will be a savory dish chosen by the judges. Lastly, the final challenge will be a dessert showing off each team's abilities in the kitchen," she informs me.

Her southern accent makes it sound like an easy feat anyone could do. I'm terrible in the kitchen, so I know this isn't the case. The people who applied and were chosen to compete are of a caliber far above mine.

Taking a deep breath, I try to think of any other questions. "Alright. So, my only task is to ensure no cars are parked in the field you're looking to use?"

"That's right, Declan," she replies, and I can hear the smile in her voice. "Try not to worry. We will make sure everything runs smoothly from our end."

"I'll see you in a couple of weeks. Have a great day, Dorine," I say, waiting for her response before hanging up the phone.

At least I won't be competing. I'm looking forward to watching from the sidelines and maybe sampling some of the baked dishes the contestants create when the camera isn't rolling. I'm happy to volunteer as an official taste tester for this event. Apples are in my blood, and I've never met an apple dish I didn't like.

Chapter 5

Julia

Friday, September 27

The croissants look magnifique. They're hand laminated with three full folds, then cut and rolled into perfect crescent shapes. Now that they've proofed, I can bake them. Still, I'm frozen in place with my hands holding the tray. My arms are shaking as I stare at the oven. Placing one foot in front of the other, I unsteadily walk to the stove. The pan clanks against the surface as I ungracefully plop it on top of the heating elements. With a trembling hand, I reach out and turn the oven on so it can preheat. I've put off starting the oven long enough. I need to get past this fear of industrial kitchen stoves. I don't struggle as much when I cook and bake at home.

Britt and Elin will be here any minute. They promised to join me for lunch, and I hoped to surprise them with a ham and cheese croissant. But if I don't get them in the oven, they won't be done in time.

Bracing my hands on top of the cold stovetop, I close my eyes as my head starts to pound. The heat from the oven is leaking out just enough that I can feel it wafting around my face. *Not now, Julia. You aren't in Paris. You are the only one here.* Unfortunately, no amount of self-coaching helps.

The stove announces it's ready, so forcing my hands to pick up the tray, I grab the oven door with a death grip and slowly lower it. A wave of heat licks against the exposed skin around my neck and face. I quickly place the tray on the center rack and slam the door shut. My breathing gets shallow, and even though it's irrational, it feels like I'm about to start hyperventilating. I don't know what to do. Reaching for my aunt's little egg timer, I quickly twist it to twenty minutes and roughly drop it on the counter, so I don't lose track of time and burn the croissants. My knees buckle as my hand finds the wall. Stumbling backward I start choking as air refuses to fill my lungs. Throwing my back against it, I slowly slide to the floor.

    I didn't make it to a chair. I frantically look around, but my eyes struggle to focus as my vision swims. Images, sounds, and smells from that night assault me, playing on repeat before I can stop them. Immediately, I'm thrown back to the fire. Haltingly, I draw each knee up, wrapping my arms around my shins and dropping my head between my knees. The only type of breathing I can think of right now is the Lamaze breathing technique my best friend in Paris had to do last year when she was pregnant. We used to jokingly practice it so that it would feel like second nature to her in times of stress. Well, guess what? This is a time of stress, so it looks like I will give it a whirl. She birthed a baby the size of a watermelon, so if it worked for her, it better work for me.

    There is a pounding on the front door, and I can't bring myself to stand. My ears are ringing, and it sounds like I'm underwater. Those underwater fights in *Aquaman* where the thumping sounds deep and muted; that's what my front door sounds like now. The sights and sounds clash around me hitting an unbearable peak, where I know I'm close to delirium if I don't think fast. My breathing is still shallow and erratic, and Lamaze is clearly not doing a darn thing.

    Hurried footsteps rush toward me, and I hear Britt's garbled voice. Soft, trembling fingers grasp my wrists, pulling on my hands, which I hadn't realized I'd placed over my ears. I shake my head, trying to seal my eyes and ears shut. The egg timer blares that the croissants are done, and my eyes cut to it as if willing the alarm to stop. It's sitting so close to the oven, though, that the waning panic increases again, and I clasp my hands over my ears.

Britt directs Elin to do something and then talks hurriedly into her phone. Screwing my eyes shut, I press harder on my ears to block out all the noise as if my palms were noise-canceling headphones. I try to blink through the fear making my veins feel like liquid nitrogen is coursing through them, but I can't.

After what feels like minutes, calloused palms, which are definitely not Britt's or Elin's, firmly grip my wrists. They are warm and commanding, immediately settling something inside of me. I suck in the first deep breath I've taken since the panic attack started, and my eyes blink open. I'm staring into the most beautiful pair of ice-blue eyes I've ever seen. They're so light they look like ice chips. Framed in dark black lashes, with thick black eyebrows. Mussed black hair hangs across the man's forehead, and he looks like he should be trying out for *Magic Mike*, not squatting on the floor of my aunt's bakery.

I swallow thickly, wondering where this man came from, because he wasn't here when I unlocked the front door this morning. His gorgeous mouth is moving, and I watch in a trance as he licks his lower lip. Did I black out? The roaring sound of blood sluices in my ears.

He tugs on my hands hard enough to lower them to my knees. Sound rushes in, assaulting my ears as I try to focus on what he's saying. Many voices filter around the room, and I struggle to decipher what he wants. "*Pourquoi cela continue à se produire? Qu'est-ce qui ne va pas avec moi?*" I mutter to myself, fighting the urge to bang my head against the wall to make it all stop.

Then it hits me. His voice rumbles, *"Bonjour mon cher. Peux-tu me regarder? Bien bien. Maintenant, peux-tu respirer profondément? Essayez de respirer comme je le fais. Suis-moi."* That's great, sweetheart. Take a deep breath. Focus on my voice. Are you with me?"

"What the hell, Axel?" Britt screeches, causing me to wince and break eye contact. Oh no. The man I was just fantasizing about on a stripper pole is Britt's brother, Axel. Mr. Panty-melter himself. He looks darn good and so much different than I remember. But sisters before misters or whatever Britt used to say in high school. He is very much off-limits during this three-month stay.

"What?" he rumbles as he stands up to face her. My eyes follow him as he goes up and up and up. Considering how short she is, I didn't expect her brother to be over a foot taller than her. As he crosses his arms over his broad chest, his t-shirt pulls across his back, and for a brief moment, I rethink the brother rule. Is there really a rule? He could be the one that makes me forget about Chauncy and Declan; I have no doubt about that. Glancing between the two of us, Britt throws her hands up in the air. Oh darn, did I say all of that out loud? Mortified, I press my lips together and focus on Britt. If Ian Somerhalder had about twenty more pounds of muscle on him, Axel could be his stunt double.

"Don't you what me, mister. Since when do you speak perfect French?" Britt demands.

Oh, thank goodness. My internal monologue was not broadcast to the room.

"Britt, I'm a Navy SEAL. Part of my extensive training was in linguistics, which is not a type of pasta. I spent quite a bit of time in France at one point. My French isn't perfect, but it got her attention." When she looks like she's about to say something else, he holds up a finger that he slowly directs at me. "What is going on, and who is this?"

"Oh, right." Britt sighs. "Sorry. This is Julia Fournier, my friend from high school. She is Rita Boulanger's niece and the new baker in town." Crossing her arms, she mutters, "I can't believe you know French. I thought you failed French in high school."

"Nope," he replies, leaning back against the metal prep table in the center of the room. "If I remember correctly though, you did."

"My croissants," I shriek, remembering they were in the oven, the whole reason I had this blow-out panic attack.

"Don't worry, Julia," Elin says calmly. "I removed them from the oven and turned it off."

A throat clears on my other side, and I quickly look to my left, finding a handsome man with deep auburn hair leaning against the wall. His assessing eyes strip me bare without him having to say a word. Adjusting his black-rimmed glasses, he pushes off the wall. He slowly approaches me as if I were a wounded animal, cornered and in shock.

"Hello, Julia. My name is Dr. Trent Walsh, and I'm the psychiatrist at the equine-therapy ranch. Would you mind if I had a word with you?" he asks, crouching down to be at eye level with me. His hands are clasped in front of him as he rests his elbows across his knees, looking relaxed but authoritative.

Nodding, I extend my hand. "It's a pleasure to meet you, Dr. Walsh."

"Please, call me Trent," he says softly, and my ears automatically focus on his words, tuning everyone else out around me. "Would you like them to step out to the front of the bakery? Or would you prefer they stay near you?"

Licking my lips, I look at Britt and Elin, then briefly glance at Mr. Panty-melter. Nodding, I reply, "No. It's okay. Go ahead."

"It appears you had a panic attack. Do you get these often?" His eyes search mine, seeking out all my truths.

I slowly shake my head and reply, "This is all new for me. I've had a handful of them in the last six months after I was trapped in my burning bakery in Paris. Firefighters rescued me, but I still had physical and emotional trauma."

Adjusting his glasses, he lowers himself to the ground, mimicking my pose as he gently drapes his arms around his knees.

"Have you seen someone about processing what you've experienced?" he asks gently.

Swallowing, I lay my chin on my knee and mutter, "I tried. I did six weeks with a therapist, but they weren't exactly helpful. I was offered some breathing techniques, but when I panicked before Britt got here at the feel of the hot oven, the only breathing technique that came to mind was Lamaze breathing."

Trent chuckles before handing me his card. "If you want to come out and try a few weeks at the ranch, I'd be happy to try to help you through this new obstacle. Have you tried cooking in a commercial kitchen since the accident?"

I don't correct him since, after receiving the police report, I now know it wasn't an accident. "No," I whisper. "My bakery in Paris was not usable. This is the first bakery I've had access to since the incident."

He seems to notice my choice of words, and when my gaze flicks to Axel, I see his eyes narrow slightly.

"I'll think about it," I whisper. "Thank you both for coming."

"When Britt called, we were just pulling into Mama M's for lunch. We were only a block away, and I'm glad we could help. I don't know French, but if you decide to come see me at the ranch and would like to work in French, I can pull Axel in for your sessions."

My eyes widen slightly in shock. When I flick my eyes to Axel, he gives a small nod of agreement. I had hoped to get back to Paris without anyone knowing how broken my mind and body were from the fire. In less than a week, four people already know some of the story.

"Please don't let anyone else know I'm struggling to bake," I plead. "It could ruin my chances of running the bakery if people don't believe in my abilities. If I can't figure out how to get past these issues by opening day, I will hire someone to man the ovens while I bake on the opposite side of the kitchen near the doorway to the front area."

Britt bends down. "We won't say anything. I am well aware people think I'm a gossip, but I just don't have a filter. I can keep a secret."

Axel raises an eyebrow at her, and she sticks her tongue out at him. "What? It's true! I didn't tell anyone you spoke French, did I?"

He barks out a laugh. "Britt, until ten minutes ago, you didn't even know I could speak another language. The secrets you keep best are the ones you don't know." Turning his attention to me, he says, "I can keep a secret. Yours is safe with me."

"Me, too," Elin murmurs, offering me a kind smile.

Trent holds up a hand. "I take patient confidentiality very seriously."

All eyes turn to Britt. "Oh my gosh. I can keep a secret. I swear. I know how to play my cards close to my chest."

Snorting, Axel mutters, "Bad simile, Britt. You suck at card games."

"I do not have a bad smile! I'm cute as a cupcake," she says with a cheesy grin.

Under his breath, Trent whispers, "I'd keep your secrets away from Britt."

"Don't worry, I typically do," I mutter, trying not to smile.

Chapter 6

Declan

Saturday, September 28

Dust particles dance through the beams of light filtering through the barn wood of our storage shed. Anders arrived right on time and is currently pouring over the clipboard of information and spreadsheets my mom uses to do orchard inventory. Reaching behind my head, I rub the hair at the nape of my neck, fighting the urge to fidget under Anders' scrutiny. With a pen in his mouth, his brown eyes assess the page. He looks between the shelves and the clipboard several times. It feels like he's been doing this for hours when, in reality, it's probably only been a few minutes. I struggle not to yawn, knowing he's taking time out of his Saturday to help me with something I should be proficient at already. But sitting around here is boring. All I want to do is get back out in the orchard.

Tapping the pen on the sheet of paper he's examining, he presses his lips together. "Alright. I see what your mom's doing here, and I think we can pound this out today."

Nodding slowly, I blow out a deep breath. "Hit me with your questions."

"I'm not sure how many questions I have as your mom has great record keeping here. I'm assuming this is the tree count for the orchard. This document is a detailed record of tree varieties, their individual planting dates, their location on the orchard, and whether they are healthy or sick. She has a red checkmark next to ten trees in the northeast field," he says, lifting a brow.

Clearing my throat, I respond, "Yeah. Those trees in the northeastern field have fire blight. I'm treating them with copper fungicide. We'll hopefully finish next week. I need to prune away any affected branches, so it doesn't spread."

Lifting his chin in acknowledgment, he flips to the next page. "This appears to be your current fruit inventory. Do you need help recording the quantity of apples being harvested? It looks like your mom tracks them by variety. There is a section for storage apples, cull apples, and processing apples. What is a cull apple?"

Grinning, I tap the current form. "This is the one form I understand. Since I'm out in the orchard with the crew harvesting the apples, I help fill this out each season. Cull apples are bruised or damaged in such a way we can't use them for processing or sale. They typically go to the various ranches in the area to be used in animal feed. I have to do a final count with the processing apples, as several bushels will go to a Channing up in Topaz Crest. He owns Growlers Alley, and they use our apples to produce hard cider."

"Is Channing coming down to pick them up, or do you also have to arrange transport?" Anders asks.

"He and a few friends will pick them up next week, which is why I need to get this done. The rest of the apples will be used to make apple cider and sell during our harvest festival. We also supply apples to various vendors in the state." I groan.

"Based on this footnote, a bushel of apples is one hundred and twenty-five apples." Pulling out his phone, he quickly types something in or makes a calculation. "Alright, a bushel of apples makes approximately four gallons of cider. You need to know how many bushels to set aside for cider during the festival and how many go to Channing. You also wanted my help determining other supplies for your harvest festival, correct?"

"That sounds about right," I mutter, having no idea if that's true because I honestly am unsure what exactly I need.

Tipping his head back, he closes his eyes and mumbles, "If each gallon is one hundred and twenty-eight ounces, and there are four gallons per bushel, that gives us five hundred and twelve ounces per bushel." Opening his eyes, he looks at me, and I'm sure I've got a bewildered expression on my face. The man is a savant with fluid ounces or something. "Do you give out four-, six-, or eight-ounce cups of cider?"

Wrinkling my nose, I reply, "Does it say on the form?"

"Ah. Good thinking." Flipping through the sheets, he comes to another form. "It looks like last year you ordered two thousand six-ounce cups." Closing his eyes again, he taps the pen against his chin. "So, if each bushel gives you that many ounces, you can get eighty-five servings of cider per bushel using six-ounce cups. If you need approximately two thousand servings, you need about twenty-four bushels. I'd round up to thirty bushels so you don't run out and order the equivalent amount in cups. How many bushels of processing apples do you currently have?"

"Well, the average mature tree in our orchard produces about fifteen bushels. We have one hundred and fifty trees planted per acre," I reply.

"And how many acres?" he asks, not looking up from his notepad where he's making notes on the margins.

"Um, fifteen, I believe is the apple orchard. The rest of the property is about forty acres for our houses, barns, and fields. Doesn't the paper say?" I ask, pointing at the clipboard.

Winking at me, he says, "Yeah, it does. I was just testing you."

"I'd rather you didn't," I grumble.

"Alright, so fifteen acres with one hundred and fifty trees per acre gives you approximately twenty-two hundred trees. If you get fifteen bushels per tree, you should have—" he pauses, screwing his eyes closed as I watch him in fascination. "Holy shit, dude. You have thirty-three thousand bushels of apples each harvest! How do you even harvest that many?"

"We have a lot of hard workers that make it happen. Wait. Did you seriously just do all that math in your head?"

Furrowing his brow, he replies, "Yeah, it was just estimating and basic multiplication. Anyway. Okay, so you need to have about fifty bushels set aside for Channing to pick up next week, based on this footnote here about how many apples he'd like to purchase." Scratching his temple, he lets out a low whistle. "That would make about two hundred gallons of cider. A growler is sixty-four ounces, so they're looking at getting at least four hundred growlers worth of cider. I wonder if the cider loses volume during the fermentation process. I'll have to ask him the next time I see him."

For the first time since stepping in the storage barn, I click my pen and scribble the reminder for Channing to pick up fifty bushels of apples.

"Have you considered using a barcode system or RFID tags for trees and bins? This would really streamline your inventory management system," Anders says, underlining something.

"I honestly have no clue. Maybe my mom has that set-up, but she never showed me how to use it."

"Well, it looks like we need to do supplies inventory next, and you have to have orders in by the first of the month, right?"

"Yeah." I nod and fist my hands against my hips.

"Do you have what you need for pesticides, herbicides, fungicides, and fertilizer?" Anders asks, ticking off each one as we cover it.

"Yeah. Those are fine." I think. Yeah, no, they are.

"Equipment and tools? Do you have the pruners, ladders, and all these tools you need for orchard maintenance?"

"Yes. We have what we need there. Next," I reply.

"The last two sections are packaging materials and harvest materials," he says, sitting down on some empty crates.

I sit down beside him, and we spend the next twenty minutes finishing up the inventory. He helps me fill out all the order forms. As we wrap up, I sense he wants to change the topic. I don't blame him; I'm tired of this, and it's my job. He's here because he's a good guy and a great friend. The best part is that Ingrid and Lachlan won't know their little brother is pathetic and unable to do basic inventory.

"What do you know about the bakery reopening?" he asks, throwing me off guard.

A small whine, as high-pitched as microphone feedback, threatens to escape my throat. "Why?" I grouse.

Tapping his pen against the clipboard, he rotates toward me. "I met the new owner yesterday, then heard some rumors she might only be operating it for three months before she sells it."

"I heard the same thing," I grumble, leaning my forearms against my thighs. I stare at the dirt accumulating below the toe of my boot as I push it around the wood flooring.

"I think I'm going to approach her and offer to get an agreement going so that the sale will be finalized when the three-month mark hits. I don't want the bakery to close again or end up in the pocket of some random investor. Do you know the new baker?"

Grunting, I reply, "Yeah. I know who she is."

"And?" he asks, arching a brow.

Pressing my lips together, I look up at the ceiling. Finally, I reply, "If she wants to sell after three months, then I'm sure she'll consider your offer. She's smart. Are you going to use Mark as your commercial broker? Hopefully, if you lock her into contract early, you'll beat the rest of the people looking to scoop up the corner bakery. I know for a year there you were struggling to get your offers accepted for some reason."

"I might approach Mark after I speak with her and get some of the specifics narrowed down. I'd like to take him our mutually agreed upon conditions so that when he draws up the purchase and sale agreement, he can fill in the blanks. Also, it's weird. For the last year, I've had no issues with my offers. Oddly, it corresponds with the timing for when Elin left Mark's brokerage office. I think she sabotaged all my offers for the two years she worked there."

My eyebrows lift toward my hairline in surprise. "You can't possibly think Freya had anything to do with that. She was just his assistant and she's always been incredibly nice."

"She did all his intakes for prospective buyers and sellers," he says with a shrug. "It would've been easy for her to slip my offer into the shredder before Mark even looked at it."

Frowning, my gaze cuts to his. "Freya's a sweetheart. I can't see her doing anything underhanded to potential clients."

Shaking his head, he mutters, "She's not a sweet, toasted marshmallow. No, the woman is basically Lilith reborn."

Snorting, I realize he isn't joking. "You're the only one I've ever heard of who doesn't love her. Plus, why does some of the town call her Elin?"

Frowning, he rubs at the back of his neck. "I grew up with her. Her grandma was the school librarian and was also named Freya, so back home she went by her middle name Elin."

"Does she prefer to be called Elin? Have I been using the wrong name all these years?" I ask with wide eyes.

He shakes his head. "No. She goes by either. I've only ever known her as Elin though." Pressing his lips together into a firm line he clears his throat and stands up. "You coming to Glaciers tonight?"

Standing up, I stretch my arms above my head. "We'll see. I hadn't planned on going out at all tonight. Maybe next week. I have a lot to get done around here. Now that I know what needs to be ordered, I can finish the forms you helped me fill out and get them emailed or faxed. Hell, I don't even know how I'm supposed to turn them in. For all I know, I have to deliver them in person."

Chuckling, Anders replies, "Most of the stuff I do is filed online through a vendor portal or a quick email to my account rep."

Scrubbing my hand along my jaw, I groan. "Looks like I'll have to call my mom anyway. I don't think she left me login instructions." Smirking, Anders turns the clipboard toward me and flips to the last page. "Well, would you look at that. Maybe my mom did plan ahead, either that or she struggles to remember this stuff as much as I do and needs all the reminders."

Chapter 7

Julia

Sunday, September 29

The batter is ready for some traditional American cupcakes. I figure I owe Britt after she helped me at the bakery. Setting the oven's temperature, I patiently wait for it to preheat. Why is it so much easier to cook at home? My pulse is racing, and my hands are shaking, but I can handle this. If I don't calm down, my piping skills will leave much to be desired and probably look like a kindergartner decorated them.

Stalking over to the fridge, I pull it open and remove a chilled bottle of Rosé. It isn't from my favorite vineyard, but I hope it will take the edge off before handling the piping bag. After pouring a few ounces into my glass I bring it to my lips, taking a large gulp. I savor the cold tingle as it travels down my throat.

The oven dings, alerting me it's up to temperature. Screwing my eyes closed, I fist my hands to ward off the shaking and nerves. *You can do this!* Cautiously approaching the hot oven, I subconsciously rub my palm along the fragile skin on my right arm. Flashbacks from the night assault my mind as they filter past my closed eyelids, unbidden.

My eyes widen in shock as my aunt's kitchen comes into focus, and my patisserie in France fades from the forefront of my memory. Forcing out a harsh breath, I grab the tray of cupcakes and quickly place them in the oven, closing the door before I can comprehend the heat emanating from inside. I hastily turn on the timer and walk to the other side of her small butcher block kitchen island, putting as much distance as possible between me and the oven. From this location, the back door is also closer. An exit it more accessible. Just in case.

Drumming my fingers against the countertop, I look around. I have fifteen more minutes until they are done. My eyes peruse the kitchen counters, looking exactly how I remember them all those years ago. At the end of the counter, Aunt Rita's junk drawer can barely close. It's so full of odds and ends. Everything in it was something Aunt Rita insisted might come in handy one day. My favorite was the collection of white pizza savers, which came in her pizza boxes. I'm sure she thought they'd make perfect fairy house tables. I've always thought that if it hasn't been used in the last year or two, it doesn't need to live in my home. I might feel differently if I'd grown up here instead of the small flat my parents and I had in France. Space was limited and tight growing up, so if I wanted something new, something old had to leave.

My eyes land on the bag of sugar. Frowning, I tilt my head to the side, wondering why something in my subconscious is begging me to pay attention. Furrowing my brows, I glance at the other side of the kitchen, where the mixer is stationed. A bag of flour sits open with the handle of my measuring cup sticking out. Biting my lip, I groan as hot tears threaten to spill. Sitting on the counter beside the flour is a container of salt.

Merde.

If the salt is there and an unopened bag of sugar is on the opposite side of the kitchen, that means the cupcakes have a cup of salt in them.

What is wrong with me? This is getting ridiculous. Maybe I won't need to worry about the bakery making it three months. At the rate I'm screwing up my baking, I won't have any business after the first day. Striding over to the oven, I turn it off, grab an oven mitt, and pull the tray of ruined cupcakes out of the oven. Plopping them on top of the stove, I growl at them, trying to place the blame for screwing up a basic cupcake recipe on anything but me. Unfortunately, it doesn't make me feel any better.

On the corner of the island sits the business card for Dr. Trent Walsh, the Ambarsan Equine Therapy Ranch psychiatrist. It's been taunting me since he extended the offer to work with me on my issues. The therapy I attended in Paris clearly didn't resolve my baking problems. I was so distracted by the idea of using the oven I mixed up sugar and salt—such a rookie mistake.

I pick up my cell phone and type in Dr. Walsh's phone number. It rings twice before his deep voice filters across the line. "Dr. Trent Walsh speaking. How can I help you?"

"Uh, hi," I murmur. Clearing my throat, I allow my eyes to fall shut as I take a deep breath. "Hello, my name is Julia Fournier. We met at my bakery the other day. I had a panic attack, and you arrived with my friend Britt to help. I'm not sure if you remember me, but I kept your card and was hoping you had time in your busy schedule to help me. I can't keep living like this."

There is silence on the other end of the line, and I'm afraid the call dropped or he hung up because I sound like a basket case. But then I hear the unmistakable sound of a door closing.

"Yes. I remember you, Julia. Sorry, I wanted to step into my office for privacy. I'd be happy to help. Are you able to come out to the ranch on—" There is a slight pause as I hear pages rustling in the background. "Does Thursday at 4 p.m. work with your schedule?"

I start to nod, realizing he can't see my response. "That works. Right now, my schedule is wide open. Thank you. I appreciate your flexibility and for squeezing me in on such short notice. I'm at my wit's end. I can't work like this."

"You're welcome. I hope you enjoy the rest of your weekend, and I'll see you next week. I'll text you the ranch address after we get off the phone."

"Thank you so much, Dr. Walsh," I whisper. "I'm sorry I called on the weekend. I didn't mean to disturb you. I'm a little distracted."

Chuckling softly, he replies, "It's not a problem. I put my cell phone on my cards so patients can get a hold of me any day of the week. I wouldn't have put it on my business card if I didn't want to receive calls on my cell. Sometimes, the difference between life and death can be a compassionate listener on the other end of the line."

I smile when I end the call, knowing this is the right first step toward getting control of my baking and moving on from the incident. The fire was the third life-altering event that changed my very being. Once again, I'll be reborn and rise to overcome my problems. The first two may have shifted my future, but I won't let the fire be the straw that breaks me.

It's time to take my mind off the kitchen. It used to be my happy place, and I know it will be again with more time. Padding up the stairs, I look around at what I could accomplish. I need to have this house cleaned out in three months and ready to put on the market. There are three bedrooms and two bathrooms on this floor. I'm not prepared to tackle my aunt's room yet.

Looking at the one door, which I haven't opened since coming back, I tentatively twist the glass knob and pull it toward me. The hinges creak as the door opens, causing a small shudder to travel down my spine. My eyes try to adjust to the pitch-black stairwell. The soft light from the hallway behind me illuminates the base of the stairs, hardly nudging the blackness away. The elongated shadow of my silhouette casts an eerie image like a black Salvador Dali painting melting onto the stairs.

My fingers fumble against the wall for the light switch, brushing against the textured wallpaper. When I flip it on, the weak hanging bulb in the center of the attic blinks to life. I cautiously step on the first stair, not knowing how strong the wood is after all these years. Aunt Rita updated parts of the house and kept the exterior well-maintained, but I doubt she saw the need to fix the attic. She always used to say, "If it ain't broke, don't fix it, dear."

With each step, the musty smell of old paper and textiles assaults my nose. When I'm far enough up the stairs to peek my head around like a prairie dog, I take stock of what's up here. Before I can sell the house, this all needs to go. The attic is full of dust and debris, but at least I haven't seen any signs of furry critters. Aunt Rita has trunks and bins stacked in all the corners up here. I check the board before transitioning my weight off the staircase. It seems sturdy enough, but I'm probably not the best judge of construction since I can't even build a birdhouse.

I grow more confident with each step, ignoring the groans from the support beams. At the first trunk, I kneel down and pop the lock. When I lift the lid, I come face to face with material covered in lace and beads. Pulling out the blue one on top, I raise it in front of me and gasp at the gorgeous dress. I don't know historical American fashion, but these are stunning and vintage. Maybe I could donate them to the high school theater department or see if a local—local what? Who could use gorgeous vintage dresses in a small country town in northwest Montana? It's not like women go grocery shopping in floor-length beaded gowns. Placing it gently back inside, I cross my fingers that no spiders are hiding amongst the fabric and close the lid.

The next trunk is small but beautifully painted. Opening the lid, I'm surprised to see hundreds of black and white photos. The first one my fingers hold up is of two little girls in pinafore dresses. White cardigans cover their arms, and their hair is cut in perfect little bobs. They are standing in front of this Victorian house, each holding a porcelain doll. They remind me of the American Girl doll named Kit, which my mom brought me back after visiting Aunt Rita when I was eight. What year would this photo have been? Turning the image over, 1936 is written in elegant cursive with the names "Reina, age six, and Dorothy, age four."

Gasping, I flip the photo back over. I bet this is Grandma Dottie. Pulling out my phone, I snap a few pictures to message Mom later. Laying the phone down, I gently push photos aside, admiring the hairstyles and outfits of relatives over the decades. Some of the pictures are colored, but the majority are not, making me think most of these photos are from pre-World War II. Mom is going to love these. She is obsessed with genealogy and our family tree. I wonder if she's ever seen most of these. If not, I wonder why Aunt Rita had them stored away so chaotically.

Out of the corner of my eye, I spot a thick leather-bound book with yellowed pages sticking out from all three sides. There is the distinct handwritten scrawl of Aunt Rita's purple pen on one of the visible sheets of paper. I wonder what it is.

Standing up, I brush the dust off my hands and close the trunk. I take a step back and head toward the book. Before I can process the sound, a large crack echoes through the large space, and my breath leaves me as the floor beneath me gives way. A scream escapes my throat. My arms flail, trying to grasp anything. My torso hits the plywood attic floor with a thud, my palms smacking hard against the unforgiving surface, making them sting. I bear down with all my might, fighting to hang on to the flat board as my legs aimlessly swing below me. I try pushing up against the flooring, but no matter how much I kick, I can't get enough momentum to propel me back up through the floor.

Merde.

I am stuck. With shaking arms, I slowly scoot my right hand toward my phone, trying to bear all my weight on my left side. I start to slip and readjust my torso. The phone is just out of reach.

"Hey, Siri. Call Britt Larson on speaker," I say with a grunt as I try to slow my erratic heart rate.

"Calling Britt Larson, mobile," Siri replies. I sigh in relief when I hear ringing on my end.

"Hello, Frenchy!" Britt shouts through the line. It's loud, and I can hear many voices around her.

"Hey, Britt. Are you close to my aunt's house?" I ask, my voice strained as my arms struggle to hold my weight.

The wood cuts into my stomach, making me glad I wore a thick sweatshirt and jeans. Hopefully, I'm not bleeding all over the room below. Nothing stings and based on how furiously I was swinging my legs, I don't think anything is broken.

"You okay?" Britt asks. "I'm just leaving Sleepy Mountain Roasters. I wanted to bring you a coffee."

"Yes," I grunt. "Well, no. I fell through the attic floor, and I'm stuck in the ceiling of the room below. I think I'm over the guest bedroom, but I'm not positive. I also can't tell if I'm injured with the adrenaline pumping through my body. For all I know, I'm bleeding all over the guest bed."

"Oh, my goodness! We'll be right there!" Britt says, hanging up before I can ask who all she's referring to with the word 'we.'

I try to patiently wait, but my arms tremble with exhaustion from supporting my weight. My mind is spiraling, too, knowing there could be creepy crawly spiders everywhere. Suddenly, I hear a muffled thud, followed by pounding footsteps as multiple people, other than Britt, ascend the staircase.

"Frenchy?" Britt shouts. I cringe at the nickname that continues to follow me long past graduation.

"In here," I yell back, fighting the urge to growl. Who all did she bring?

"Well, well. If you'd wanted to fall into my arms, all you had to do was ask," a masculine voice teases. He sounds like he's standing directly below my feet, but the sound is too muffled to clearly tell who it is.

"Axel." Warns another deep voice. Ah, yes, Britt's smokin' hot brother. Of course.

"Man, I'm always ready for a rescue," Axel says.

Give me strength.

Footsteps rapidly ascend the attic staircase. I rotate my head and watch as Britt's mass of bleach-blonde curls bounce into view. She gasps. "Julia!" Then, her head disappears as she runs back down the stairs.

"Axel, she's barely hanging on. Do something!" Britt screams.

"Britt. Calm down. I'm standing right below her. If she falls, I'll catch her. I'd rather see if we can edge her back through the hole so she doesn't risk scratching her upper body and face."

"Did you hear that, Frenchy?" Britt shouts from the bottom of the attic staircase.

"Yes," I grind out. He is literally right below my feet. His voice is muffled, but I can hear every word.

"Alright. Julia, I will stand below you and put my hands below your feet. Use my hands to stand up, and when you're ready, we can count to three, and I'll push upward. You should be able to get enough leverage that you can hoist your butt up onto the floor and crawl away from the edge," Axel says.

"Like hell, you will," the other man says, and I wince when it clicks.

"Declan, what's your problem? I'm just going to grab her feet and push her up," Axel replies.

"I'm taller. I should be pushing her through the ceiling," Declan replies. Lordy, his voice is warm and deep, sparking heat to spread through every inch of my body. The growly undertone is better than I remember, which doesn't seem possible because his voice always sounded like a dream. Maybe the attic fumes are getting to me. Did I fall into asbestos?

"Seriously? One inch? You are one inch taller than me. For all we know, my arms are longer," Axel says, and Britt snorts out a laugh.

"I have an idea. Why don't you each grab a foot so she has a wider base to stand on," Britt suggests.

"I don't care who grabs my foot, but if someone doesn't do it now, my arms will give out. I haven't worked out in months, and my muscles are quivering. I'm shaking so hard I probably look like a butterfly chrysalis ready to hatch."

Suddenly, two sets of warm hands grip my socked feet, creating a small platform for me to stand on. I use my legs to take the weight off my arms and rest for just a moment.

"Alright, Julia. Straighten those legs like a flyer in cheerleading," Axel says.

"What do you know about cheerleading?" Declan scoffs.

"I paid attention in high school, during football games. When I was on the bench, I watched them closely."

"I have no idea what a flyer is," I admit, flattening my palms against the floor. Bending my elbows, I call out, "Three, two, one." With a grunt, the guys thrust my feet toward the ceiling, and I use the upward momentum to heave myself out of the hole.

I fall to my back, sucking in deep breaths, before rolling away from the opening. I lie on my back like a starfish when I get to the top of the stairs. Hopefully, if I disperse my weight, I won't fall through. Heavy footfalls land on the stairs. Tilting my head backward, I lock eyes with Declan. My cheeks flame in embarrassment that he saw me like that, probably looking like something out of *Grimm's Fairy Tales*.

"Thank you," I murmur.

"Are you okay?" he asks. Sitting on the top step, he slowly sweeps my hair away from my forehead.

Nodding, I mutter, "I think my butt suffered a mild concussion."

"Want me to rub it?" he replies with a wink. Sobering, he whispers, "Are you sure you're okay? Do you need the hospital?"

"I'm fine. Really. Why did so many people come?" I ask.

"Britt was having coffee with Axel at the coffee shop when you called. They were waiting for their order, and I was beside them, talking to the owner. The three of us rushed over as soon as we heard you were in trouble," he says softly.

I look away, struggling to process the emotion in his voice.

"Thank you for coming to help," I whisper.

Under his breath, he says, "I'll always come, Julia."

My breath hitches as my eyes cut back to him. Before I can respond, Axel fills the attic doorway below. "Any injuries need tending to?"

Grumbling, I reply, "I don't think so. I will lie here for a minute before attempting to climb down the stairs. I wouldn't want to fall headfirst."

"I'd be happy to carry you, sweetheart," Axel says, wiggling his eyebrows.

"If anyone's going to carry her, it's going to be me," Declan grinds out.

With hands raised, Axel winks at Declan. "I'll head downstairs with Britt and make us all a drink."

The sound of Axel and Britt heading downstairs is the only sound besides our shallow breathing. "Uh, when Axel makes a drink, he isn't referring to tea or coffee. He's probably looking for hard alcohol in your cupboards," Declan mumbles.

"Yeah, let's get down there before he finds my aunt's liquor cabinet," I reply, sitting up. My whole body aches. I scoot and reach for the leather-bound book so I can take a closer look at it in the safety of the downstairs. Hugging it to my body, I inch to the top step and slowly stand.

Declan wraps his arm around my waist, guiding me down the stairs. I lean into his warmth, taking a deep breath of his woodsy, spicy cologne. When we pass through the narrow doorway, he swings me into his arms and carries me to the top of the main staircase. A choking sound comes from the kitchen.

Axel splutters, "What the hell did you do to these cupcakes? They taste like hardtack."

"Oh, no. My cupcakes," I hiss. "Don't eat those! The recipe is bad!"

"Yeah, a little late for that, sweetheart. I wouldn't serve these to the public if I were you," Axel shouts back.

"What happened?" Declan whispers against the shell of my ear as he pulls me tighter to his broad chest.

"I accidentally switched the salt with the sugar," I say so quietly I'm not sure he hears me until he tips his head back and barks out a deep laugh. Something warms in my chest at the sound, and when I snuggle in closer, I tell myself it's so he can carry me easier. I might have sprained my ankle, for all we know.

Chapter 8

Declan

Monday, September 30

The morning is off to a rough start, which seems to be the norm for me after my parents' quick departure. Since the accident, I feel like the kid whose parents threw him in the deep end so he'd learn to swim or the baby bird pushed from the nest to learn to fly. I'm constantly flailing these days, and I don't like it.

A few of us spent the first few hours of the day separating out the bushels for Channing. He plans on coming to the orchard tomorrow, so we need to be ready. My parents would kill me if we lost his account. I doubt he'd make a big deal about it, but I don't want to risk it.

The worst part was getting out to the southwest orchard, only for me to realize I forgot to bring the clipboard with all of Anders' notes. I couldn't remember the amount Anders calculated for me on Saturday, so I had to hike back to the office and find where I put it.

After we sorted the bushels for Channing, it was time to put in the final orders. Now, I'm sitting at the computer triple-checking every form I fill out through our online portals to ensure I order the correct items. I forgot we had a s'mores night planned on the festival's last day; therefore, I didn't have Anders' help calculating how much

I needed to order for graham crackers, marshmallows, and chocolate. I'm sure this seems trivial, but each time I divide the number of projected attendees by the servings in the bag, I get a different number. As I push 'order,' I only hope I did it correctly. I went with the amount I got twice for each item.

I hate not having someone look over my work like Mom usually does. I'm too embarrassed to ask any of the other staff for fear they'll see me as a fraud. I'm having major imposter syndrome these days. I can only hope that when Dad decides to pass me the torch, it will be a long and slow transition period.

All these numbers are crucifying me, taking their sharp claws and tearing me apart, limb by limb. If I'd figured out how to make it to college, a few math classes would have nullified all these problems.

The glow of the computer screen illuminates my skin as the laptop stares back at me. I think it's about time I take a break from the nightmare that is ordering. At least Mom didn't say I needed to reconcile anything. Perhaps being the only Ambarsan sibling willing to take over the orchard was my first mistake. I spent my whole life in the shadow of my two older siblings. Maybe I should rethink the idea of inheriting the business when Mom and Dad want to retire. I might not be cut out for this line of work like I thought I was.

I keep hoping my awesome ideas will make us millions overnight. If they do, I can hire out the stuff I don't want to do, like anything involving numbers. I've heard AI makes art, creates music, and writes books, which seems stupid to me. Why would people want AI to do the fun stuff? I'd much rather they train AI to inexpensively take over all the mundane work I don't want to do so I have time to do what I enjoy, like working with clay.

I'm curious if people are working on that or whether I should pitch the idea to one of those AI companies. No. I'd rather hire a real person to do all this. Ugh, brain. Please focus—no more tangents.

Shrugging on my coat, I step outside into the midday sun. What to do? I should check on Mira and Cameron. They were talking about the bushels of apples required for the Apple Harvest Festival. As I walk toward the storage barn, my phone rings. "Bad Apple" by Mary Kutter blares from my cell into the quiet of the orchard, scaring some birds in the tree above me and causing them to take flight.

Pulling my phone from my back pocket as I dodge the birds, my fingers fumble against the cumbersome case, which Mira insisted Cameron and I get for our cellphones to make them indestructible after they fell from a tree for the third time last week. My grasp on the device slips, and before I know it, the phone falls face-first into the mud. Hopefully, the new case did its job. At least we aren't at the equine ranch because my phone probably would've fallen in manure, not mud. A round of applause for small wins around here. The apple orchard doesn't seem so bad at the moment. Reaching down, I quickly wipe it off on my jeans and press the answer button several times until my finger swipes in the correct direction.

"Hello?" I say hurriedly.

"Hi, Declan? This is Dorine Metcalf from the Baking Network. Do you have a moment?" she asks, her voice sounding distracted.

Clearing my throat, I look around nervously. Ducking behind the nearest tree, I attempt to create some modicum of privacy in an open field. Glancing back at the office, I furrow my brows, wondering if it makes sense to go back there. I don't want to ask her to hold while I race back to the office, nor do I think there is anything she'd say I'd feel compelled to keep from any staff passing by me.

"Yes, please. Go ahead. How can I help you?" I ask, schooling my tone so she doesn't hear the nerves threatening to bust through.

She anxiously chuckles on the other end. "You see, one of the couples dropped out of the bake-off competition. Usually, we ask another team that didn't make the original cut, but no one could change their plans at the last minute. We'd made the original choices and notified the groups back in June. The other couples all said they'd found other arrangements for October."

"What does that mean? We just have one less team competing?" I ask.

"Well, no. We need to fill the last space. Two teams need to be voted off in each round. Is there anyone in the community who enjoys baking and would like to participate in the event at the orchard? We could call them the Home Team or something. Make it about the small-town camaraderie, which I'm sure Topaz Falls possesses in droves."

Pressing my lips together, I think through the options. Ingrid can bake cookies but not an array of desserts. Lachlan cooks. I've only seen him bake if Aislinn is involved. Aislinn loves to bake, so she could be an option. Mama M might want to do it, and the competition would be free advertising for the cafe.

"I have a few people in mind I could ask. Let me get back to you a week from today with the names of the participants for the Home Team."

Dorine hums in approval. "Sounds great, Declan. Thank you for being flexible. We were shocked the other entrants weren't available. Still, I can understand how thirteen days isn't a lot of time to plan and fly out since most teams were from California, Texas, or New York and had their own bakeries or catering companies to consider."

"Happy to help. I just want our small-town harvest festival to be a smashing success. My goal is to bring tourism here with the cool autumn weather."

"I look forward to hearing who the new couple is next week. Keep me updated. If you get two people to agree this week, please let me know as soon as possible so I can send over the waivers and disclaimers they need to sign in order to participate in the show."

"I understand and will let you know as soon as I do," I reply.

"Good. Good. I have another call coming in, so I will have to let you go. Have a good day. Bye, Declan." Before I can respond, I hear the click of the phone disconnecting and look at it in my hand. She is always in such a hurry. I suppose that is one benefit to the orchard. For the most part, life is pretty laid back, and I get to plug along with my to-do lists.

Shoving off the apple tree, I continue toward the barn, searching for my team. The hand-hewn wooden door sits propped open as darkness yawns from inside the large barn.

"Mira and Cameron? Are you two in here?" I ask, knocking on the door frame.

"Over here," Mira calls from the belly of the barn.

Ducking through the door, I squint my eyes, trying to see in the dim light of the bulb hanging idly over the hunched figures of Mira and Cameron.

"How's it going?" I ask, placing my palm at the back of my neck and gently tugging it to relieve the uncertainty rolling around in the pit of my stomach. I had hoped that by having them stay out here while I stared at the unforgiving computer screen for hours, everything would be organized according to our order forms and the amount Anders calculated.

"We're just about done," Cameron says, standing and arching his back against his fists. I fight the urge to whoop in excitement that I won't be needed.

"Can you sign off on this? I managed to finish the cull apples ordered by the various ranches in the area," Mira says, stepping up beside me. She smells of the earth with the underlying sweetness of apples. It may sound like I think she smells like dirt, but it's hard to describe. I'm sure Cameron and I smell similar. Julia was the one who pointed it out to me, saying it was a calming smell she'd never experienced before. I wonder if she still thinks that when I'm near her. Does the scent bring back long-forgotten memories? One of the benefits of working at the orchard during harvest time is you smell like fresh apples.

Grabbing the pen, I scribble my signature, approving the amount, knowing there's no point in me checking her work since she's probably better suited for the job than I am. If she's still working here, maybe I could offer her the manager position when my parents retire. She has a knack for detail and is incredibly organized. I'm surprised my parents haven't given her more responsibilities. When they get back, I might bring it up with them.

"Hey, this is off-topic, but can I ask you both a question?"

"Sure," Mira responds as Cameron lifts his chin in acknowledgment.

"The Baking Network said one of the couples dropped out of the competition. They asked me to find two people to be the Home Team from Topaz Falls. Who should I ask? Do you two bake?" I ask.

Mira winces as Cameron looks at me in disbelief. "Dude, I can barely make toast. Ask Mama M. I bet she'd love to do it."

"I'm a terrible baker. I can grill just about anything, but pastries are not my expertise. I saw the new bakery is opening soon. The owner might like the free publicity. You should ask them," Mira replies.

My shoulders tense as I try to think of approaching Julia about this. She left me the last time I asked her for something big like this. I'm not sure I can put something this important in her hands only to risk her dumping me at the last minute. Who would she even ask to be her partner? Perhaps I could see if she would do it with me. I can't bake, but if she tells me what to do, I could be a second set of hands and spend more time with her.

"Declan? Earth to Declan?" Mira calls, waving her hand in front of my face. "We need to review the apples set aside for our harvest festival to ensure we picked the variety you want for the cider press."

My excuse to call Julia gets postponed because duty calls.

Chapter 9
Julia

Setting all the ingredients out on the counter for scones, I grab a mixing bowl and pull the butter out of the freezer. I thumb through the pages of the book I found in the attic, thrilled to have Aunt Rita's cookbook. Sitting on the couch last night, I poured through it from cover to cover twice. I think it must have recipes from my grandma and maybe even my great-grandma, as there are two other distinct writing styles other than Rita's in here. One of them wrote down a recipe for fair scones. I remember making these with Rita, but this isn't her handwriting.

A knock on the door startles me. Putting the butter on the kitchen island, I brush my hands over my apron and walk to the front door. I pull it open and come face to face with Britt and Elin.

"Britt. Elin. Nice to see you. What brings you over?" I ask, ushering them inside the foyer.

Britt offers me a warm hug, and I return the gesture, my face smooshing into her curly hair.

"We just got off work and saw the bakery lights were off. Elin and I thought maybe a girl's night might be in order. We brought wine! I have no idea if it's any good, but the label is gorgeous. Look," Britt rambles, her words flying from her mouth faster than I can process them.

"You stopped at the bakery?" I ask, backing up the conversation.

Elin steps in and places a hand on my forearm. "We were worried you might have trouble baking and wanted to check on you. When we saw the place was empty, we assumed we could have fun baking in your kitchen here and get some free treats if we brought wine."

Smirking, I wiggle my eyebrows at Britt. "Well, you both arrived at the right time. I'm making fair scones with preserves. I thought maybe if I tried making an American treat instead of a French pastry, I wouldn't have the same mental block."

"Um, not to rain on your parade," Britt says, holding up her finger. "But didn't you try making cupcakes the other day? Axel said the one he tried was pretty awful." Her gaze darts to her shoes.

"Well, maybe with a glass of wine in my system and you two distracting my mind, it will have a different outcome," I say with a bit of false bravado. How did I already forget about the cupcakes?

"I actually make scones all the time because my mom loves them. It's a treat I can easily transport to her residence," Elin says softly, a small smile gracing her lips.

I wash my hands in the kitchen sink, then return to the kitchen island. As conversation flows between us, I begin putting the ingredients together, my body on autopilot. After a few gulps of wine and lots of laughter, my nerves start to calm down. Without hesitation, I turn on the oven, returning to the island before I can focus on the heating element behind me.

"Chocolate chips, blueberries, or blackberries?" I ask as I look at the mound of dough.

Elin motions to Britt. "I really don't care. I like all those toppings. Britt, you pick."

Tapping a hot pink fingernail against her lower lip, Britt stares at the dough. "Is this like a free treats girl's night?"

With a raised brow, I reply, "Sure."

"Can you separate the dough into three chunks and make a couple of each, or is that too hard?" Britt asks with a furrowed brow.

Laughing, I shake my head. "Completely doable."

I divide the dough, add the toppings, and cut them into triangles. My spatula places the last scone on the baking sheet when the oven dings.

My hands start to shake as I grip the edge of the island.

"Okay, what's your favorite Disney movie?" Britt asks Elin and me. My eyes snap up to her in confusion. "You need a distraction! I'm providing said distraction."

I look at her wide-eyed as I try to remember the Disney movies I watched as a kid. Growing up, we didn't get to watch many movies because we didn't have a DVD player, only my mom's old VHS player.

"I'll start. My favorite was *Cinderella*," Britt says.

Elin gasps, and we all look at her. "You mean you like the one where the guy doesn't recognize her because she doesn't have her hair and make-up done? Nope. I want a guy who likes me better with my hair piled on top of my head in sweats than when I'm in a fancy dress."

"Well, when you put it that way—Wait, no. I like *Cinderella* because of the mice," Britt says in defense. When Elin simply raises her eyebrow, I hide my smile behind my glass of wine. "Well, Elin, which Disney movie is your favorite?"

Clearing her throat, she rubs her fingers against her jaw. "*Mulan*, hands down, because she sets out to prove that women are equal to men. She also put the life of her father first as he was too injured to fight, and I think that showed incredible courage. Not to mention, Mushu is hilarious. It's him or Genie as all-time best comic relief."

Sighing, Britt nods. "Yeah, alright. I see your point." Both sets of eyes turn to me. "Julia?"

"I didn't really watch a lot of television and movies growing up. I was more of an ink drinker," I reply.

Britt chokes on her wine. "A what?"

I furrow my brow. "An ink drinker. You know, someone who reads a lot."

Mashing her lips together, Elin snorts. Her hand covers her mouth as she blushes profusely. "I think what our dear French maiden is trying to say is she was a bookworm."

"Ah, okay. Ink drinker. That's a good term. I think I like that better than bookworm." Britt's voice comes out hoarse as she struggles to keep a straight face. The lovely language barrier.

I quickly get us back on topic. "*Beauty and the Beast* is the best. It's set in France, so how could it not be amazing," I reply with a wink and sip my drink.

"Ah, so you want the morally grey jerk as long as he gives you a library," Elin replies evenly.

I narrow my eyes at her as I think of what books are on my Kindle, and I guess I am in my morally grey era. "Libraries are great, but I'd prefer a stunning kitchen."

Snorting, Britt faces me and leans her hip against the kitchen island. "Belle gets the library and the kitchen with a staff to help." She starts humming, "Be Our Guest." I take that as my hint to finish making the free treats. This definitely relaxed my body and distracted my mind. I look down at the kitchen island and realize I put the pans of scones in the oven without freezing.

"What are your thoughts on Ariel, Elin?" I ask, trying to remember my princesses.

"Honestly, I feel like the movie's entire premise was misleading. We repeatedly hear that Ariel is sixteen and should be old enough to make her own decisions. In reality, she is under eighteen and, therefore, unable to legally enter into a binding contract. Her father should have pointed out the contract was null and void because Ursula had an underage girl sign it without a guardian present, yet he approves of her getting married."

I cut in. "But remember, *The Little Mermaid* was originally set in the mid-1800s when girls were out doing adult activities much younger than today's world. It was also set in Denmark, and I don't know what their contract laws were back then."

Pressing her lips together, Britt replies, "Both of you have made valid points. Now, where do we stand with *Snow White* versus *Rapunzel*?"

"I'd much prefer living with the chameleon. They're both required to do chores for other people, like a maid. At least with Rapunzel, she's given ample time to do her hobbies and read books," I reply.

"Plus, Rapunzel gets to choose who she lets up, whereas Snow White falls into a coma and then proceeds to be kissed by a random stranger. I'd rather stay in a dreamless sleep forever than get kissed by a crazy person," Elin replies, taking a long sip of her wine. "Yet, I'm not sure Rapunzel had it much better when she was consistently misled with false promises by the narcissistic thief."

With wide eyes, Britt slams down her glass with enough force to make me wince and replies, "First, with both Snow White and Aurora, true love's kiss is what brought them out. It's not some random guy, it's their soulmate. Second, you both are in danger of ruining

Disney movies for me. I'm never letting you watch them with my little sister. She'd probably cry."

Elin arches a brow. "Isn't she in high school?"

"Yes," Britt grits out. "But, we love our sister movie nights where we watch Disney."

"Alright." Elin raises her hands in surrender. "*Aladdin* is pretty well-rounded. Jasmine gets to make her choice, although she is super young. Yet, we still have issues with a misleading thief."

"Moana and Elsa, too." Britt huffs, worrying her lip between her teeth. "Elin, you are such a pessimist about love."

"And you have always been a romantic." I wink and lift my glass.

"If she's the pessimist and I'm the hopeless romantic, where does that leave you, Julia?" Britt asks, looking at me over her wine glass.

The oven dings, and I ponder what I am. Is jaded romantic a term? Or pessimistic romantic? I try to focus on other movies with strong females who encourage the young minds of the next generation and move on autopilot, putting ideas of romance and love out of my mind for the moment. Pulling the trays from the oven, I set them on the stove and smile at my work. They look amazing.

"You did it!" Britt cheers. "Let's do a taste test to see which ones you should have on the menu. You know fair scones will sell better than hotcakes, right?"

I place a sample of all three scones on each plate and slide them over to Elin and Britt. Slicing my fork into the chocolate chip scone, I lift it to my mouth. As I bite into it, Elin asks, "Did you play any sports growing up?"

Shaking my head, I fight a groan when the buttery pastry melts against my tongue. I swallow before replying, "No. The only sport I did growing up was ballet. All the girls in my primary school attended ballet twice a week. My mother wanted to get along with the other mothers, so we went. I was quite good. I begged my mom to let me do karate because I loved Jackie Chan. One night, I put together a storybook with pictures depicting a burglar breaking into our house and somersaulting through our skylight. I drew myself in a karate outfit, kicking and using nunchucks against the bad guy. My dad was wheezing from laughing so hard. In my drawings, my nunchucks were bright purple with rhinestones on them. All the American magazines my mom read featured ads with a bedazzler. I wanted one so badly."

"Did you get to do it?" Elin asks, around a mouthful of scone. "By the way, this is amazing," she says, tapping her fork against the chocolate chip scone.

"Do what? Karate or bedazzle nunchucks?" I ask, fighting a grin.

"Karate," she deadpans.

"No." I huff as I press my fork against some stray crumbs. "I probably had a better chance of getting to bedazzle nunchucks. I had to continue taking ballet. When my parents told me I couldn't take karate, I let them know that if an intruder somersaulted into our flat, I'd just pirouette him to death. My dad told me to add a grand jeté for good measure."

"A grand jeté?" Britt stops chewing as the words roll oddly off her tongue.

"A big jump. He told me to twirl and jump when I could've done kicks, chops, and punches if I'd become a black belt."

"Well, you are really bendy," Britt drawls. "I remember when Coach Athail told us to stretch before doing the fitness testing senior year, and while I struggled to touch my knees, you had your head between your knees and your arms flat against your calves."

Clearing my throat, I respond, "Yes, I'm quite flexible. Or I was. Can't say I do much more than stand over a kitchen island anymore, but I used to be very flexible."

"Not to change the subject, but I want to point out that all three of these are amazing. I think you should make all these flavors for the bakery," Elin says, drawing my attention to her empty plate.

"I think I will. Thank you for being here, you two," I whisper as a smile tips the corner of my mouth.

"How is Madeleine liking her stay in this old Victorian house?" Britt asks, jamming another bite in her mouth as crumbles fall to her plate.

"She's adjusting just fine. My aunt had a bunny once so I'm using the cage she had in the attic, which Madeleine fits perfectly inside."

"Maybe your bunny can convince you to stay in Topaz Falls," Elin says with a wink.

Shaking my head, I take notes in the margin of the recipe, adding the amount of cinnamon I added in the batter. I stare at the remaining scones, and pride flows through me. I did it. I baked something without having a panic attack. If I did it once, then I can do it again. I just need to rebuild my confidence, and I'll return to normal in no time. Hopefully, I'll be able to do it alone next time because I don't think Elin and Britt can come to the bakery with me every day.

Chapter 10

Declan
Tuesday, October 1

The smell of cinnamon and butter is so thick I can almost taste it as I walk into Mama M's for breakfast. I texted Lachlan and Aislinn last night to see if they had time to meet me for breakfast before they had to be at work this morning. There is a soft drone of conversation as the patrons at each table lean in toward one another, cradling coffee mugs and shoveling food in their mouths.

My stomach audibly growls. Since Mom and Dad went to the rehabilitation center, I've been living off Pop-Tarts and cereal for breakfast. I may be a grown man with my own house, but that doesn't mean I know how to cook, nor do I have any desire to learn. I hate cooking and baking. I swear the recipe changes between when I read what the measurement is supposed to be and when I dump it in the bowl. One cup becomes half a cup, or four teaspoons magically change to a quarter teaspoon. If I believed in mythical beings, I'd assume I have kitchen elves messing with my recipes because it doesn't matter how many times I stare at the stupid recipes; the food never comes out as they say it should in the reviews.

Aislinn and Lachlan are snuggled up to one another on a bench seat in the far corner of the diner. I love my brother and sister-in-law, but at the same time, I'm wildly jealous of what they have. Do I want to settle down? Hell, yeah. Do I want to settle down with anyone I've dated in the last five years? Definitely not. Now that Julia is back, my hope is restored. During my senior year, I assumed it would be the two of us forever. I still don't know what happened between us that made her hightail it out of here, but I'm desperately hoping for a second chance. I'm sure she's changed since the fresh-faced eighteen-year-old, but so have I.

Lachlan lifts his hand when I arrive at the table. Aislinn scoots out of the booth and wraps me in a tight hug. It's hard to believe they've already been married for almost five months. She may have only been in our lives for the last year and a half, but it feels like she's been family forever. Patting her on the back, I savor the familiarity of her embrace. It makes me miss having someone to wrap in a tight hug whenever I crave human contact or affection.

"What are you guys having?" I ask as I step away from Aislinn and slide into the opposite side of the booth.

"Omelet," Lachlan says as he lifts his mug of black coffee to his mouth.

Aislinn taps on the center of the page. "Pigs in a blanket with maple syrup," she replies. "You?"

I think a large protein order is necessary for my well-being because my breakfast has consisted of Pop-Tarts and Frosted Mini Wheats for the last few weeks. "Depends. Are we splitting the check, am I buying, or are you buying?" I wiggle my eyebrows at her so she knows I'm joking.

Pressing her lips together, she shakes her head. "Our treat, Declan."

Laughing, I let out a low whistle. "Well, then, in that case, I'll have to order one of each." Lachlan's boot connects with my shin, causing me to inhale sharply. "I was joking," I grind out. "I'll probably get the Glacier Lumberjack Stack. It's pancakes with eggs, bacon, and sausage. I have planned a long day in the orchard today, fighting blight."

Mama M appears out of nowhere with a coffee just the way I like it. I need half an inch of cream on the top of mine to make it palatable. "Alright, I heard you wanted the G.L.S., Declan. What about you, two?"

After we order, I make awkward small talk about the ranch, veterinary clinic, and orchard. When I mumble errant observations about the weather, Lachlan raps his knuckles against the table and raises a brow at me. "Do you need money? Help reconciling the accounts? Spit it out, man. This is getting painful," Lachlan mutters.

Clearing my throat, I reply, "Alright. So, you know how the orchard is doing a televised harvest bake-off with the Baking Network?" They both nod, Aislinn's brows furrow in concentration. "Well, the lady I've been working with at the network called the other day. One of the teams backed out, and she asked me to find two people from Topaz Falls to compete as the Home Team on the show. It's three Sundays starting in less than two weeks."

I take a deep breath as Lachlan replies, "And what? You need our help brainstorming who to ask?"

My eyes meet Aislinn's steady gaze. "Actually, I was hoping to ask Aislinn and see if she could partner with Ingrid or something. I don't know. I'm at a loss of what to do."

"I haven't watched the show yet. Do I need to make cookies and muffins?" Aislinn asks.

"Well, you can make those for your choice of breakfast food. There is also a savory lunch bake, where the judges ask you to make something with a required ingredient. Then there is a dessert piece," I explain, hoping I'm describing it correctly.

Aislinn presses her lips into a hard line as her eyes volley between us. Reaching up, she massages her forehead, closing her eyes. "That's really sweet of you to think of me, but I don't know the first thing about technical baking. I can make muffins, cookies, and cupcakes, but I wasn't classically or professionally trained. I just enjoy baking, but I need a recipe to follow. I'd ask my brother, but he's working weekends the entire month of October. Have you asked Mama M?"

"Asked me what, sweetheart?" Mama M asks, sliding our plates of hot food in front of us. She moves like a kitchen ninja.

"I need to come up with a team of two people to participate in the bake-off during the last three Sundays this month. The network wants the participants to be from Topaz Falls. Would you want to do it?" My voice sounds like I'm on the verge of begging Mama M, who looks like Mrs. Potts from *Beauty and the Beast*. Like a coin, she's as tall as she is wide, and her once amber hair is now shot through with silver. Coral cheeks against her alabaster skin make her look like one of the porcelain dolls my grandmother collects. She's rarely not smiling, and the frown marring her face tells me she isn't the answer to my problem.

"Sorry, sugar. Sundays are our busiest days. I'd love to help, but Kyle is the only person I can think of as my teammate. Unfortunately, he's on the grill when we open every Sunday. What about that sweet new baker, Rita's niece, who's taking over her bakery? I bet she would love the free advertising for her abilities. I remember Rita telling me she attended some fancy culinary school in Paris."

"Yeah," I grumble, staring at the swirling cream in my coffee. "Looks like that might be my only option."

Lachlan furrows his brow. "Wait, didn't you date Rita's niece senior year of high school?"

Mama M snaps her fingers and crosses her arms over her chest. "That's right, he did. Now, how did that slip my mind." Her eyes bore into me, hoping I'll give her a bit of information. Any information about where Julia and I stand currently. Hell, I don't even know. I know where I want us to stand, but I'm unsure how to convince her. It's not like I became a catch over the last decade.

"Well, you all enjoy your breakfasts, and let me know who will be representing Topaz Falls in the bake-off." She spins on her heel and strides back to the kitchen as Kyle's deep voice notifies her that another order is ready.

We eat in silence, and I fight the pull to meet Aislinn's gaze as it drills into the top of my head. I stay hunched over my plate, scooping food into my mouth so I don't have any opportunity to talk. She is dying to ask me questions but is too polite to initiate the conversation. Lachlan was getting his graduate degree when I was a senior. Because he was doing internships every chance he got, he didn't come home more than a handful of times that year. He never met Julia, but I'm sure he overheard my mother and Ingrid gossiping about my failed relationship on numerous occasions.

Once our plates are cleaned, I drop a twenty on the table to cover my bill and slide out of the booth. Lachlan and Aislinn follow suit and walk with me to the front of the diner. Saying goodbye to Mama M, we push through the door, and luckily, I'm parked right in front, so I won't need to make more awkward small talk. I spin and hug Aislinn tightly before she can ask me anything pointed. "I'll see you guys at Glaciers this weekend?"

Pressing her mouth into a firm line, Aislinn replies, "Sure. But you hardly ever go to Glaciers."

Lachlan chuckles as he wraps an arm around her shoulders. "Mom isn't home to cook, so he has to eat out somewhere unless he wants frozen pizza, burritos, or Pop-Tarts for the four hundredth time."

I wrinkle my nose, pissed my brother knows me that well. "Yeah. I'll be there. The fact they make a good burger is an added bonus. Ingrid texted me she was playing, so I wanted to see her. Look, I've got to get back to the orchard. I'll talk to you later."

Lachlan's smug grin is the last thing I see as I put my truck in reverse and haul ass back to the orchard. Glancing at the clock on the dash, I groan. I totally lost track of time. Channing is due at the orchard in ten minutes. I smack the steering wheel in frustration as one of the only lights in this entire town turns red when I approach the intersection.

My phone rings, and I answer it hastily. "Hello?"

"Dec? It's Channing. Camille and I are about twenty minutes out. One of our deliveries got screwed up, so I was stuck on the phone for the last hour trying to hash out the issue. Will you still be around?"

"Not a problem. Are you and Camille each bringing a truck? I've got fifty bushels set aside for you. Each box weighs about forty-five pounds. Will you be able to get them all in one trip? Your truck can only hold about sixteen bushels, right?"

"Yeah. I've got two more friends meeting us there. Do you remember Connal and Dylan? They'll be there at the top of the hour," he replies, his deep voice rumbling over my Bluetooth.

"Sounds good. See you in a few." Clicking off my phone, I turn into the orchard. I wonder if Camille and Channing can bake. They may be from Topaz Crest, but at least I won't have to approach Julia about the competition. I already hate who she'd choose as her partner anyway because I want to be the one who spends copious amounts of time shoulder-to-shoulder with her. Maybe if I ask, I should tell her the Home Team is women only, so she can't pick some dude I don't know.

Channing pulls his huge dually into the gravel beside the storage barn shortly after I get the doors open to the loading ramp. "You sure the three of us can load the first thirty bushels alone?"

"They're only forty-five pounds, right?" Camille asks, hopping down out of her truck. Her dark blonde hair is woven into an intricate braid down her back. Her upper body strength rivals mine as she easily heaves the first crate into her arms and strides back to Channing's truck bed. Her deep brown eyes assess me as she passes me for the next crate. Clearing my throat, I hoist a crate and follow her to the tailgate. Sliding it in, we all work in companionable silence until both trucks are full.

"Hey, Channing? Do you or Camille bake?" I ask before I lose my nerve.

"Definitely not. We run a pub for a reason," Camille replies for them. "We can grill meat like pitmasters, but we suck at baking."

Hrm. Damn. "Okay. Another question for you guys. Being a brewery and pub, have you ever considered doing an Octoberfest or Brewfest? We could call it Growler's Brewfest or Bigfoot Brewfest. Something fun for the fall? Next year, if you want to set up an area on the orchard during the Apple Harvest Festival to get Growlers Alley some exposure, I'm sure it would be a hit. Fresh pressed cider for the kids and hard cider for the adults."

Nodding thoughtfully, Channing widens his stance. "That might be a fun activity. I'll think about it and talk it over with my team. Big events aren't really our scene, but we can discuss the idea."

"Awesome."

At the top of the hour, Connal and Dylan back their trucks up to the loading ramp. I shake hands with Connal first, a mountain of a man who makes me feel small even though we're the same height. His thick blonde hair is tied into a loose ponytail at the nape of his neck as he wordlessly studies me. With a tight smile, he turns and effortlessly heaves a crate into his meaty hands before silently striding to his truck.

Dylan offers me a tight smirk. Ingrid always refers to him as a semi-reformed bad boy. I'm shocked to see he owns a truck. I've only ever seen him riding a red Harley. Ink peeks out from below the cuffs of his black leather jacket and under the collar of his white t-shirt. His dark brown hair is spiked unruly, making Axel's hair look tame. "Good to see you, Dec.'"

"You too, Dylan. Thanks for moving all these apples. With my dad out of commission, I don't have a lot of delivery people on hand."

"No worries. We've got this covered. You smell, I mean, look stressed. Why don't you get back to what you need to do? We'll handle it from here, man," Dylan says, grabbing a crate with ease and walking to his truck effortlessly.

I haven't met many people from the Topaz Crest, but they seem to be a different breed. The biceps on Connal make mine look measly, and by normal guy standards, I know they aren't. Rotating my arm slightly so as not to look like I'm checking out my arm, I glance up at Connal and internally shake my head. Nah, these guys are just huge. I don't think they all are. Maybe I should visit Channing's bar, Growlers Alley, and meet a few more from the community. These guys have always been loyal to a fault.

"Well, if you guys have it from here, I've got some branches that I treated for fire blight to trim," I say, rolling up the sleeves of my flannel.

Slowly nodding, Camille gently squeezes me on the shoulder. "Don't forget to take a bucket with alcohol to dip your shears between cuttings. Wouldn't want that shit to spread, you know?"

Smiling tightly, I pat her on the upper back. "Thanks. I probably would've forgotten."

She throws me a wink before walking back up the ramp to grab another bushel of apples. Man, what I wouldn't give to have a set of workers on staff who are as strong as those four.

Alcohol—don't forget a bucket of alcohol. I'd hate to get to the far end of the field only to realize I forgot it. Maybe I should write it on my hand. Shears—can't forget those damn things either.

Chapter 11

Julia

Wednesday, October 2

Marching over to the trash bin, I dump another tray of macarons. They aren't usually this finicky. What is wrong with me? I did fine with Elin and Britt on Monday. Digging my nails into the palms of my hand, I fight the urge to growl in frustration. I thought all of this was behind me now. What could possibly have changed that made me bake like an imbecile two days later? Are French pastries really no longer an option for me? Do I need to switch gears and only bake American treats? How will I sell this place and return to France if I can't bake French desserts? No one will visit my shop if I can only make American fair scones. I know I screwed up the cupcakes last week, but I'd like to think that was an honest mistake. It wasn't because of my fear of the oven. I was just distracted.

My phone rings through my Viber app, and I pick it up, needing to forget about the ruined batch of cookies. "Hello?"

"Sweetheart?" My mom's melodic voice brings an instant smile to my face. "How are you? Is Topaz Falls treating you well?"

"Ask her if she is doing okay in the kitchen," my dad's voice calls from somewhere in their flat.

"I'm alright. I've made some progress with the ovens. I made a batch of scones," I reply, forcing myself not to sigh in defeat. Mom would hear the frustration in my voice and probably book a plane ticket tomorrow.

"Scones? Were they from Rita's recipe book?" she asks, and I can hear the smile in her voice. "We would make those with my mom and grandma."

"They were! I added three different toppings, and they got rave reviews from my friends. I'll probably add them to the menu."

"Wonderful sweetheart. Are you doing okay in Rita's house?" Mom asks. Even though I can't see her, I know she's twisting her fingers into the hem of her house sweater.

"Yes. I actually found an old family cookbook and a trunk full of old photos. I'll be sure to send you scans or photos of what I find. I even found a photo of Grandma Dottie and her sister Reina standing in front of the house." With the excitement of falling through the ceiling, I completely forgot to send Mom the photo of them. Luckily, there was a carpenter from Larkspur Canyon, which is the next town over, who was able to stop by this afternoon to assess the damage.

"I think the cookbook originally belonged to Grandma Dottie's mother, Desolee. They're the ones who built Rita's house. I'm glad you're exploring the house. Is there a lot of work to do?" Mom asks hesitantly.

"Yes," I sigh. "There is so much stuff. But I will get it sorted and I promise not to throw out any family heirlooms or photos. I need to de-fairy the downstairs. I feel like I'm in fairyland when I'm sitting in the living room. It's a bit unsettling."

Mom chuckles. "Yes, please do not ship any fairy trinkets to your father and me. Have you seen the Ambarsan boy?"

I stiffen. I knew she was going to loop around until we spoke about Declan, but I hoped I had more time. "Yes. I've seen him a couple of times."

"As in glances from across the street or dates?" Mom can pry better than a professional interrogator. I'm not even in the kitchen where she can ply me with her cookies to loosen my lips.

"Across the street and stuff," I grumble.

Her voice catches on a rapid inhale. "Are you still planning to come home in January?"

"Yeah." My voice wobbles a little at the thought of never returning after I sell the only things left attaching me here.

"Sweetheart, I have to go. Your father just reminded me we have to leave for the theater. Be good and we'll talk to you later. We love you."

"Love you both. Have fun." I hang up and my eyes quickly find the ruined tray of macarons.

I'm pacing in the kitchen as I try to think of what else I could do before meeting with Dr. Walsh. My mind drifts into a daydream of Paris streets. I have the perfect place picked out for my shop on Rue Saint-André des Arts. It is the ideal place for my new patisserie. Maybe if I turn on some music, it will distract me like Britt did so effortlessly. I could also put a television back here. Maybe some daytime soap opera would numb my mind enough that baking would flow naturally.

A gentle knock pulls me from my downward spiral. When I glance up through the kitchen doorway, I lock my eyes on the man from the coffee shop. Britt likes him, but Elin seems to hate the guy with as much vehemence as I do Chauncy. I was convinced it was due to a lover's quarrel, but she made it very clear the two never even dated.

What was his name? Andrew? Andre? Antoine?

Untying my apron, I stride toward the front door, lifting it over my head and laying it on a table. The bright sun is high above the horizon, and I swallow the emotions of frustration threatening to bubble out of me as I step into the warm sunlight bathing the front of the shop. My fingers pinch the cold metal of the deadbolt as I crank it open and yank the door toward me.

I offer a hesitant smile because I'm unsure whether to be on team Britt or team Elin regarding the man with thick golden hair and soft brown eyes, which remind me of cups of hot cocoa. He towers over me in his hiking boots, cargo pants, and flannel shirt. The smile he offers me is kind and understanding. Sorry, Elin, but I don't think this man has a cruel bone in his body, and we haven't even had a proper conversation yet.

Goodness, what is his name?

Reaching out a hand, hoping it will get him talking like it does most Americans, I say, "Good morning. How are you doing today?"

Clearing his throat, he grasps my hand and offers me a steady shake. "I'm good, Julia. I don't know if you remember meeting me at my coffee shop the other day, but I'm Anders Tollefson."

Grinning, I reply, "Hi, Anders. Yes, I remember. It's good to see you again. Is there something I can help you with? I don't open until next week."

He offers me a cheeky smirk, which I force myself not to blush over. "Actually, I was stopping by to discuss the shop with you. Correct me if I'm wrong, but I heard your aunt's will stipulates you need to run the bakery for three months, and then you could sell it and move back home. I wanted to approach you with an offer to purchase the bakery when the time comes. You see, the town desperately needs a bakery. I don't want to see this place end up in some investor's hands who will turn it into something else." He takes a deep breath before continuing, "I love this town and am willing to purchase the business from you at above market value if it means keeping it in the hands of the community who will love it as deeply as your aunt."

Furrowing my brow, I tilt my head. "You want to start a contract to purchase a bakery, which hasn't run in two years? What if I can barely survive three months because the town isn't big enough to support a bakery?"

He rubs his palm along the scruff of his jaw as his eyes rest unfocused on the far wall. "I want what's best for this town and the people who love living here. Money isn't an issue if it means keeping the heart of Main Street bustling with small businesses. It allows more jobs for our high schoolers and returning college students during the summer when tourism picks up with people traveling to Glacier National Park. I don't want to be one of those quaint towns that loses themselves to strip malls and high rises."

Worrying my lip between my teeth, I get what he's saying, but it's hard to grasp the concept of unlimited funds.

"Have you found a place in Paris you'd like to purchase or lease?" he asks softly as he settles down into one of the colorful wooden chairs sitting mismatched around the table.

Slowly nodding my head, I glance out the window. This is the out I needed. It literally fell into my lap. His offer to buy the bakery means I won't have to hire a broker or look for a buyer. Why does it leave a knot in the pit of my stomach?

"I want a place on Rue Saint-André des Arts. There are so many historical cafes and bakeries in the area. People stroll along the street, meandering from bakery to bakery. I want to have some traditional French bakes and nouveau modern takes on the classics," I explain wistfully.

With each day that passes here, I'm struggling to see myself behind the bakery case in my daydreams of Paris.

"What would it cost you to open a bakery in Paris?" he asks so quietly I almost think I misunderstood him.

"I was hoping to get seven hundred thousand for my aunt's house and the bakery," I murmur, wiggling my nose.

Surprisingly, he doesn't look shocked. He narrows his eyes as he assesses me. My soul feels flayed, and his gaze seems to uncover my deepest fears and strongest desires.

"You realize the house alone would be about four hundred thousand, right? You could probably get five hundred thousand for the building with the living unit above. The bakery with fixtures, furniture, equipment, and your aunt's recipes could probably sell for one hundred and fifty thousand dollars," he explains. I can't tell if he thinks I'm an idiot or desperate to get out of this town before it threatens to keep me here and throw away the key.

Smiling tightly, I fold my arms over my chest. "I'm well aware, but I wanted this sale to happen with as little effort as possible on my part. When the three-month mark hits, I want a sale to be final and a plane ticket to Paris in my hands. If I try to get what it's worth, I may be here much longer than I want."

"What do you think of my offering you seven hundred thousand for the business and building? You could keep the house, so you'd have a place to stay if you came back to visit, or you could rent it and have an additional income."

Nodding, I reply, "That sounds too good to be true, Anders."

"I want to be fair. I also don't want you to lose your connection to this town by selling all of your aunt's possessions and properties."

Stepping forward, I wrap my arms around his shoulders and sigh. "Thank you. I can't tell you how much stress this will remove from my shoulders."

Stiffly patting me on the back, he replies, "I'll have the escrow attorney I use for all my business deals draw up a neutral Sale and Purchase Agreement. Once he has a draft ready, I'll bring it by, so you have time to read it. If you want an attorney to review the agreement before you sign it, I can recommend some possible people. I'm offering all cash, so there's no need for a bank loan or promissory note. I also know your aunt owned this outright, so there will be no third-party payoffs. I believe the estate's attorney kept the personal and real property taxes current, so I will pay the advance tax and use tax on the equipment. I have a rough idea of the equipment amount, so I'll plug in the allocations for the purchase price that you can alter if you feel they are off. Because you will return to France, I won't add a non-compete clause. Does that sound okay?"

Widening my eyes, a drip of sweat trickles between my shoulder blades. "I may have been raised by an English-speaking parent, but I have no idea what you just said or are talking about."

With raised hands, he offers me a boyish grin. "Sorry. I get a little carried away with business deals. How about I give my terms to the attorney, and when I bring you the agreement, you can look it over and seek legal counsel if you see the need?"

Licking my lips, I reply, "Alright. Let's start small and work our way up." Something he said clicks, and my jaw drops. "Wait. Did you say you were going to pay cash?"

Tugging at the back of his neck, he swallows audibly. "Yes. I will pay cash, so we don't need to worry about bank or seller financing."

Nodding, I press my lips together hard. "Okay," I say on a slow exhale. "You've convinced me to take your offer."

"Oh, and also, if you decide you don't want to sell and would rather stay in Topaz Falls, just let me know. I'll ensure there is wording allowing you to cancel the deal at any time in the next three months."

"Wow," I reply, my tongue feeling tied. "Seriously? Why?"

"Because Topaz Falls has a way of keeping those who are meant to be here. I think you're meant to stay, and your aunt knew it. She talked about you all the time, you know?"

I shake my head and whisper, "Topaz Falls chewed me up and spit me out a long time ago. I'm just here to deal with my aunt's affairs. Don't worry, I won't be staying. The bakery is as good as yours, Anders."

"We'll see," he murmurs as he opens the front door. "It was good to see you, Julia."

"Same," I reply, my gaze following his frame as it strides toward the coffee shop.

He may know business, but he doesn't know me. I won't be staying longer than necessary. Topaz Falls didn't want me back then, and it certainly doesn't want me right now. Aunt Rita just made it difficult to walk away untethered. Luckily, Anders offered me the perfect escape.

Chapter 12

Declan
Thursday, October 3

Shaking out my hands, I grip the door and tug. The glass rattles, and I step back, noticing Julia has no open or closed sign in the window. I know the bakery doesn't officially open for another week, but the kitchen lights are on, and music is playing.

Stepping back up to the door, I cup my hands around my eyes and peer through the glass. Before I lose my nerve, I straighten my back and rap my knuckles on the metal frame. Stuffing my hands in the pockets of my oiled canvas coat, I rock back on my heels attempting to look calm, cool, and collected. I am none of those things. My eyes dart to the ground and follow a hairline crack in the concrete below my feet. I wonder if I should call and get someone over here to fix it before it gets worse.

After a moment, I lift my hand and knock loudly on the glass. A piercing scream echoes through the bakery, sending a jolt of ice through my veins. Julia. Without thinking, I turn and thrust my shoulder against the door. The glass rattles, but the door doesn't budge. Her continuous screams of panic gut me as my eyes wildly search for a way to get inside. I have to get to her. Taking a step back, I ram my upper body into the glass again. This time, the door shakes, but an impenetrable barrier blocks me from getting to my girl.

Pivoting, I sprint to my truck in the front row space behind me and leap into the truck bed. I hastily grab a wrench from the tool compartment and jump out, racing to the door. My toe catches on the damn crack in the concrete, causing me to stumble. The stupid door breaks my fall as I ram into it. Sucking in a sharp breath, I wind up, bring the wrench back, and ready myself to break the glass. Before I start to swing, Julia comes running out of the back room, waving her hands at me in panic. Heaving, I drop my arm to my side, trying to steady my breath as the jolt of adrenaline arcs through me.

With wide eyes, Julia undoes the lock and yanks the door open. "Dec? What are you doing?"

My voice is guttural as I stumble toward her, wrapping her in my arms and pulling her flush against my chest. "You screamed, and I couldn't get to you."

Her arms hug me close as I bury my face in her hair. She smells like spun sugar and apples.

All too soon, she gently pushes me away and steps back. "Dec. I'm fine," she whispers, reaching up and tugging on her braid to steady the shake in her hands.

"Why'd you scream, blossom?" Her cheeks heat, and something thrums in my chest. I love watching her smile twitch when I use the nickname I gave her senior year.

Clearing her throat, she wraps her arms around her waist. "I, uh, saw—" Her voice becomes too soft for me to make out the words.

"You saw what? Was someone threatening you in the kitchen or alley?" Ugh. The alley. I bet the door back there was open. I should have run to the alley door when she screamed. Instead, I attempted to break down her bakery's front door like an idiot caveman.

At first, she doesn't answer, mashing her lips into a hard line as her eyes dart left and right, avoiding me at all costs. Placing my finger under her chin, I tip her face toward mine to see those gorgeous eyes that look like highballs of Grey Goose in the soft glow of the overhead lights.

Her cheeks heat with embarrassment this time, and a memory tugs at my subconscious. Her biggest fear is spiders. She refused to camp with me during senior year, always opting for my family's cabin up north. If we wanted to star gaze, it was on blankets in the back of my truck, never on the grass out in the orchard. When we went to the treehouse at the edge of the property, she would make me do a quick sweep for creepy crawlies before climbing up the ladder.

Smirking, I lean in so my breath fans against her cheek. The hitch in her breathing has me aching for her touch. "Was there a spider, blossom?"

"Maybe," she whispers with a hint of defiance lacing her tone. She hates to be teased. All her little nuances come flooding back to me. Things I thought I'd never forget are resurfacing after years of dormancy. Her fear of ice during the ALS ice bucket challenge after a terrible ice-skating accident when she was little. Standing in her aunt's kitchen making nutellasagna and pizza cake. The hot pink cargo capris she wore whenever the sun was out.

"Dec?" Her voice is barely audible but brings me back from the cobwebs of my brain. She's looking at me curiously as her head tilts to the side. "Why are you smiling like that?"

Shaking my head, I lean down and press a kiss to the top of her head. Reaching out, I gently wrap my fingers around her wrist and urge her to follow me back to the kitchen. "Come on. I'll get it for you and protect you. Where is it, blossom?"

Her warm hand finds the small of my back, and her fingers tighten around my belt loops. I will come slay spiders here any time of the day if it means getting this close to her. I bite my lip to keep from laughing. Her hand trembles when it reaches past my hip, pointing toward the sink at the back of the kitchen. My shoulders struggle not to shake in silent laughter.

I shuffle us toward the sink and spot the brown spider on the wall above the faucet. I bet she went to wash her hands and about fell over when she spotted it there. "Let me just grab a glass and a piece of paper. I'll release it out back, and your kitchen will be spider-free again."

"Thanks, Dec," she whispers as she presses her forehead into the center of my back.

Spotting an empty water glass in the sink, I pick it up and then search the counter for a piece of paper. A notecard sits on the kitchen island, so I snap it up and approach the eight-legged creature. I owe this little guy for making me look like Superman. As I get closer, it takes off like a shot, and I hold my breath. Shit, it's a baby hobo. Glancing over my shoulder, I meet her wide-eyed stare as Julia nibbles on her bottom lip. I tightly smile so she doesn't worry, but I will call the exterminator to ensure he can treat the kitchen when I leave here. Where there's one hobo, there are usually more. She's already struggling with her baking for some reason. I don't need to add a spider infestation to the problems she's having to face.

The spider stops, and I quickly press the glass against the wall. Sliding the notecard between the wall and the glass, I capture the spider and walk it back to the alley. In the daylight, I hold the glass up and check the pattern on its back. Just as I thought, medium brown with a pale-yellow chevron pattern. I walk it to the far end of the alley and release it. Julia gasps when I return to the kitchen door with the glass and notecard in my hand.

In disbelief, she rasps, "You used my aunt's recipe card to catch the spider?"

"No? Yes? Not on purpose," I reply with my hands raised.

She throws her arms around my waist and hugs me tight. My body relaxes into her embrace, feeling so familiar as if the last eight years have melted away. This is what we could've had if she'd just stayed here with me.

"I appreciate you coming to save me from a spider, but what brought you here?"

Clearing my throat, I tug at my collar. "Actually, I have something important to ask you."

Her eyes brighten with a hint of excitement. "Yes," she says on a breathy inhale.

"You see, the orchard is having its second annual Apple Harvest Festival. This year, I got the Baking Network to come and host a harvest bake-off. The other day, the network representative I've been working with informed me one of the couples backed out, and they've asked me to get two locals to be the Home Team." Taking a deep breath, I continue, "I was hoping I could convince you to be on it." Jamming my hands into my back pockets, I finally look up and meet her gaze.

Her shoulders slump ever so slightly as the brightness in her eyes dim. "That's what you wanted to ask me?"

Grabbing the back of my neck, I shift awkwardly. "Yeah. I really need you."

She takes a small step back, and the distance feels charged, like we're two magnets fighting the pull.

Swallowing audibly, she stares at my chest, not meeting my eyes. "I'll think about it. Can I let you know in a few days? I need to ask around and find myself a teammate."

I quickly step forward, wrapping her in a hug. She melts into me, and this time, when I step back, the heat in her eyes is unmistakable. My palms gently brush against the skin of her upper arm. Her right side tenses slightly. I wouldn't have seen it if I wasn't staring into her eyes, refusing to blink for fear of missing a moment of this.

Tentatively, I bring my hands up, cupping her face. Her eyes flutter closed as she leans into my palm. My thumb gently brushes her cheek. With a shallow breath, I hesitantly lower my mouth toward hers until our breaths mingle. When I can feel the warmth of her lips a hair's breadth away, static sparks between us. God, I've dreamt of this moment.

A pounding on the glass startles me, and we jump away like opposing magnets. My breath is heaving even though we haven't done anything. The mere thought of kissing her has my adrenaline pumping through my veins like a thirteen-year-old kid.

I shake my head to clear my thoughts as Britt's sing-song voice enters the kitchen. "You left the front door o—" Elin skids into her back as they see Julia staring at me with a heavy-lidded gaze.

"Well, well, well. What do we have going on in here? Is he morally grey enough for you, Julia?" Elin asks, the side of her mouth tilting up.

Julia chokes as her eyes narrow at Elin. Am I morally grey? What the hell? No way, I'll treat her like a fucking queen. She deserves ruby necklaces, not hand necklaces, and I'll kick anyone's ass who tries to give her either kind.

"Hey, you two," Julia splutters, smoothing her hands down the front of her jeans. "What brought you by?"

Britt wiggles her eyebrows. "If I remember correctly, you were making macarons today. Elin and I wanted to see if you needed any help. With, uh, the—"

"Washing," Elin shouts, cutting Britt off. Britt glares at her as she crosses her arms over her chest.

"Yeah. Elin told me she wanted to wash the dishes while I helped arrange the cookies on a platter," Britt grinds out.

Arching a brow, I blow out a heavy breath. "Well, you're about as subtle as an elephant in a hen house, Britt." Raising my hands, I wink at Julia and walk toward the front. "I'll see myself out and let you all get back to washing and platter decorating."

As I pass Elin, something hard and mental hits me in the gut. "I think this might be yours? It's not a good idea to leave your expensive tools lying around."

Chuckling, I grip the wrench and walk out of the kitchen. Julia's lilting voice calls out, "I'll get you an answer by the end of the week. Promise."

"I never doubted you, blossom," I murmur, facing away from them.

I never doubted us, either.

Chapter 13
Julia

I can't believe I almost kissed Declan, or should I say let Declan kiss me. I'm such an idiot to let my heart get entangled with him again. I'll just end up with another broken heart. The outcome is inevitable. You'd think I'd get it through my thick skull at some point. I need to keep my head on straight and a brick wall around my heart for three months. Afterward, I can go back home and focus on my patisserie. I don't need the distractions of letting men into my thoughts.

Now, I'm on my way to my first appointment with Dr. Walsh. There is also a chance I will run into Declan's siblings, Lachlan and Ingrid. Topaz Falls might be small, but I have no idea where I'm going. Britt told me the ranch used to be Declan's grandfather's land, and it's the opposite direction from the orchard, which I remember like the back of my hand. I recall his grandfather passed away a couple of years before I came here as a foreign exchange student.

Luckily, Aunt Rita's car is a newer Kia model with GPS. She bought it a year before she passed away. When I notified the law office I'd be coming to Topaz Falls, they took her car in for a tune-up. I guess it's technically my car, which is hard for me to consider. I've struggled to accept Rita isn't coming back. My gaze darts to the back door whenever I stand in her kitchen, thinking she'll walk in and start baking. I know it's been two years, and I've mourned her death, but being here, it still doesn't seem real.

The voice in the car tells me to turn at the next driveway. I slow the car down and pull across the cattle grate through a substantial wrought iron gate. A row of horses running is etched into the top with Ambarsan Equine Therapy Ranch in bold letters. At the fork in the road, I take a left, my car bouncing on the gravel and dirt-packed path. I pass a farmhouse with a truck and Subaru in the driveway. A little further down the path, an open barn containing several parked cars sits to the left. Directly in front of me is a large structure with a bold print sign above the door identifying the office. To the right of the office is a huge barn with a covered arena. The entire right side of the property is gorgeous, fenced pastures. This place is enormous and stunning.

I pull my car into one of the unmarked parking spots in front of the office. After shutting off the ignition, I grip the steering wheel and lower my forehead to the unforgiving leather. The coolness of the steering wheel grounds me before I have a chance to spiral. I lift my head just enough to look at my watch. Three minutes until my appointment time. Dr. Walsh didn't seem like the type who appreciates tardiness. Sucking in a deep breath, I climb out of my car and grab a bag of baked goodies I brought as a thank you to Trent and Axel. Slowly, I walk to the door.

Gripping the wooden handle, I push the door open. I'm hit by the smell of cinnamon as I duck through the threshold. My eyes adjust to the dim light as they dart around the room unfocused. A comfy couch sits off to the right under a window facing the barn and pasture. Straight ahead is a long counter, which separates the waiting area from multiple desks and people in chairs working on computers.

A woman with medium brown hair and a bright smile stands to greet me. She looks so familiar, and it isn't until she's right in front of me, when the light hits her eyes, that I realize she has the same color eyes as Declan.

"Ingrid?" I ask hesitantly, my voice sounding strained.

Her smile widens further, and she comes around the end of the counter into the waiting area. I tug at the sleeves of my shirt, trying to cover the back of my hands as much as possible.

"Julia," she says softly. "It's so nice to officially meet you. I've heard a lot about you over the years, though most of the information is almost a decade old. It is a rare occurrence for someone to catch my baby brother's eye, and you had them bugging out of his head."

Shaking my head, I bite my lip. "All good things, I hope? Honestly, I don't think I've changed much since then, so the information is all probably valid."

"I'll keep that in mind. What brings you to the ranch? Declan isn't here. He only stops by if there's food involved." She glances over her shoulder and frowns. "Actually, Lachlan brought in cinnamon rolls today, so maybe he is stopping by, but no one told me."

Before I can correct her, Dr. Walsh steps out of a room at the back of the office. "Ingrid. Julia is here for an appointment with me." I fight not to recoil at the thought of everyone knowing I'm here to see a shrink. He notices my flinch and his stoic expression softens. "It's okay. You are in a safe space."

Ingrid schools her features when she turns back around. "You are in great hands with Trent. I'll let you get on with your meeting. If you ever want to catch up or are looking for a new friend in town, please reach out to me. I've wanted to meet you forever, and I'm thrilled you returned to Topaz Falls." She wraps her arms around my shoulders and whispers, "Everyone needs some form of help. Trent is amazing at what he does. If you need anything, just let me know."

I swallow the thick lump at the back of my throat. I forgot how open Americans are with their emotions. I've read all about the mental health awareness they're pushing here. I had hoped I could scoot under the radar.

Ingrid heads back to her desk, and Trent takes his place before me. "Hi, Dr. Walsh," I murmur, struggling to make eye contact. I can feel his intense gaze as he simply watches me.

"Hello, Julia. Where would you like to have our introductory meeting? We could meet in my office, the lounge, or the stables." He folds his arms across his chest, pushing his black-rimmed glasses up the bridge of his nose. Lord, does this man know he looks like an auburn-haired Clark Kent? Oh goodness, he said something else while I was obsessing over his Hollywood doppelganger. My palms feel clammy as I think of what this meeting means. I'm seeking help. This is good.

"Are the horses an option?" Hopefully, that response makes sense. Briefly closing my eyes, I force myself to focus on him. Reaching the bag of treats toward him, I say, "Also, these are for you and Axel as a thank you for your help the other day."

He accepts the bag with a smile. "Thank you for these. I will make sure Axel gets a few. To answer your question, yes, of course. The horses are always an option for therapy. Would you feel more comfortable having Axel here? Your English is flawless, but I observed how you responded to Axel speaking French to you in the kitchen," Dr. Walsh says. His eyes are assessing my every movement.

Shaking my head, I reply, "No. I was raised by an English-speaking parent. I think it was more the shock of hearing fluent French in Topaz Falls, which pulled me out."

Motioning to the door, he opens it and allows me to step outside. I match his stride as we walk to the barn. The tall grass is golden this time of year, dry from the warm summer months, which have now ended. The leaves on the trees surrounding the pasture are an array of reds, oranges, and browns, reminding me of the many autumns I spent in Alpes-Maritimes. The trees look like they're on fire in a sea of gold. We pass the barn doors and arrive at a split rail fence. Dr. Walsh whistles sharply into the field. A moment later, a stunning horse runs in our direction. In the waning sunlight, it looks navy blue. The mane and tail whip wildly in the wind as it approaches us.

"This is my ranch horse, Tsunami," Dr. Walsh says when the horse snorts at us over the fencing. It shakes its head up and down until Dr. Walsh rubs his hands on the bridge of the horse's nose. "Tsunami, meet Julia. Come over here and let Tsunami get used to your presence. He can be a part of any of our sessions. Horses have a calming effect on us. He might help you talk out what is bothering you."

"Okay. I'd like to use Tsunami, Dr. Walsh." I approach slowly as the horse simply stares at me.

"Please call me Trent. There's no need for the formalities," he says. I nod in response, offering him a timid smile. As I pet its nose and slowly stroke down the neck, Trent begins to talk. "This first meeting can just be introductions, or we can dive right in and see if we can begin working on overcoming the mental hurdle of using an oven. The choice is yours."

Blowing out a deep breath, I close my eyes. "Let's get this started. I actually have something to run past you, and I'd like your opinion from a psychological standpoint. I'm wondering if it will set me back or push me forward."

Trent nods slowly. "Ask away. But first, do you feel comfortable giving me your back story? If this was a recent development, can you explain what the trigger was for you?"

"I was afraid you might ask that," I mutter. Squaring my shoulders, I give my full attention to Tsunami so I don't have to look at Dr. Walsh. "Back in February, I was at my bakery in Paris. I was pulling a late night, trying to balance our accounts. I must have fallen asleep at some point because I woke up at 2 a.m. to smoke coating the ceiling of the small office I used at the back of the shop. Firefighters were able to get me out, but I suffered severe burns. In May, I found out my fiancé was a con man. They think he started the fire in the ovens with rags coated in accelerant. The insurance policy was in his name, so when the payout came through, all the money disappeared along with him. My only option was to come back here. If I'm not distracted by Britt and Elin, I have a panic attack when I use the oven. I'm reopening the bakery in less than two weeks, and I don't know what to do if I can't even bake." I drop my head in defeat, smirking when Tsunami bumps his muzzle into my forehead.

Out of the corner of my eye, I see Dr. Walsh look at the notepad in his hand. He thoughtfully asks, "Why was Topaz Falls your only option?"

"My aunt was named Rita. She owned the bakery for decades. When she passed away, she left her entire estate to me. Unfortunately, there was a stipulation where I had to run the bakery for three months before I could sell the house or business."

"I see. Can you hire other people to work the oven while you create the batter or dough?" He crosses his arms over his chest, tapping his pen against his jaw.

"I could," I say, pausing as my train of thought mulls this over. My hand stills on Tsunami's muzzle. "I don't have extra cash right now, but I think the bakery had enough funds to hire some people."

"Does it make a difference whether you are in a commercial kitchen versus a home kitchen?" Dr. Walsh asks softly.

Quirking my mouth, I think of how best to describe it. After a moment, I respond, "Yes and no. It seems I am less likely to have a panic attack at home, but other things distract me there, so I'm not completely sure."

"Alright, so to reduce your anxiety and stress in the kitchen, how about you look to hire an assistant who will keep you distracted in the kitchen and work the ovens. Then, hire a second person to work on the bakery case and cash register. Speak with the estate lawyer to confirm there is enough in the accounts to hire temporary employees. What was the other question you wanted to run by me?" Dr. Walsh asks, stepping to the other side of Tsunami's muzzle so he can look at me directly.

My eyes dart to him before returning to the corn spots on Tsunami's blue roan coat. My finger nonchalantly traces the marks like a dot-to-dot. "Declan Ambarsan asked me to partake in a baking competition at the Ambarsan Apple Orchard. I have to find a partner for the event. Do you think it's wise for me to be in the competition when I can't even use an oven?"

"Interesting," he muses quietly. "Declan's told us about the baking competition he set up with the Baking Network. It's an outdoor event with all the baking completed outside under a large tent. My opinion is you give it a try. Since it is outside, your nerves might be less on edge because you won't feel trapped. I think a large part of your panic is your fear of being trapped inside again. You'll also be with a partner. You could have the partner man the oven. I truly think this would be a good way for you to begin overcoming your fear in a safe environment."

Nodding, I reply, "I was leaning toward accepting the offer. I'm not sure who to ask."

Dr. Walsh rocks back on his heels. "Aislinn and Freya, or Elin as you call her, love to bake for the veterinary clinic and the ranch. You could try asking one of them."

"I'll ask Elin this weekend. We're going out for girl's night at Glacier's on Saturday," I reply. "Thank you for your help."

"It's my pleasure. I'm glad I can offer you some guidance. If you'd like to meet regularly, we can return to the office and sign you up for a few more sessions."

"Sounds great. I appreciate your time today. Thank you."

"If you need anything else, please contact me day or night. Don't suffer alone if you find you're having a panic attack," he says, placing a reassuring hand on my shoulder.

"I won't. You'll be number one on my speed dial until I can successfully bake again," I say, smiling brightly at him. For the first time in months, I have hope I will overcome this setback and become stronger than ever.

Chapter 14

Declan
Friday, October 4

You've got to be kidding me. I slam my boot into the box of s'more supplies, shoving it to the far side of the floor. The first thing I attempt to order on my own arrives, and I screwed it up.

"Declan, it's not the graham crackers' fault you accidentally ordered double the amount we need. Speaking of which, why did you order double the amount?" Cameron asks, folding his arms across his chest as he leans against the wall. "Or maybe I should ask how you managed to order double the amount of graham crackers."

Fisting my hands on my hips, I tilt my head to the ceiling. I should have swallowed my pride and asked Anders for help. The dude is nicer than Mom's apple pie. He'd have looked over the order form without asking any questions. I don't think I'm capable of doing this job. Mom and Dad's sudden absence makes this fact glaringly obvious.

"Well," I say, clearing my throat. "I took the number of crackers per box—" I pause, pressing my lips into a firm line. Cameron lifts his chin, urging me to continue, but I can't. I have no idea how I got the number I did. I calculated it a bunch of times, but each time, I got a different amount. I think I just went with whatever I got twice and called it good. "Then I doubled it since each s'more needs two crackers. One for the top and one for the bottom."

"Right, but each cracker is split in half to create the top and bottom, so you actually needed half the number of boxes," Cameron replies, looking confused as hell. Trust me, man, I have no idea what I'm talking about. You think you're confused? Take a look in my head. You'll be more lost than Harry Potter was in the magical maze.

"Alright. How about you pull up the calculator on your phone?" I suggest. I go over to the cardboard box, open it, and pull out the box of graham crackers. I remember looking at the nutrition facts when I ordered them and being utterly baffled.

Cameron pulls out his phone and motions for me to give him the box. Sighing, I hand it over. "Alright, it says there are fourteen servings per box. Eight crackers make a serving, and there are two sheets per serving. How many s'mores are you planning for?"

Scrubbing a hand down my jaw, I sigh. "Five hundred."

"And how many boxes did you order?" Cameron asks.

"Thirty-six." I pause and look over the invoice to confirm before nodding. "Yeah, thirty-six boxes of graham crackers."

"Dec, that's enough for one thousand s'mores. There are twenty-eight crackers per box. One cracker makes a s'more because you snap it in half," Cameron says, exasperated.

"It says there are fourteen servings. A s'more uses two servings," I bark back.

Cameron fights to roll his eyes before redirecting the conversation. "Okay, whatever. What about the marshmallows."

"The packaging said there were about sixty-four marshmallows per bag, so I rounded up and ordered ten bags," I say.

"That isn't rounding up. Rounding up would be getting eight bags because it would be just over five hundred," Cameron says, massaging his temples. "You ordered six hundred and forty marshmallows."

He stands up and strides over to the chocolate box. "Should I even ask how many chocolates you ordered? Wait," he says, holding up the bag of individually wrapped chocolates. His brow furrows before he turns his gaze back to me. "What the hell are these?"

Jamming my hands into my pockets, I take a deep breath. "Okay, so I didn't have a Hershey's bar in the office, so I had no idea how many s'mores I could get from one bar. I figured it would be more sanitary to have the individually wrapped chocolate bars for everyone, too."

"Okay. I get the sanitary thing, but Dec, these aren't Hershey's bars. This is the Halloween assortment. There are Mr. Goodbars and Krackels in here. What kid will want a s'more with a damn Krackel in it? What the hell is a Krackel anyway?"

"Kids eat a shit ton of candy. They don't care what it is as long as it has milk chocolate and sugar. These have both in large quantities," I retort. "It says there are about one hundred pieces in the bag, so I rounded up to six bags just to be safe. I figure whatever we don't use can be used on Halloween. Problem solved. It's not a big deal."

Cameron shakes his head and takes a steadying breath. "Well, you have enough to make six hundred s'mores. Can you return the other fourteen boxes of graham crackers we won't need?"

I give a sheepish one-shoulder shrug. "Each box is only about four dollars. I'm sure I can figure out something. Don't worry about it. It's like a fifty-dollar mistake."

Placing his hands up in defeat, he mumbles, "You know what? You're right. It's not a big deal." His eyes look at me with pity. It's not the first time someone has noticed I'm terrible at math and looked at me like I'm an idiot. I'm not stupid. Math and I are like parallel lines; we never meet, no matter how hard I try. I think my mental calculator is broken as it only adds more confusion to the situation instead of solving problems. It's frustrating and annoying, but it's all I've ever known.

Before I can respond, my phone rings, and Cameron slips out the door, eager to return to his tasks around the orchard. This time of year, our to-do list is longer than Dad's honey-do list.

"Hello?" I say, not recognizing the number.

"Declan?" Julia's soft lilt comes across the line, and my world stops. My grip loosens, and the phone almost falls from my grip at the sound of her lyrical accent.

"Blossom?" I whisper in disbelief. "How did you get this number?"

"Your phone number? Well, I took a chance you had the same phone number as it was in high school," she replies.

"You remember my phone number from high school?" I can't hide the shock in my tone.

"Uh, yes. I dialed it almost every day. I bet you remember my old one, too. When I arrived last month, I got a new phone with a new number," she responds.

No, I don't remember her phone number from high school. I remember the area code. It was the same for everyone in Topaz Falls. I can barely remember my number, let alone one from eight years ago.

"Is this your new number?" I ask, looking down at a number that seems vaguely familiar.

She pauses for a moment, then responds. "No, this is the bakery number. It's the same from when Rita worked here."

Quickly, I change the topic. "How are you?" I ask, steering the line of questioning away from my terrible memory for all things numerical.

"Very good. Thank you. How are you?" Her voice sounds formal and hesitant, not like the effortless conversation we had years ago.

"I'm alright. Can you think of anything I could make to use up fourteen boxes of graham crackers?" My palm rubs along the scruff of my jaw as I stare at the cardboard box filled to the brim with crackers.

"I could make pumpkin cheesecakes with a graham cracker crust. It takes about two cups of graham crackers per pie. I don't know how many boxes that would take, but I'd be more than happy to try. I'm guessing it will make at least ten to fourteen cheesecakes." Julia's voice trails off. I can picture her nibbling her lip as she looks up at the ceiling to think, just like she did in physics senior year. "What if I bought the graham crackers from you and used them to make pumpkin cheesecakes for opening day next week? I'd just need some pie tins. I don't think Aunt Rita has enough to make that many pies."

"Our storage shed has a box of pie tins from when Mom did an apple pie sale years ago. Why don't you come to the orchard on Sunday, and we can grab them." I try to tamp down the excitement coursing through me at having her back at the orchard. Maybe the apple trees will bring back memories she's fighting to keep locked away.

"Sounds like a plan. But I actually called to tell you something important," she says, sucking in a deep breath. "I wanted to let you know I'm in for the competition at the orchard."

"Really?" I ask, surprised. It seemed like this day was heading down the crapper, but if I have one less thing to worry about, I guess my day is trending upward now. "Have you found a partner yet?"

"Actually, I was planning to ask Elin when we go to Glaciers tomorrow night," she replies.

My molars grind as I think of her at Glaciers. Sadly, it didn't occur to me that she'd go anywhere other than the bakery or her aunt's house. At Glaciers, guys like Axel and Noah will be there, possibly asking her to dance or using cheesy pick-up lines on her. I'd been planning to watch Ingrid play, but now it seems I'll arrive early and stay until Julia is safely in her car heading home. Alone.

"Dec?" Julia asks, pulling me back to the conversation.

Clearing my throat, my voice sounds rough as I reply, "Yeah. I might see you there. I'm going to watch Ingrid play tomorrow night. Save me a dance?"

"You dance now?" Julia's shocked response makes me smile. I had two left feet in high school, but that was because I hit 6'3" before I filled out. Wearing size fourteen shoes didn't help either. I felt like a giraffe trying to dance.

"Of course. So, is that a yes, then?" I probe, trying to decipher whether there will be any guys with her.

"Yeah, sure. It sounds fun," she murmurs. Before I can respond, she continues, "I'll see you around and let you know if Freya, I mean Elin, can be my partner. Bye."

The phone clicks off, but a huge smile overtakes me as I think of her blushing and flustered from the phone call.

Opening my contact list, I scroll down to Dorine Metcalf's info at the Baking Network. After two rings, she picks up. "Dorine Metcalf here. How can I help you?"

"Hi, Dorine. This is Declan Ambarsan. I wanted to let you know I found a Home Team for the baking competition in a couple weeks."

"That's great news. The producer will be thrilled. We look forward to seeing you. Was there anything else you needed?" Dorine asks. Her voice sounds happy, as if finding an additional team for the competition weighed heavily on her shoulders.

"No, I'm good. Thank you, though. I have some work to do, so I'll let you go. I just wanted to let you know I found a replacement team. Have a great day and a good weekend."

"You too, Declan." She hangs up before I can press end. I pocket my phone and pick up the bucket by the door with a pair of shears and a container of alcohol. Time to fight the blight so I can spend tomorrow evening at Glaciers watching over my girl.

Chapter 15
Julia
Saturday, October 5

I have two more interviews to complete today for the bakery staff positions. The next one should arrive in five minutes. Opening day is in two days. I'm freaking out inside. I posted a few fliers and a social media post about wanting help, and five people called or emailed to inquire about the position.

Three have stopped by, and although I'm desperate, I'm not sure I'm that desperate. One girl spoke so fast, I couldn't understand a word she said. Another girl seemed nice but so shy she almost refused to speak. It didn't matter my question; I was lucky to get a one-word response. The third was a teenage boy who was a senior in high school and could only work from 4 p.m. until 6 p.m. When I reminded him this was a bakery and I would be done by 4 p.m. each day, he told me to keep him in mind if I expand to desserts. I didn't have the heart to tell him the hours he could work fell into the dinner hour, not the dessert hour. I feel like I'm striking out with less than forty-eight hours until we open. I need this place to survive the ninety days so I can go home with my head held high.

I take in the worn, checkered flooring and the cream and aqua-stripped walls. I also notice the large bakery case my aunt meticulously kept clean. The cream tables with the mismatched chairs coordinate and give the place a shabby-chic style. It always felt welcoming and whimsical in high school. I'm afraid now it looks worn and in need of some love. Hopefully, when people arrive, they will be filled with nostalgia from my aunt's reign here, and they'll overlook the obvious flaws.

The door clanks open, and my gaze snaps to the entryway. I stand from my distressed aqua chair and greet the large man before me. He has a full head of golden-brown curls most women would pay good money for at the salon. Natural highlights are streaked through his hair, and his skin is the color of a toasted marshmallow. He must spend a lot of time in the sun. The faint lines around his eyes crinkle when he offers me a boyish grin.

"Hello," I say, reaching my hand confidently toward him. "My name is Julia."

His deep baritone echoes off the bakery's walls as his hand engulfs mine. "Hi, Julia. My name is River. Thank you for the opportunity to interview. I usually get turned away pretty quickly."

My head cocks to the side as my eyes assess him. "How come?"

Grabbing the back of his neck, he gently tugs as his eyes dart to the ground. "I did some time and am out on parole. While I was inside, I learned to bake. It calmed my mind and brought me joy. I was hoping I could find a job at a bakery once I was out, but the ones in Whitefish weren't hiring, and the one in Larkspur Canyon chose someone else. I assume it was more related to my past, but they let me down easily."

I force myself to stay grounded. He may have been in jail, but I don't know why, and if it was for something like murder, I'd hope he'd still be in there.

"How old are you?" I ask, forcing a smile that doesn't quite reach my eyes as my lower lid ticks with nerves.

"Twenty-nine. I did five years for being with the wrong crowd. I was with an MC group out of Larkspur Canyon," he explains, not moving closer to me. He's giving me space, but his eyes are pained as he looks at me with hope.

"What is an MC group? Are you a singer?" I ask, genuinely confused. Maybe his band members were dealing drugs.

Wincing, he shoves his hands in the pockets of his thick leather coat. "Motorcycle. Not master of ceremonies."

"Ah. I see. Well, did you do the crime you were accused of?" I ask, narrowing my eyes ever so slightly.

"No, ma'am," he says, shaking his head profusely, his thick curls bouncing around his face. It makes him look younger than twenty-nine. Almost angelic.

"First of all, please don't call me ma'am. I'm younger than you. Julia is fine." When he smiles in confirmation, I ask, "So, do you like to bake?" I play with the straps of the apron I have around my waist.

He nods. "It brings me so much peace. I love to bake bread the most. Kneading the dough is therapeutic for me."

"Excellent. Are you able to do 5 a.m. to 2 p.m. with an hour lunch?" When he nods, I hold up my finger and cringe. "Are you able to start Monday morning?"

"I'll be here to help you open," he says, then pauses. Looking at me through his thick lashes, he murmurs, "If you'll hire me."

Reaching out my hand, I smile wildly. "I'll see you bright and early Monday. I look forward to working with you, River."

"Thank you for taking a chance on me. I promise I won't let you down. This bakery is going to be the talk of the town." Before I can respond, he's striding out the door, allowing it to fall shut behind his retreating form. He hops on his motorcycle and pulls away before I can blink. The roar of his engine echoes around the empty space as I stand there in silence.

Huh. That went better than I expected. He felt right for the bakery. It seems to hum with his presence. Just as I lower myself into the seat, a woman with white-blonde hair streaked through with pink rushes through the door. She's dressed in a boho skirt and crocheted sweater. Her fringe suede boots click on the linoleum as she rushes toward me. Her bright blue eyes are wide with excitement. I brace myself for the verbal monologue, which I'm sure will explode from her tiny body in less than ten seconds.

When she gets to the chair across from me, she stops, placing both hands on the back of the seat. Taking a deep breath, her chest rises and falls. "Hello," she says in a surprisingly soft voice. "My name is Maria. Are you Julia?"

A genuine smile spreads across my face. "Hi, Maria. Yes, I'm Julia. Thank you for your email. I'm glad you could make it down here today. I'm sorry this interview is coming with such short notice. The bakery will open on Monday, and I need someone to work at the front counter and cash register while I bake. If items are in the oven or waiting to cool, I'll be upfront helping clear tables and take orders, but I need a permanent person to be at the counter."

She nods and smirks at me as a lock of pink hair falls across her left cheek. "I worked for a deli in Whitefish. I just moved here last month, and the commute isn't far, but I'm spending more on gas than I'd like. I've kept my eyes open for a position in Topaz Falls, and when I saw the ad you posted, I was thrilled. I've worked the deli case and cash register for the last six years. I'm a pro at it!" She points a fingernail at her chest and smiles so wide I can see her molars.

"Can you start on Monday at 7 a.m. when we open? River and I will arrive at 5 a.m. to start baking. If you can work until 4 p.m. with an hour lunch break, that'd be ideal." As I think about her and River being part of my small team here, I am hopeful.

Gnawing on her bottom lip, she replies, "I think that'll work. I'll ask if I can work weekends at the deli for the next two weeks until they can find a replacement for me."

Palming my forehead, I groan. "Weekends. I forgot about the weekends. I'll need to hire the other three people as well. Let me know what days work for you, and we'll make it work until your job can comfortably let you go. I don't want to put a strain on another local business."

After Maria leaves, I call Vincent, Celeste, and Poppy. Vincent informs me he can do weekends, which won't affect his school schedule. Celeste would love to work any day, so I told her to start next weekend, and then we can add days depending on how busy we are. Poppy was the quiet one. She hoped to work in the kitchen, so I asked if she could work Wednesday through Sunday, overlapping with River. I know this will be a bit of trial and error, but I want to hit the ground running.

After hanging up with Poppy, I walk out the front door and lock up. I am thankful I dressed cute before coming in for the interviews this afternoon. I'm exhausted, but I promised Britt and Elin I'd meet them at Glaciers for live music and dancing. I feel more confident with the five new hires, and tonight, I plan to ask Elin to join me for the baking competition. Maybe River or Poppy could be a backup choice. Still, if the competition is three Sundays in a row, I'll have to rely on Poppy to work Sundays. I feel River will be exhausted after working Monday through Friday and have no desire to bake more with me on his supposed days off.

Pushing my fingers through my hair, I finger comb my locks quickly as I approach the door to Glaciers. Shoving it open, I step inside, and the smell of beer assaults my nose. It's such a different smell from the bakery, which has years of cinnamon, butter, and vanilla baked into every surface. No matter how long it's been since Rita baked or how many times the surfaces are cleaned, it still smells like pastries inside.

My eyes slowly adjust to the dim lighting as I take in the large bar top to my right. The mirrored wall reflects the stage lights on the left. Rows of liquor line the mirror as two people move with practiced ease behind the bar, filling glasses and sliding them as fast as people can order.

The center of the bar is a large wooden dance floor, with tables on the far wall and to my left, along the wall of windows facing the street. On the left side of the stage is an archway leading to a smaller area with pool tables and dart boards. My gaze lands on Britt's bouncing curls as she throws her head back and guffaws at something Elin said. I weave through the tables and patrons while focusing on the two people I'm here to meet.

I sidle up next to Britt, bumping my shoulder against her bare arm. "Aren't you freezing in that tube top?"

She arches a brow at me, looking over my sweater. "You'll be stripping down by the third song. This place gets packed on the weekend. It'll be almost standing room only. My brother and his coworkers are at the table behind us."

Looking over, I see Trent and Axel hunched over beer bottles, deep in conversation. Axel feels my gaze on him, causing his eyes to snap to mine. I offer him a small smile and wave. He grins before lifting his beer bottle in acknowledgment. Trent turns and provides a small salute before returning to his conversation with Axel.

A man who could be Declan's twin is seated beside Axel with a beautiful brunette on his lap. His arm is draped around her waist as she lays her head on his shoulder against the crook of his neck. The only reason I can tell it isn't Declan is he's wearing a wedding band and has fine lines around his eyes. He must be Lachlan, which means Ingrid is probably close, too. Moving my gaze around their table, I see Ingrid sitting beside a massive man with blonde hair and crystal blue eyes. His arm is wrapped around her shoulders as he presses a kiss into her temple. Before I can draw my gaze back to Britt and Elin, a stunning redhead plops down beside Trent and places a loud kiss on his cheek. His gaze softens as he wraps an arm around her shoulders and pulls her tight to his side. I want what each of those couples have—a perfect counterpart.

Snapping fingers in front of my face jolts me back, almost tipping me off my stool. "Earth to Julia," Britt says, putting her face in front of mine.

"Sorry. I was looking around. This is my first time here." Nice save. Taking a deep breath, I close my eyes. A tingling sensation tickles my cheek. When I open my eyes and glance at the table with Trent and Axel, I see Declan's green eyes boring into me. Lifting his drink to his lips, he takes a long gulp before placing his pilsner back on the table. A bit of foam graces his top lip, and I fight the urge to rush over there and wipe it off with my thumb. The corner of his mouth tips up as he watches me shiver.

"Elin, I have a question for you," I say, forcing myself to look at Elin and Britt, cutting off Declan's trance over me.

"Yeah. What's up?" Elin asks, taking a sip of wine.

"Would you want to be my partner in the harvest bake-off at the orchard in two weeks?" I ask sheepishly. We haven't been friends for long, but she is one of only a few people I even know in this town.

"Hey," Britt cuts in. "What about me? How'd I get leapfrogged?"

"Simple. You can't bake, Britt. You've told me yourself—multiple times," I reply, grabbing her wine glass and taking a small sip.

"True, but I'd look cute on camera," she says with a wink.

Elin nods. "I'd be happy to. When is the first day?"

"Declan told me the thirteenth, but I'll have to verify the time. Thank you!" Standing up from my seat, I point to their wine glasses. "I'm going to grab one of these before the music starts. I'll be right back."

Zigzagging through the tables, I belly up to the bar, and a woman with a pixie cut pats the bar top. "What can I get you?"

"I'll have whatever red wine you have open. Thank you." I tap my fingers at the bar. I still when a large hand lands between my shoulder blades. Warm breath fans against my neck, causing a stuttered breath to escape my lips.

What happens when your life is on the verge of crumbling beneath you, but you keep running into your dream guy? You panic, flirt, and fall. My legs barely keep me upright as I try to come up with a witty comment. No matter how much my mind knows I should leave and never look back, my body has a different idea. Embers swirl in my stomach.

"Hey, blossom," Declan says, pressing his lips into my hair. Any resolve I have to keep this man at bay fractures, falling like sand through my fingers as I suck in air.

Chapter 16

Declan

Her body stiffens slightly before she relaxes into my touch, arching her shoulder blades against my palm. The heat radiating off her skin feels like static hovering in the air before a thunderstorm. You want to embrace it, yet you know lightning could strike at any moment and illuminate the sky. My nerves dance beneath my skin, awaiting her response.

"*Mon autre*," she whispers under her breath. If I wasn't pressed against her temple, I wouldn't have heard my nickname fall from her pouted lips. Her heavy-lidded eyes find mine in the mirror behind the bar. Reaching up, she tugs her hair over her right shoulder, exposing the left side of her neck. I fight the urge to nuzzle into her pulse point, pressing kisses against the tender skin as her blood thrums beneath my lips.

Squaring her shoulders, she rotates into my body, pressing her chest against mine. Her fingers gently push against my lower abs, just above my belt buckle. It takes every ounce of me not to close my eyes and sink into her touch.

"Your wine is ready," I murmur, reaching for the glass. I firmly place a twenty-dollar bill on the bar top, sliding it to Alexa before she moves on to the next patron. She winks at me, wiggling her eyebrows at Julia's back. I wrap my arm firmly around Julia's waist and tug her toward my table.

"Wait, I'm sitting with Britt and Elin," she says in a panic.

"Don't worry, blossom. I won't steal you away, but I expect a dance with you," I reply over the music from the sound system. The Buckshot Rebels should start playing soon, and once they're plugged in, it'll be impossible to hear over the bass.

Her cheeks blush as she subconsciously rubs a hand up her right arm. She must be boiling in the long sleeves. Hell, I'm about five minutes away from unbuttoning my flannel shirt as more and more people fill the bar.

I sit beside her across from Britt and swivel my lower body so my knees cage her stool. "What did you do today?"

"Well, other than cleaning out my aunt's house a little more, I interviewed for positions at the bakery. Trent reminded me I needed workers; otherwise, I'd kill myself trying to be in three places simultaneously." She beams at me, excited about the reopening.

For the first time since she arrived, it doesn't seem like the bakery is a burden to her. The happiness in her eyes shines bright like it did in high school when she spoke of her aunt's bakery. I always knew she'd take it over, but back then, I assumed she'd work there full time right out of high school, then transition to the owner as her aunt reached retirement age. Unfortunately, neither she nor her aunt followed the path in my head. Not many do, but I'm never sure if it's because the paths I visualize aren't meant to be followed or I don't understand people well enough to make a plausible plan for them.

Life seems so black and white to me. Calculating numbers is the only thing in my world that lives in the shadows. But I don't plan to shine a flashlight on that situation anytime soon. I sorta shoved all that crap in the corner of my mind the moment I graduated high school.

I've known since kindergarten I would work on the orchard and one day take it over. In sixth grade, I told my parents I'd build a house on the far end of the property, so I'd be close but out of their home. By the end of ninth grade, it was obvious that I wouldn't be smart enough to attend college.

When my plans involve others, that's when shit hits the fan. Lachlan and Ingrid abandoned me, leaving me the sole heir to the orchard. Julia left without looking back for reasons I still don't know. As I stare at her, I'm not sure I care anymore. She's back, and that's all that matters to me.

Fingers wiggle in front of my face, causing me to blink. "Dec, you were staring at Julia like she was the tastiest looking apple pie you'd ever laid eyes on," Britt says, cackling at the dazed expression on my face.

Standing up, I pat the top of their table. "I'll head back to my seat before the music starts. But remember, blossom, your dance card only has my name on it."

The lights blink a few times as I lower myself on the bench beside Axel. He leans in and asks, "Britt behaving?"

Scoffing, I mutter, "Of course not."

"Yeah, she's always been difficult. Understanding Britt is like trying to catch lightning in a Mason jar. I pity the son of bitch that gets shackled to her for life," Axel grins, lifting his bottle to his mouth. "She'll give him a run for his money."

"Only because he'll have to deal with your bs all the time," I say, raising a brow.

"On their wedding day, when they do the first look with the bride, I already told Britt I'm dressing in a hideous white gown so when her future husband turns around, he sees my beautiful mug first." Axel pins me with a smoldering look, which I'm sure the ladies love but does little more than intimidate the hell out of me.

"Well, that man won't be me," I deadpan.

"I know. You have your eyes glued to Julia like you're afraid she'll float away the next time the wind picks up. You do realize she isn't a dandelion," he says, narrowing his eyes at me over his beer bottle.

I pick at the label on my beer bottle, wondering how much to tell him. He was a SEAL when Julia was here for our senior year, so he never met her. "That's basically what happened. The day after graduation, she flew out without even saying goodbye. We'd dated our entire senior year. I thought I had forever and a lifetime with her. Still, after I stopped by her house to find her aunt's eyes red-rimmed and puffy, I realized there were so many things I didn't get a chance to tell Julia. I won't make that mistake again. I didn't go after her last time, and it was the biggest regret of my life. Before I know it, I'll be thirty. I'm not getting any younger."

Axel makes a humming sound in the back of his throat as his eyes roam my face. "When's your first date?"

My eyes widen. Damn. I haven't even asked her on a date yet. "Soon." Quickly changing the subject, I ask, "What about you? When are you going to settle down?"

He barks out a laugh and shakes his head. "Women are too smart to end up with a man like me. I'd have to be their last option, or they'd need to be desperate for an out."

Before I can question him further, Mark speaks into the mic. "Welcome to Glaciers. We are the Buckshot Rebels. With Sylvie being out of town for the next two weeks, we asked Ingrid to be our special guest tonight as we play Taylor Swift songs all night long."

The crowd cheers. Aislinn and Lachlan pop up and move onto the dance floor, lost in each other's gaze as "Safe and Sound" begins to play. It's moments like these where I envy my brother. They move across the floor with practiced ease, wholly wrapped up in themselves.

My gaze cuts to Julia, only to find her grinning at the stage. Her foot taps the floor beneath her stool in rhythm with the music. After she left, I took dance lessons. No one knows about it because I went into Kalispell. My eighteen-year-old brain assumed she left because I didn't do much more than sway at prom the week before. I remember her pleading eyes as she begged me to dance with her to every song. Logically, I know that wasn't her reason for leaving, but I still want to prove myself tonight. Back then, I had no sense of rhythm. Watching my brother, I have no idea where he learned to dance.

Before I know it, the song is over, and Mark's voice fills the building. "Alright. The next song is 'Back to December' for all the people out there hoping for a second chance at love or regretting their lost love."

My gaze automatically cuts to Julia just as a tall, built man I've never seen approaches her table. He has thick blonde hair tied in a bun at the back of his head, the sides shaved short. His eyes dance with mirth as he saunters toward the three women. Women who I should've never left unattended. I rake my teeth over my bottom lip. My frustration builds as I watch him place his drink on their table and strike up a conversation with them. Straight white teeth blink in the overhead lighting. Teeth which I'd like to rearrange if he doesn't move to the next table soon. When he leans down into Julia's personal space, I see red.

Without thinking, I stand and maneuver through the tables. My hand brushes against Julia's shoulder as I lean in and whisper, "I think this is our song, blossom." My eyes glare hard at the manbun dude, letting him know Julia is off-limits. I know I'm basically peeing on her, but I can't let some asshole butt in on what I'm working toward.

Oddly, he doesn't even register my appearance. His eyes are focused on Britt. She places her hand in his, allowing him to lead her on the dance floor. I feel eyes on the side of my head, and when I glance up at Elin, I frown. She lifts her wine glass to her mouth in a failed attempt to hide her amusement.

Julia's doe eyes blink up at me as water fills along her lower lid. She softly nods before standing and intertwining our fingers. We arrive in the middle of the dance floor, and with practiced steps, I pull her flush against my body and lead her through a simple two-step. "I thought the guy with the man bun would ask you to dance. I about lost my shit over it."

"Who?" Julia asks, looking around, confused.

"Never mind, blossom. Just remember, you're mine." She stiffens slightly in my grip.

"I'm only here for ninety days, Declan," She murmurs into my chest.

"Then we need to make it count. What are you doing next Friday night?" I ask, tugging her closer into my frame.

"Nothing?" Her chin tilts up as she tries to search my eyes.

"Good. Can I pick you up at 6 p.m. for a date?" My voice threatens to crack as nerves settle into my vocal cords. Until now, it hadn't occurred to me that she might turn me down. The last time she was here, we were a team. She was my perma-date.

"I'd like that," she whispers, nibbling on her bottom lip as her eyes dart between mine.

As the last note draws across Ingrid's strings, I realize I've stopped us in the middle of the darkened dance floor. Her tongue darts out and licks her lower lip. My heated gaze follows the motion. The pads of my fingers dig into her hips with bruising strength, afraid she'll slip away again. I tentatively lower my head, mesmerized by her lashes fluttering as her lids fall closed.

The sweet scent of wine floats on her exhale, and I can barely control the anticipation of kissing her again. I've dreamt of her kisses more times than I care to admit, assuming I'd only experience her soft lips once my body was fast asleep. Just as the static between our skin jumps between us, Britt calls, "Julia! I'm heading out! Let's go. I'll give you a ride back to your car."

Her body goes rigid, and her vision clears, coming into extreme focus. She blinks at me, the heat completely gone.

"Stay," I plead.

"I can't. We're riding together," Julia murmurs, her body retreating further from me.

"I'll give you a ride back," I say hurriedly. My eyes bounce between hers, willing her to stay with me. To not choose someone else over me again.

Her palm lands on my chest. "Not tonight. Not yet, Declan. I'll stop by the orchard tomorrow to get the pie tins," she whispers. "Let me give you my cell number."

I yank out my phone and she rattles off the seven digits faster than I can type. A smirk creeps on my face as I save the contact name as Blossom. Angling my phone to her she dips her head, a deep blush tinting her cheeks. When she turns to leave, I say, "Sure I can't convince you to stay?"

She shakes her head and follows Britt out the door, mouthing, "I need to go."

"Tomorrow," I reply to her back, defeat lacing my tone. Dropping my head, I refuse to watch her retreating body. Always walking away from me. That will change soon. Our date is a few days away.

Determination thrums through my veins, forcing me to remember this is a long game. Patience and persistence. I'm not letting her go without a real fight for us, but I'll let her set the pace until that time comes.

Chapter 17
Declan
Sunday, October 6

Two times now, I've almost kissed Julia. Both attempts have failed miserably. Maybe this is some higher power telling me to take the woman on a damn date before attempting to kiss her because clearly, we weren't meant to pick up where we left off almost a decade ago like I'd optimistically hoped. I'm a stubborn man, so a part of me refuses to admit we have to start over when what we had was perfect.

As I stand among the trees near the edge of the parking area, I hum in agreement as the wind whistles through the branches. The orchard knows Julia is coming. I can tell by the way a calmness falls among the rows of sentinel trees, waiting for her return as much as me. I'm sure it's all a figment of my imagination, but I desperately want the orchard to bring her the same peace I feel here.

Closing my eyes, I listen for the distant sound of tires on gravel. When the faint crunch of wheels pulls into the long driveway, I lean back against the tree. It's providing me shade from the afternoon sun, which is just warm enough to heat my back on this mild October day.

My eyes snap open when the whir of a car engine stops in front of me. My gaze locks on Julia's grey eyes, which look almost silver through the glass of her windshield. Pushing off the tree, I stroll to her car with my thumbs tucked into my front pockets. The door cracks open, and she gracefully slides out of her aunt's car. Rounding the hood, I don't stop until she's enveloped in my embrace. I pull her against my chest so her cheek can feel my heart beating for her. My hand cradles the back of her head as my other arm wraps around her small frame.

"Blossom," I murmur into her hair, inhaling deeply her apple scent.

"Dec." Her muffled reply is barely audible with her face pressed into my flannel shirt. I smile when I feel her back expand as she sucks in a breath of my cologne.

"Pie tins?" I ask, knowing she came here mainly to get my mom's pie tins to make a ton of cheesecakes for opening day with all the extra graham crackers I stupidly ordered. I guess it was a happy accident. Bob Ross would be proud of me for turning a mistake into something positive.

Rubbing my palms along her upper arms, I frown when she suddenly stiffens and haltingly pulls away. Her left hand tugs at her right sleeve, pulling it over her fingertips. I look pointedly at her nervous habit, but she looks anywhere but at me. My fingers softly grip her chin as I lower my eyes to her level. When her gaze meets mine, she offers me a watery smile. My eyes are full of questions, but she shakes her head.

Without another word, I lace my fingers with hers and guide her down the row of trees. A whisper of a smile graces her face as her eyes flutter shut, and she takes deep breaths. "I've missed the serenity of the orchard, Dec. It's not like this in the city. The trees seem to mute the world around us. It feels like just you and I exist in this world when we're here."

I like the sound of that. A grin tugs at the corner of my lips as I watch in rapt fascination at her expression as she looks up into the tall trees above her head. After a ten-minute stroll, we end up at the shed I built this summer. I'm damn proud of it. It's about twenty feet by twenty feet and made from reclaimed barn wood, which I recovered from a collapsed structure at a farm down the street. The muted gray tones are a stark contrast against the green grass and apple trees surrounding it in every direction.

My house winks in the distance, and it takes all my strength not to take Julia there instead. I want to see her barefoot in my kitchen dusted in flour, snuggled under a blanket on my couch, or reading a book on the porch swing while she sips a cup of tea.

Her small hand presses into my lower back. Blinking, I realize we're at the door to the shed. Lifting the lever, I unlock the door and slide it open. Beams of light filter through the cracks in the wood, illuminating the interior just enough for us to see as we step inside. Striding to the back of the unit, I find a box labeled pie tins in my mom's handwriting. I flip open the lid to make sure it wasn't mislabeled. Sure enough, dozens of well-loved pie tins are stacked inside.

A loud boom makes me jump, and I push Julia behind me as I turn toward the source of the sound. The door slid shut, banging against the stopper from the force of it gliding along the track. There is a distinct click, which causes my eyes to widen in panic.

"What happened?" Julia whispers, her fingers gripping my belt loops.

"The door shut," I reply simply, but my voice is hoarse.

I shake off the unease settling in my gut and stride to the door. With shaking hands, I feel for the door handle, releasing a slow breath when I find it. With a firm grip, I yank the piece of metal. My breath catches in my throat when I tug on the handle, and the door merely rattles. Adjusting my grip, I pull harder, but nothing happens.

Thudding my head against the wood, I mumble profanities under my breath. In an attempt to regain my composure, I roll my shoulders back and turn back toward Julia, stumbling when I find her directly behind me.

"Shit, blossom. I didn't realize you were so close," I mutter.

"I—I don't like being trapped, Dec. We need to get out now," she murmurs, her voice verging on a whispered panic. Fear seems to clog her throat as her nails dig into the flesh of my forearm.

"It's okay," I breathe out, but even in the dim light, I see her eyes wildly looking around like a trapped animal. What happened to her? She used to climb into barrels during hide-and-seek or shimmy under the crawl space to play pranks on Britt.

Cupping her cheeks in my hand, I lower my lips to her forehead and press a kiss against her clammy skin. I pull out my phone and sigh, relieved I still have battery left. Having an empty battery in this situation would be just my luck.

"Can't you, like, take off the door at the hinges or something?" Her voice cracks as her breaths come in short puffs.

"No. The barn door is on a sliding track. I built it to automatically lock when the door shuts, so I wouldn't accidentally leave it unlocked." Biting my lip, I glance back at the door. "I don't know why it shut in the first place, though. It was wide open when we stepped inside."

A whimper leaves her lips. "Do you think someone trapped us in here on purpose?"

Tugging at the back of my neck, I frown. "No. I think it was just an accident."

I dial Cameron's number, but it goes straight to voicemail, along with Mira's phone. Where could they be? Trying not to feel panicked, I dial Axel's number. The guy always knows what to do.

After two rings, Axel says, "A-X-E-L, what's your emergency?"

"Funny you should ask," I respond, clearing my throat.

"Shit, dude. What'd you do now? Please don't tell me you stapled yourself to something," Axel says in mock disbelief since that actually happened last Christmas. Still, I won't admit that to Julia any time soon.

"No," I grind out. "I was wondering if you were near the orchard?"

Chuckling, he replies. "I could be. Why do you ask?"

"Well, I'm locked in a storage shed, and neither Cameron nor Mira answered their phones. I really don't want to call Lachlan or Ingrid, and my parents are obviously not around. Think you could come get me out?"

Barking out a laugh, he responds, "Sure. But it will cost you."

"Name your price." I groan.

"A beer at poker night this week," he replies, the smile on his face evident in his tone even though I can't see him.

"Yeah, yeah. Okay. I'll get you an entire six-pack," I grumble.

"Naw, just one is fine. I've already got a six-pack." There is a faint patting sound as if he's smacking his stomach.

"Can you just hurry, please?" I fight the urge to plead. I don't need him rushing to my aide, but the wide-eyed look from Julia tells me she does.

"What's the rush, princess? Need to pee or something?" He says, but I hear the sound of his truck engine and sigh in relief that he's just teasing me or trying to lighten the mood.

"No, I don't need to pee. I just need to get out quickly. What's your ETA," I grind out, enunciating slowly, hoping he'll get the hint.

"Oh, maybe an hour," he says flippantly.

Julia squeaks beside me, and my hand immediately rubs small circles on her back.

"What was that?" Axel asks, his voice turning serious.

"I'm here with Julia," I respond.

"Shit," he hisses. "Declan, distract her. I'll be there in less than ten minutes. Are you in the shed a stone's throw from your house? The one you built earlier this summer?"

"Uh, yeah," I reply, surprised by his verbal whiplash.

"I don't care what you do, but don't let her spiral. Distract her. I'm coming." The phone clicks off before I can figure out what he's talking about. How does he know she's panicking? All from a squeak. Staring at my phone, I narrow my eyes, wondering what I'm missing.

Stuffing the phone back in my pocket, I step closer to Julia. A sheen of sweat glistens on her forehead. Her shoulders softly shake as fear grips her body. I cradle her face in my hands and bring her gaze to mine. "Blossom. I need you to look at me. Take some deep breaths. Axel is coming and will be here soon."

"Not. Soon. Enough," she rasps. Her legs buckle, and she pulls on my shirt, bringing her face firmly into my chest. I walk us backward to a stack of crates on the side of the shed. Sitting down, I pull her into my lap, allowing her legs to drape along the side of my thighs. Her breath hitches at the change in position. Tears silently track down her cheeks as she looks at me, bewildered. My thumbs gently swipe the tears away as her gaze struggles to focus on me.

Her throat contracts as her eyes fall to my lips. I'm mesmerized by the sight of her tongue darting out to swipe against her plump lower lip. "Distract me, Dec," she whispers.

"Fuck it," I mutter, tugging her face to mine. Our lips collide in a detonation of electricity, filled with pent-up charge. Her lips are softer than I remember, and it blindsides me that I forgot the feel of her mouth. She tastes like mint, and I close my eyes as I inhale her, moaning when she deepens the kiss.

If I didn't know better, I'd assume I was dreaming, but this is better than my imagination could ever envision. Her small hands work their way up my chest, gripping the collar of my flannel shirt as she tugs me tighter.

She begins rocking against my hardening cock as she thrusts her tongue into my mouth. My fingers tangle in the hair at the nape of her neck, drawing her closer with each ragged inhale. I want to consume her with every ounce of my being because I will never get my fill of this woman.

Her nails scratch a burning trail across my shoulders, dipping below my neckline as she digs them into my lats and giving her more leverage in my lap. A groan filters up the back of my throat, which she captures. Her lips move in a frenzy as embers swirl in my stomach like a bonfire during a gust of wind. I can feel my restraint losing control as my other hand sinks into the skin at her waistband.

My fingers dip below the hemline of her shirt, trailing along the soft skin of her ribcage. Over the top of her cotton bra, I roll my thumb over the stiff peak of her nipple. She moans into me, pressing her breast into my palm with unrestrained force.

There is a pop, and light floods the small building as the door slides open. I quickly remove my hand, tugging on her shirt to right it. Her creamy skin is for my eyes only. She whimpers at the loss of my touch, making me want to smile with the cocky sense of pride I'm feeling.

Julia blinks slowly as her eyes attempt to adjust to the onslaught of harsh sunshine.

A deep throat clears in the doorway, and I can see the silhouette of Axel's broad frame. "Based on the windblown look you're both sporting, I'm gonna take a wild guess and assume you figured out a decent distraction technique." When my gaze narrows at him to shut up, he continues, "And it doesn't appear it was a game of Backgammon. Pity. I was hoping to take on the winner."

Julia stumbles off my lap, her legs looking like she was out at sea for the last few weeks as she carefully steps back so I can stand. It makes me glad I seem to have the same effect on her as she possesses on me. I tuck her into my side and grab the box of pie tins before we walk outside.

"Thanks for coming, Axel," I reply. Turning to Julia, concern laces my tone as I softly ask, "Are you okay?"

Nodding slowly, Julia replies, "Yes, I'm perfect. Thank you both. But what happened?"

She turns and looks up at the sliding barn door. Axel responds first. "I don't have a level with me, but my guess is Declan didn't either when he built the shed. It looks like the track angles toward the lock, so it slid shut and automatically locked once you stepped inside."

Julia covers her mouth as her eyes dance with delight. A small giggle escapes her lips, and she replies, "It's like the birdhouse you tried to build in shop class. Remember the teacher called it the Winchester mystery birdhouse because it was disjointed and not level?"

Frowning, I grumble, "You're right. I didn't use a level, and my birdhouse sucked, but Mr. Bronson should eat his words because it's still on the fence post and has housed multiple bird families." I cross my arms over my chest in defense.

Julia's soft grip tightens on my forearms as she gazes into my eyes. When I glance up at Axel, he smirks at me. He winks, then silently turns and walks away.

"Thanks, man," I call out to his retreating back.

"Don't forget I want a blonde for poker night!" Axel shouts, and I shake my head.

"Come on, blossom. Let's get these pie tins back to your car. I remember you said you needed to start on the cheesecakes as soon as possible. I'll get the graham crackers for you, too," I whisper.

She wraps her arm around my waist as we trek back to her car. I can't help but place a kiss on the top of her head.

Our date can't come soon enough.

Chapter 18

Julia

Monday, October 7

It's only 7 a.m., and it already feels like the longest day I've ever had. I baked cheesecakes well into the evening last night. Darkness bathed the silent streets when I finally called it quits. When my alarm clock started blaring at 4:30 a.m., I was shoved out of my dream like I'd been hit by an Amtrak train.

After we sell the last slice of cheesecake, I'm never again making a s'more or buying a box of graham crackers at the store. By the time I locked up last night, I'd made two dozen cheesecakes and a batch of gluten-free, vegan muffins for the sweet couple who made the special request last week.

River arrived ten minutes early and got right to work this morning. I made a list of items I wanted to make for opening day. I've been working on cinnamon rolls, scones, and croissants. River is in charge of Danishes, bread, and muffins. After we finish the breakfast items, we will switch to cookies and cupcakes for the after-lunch crowd.

I'm shocked at how easy it is to bake beside River. I'd never have guessed this was our first day sharing a kitchen. Maybe we should have done a trial run, but I don't think we needed any practice working together. We've already managed to fill the bakery case with one of each type of item.

He works quietly, softly singing as he does so. His deep and melodic voice keeps me unexpectedly calm.

He didn't seem surprised when I asked him to be in charge of the ovens. With the way our island counter sits lengthwise in the kitchen, it is safer if I'm on one side and he is on the other. He took the oven side of the island without questioning my motives when I suggested it upon arrival. We use the stainless steel countertop behind me as a proofing and cooling area.

All too soon, the first customers are strolling through the door. The couple who requested the special muffins supposedly bought half a dozen. Maria was so excited she ran back after they left, squealing with the news.

At 7:45 a.m., I bring out another tray of cinnamon rolls. The first tray went fast and seemed a popular choice among the older crowd. With my back turned to the customers, I offload the cinnamon rolls. Suddenly, I'm startled by a deep voice. The tone is familiar and catches my attention.

"Can I get a cupcake?" asks the man. I can't pinpoint where I recognize the voice, so I cautiously look over my shoulder. My eyes widen in surprise seeing the guy with the manbun from Glaciers standing at the counter.

Turning, I put a smile on my face and step up beside Maria. "Morning. Tristan, right? It's good to see you again."

A smile beams on his face, making his seafoam eyes sparkle. "Jules?" The wince tells me he doesn't quite remember, but at least he was paying enough attention on Saturday to get close. At least he didn't call me Sarah or Tammy.

"Julia, actually. We will have cupcakes and cookies available starting around 11 a.m. Only breakfast items right now. Cupcakes have to completely cool before I can frost them, and my blast chiller is only so big." I offer him a consolatory shrug.

Grinning, he replies, "You know what I never understood about breakfast? Society frowns upon cake and cupcakes before lunch. Still, a cinnamon roll with cream cheese frosting or a crepe with Nutella and whipped cream is acceptable?"

Valid point. Before I can open my mouth to respond, he continues, "Also, why can't I get fries before 11 a.m. when I can get hashbrowns at 6 a.m.? I know fries use a deep fryer, but come on, it's potatoes. Don't get me started on hotdogs. People look at you weird if you're in a restaurant and ask for a hotdog with ketchup during breakfast, but sausage links with maple syrup are okay? They are both cylinders of pork."

Biting my lip to fight the smile I know he's aiming for, Maria replies, "Maybe it isn't the hotdog people think is weird, but the hotdog bun?" She taps her glittery pink nail against her lower lip and stares up at the ceiling thoughtfully.

Crossing his arms across his broad chest, he draws my gaze to his mechanic coveralls with his name embroidered across his left side. "Yet, pigs-in-a-blanket are appropriate because the sausage is wrapped in a pancake. Nope, I'm not buying it." He winks at me as Maria looks at him with her mouth hanging open.

"He's right," she whispers, her eyes wide with disbelief as she looks at me.

"I think he should ask Mama M to make him a hot dog and French fries for breakfast. I'm sure Kyle would do it," Britt says as she and Elin approach the counter.

"You guys came!" I shout and rush around to kiss their cheeks.

"Of course, we came," Britt says. Turning to Tristan, she motions her finger up and down his outfit. "So, are you working at Bubba's Auto for Coach?"

"Coach is my uncle. I'll be here helping for a couple of weeks. I'll be taking over the shop in the new year when Coach retires," Tristan says, his arms barely contained under the long sleeves. His bun is tied at the nape of his neck, and the sides are freshly buzzed. He can't be much older than thirty-five if I had to guess, but there are faint lines at the corner of his eyes.

Axel strolls in with Trent. "We came to get two dozen pastries to take back to the ranch," Trent says as Maria pulls out a large box. He offers me a pleasant smile. "Julia, it's nice to see you. Congratulations on the grand re-opening."

"Thank you, Dr. W—I mean Trent," I reply, blushing profusely at using his professional title. I haven't really told anyone I've sought out therapy. Especially since I haven't openly shared my recent history.

Axel turns and watches in amusement as Tristan stuffs the cinnamon roll in his mouth, taking a massive bite. "Not sure whether I should call you Manbun or Cinnabun since I don't know your name. I'm Axel. You new in town?"

Tristan starts to talk around a mouth full of food but catches himself. Holding up a finger, he waits until he's finished chewing before replying, "I'm Tristan, but I'm not too picky about names. I'd probably respond just as easily to Manbun or Cinnabun." Holding up his cinnamon roll, he beams at me. "These are really good. What time did you say I could return for dessert since this counts as breakfast? I will have to keep up with running daily if I eat this much food. What magic ingredient is in this?"

"Butter. The secret is lots and lots of butter," I whisper loudly, giving him an exaggerated wink. "Feel free to come back any time after 11 a.m." After a brief pause, I remember all the cheesecakes. "Wait, I have cheesecakes, too!"

"I've already sold five," Maria announces with a fist pump. I bop her fist with mine and can't help but return her grin.

"I'll take a cheesecake. The guys at the shop will love it. Can I get six forks for it, too?" Tristan asks, setting his dirty dish in the bus tub by the garbage.

After boxing up the cheesecake, I step around the counter and motion for him to lead the way outside. I assume he'd rather not answer a million questions from Britt, so I make it my job to get him out of the bakery. He seems like a decent guy, and she's a lot to handle in the morning. As my feet hit the sidewalk, Declan's voice filters over us.

"Blossom," he grinds out. "Who's your friend?"

"Tristan, this is Declan. Declan, this is Tristan. His uncle owns the auto shop in town, and he bought a cheesecake to take back," I state slowly.

Without taking his eyes off Tristan, he reaches out his hand and firmly shakes it. When they release their grip, Declan skeptically looks at his palm. "Sorry, man. My hands are sticky from jamming a cinnamon roll too fast," Tristan says apologetically.

I snort when Declan wipes his hand on his jeans dramatically. The guy spends most of his day in muddy fields. For all I know, Declan's hand was sticky, too. I press my lips together to fight my smile.

Taking the box from me, Tristan strides to his motorcycle, awkwardly tethering the box to the back. That man is a beautiful specimen of the male form, but I don't think there's much going on upstairs. It's like the hamster wheel is turning, but the hamster is on vacation.

A warm arm wraps around my shoulders. I stiffen. "Dec. You can't act all growly and possessive over me at the bakery. We aren't seeing each other."

"Like hell we aren't," he grumbles under his breath, and I bite my lip to keep from laughing.

The front door flies open, and Britt strides out with Elin. She holds up a pink box. "We will arrive at the vet clinic with sweet treats to bribe Aislinn."

"Bribe your boss? Why?" I ask, narrowing my eyes at Britt.

"Because it's Monday, and I don't want to work very hard. I hope it will butter her up so I don't have to do inventory or some other mundane task," Britt retorts.

"Thanks for coming," I say, so thankful for friends like Britt and Elin. They've helped me so much since arriving that I don't know how to thank them.

Declan tugs me toward the bakery. River steps out of the kitchen with a tray of scones. "What is up with all these guys flocking to you, blossom? Don't they know you're mine?"

My gaze flicks to him. "I belong to no one, Dec. Remember. Only here for a few months."

"We'll see," he says cryptically. Marching up to the cash register, Maria's eyes widen when she drinks in Declan's flannel-clad form. Down, girl. Even though I know he isn't interested in Maria, my eyes narrow, and I know I'm about two seconds away from going She-Hulk in here, as my skin tints green with jealousy. He's mine. Frowning because he isn't mine, can't be mine, and won't ever truly want me since I can't give him what he wants most in life. Not to mention, I just verbally told him it wasn't an option. I'll consider something casual, but I'm afraid my heart won't survive losing him twice.

Stomping to the kitchen, I pass River in a huff, causing him to jump, the words to his song catching in the back of his throat. A huge ball of dough lands on the counter in front of me.

"I've found kneading dough is meditative," River murmurs without looking up at me. His hands push into the ball of dough in front of him, and I take that as my cue to give it a try.

Before long, we are back to working in companionable silence. Without turning around, I know without a shadow of a doubt that Declan is leaning against the door frame, watching me work as my neck prickles with awareness. River's eyes flick over my shoulder every few minutes, and a part of me hopes Declan stays there all day. That She-Hulk feeling immediately dissipates, and I scrunch my eyes closed at how messed up this is.

Chapter 19
Declan

I could've stood and watched Julia bake all day. Watching her hands shape the dough was mesmerizing. Embarrassingly enough, the longer I watched, the more jealous I became of the damn dough.

My original goal was to ensure the new guy didn't hit on her and knew she was off-limits. Lucky for him, he didn't seem interested in her. The entire thirty minutes I stood watching her in the doorway, he sang under his breath and worked hard. The couple words they exchanged were purely job-related. Hell, by the time I left, I admired him for not gossiping like a magpie since I assume that's how most kitchens are. One of the reasons I hate working in the orchard with Mira is because there are days she never shuts up.

When I finally pulled myself away from Julia, it was like walking into a strong headwind or pulling apart two magnets. As I left the kitchen, Maria waved goodbye to me like we were old friends. It was unsettling because I felt like I knew this entire town, and I didn't recognize either of the people working for Julia.

During the entire walk to the grocery store, I contemplated turning back. I might have if my cupboards weren't completely bare, but I desperately need food. At least Mom can't complain that my pantry is full of expired food. Over the last month, I literally ate everything. Even the Spaghetti O's I had at the back and the can of tuna are gone. It's bad when you don't even remember buying something; it makes you wonder how long it's been there.

I found a container of casserole Mom placed in my freezer, which looked a little freezer-burned but was palatable. The frozen meal was my last resort yesterday because after I came home and switched into sweats, I refused to get dressed and head into town. Entering Glaciers or Mama M's in nothing but a pair of sweats would've made me the talk of the town.

I'm embarrassed to admit that I've been living on my own for years and can't cook more than scrambled eggs, toast, and Hungry-Man meals. When my mom's amazing cooking is only on the other side of the orchard, it's easy to appear for breakfast, lunch, and dinner every day. I might've moved out, but I still prefer my mom's cooking over mine.

Grabbing a shopping cart, I head toward the first aisle. I grab apples and bananas and place them in the cart, and my eyes roam over the vegetables. I should probably get something. Oh! Carrot sticks. I don't need to prep those. If they're good enough for Bugs Bunny, they're good enough for me. In the refrigeration unit, there are packages of pre-washed veggies. I throw some in my cart so Mom can't harass me for not having anything healthy in the house.

I restock some canned goods, avoiding Spaghetti O's because I think I've eaten enough in the last week to last me the year. Down the next aisle, I grab some cereals and Pop-Tarts. Next up, Oreos and fishy crackers go in the cart. I toss in a few types of chips, and then I grab a couple boxes of Eggo waffles. As I walk past the protein bar aisle, I grab a few because why not? A few of those microwavable cups of green beans, peas, and corn. I'm all set!

Turning the corner, I almost run over Mama M. Her short, squatty body jerks to an abrupt stop, causing the messy bun of auburn hair shot through with gray to bob on top of her head. I tug my cart to a halt as I look at her surprised eyes.

"Declan? I can't remember the last time I ran into you at the grocery store. You were probably only five," she says in a teasing tone. I'm sure Mom told her all about how often I still visit my childhood kitchen to eat her meals. I don't know how Lachlan and Ingrid learned to cook. It was probably something they picked up in college. The sink or swim method. Well, it appears I get to go through that form of learning now.

"Hey, Mama M. How are you? Shopping for you and Carl or the café?" I ask, placing my boot on the cart's lower rail and draping my upper body over the handle so I'm more at eye level with the short woman.

Her gaze travels over the contents of my cart, and she sighs heavily. "Sweetie, you might be able to survive off this junk food, but you can't live off it. I think it's time you learn to cook. Also, why do you have apples in your cart when you live on an orchard? Aren't those apples Ambarsan apples?"

My mouth opens, but nothing comes out. First, I know I was just thinking it was time for me to sink or swim, but I'd rather not. Maybe we could start with some floaties? Also, I think I meant to grab oranges, but I just went for apples. I'm gonna ignore that slip-up.

Swallowing roughly, I watch her pull out a little notepad from her pocket. 'Mama Knows Best' is written on the top, which tugs a chuckle from me. She glances up and winks, tapping her pen on her pad of paper.

"Can you make spaghetti?" she asks.

I shake my head and mumble, "Only the canned variety."

Scoffing, she scribbles out a list and hands it to me. Ground beef, pasta, pasta sauce, oregano, basil, and mozzarella. Well, that is a short list. She sits and explains the process to me. I borrow her pen so I can draw little pictures of the process.

"Thanks for this," I say to Mama M, holding up my paper. "And for not adding amounts. I really just dump everything of each item except for the spices, and that's just a pinch?" She nods with a warm smile and pats my forearm. Now, I just need to find these ingredients and not lose the instructions between now and dinner time. If I make enough, maybe I can take some to Julia and surprise her tomorrow.

With renewed excitement, I Bob Ross the moment, determined to turn the problem into a happy accident. I put a pep in my step until I reach the spice aisle and realize I have no idea how to find oregano and basil. I think the only spices I have in the cupboards are salt, pepper, and fry seasoning.

A few people stand browsing the options. An elderly woman has her reading glasses perched on the tip of her hawkish nose as she reads the back of one container. I notice the spices are in alphabetical order. Finding the basil at the top, I reach over everyone and grab the jar. My eyes travel down the shelf until I see oregano directly in front of the little old lady.

"Excuse me," I say, clearing my throat. The woman doesn't appear to hear me, so I reach my arm past her, and she jumps. Her bony hand slaps my forearm with so little strength I barely feel it through my coat.

"What are you doing, Declan?" The woman huffs, glaring at me over her horned-rimmed glasses. Darn, I didn't realize it was Mrs. Markham.

"Sorry. I have to get some spices. Apparently, I need oregano," I mutter quickly, snatching the spice jar and moving down the aisle as fast as possible. Edna Markham isn't my biggest fan after I repeatedly turned down her attempts at setting me up with her granddaughter. When you attend the same school with someone from kindergarten until graduation, they feel like a half-sister once removed. Not someone I want to kiss. I always sought out women from a neighboring city, never Topaz Falls. No one, except Julia.

As I stroll to the checkout area with my cart full of food, I spot the florist section. Julia always loved flowers. Each week in the spring, she'd collect wildflowers and place them in a Mason jar on the windowsill of her aunt's kitchen.

What was her favorite flower? It came in shades of pink and had lots of petals. I peer into the buckets and cringe. Damn, these all look the same. I was hoping there would be tulips, sunflowers, and then her favorite flower with a lot of pink petals. An older gentleman barely over 5'0" brushes his hands down his green florist apron and adjusts his round glasses.

"Can I help you build a bouquet?" he asks.

Scratching my temple, I fight the urge to tug at the back of my neck and stare at the ground. "I'm looking for a pink flower with lots of petals."

"Ah," he says as if he knows exactly which flower I'm visualizing. Obviously, he doesn't, but a guy can wish. He walks into the back, where the refrigeration section is, and slides the doors open. He pulls out three different stalks. "I have ranunculus, peony, and dahlias in right now."

Holding up the different flowers, I swear they all look alike. Biting on the inside of my cheek, I close my eyes and try to picture the bouquet I bought Julia senior year. She stared at them like they were the most amazing gift she'd ever received. It was the same day I gave her a promise ring. In response to her dreamy gaze, I said, "A peony for your thoughts?"

Pointing to the flower in the middle. I ask, "Can I get a dozen peonies, please? Any shade of pink works."

Nodding, he puts together a beautiful bouquet with the small white flower all bouquets have for some reason. Babies' farts or burps, maybe.

I hate grocery shopping, but the prospect of making something special for Julia has my adrenaline rushing. I can't wait to see what she thinks of the flowers, too.

Chapter 20

Declan
Tuesday, October 8

Alright. I'll be the first to admit the spaghetti didn't turn out great, but it was edible. Either that, or I was starving when I finally plated the pasta, which took much longer to cook than I had guesstimated. The sauce's flavor seems stronger than how Mama M makes it. I'm unsure what I did wrong, but no one can say it isn't flavorful. I'm nervous about delivering my first actual attempt at cooking to Julia. Still, I can't wait any longer to see her; bringing her lunch is the perfect excuse.

Luckily, I remembered to put the bouquet in a bucket of water overnight. It still looks beautiful, although my rewrapping skills leave much to be desired as I try to wrap the twine around the bunched-up butcher paper. I've already caught my finger twice in the mass of string, and I can't remember if I'm supposed to do a knot, a bow, or a double knot.

Grabbing the bouquet, I wonder if I need a degree in origami to rewrap the stupid thing. The blooms look beautiful, and some are beginning to open, which were closed yesterday. Unfortunately, it looks like two cats fought in the paper and twine, but I don't own any cats to blame the mess on. Frowning, I lay it on the passenger seat of the truck next to the bag of leftovers and pull out of my driveway.

I tried calling her number a few times, but she never answered, and the voicemail was a default mailbox robot. Of course, I was too chicken shit to leave a message for fear of sounding like a blundering idiot.

Luke Bryan's song "Scarecrows" plays in the cab. The lyrics are so close to the truth of my life that I have to roll down the windows to let out the invisible tension choking me, threatening to break me down faster than Uncle Simon's ancient tractor. On autopilot, I drive into town, humming the song that speaks so strongly to me.

I pull into an empty spot a few spaces down so I don't take up prime parking real estate in front of the bakery. I might be in front of Frida's yarn shop, but she doesn't open for another hour, so I don't think her clientele will mind.

Cradling the bouquet in the crook of my arm, I saunter to the front door with the bag of spaghetti clutched in my grip. I take a deep breath before opening the door. When I duck inside, I'm pleasantly surprised to see most of the tables are filled with people eating plates of pastries. I want Julia to succeed more than anything.

Maria's eyes widen when she sees me, her gaze falling to the flowers as she sighs longingly at them. The reaction might make me straighten my back and shoulders even more. "Is Julia in the back?"

She fights a grin but says, "Yep." Throwing me two thumbs up. She gives me a wink, then turns back to the cash register, whistling a song I don't recognize.

"Maria! Why are you humming 'Still In Love With You' by Sade? How do you even know that UK song? Were you even born when it came out?" Julia calls from the back room, and I press my lips together in amusement and confusion.

"Yes! I'm older than thirteen! Geez, I'm only a year or so younger than you!" Maria replies. With a shooing motion, she points to the kitchen.

"Hey, blossom," I drawl, coming around the corner to lean against the door frame.

She whips around, her caramel brown hair swishing in the ponytail behind her. Wide-eyed, she puts a hand on her chest. "*Mon autre*, you scared me!"

"Who else do you think Maria was humming that song for?" I reply with a wink.

She drinks me in, her eyes starting at my boots and slowly moving up to my backward hat. "Lordy, the books are right. The whole door lean thing is hot," she murmurs under her breath. Bringing her hands up, she fans her flushed face when she sees me staring at her.

With a chuffing laugh, River mutters, "Damn. I'm straight, and I'd even agree with that statement."

Pushing off the wall, I slowly stalk toward the kitchen island, a knowing grin tilting my lips. With an outstretched hand, I give her the bouquet. "Peonies," she whispers, burying her face in them and inhaling deeply. "You remembered."

"I remember every damn thing about you, blossom." As she looks up at me, her gaze darting between my eyes, I whisper the same words I did eight years ago. "A peony for your thoughts?"

Her lip trembles as she beams up at me. The world fades away, and I drop a gentle kiss on her forehead. Inhaling the scent of cinnamon on her skin, I grip her hip, gently pressing my fingers into the sliver of exposed flesh beneath her apron strap.

A throat clears, and time resumes, the noises from the kitchen coming back into full sound. My gaze cuts to River, and I narrow my eyes at him. He lifts his eyebrows and then nods to the door. I look over my shoulder to see Maria standing in the doorway, biting her lip. Literally, no privacy, but what did I expect coming to her bakery?

I guess I didn't need to worry about the paper because Julia steps out of my reach and rushes to untie the twine. When the flowers are in a jar of water, Julia turns and almost skips out to the front, where she places them on the counter by the cash register with a flourish. I'm beaming with pride. She likes my bouquet.

Waiting until she turns around, I thrust the bag at her, excited to show her what else I brought. I have a feeling I'm going to want to shower her with gifts. The look on her face is addicting. She opens the plastic bag and pulls out a gallon-size Ziplock bag with the spaghetti. I frown, realizing I should have stopped by Mom's and put it in an actual storage container.

She holds it up, fighting a grin. "What is this?"

"Lunch. I thought you might like a homemade meal during your break," I reply, standing a little taller. "I made spaghetti. Mama M gave me the recipe."

"Mama M? Really?" She brushes past me, sliding the food into a microwave. When she brings it out, she dumps it on the plate. It looks a little unappetizing as a glutinous mass, but I try not to show the nerves threatening to bubble over. Grabbing a fork, she dives in but manages to look like royalty with her manners.

"Wait, it's only 10 a.m. I figured this could be your lunch," I reply, forcing myself not to grab the plate from Julia, figuring she doesn't realize how early it is.

"Yeah, Dec, I know, and I've been up since 4 a.m. today. I'm starving," she replies, stuffing the first bite into her mouth.

She quietly chews as I wait on bated breath. "This is Mama M's recipe?" Julia asks around a mouthful of food, covering her lips with the back of her hand.

"Yeah?" I say, but it comes out as a question. "It was my first real attempt at cooking, but I followed her directions exactly."

Nodding slowly, she says, "It's wonderful. There is a lot of flavor packed into the sauce." She swallows hard. "How about I come by and make you dinner one of these nights?"

I lean back against the counter and smile. I may not be opening a restaurant any time soon, but whatever I made did the trick. After a few more bites, she puts the plate down. "Here, I'll walk you out, then return and finish my lunch."

At the door, she wraps her arms around my waist. "Thank you for the lovely flowers and the nice meal, Declan."

"My pleasure, blossom," I murmur into her hair. "I can't wait for our date on Friday. Was your phone off this morning?"

She shakes her head. "No. I have it on low so I can answer if needed, but I'm not really expecting any calls. Why?"

"I tried calling you a few times before driving down here, but it kept going straight to voicemail," I reply, rubbing small circles between her shoulder blades.

"Well, that's odd. Did you leave me a message? It didn't send me an alert," she says, sucking on her bottom lip.

"I'm not a huge fan of the automatic robot voices." I wince and reach back to tug at the back of my neck.

"Robot voices? My voicemail is my voice. Dec, can I see your phone?" Julia asks, placing her palm out.

I hand my cell to her. She holds it up to my face to unlock the screen, then opens the recent calls and frowns. It shows I called Blossom three times, all lasting ten seconds. When she opens the contact information, she grimaces. "This isn't my number, Dec," she whispers, rotating my phone. After the area code, she points to the first three numbers. I typed in 6-9-6, just like she told me at Glaciers the other night. "My number is 9-6-9."

She quickly changes it and calls her phone from mine. A second later, a song plays from her back pocket. She pulls out her phone and I see my nickname scrolling on the screen, which makes me smile. "I'll see you in two days, blossom." My fingers gently tug on her ponytail before I turn away. If I don't leave now, I'll never get any work done today, as I'll want to spend the entire day watching her move around the kitchen.

I halt as I step onto the sidewalk so Mr. Manbun can run past me. He's in a pair of running shorts with no shirt. His golden hair is tied into a bun at the back of his head. He winks at Julia as he runs past. It takes all my strength not to clothesline the guy. The dude knows it's October, right? A little cold to be running around showing off washboard abs. I need to figure out this guy's story.

Chapter 21

Declan
Wednesday, October 9

Clearing my throat, I get everyone's attention around the table. Raising a finger, I nonchalantly ask, "So, does anyone have any information about the new guy in town?"

Axel chortles. "Man, that's as subtle as a pig wearing lipstick." He shuffles the deck of cards before taking a sip of beer.

Frowning, I shrug. "I was just curious about the guy."

"Because you might want your truck worked on or because you're jealous he's trying to work on something with Julia?" Axel chides.

I growl, "What?"

Tapping the deck of cards on the velvet table, Axel leans forward. "Well, I call him Cinnabun because he's obsessed with Julia's cinnamon rolls."

"You better be referring to the pastry and not a body part," I grind out, almost creasing the cards in my grip.

"Hey, now. Easy on the cards." His eyes narrow on my hand, and I relax my grasp. "I did some background on him. Other than the fact he's a dead ringer for Kevin Creekman with more tattoos than me, he seems like a pretty simple guy. He's from the Seattle area. From what I've gathered, he's here visiting an uncle who is not blood-related and owns the local auto shop."

"He's here to see Coach? Why?" I demand.

"Down, Cujo," Axel deadpans, raising an eyebrow. "This is poker night, not some debriefing. Anyways, Coach is ready to retire, and Tristan Ballentyne is planning to buy it and continue Bubba's Auto."

"So, he's staying for more than a week?" I groan.

"I have no idea?" Axel answers with a shrug, but he totally does. He probably has an entire folder on the guy in the office here. Before I can ask anything further, he leans back in his chair, rocking on the back legs. "So, what do you guys think of the man cave? Anders and Declan, you two are the only ones who haven't had a chance to come for poker night yet, right?"

Nodding, I reply, "This is my first time. I like what you did with the place. Hard to believe Daniella used to live here. This looks like a bachelor pad."

"That's the point," Axel says, rolling his eyes. "I actually got quite a few of these old gas station and automobile signs from your dad, Callum. He let me browse the barn."

"What made you look into Tristan?" Trent asks, slipping into his chair.

"Ah, it wasn't because he and Declan have the same crush," Axel mutters. "Coach wasn't always a strait-laced guy. Let's put it that way. I wanted to make sure I knew what was coming to Topaz Falls."

"Always the SEAL, Axel. As the saying goes, 'Neither rain, nor snow, nor death of night, can keep us from our duty.' You sure live by it," Callum replies, sitting in the chair on Trent's other side.

Axel spits his beer as Trent says, "You just recited the Pony Express motto, man."

"No, I didn't. Their motto is 'Neither snow nor rain nor heat nor gloom of night stays these couriers from the swift completion of their appointed rounds,'" Callum states with a broad grin.

"No, that's actually the postman's motto," Trent deadpans, adjusting his glasses. He's like Clark Kent with auburn hair. The guy comes across as a grumpy professor unless Paisley is in the room; then, he looks like a less grumpy professor.

"Are you sure?" I ask because Callum sounds right. Trent is smart as hell, but it sounds right.

"Yes, I'm sure," Trent grinds out.

"Axel?" Callum asks, turning his attention to the stoic man whose looks could kill more than one of us here.

Anders lifts his finger, and all eyes turn toward him. "What I want to know is how you flawlessly recite them yet have no idea what they're for."

"Callum's dad worked for the post office for thirty years," Trent replies. "He recently retired."

Lachlan strides in from the kitchen. "What'd I miss?"

"Neither Callum nor your brother knows the SEAL motto. They thought it was the Pony Express motto," Trent points out.

Lachlan looks at me in disbelief. "Dude, it's 'The only easy day was yesterday.' How did you get those mixed up? They aren't even close. Well, the Pony Express and Postman motto are similar, but not to the SEAL motto. Axel has a huge sign in his office at the ranch."

With a shrug, I lift the beer bottle to my lips. "They both deliver shit. One just delivers bodies, the other delivers mail?" The icy glare from Axel has me adjusting my body further from him. "I didn't mean it like that. I meant because you shoot the bad guys."

Finally, he shakes his head. "You aren't the brightest of the bunch, huh?"

Lachlan chuckles. "You're just now figuring that out? What does that say about you? I have some good memories of both of them. In elementary school, Callum challenged Declan to run home to see if he could beat the bus. He took off running as fast as his legs could carry him, looking like Forrest Gump leaving the plantation. The bus arrived home a minute after him. He may've won, but we were a lot less sweaty. The next day, Callum was convinced he could beat Declan's time, so he raced the bus home. He was maybe five minutes faster, but being six years older might have been the reason. If Ingrid hadn't put her foot down, they probably would have continued racing the bus home for the rest of the school year to beat their times."

"Deal us in, harbor seal," I say, ignoring my brother's attempt at story time. Callum looks relieved, probably hating the reminder he almost got his ass handed to him by a second grader. I snicker as I glance at my cards and realize I have two pairs. I toss a few pieces of trail mix into the center, and we each place our bets. "Next time, can we do M&Ms or something? I'm not sure winning trail mix is actually a win," I grumble.

"I'd have brought chocolate-covered coffee beans if I knew we were playing with peanuts," Anders mumbles.

"I suggested we used Halloween candy," Trent replies, tossing in two cashews.

"Okay, I'm all in," Anders says, and I frown. Is it because he actually has a good hand, or is he sick of playing with the stupid prize? Hell, even pennies would be better than this stuff. I glance over just as Axel pops a handful of his trail mix in his mouth and leans back in his chair.

Snorting, I push my trail mix into the center and fan my cards. Axel throws back another handful of trail mix, and I wonder if he realizes he's doing it or whether this is his way of getting out of the game as fast as possible.

"Who brought the trail mix?" I ask.

With a raised brow, Axel stops chewing. "You did, dude. It was in the bag with my beer."

"I didn't buy trail mix. I swung into the gas station on my way here and picked up your beer. Eddie must have accidentally added it when he rang me up," I reply.

"Alright, looks like my full house wins," Trent says, gathering all the trail mix from the center and adding it to his pile. Anders and I are out of the game, and it looks like Callum is not interested in playing as he throws back another handful of peanuts.

"Well, screw this," Axel says, eating the rest of his trail mix. "Looks like I'm out. You ready for a tour since you two were late getting here?"

Anders and I stand up. "You guys can go ahead on the tour. Lachlan and I will finish the game," Trent replies as Lachlan reaches for the deck of cards. Callum remains seated and slowly munches on his snack.

Anders and I follow Axel into the kitchen. "Obviously, this is the kitchen. Help yourself to drinks and food. I try to keep it well stocked. If you dirty a dish, put it in the dishwasher. I'm not your maid." Turning on his heel, he strides down a small hallway. "This is my office. Don't go in there."

When I peek in the door, I see an entire wall of gun safes. "Man, this is like an armory. Wait, is that a pinball machine?"

Axel shrugs. "An off-limits pinball machine." Without further elaboration, he continues down the hall and opens the door. "This is a crash pad. If you get too drunk or need a place to stay, this bed is always open. If you use the sheets, strip them and replace them. There are basic clothes, large and extra-large, in case you need to borrow something."

"Alright. This is quite the set-up you have here," Anders replies.

"I'm still trying to think of a name to put on a plaque over the front door. Man Cave and Dude House seem kind of boring. I think I will hand everyone a piece of paper, and they can write down their idea for us to vote on next week," Axel says, locking his hands behind his back.

"Monkshaw Grotto?" I ask.

Axel arches a brow and crosses his arms over his chest. "What the hell kind of name is that? I don't think any of us are celibate, nor do I sing about kissing girls with a Jamaican accent."

"I'll keep brainstorming," I mumble. "What about Hummer Sanctuary." Axel wearily shakes his head. "Hemi House?"

Anders leads the way back down the hall. I lean and ask Axel, "So, what else did you learn about this Tristan character?"

Huffing, Axel shakes his head. "Dec. The guy's not Voldemort. He's thirty-six years old and from Seattle. The dude's an auto mechanic who played high school baseball. The only vehicles licensed to him are a motorcycle and an ancient truck he probably uses to haul shit." He slaps me hard on the upper back. "I don't think he's a threat to this town."

"Well, he's too old for her anyway. They're almost a decade apart," I grouse.

"First, don't say that around Trent, as he's almost eight years older than Paisley. Secondly, clearly, you aren't well versed in the bookish world of age-gap romance," Axel whispers as we approach the dining room.

"I'm not a huge reader." I wince when it looks like Axel is about to take three deep breaths. "We have a date Friday night. Everything will be fine," I grind out. Whether I'm trying to convince myself or Axel, I'm not really sure.

"I have no doubts. Britt says you two are meant to be as long as you can get her to stay in the same country as you," Axel says with a wink. I wish I could wipe that smirk off his face, but he'd hand me my ass in less than three moves.

"Yes, we are. Even if Julia leaves, I'll follow this time," I whisper.

Axel stops dead in his tracks. My front almost collides with his back. Slowly turning, he narrows his eyes and slowly repeats, "You'd leave Topaz Falls?" His voice is so quiet I can barely hear him.

When I silently nod, his eyes search my face, probably looking for some sign I'm lying. Joke's on him, though, because I'm not. I'm dead serious this time. He can try his interrogation mojo on me all he wants.

"Do your parents or siblings know?" Axel mumbles.

"No. Julia doesn't even know yet because I'm still hoping this time around, she'll choose me over Paris," I mutter.

He grips my shoulder and gives me a firm squeeze. With a quick nod, he turns and walks back to the poker table. "Where'd the trail mix go? It's hard work to be a tour guide in a single-story house."

I stand frozen because it's the first time I verbalized my decision to follow Julia, even if it means leaving the orchard and Topaz Falls. Now that it's out there, I can't take it back.

Chapter 22

Julia

Friday, October 11

Frantic knocking comes from the front door. Shards of light are fracturing through the stained-glass window in the entry, casting a colorful mosaic on the wood floor. My socked feet pad toward the noise because I realize I forgot to unlock it.

I swing the door open and fight the urge to laugh at Britt's cheesy grin as she holds up a clothing bag and a tackle box. "That's a lot of makeup," I mumble.

Elin chuckles. "I brought the good stuff." She holds up a bottle of tequila and a tub of margarita mix.

"You can't be serious. I can't be blotto when Declan arrives here to pick me up. I am an utter lightweight," I whine.

With an arched brow, Elin marches toward the kitchen with her drink ingredients. "Sweetheart, the drinks aren't for you. They're for Britt and me while we help you get ready. Then, we'll stay and drink, knowing you're the one out on the town on a Friday night, not us."

Pouting, Britt says, "Yeah. We're like the ugly stepsisters. Elin, get me a drink, pretty please. I'm going to show Julia the outfit options I brought."

Unease creeps up my skin. Britt brought outfit options. Her idea of a skirt is a bandana. Hopefully, she looked in Elin's closet since she seems to be the more conservative of the two.

Britt unzips the garment bag and pulls out three dresses. "Alright. Here are the options for tonight. One, this lovely strapless red number. B, a navy maxi dress. Third, I have a mustard yellow dress."

I look at all three options. They're gorgeous and would go great with my hair and eyes, but they are all strapless or spaghetti straps. "These are a bit too revealing, Britt."

Her eyes widen in disbelief. "These are my most conservative autumn options. You are twenty-six and stunning. I'm not dressing you in a habit for your hot date. Come on, it's Declan." She shimmies her shoulders, and I growl. Not because I'm feeling possessive—well, maybe that plays into it a little bit—but because I need to show them why I need to wear long sleeves.

I tug my arm out of the oversized sweater and lift the hem around my neck, exposing my entire right side. Britt gasps, and the thud of the margarita mix bucket hitting the floor makes me wince.

"What happened?" Britt whispers as she slowly approaches me. The margarita mix is abandoned, and Elin moves around the kitchen island until she's only a foot away.

"You know how I told you my bakery burned down in Paris, so my only option was to come here?" I ask, my voice threatening to crack.

"Wait, no," Elin replies. "I think you need to start at the beginning. I knew you came here to exercise your aunt's will stipulations, but I assumed you knew about it long before she passed."

Shaking my head, I say, "No. I didn't realize she left everything to me. In hindsight, it made sense because, besides my mom, I'm her only living relative. She never married or had kids. But when she passed, I was managing a patisserie. I figured if I didn't like it, I'd come here. Then I met Chauncy, my ex-fiancé, and we opened our own patisserie. Earlier this spring, I was working late and must've fallen asleep at my desk in the back of the kitchen. I woke up to smoke billowing under the door. Firefighters got me out, but I already suffered severe burns by the time I was finally rescued. My skin is healed, but the scars remain."

"Is it along your entire right arm, from wrist to shoulder?" Britt asks, her fingers reaching out like she wants to touch the puckered skin as tears fill her lash line.

"Yes, but my side, too." I lift my right arm, exposing my rib cage and the tender skin pulling taut against my torso.

Elin's fingertips come to her mouth as her eyes categorize every little scar. The golden light above the kitchen island highlights the stark white skin.

"This is why I need something long-sleeved. I'm not used to the stares yet," I whisper, angrily wiping a tear from my cheek.

"Hey, don't do that. You're gorgeous inside and out. We didn't gasp because we thought it was hideous. We were worried about you. You're all healed, though, right?" Elin asks, and I take a shaky breath.

Nodding, I reply, "As I'll ever be. The scars may fade more over time, but they will always be noticeable."

Britt grips my good shoulder as I ease my right arm back down the sleeve. "You realize Declan won't give a crap about the scars marring your skin, right? He thinks you're a goddess in every sense of the word."

"Wait," Elin says, waving her hands at Britt to be quiet. "Did they catch the person who did it?"

Frowning, I tip my head back. "They know it was my fiancé who started the fire with accelerant, but he drained the bank account and took off before the finger ever pointed at him. I was still in the hospital recovering when he left with all our money."

"That's awful," Elin murmurs, rubbing small circles on my back.

"Well, enough of the doom and gloom. I hate that you went through this, but it's time to get back on the unicorn and ride into your dreams," Britt calls out as she heads upstairs. "If you don't wear one of mine, then I'm shopping in your closet."

Elin and I follow her to my aunt's room just in time to see two garments fly onto the bed. "Oh, this is just like prom, you guys!"

I remember prom. Aunt Rita gave me money for a dress. The night of prom, she cooked Declan and me a pasta dinner at the house before we drove to the high school gym. I glance over my shoulder at Elin to see if she understands what Britt is referring to. "Don't ask me." She shrugs a delicate shoulder.

Britt pokes her head out of the closet, her curls in disarray around her face. "Elin, didn't you get ready with a bunch of friends? Julia was my only friend with a date, so my other friends all got dressed at my house. Dresses and makeup were everywhere. My bed looked like a prom store exploded with a sequin and glitter bomb."

Elin winces. "I wouldn't know."

Narrowing her eyes, Britt says, "Didn't you go to prom?"

Huffing, Elin crosses her arms. "Oh, I barely went to prom. I have a feeling our versions of prom were very different. I went with my best friend's twin brother and his date. Being the third wheel was mortifying, especially when he and his date hit it off at dinner, so I walked home. I didn't even go to the actual dance. I had a huge crush on a guy, but he went with the most popular girl in the school."

"Huh. Okay," Britt replies, then ducks back into the closet.

"You realize these aren't my clothes, right?" I ask. "We're in Aunt Rita's closet. My room is down the hall."

"Well, her taste in clothes was awesome. Is the hole in your ceiling fixed?" Elin asks.

"There is a contractor from Larkspur Canyon who is handling everything. It will be good as new in no time," I reply, crossing my fingers. When I glance at Britt, her mouth is pressed into a firm line as a dress hangs limply from her extended hand.

"Fine, let me try this," I reply, yanking the garment from Britt's grasp.

"Watch it! Don't act like you're some old hag snagging the last loaf of bread at a farmer's market," Britt shrieks.

Huffing, I call from inside the bathroom. "Alright. I'll admit. This is perfect." I don't remember seeing her wear this dress. It's a soft cashmere sweater dress with a mock neck collar in a stunning shade of amber. My hands shakily brush the garment over my thighs, amazed at how soft it feels under my fingertips. The color brings out the highlights in my hair, making the gold really stand out. The sleeves come down to the back of my hand, and the collar is high enough to hide the scars on my shoulders. I know Declan will find out or see them in due time, but I hope I get to live in this bubble a little longer. I'm just glad he's right-handed so his distraction in the shed didn't find my torso scars. I love how he looks at me, and although I know Britt's right, I don't want to risk him looking at me differently.

When I open the bathroom door, Britt and Elin are standing on the other side, softly talking. Looking up through my lashes, I wait for them to say something. Britt extends her hand, her mouth slack. I've never heard her so quiet before. Hopefully, it's a good quiet, not a bad quiet.

"You look stunning," Elin whispers, breaking the silence. "The gold in the dress makes your eyes look like pools of silver."

"Let me do your makeup," Britt says, tugging her tackle box onto the bathroom counter.

Lifting my finger, I reply, "No red lips or dark smokey eyes. I don't want to look like a vampiric raccoon."

Arching a brow, Britt motions to the dress. "I plan on doing a warm palette. Trust me. I know what I'm doing. I'm not eighteen years old anymore. I know how to apply makeup now."

Pointing to my teeth, I say, "You have a little bit of something right here."

Panicked, Britt spins toward the mirror. "What?"

"Just kidding," I say, fighting the urge to giggle.

Britt shakes her head, a smirk tilting the corner of her mouth. "Sit down so I can beautify you."

Ten minutes later, I walk down the stairs in a pair of flats. Britt insisted I wear heels, but I won, demonstrating my lack of coordination in the heels she found in the closet. In the kitchen, the blender whirs, and I laugh at the sight of Elin dancing around the kitchen with a huge margarita clutched in her hand.

"Is that one mine?" Britt asks.

Pointing to the blender, Elin raises the glass in her hand to her mouth and shakes her hips.

"Before I forget. Julia, I got your message about the competition being three Sundays in a row. Sunday is the day I visit my mom. I can't miss three visits in a row. It would devastate her. I'm all she has left. I'm so sorry, but I can't make it work. I thought it would be one weekend, not three," Elin says, her face falling as she stares into her drink.

I place my hand on her forearm and reply, "Don't worry. I'll find someone else. I have a little bit longer until the competition, and there are plenty of townspeople we could rope into the mess."

"I think you should convince Declan to be your teammate since he's the reason you're doing the competition," Britt muses as she stares at the blender, waiting for the drink to be smooth.

There's a knock at the door, and Britt turns to answer it, abandoning the blender altogether. A little growl bubbles up from my throat, wanting to be the one to see Declan first. "You two stay in the kitchen. He doesn't need to know I needed an army to prepare for this date."

Britt raises her hands. "Cool down, chica. You don't have to lick him to claim him for yourself. He's all yours. Remember, I grew up with Declan. He's like that third cousin at a reunion where you can objectively admit he's hot as sin, but you wouldn't romantically touch him with a ten-foot pole."

My gaze narrows on Elin. Shaking her head, she replies, "No way. I know he's good-looking, and the whole age gap thing is in right now, but he is too young for me. Plus, I've got my eyes set on the blondie with a man bun. I almost swallowed my tongue when he ran past the vet clinic shirtless the other day. I may want to lick every one of his tattoos, but right now I'm going to quietly drink my margarita. Go ahead and pretend like I'm not here."

Furrowing my brow. "Tristan? He's taking over the auto shop at the beginning of the new year."

"Yeah, him," Elin says dreamily. "Take me to Valhalla."

"If he's at the bakery the next time you stop by, I can introduce you. He's really nice, and I think he said he was in his late thirties. I know you sort of met him at Glaciers, but it was too loud and dark that night to talk."

"Plus, he danced with Britt. By the time you returned from dancing with Declan, I'd already ducked out for the night," Elin replies.

"That, too," I mutter.

Elin winks as I stride to the door, smoothing out any possible wrinkle and pressing together my glossy lips. I can do this. Tugging open the door, I stare dumbstruck at the most beautiful man in the world. Lordy, he looks edible. Who needs dinner when this man is standing before me. Taking a deep breath, his woodsy, spicy cologne wraps around me like a familiar blanket.

"Hey, blossom," he murmurs, stepping closer to me.

The sky is covered in dark gray clouds, with slivers of light fighting to break through. I shiver, thinking it might rain tonight.

"You look beautiful. Instead of a bouquet, I brought you a basket of apples I picked today," Declan says. His gravelly voice makes me want to pull him upstairs and forget all about the restaurant.

Swallowing, I reach out to accept the gorgeous basket of apples. Our brief touch sends an electrical impulse up my arm, jolting me. "Thank you, *Mon autre*. You look pretty good yourself."

Chapter 23
Declan

Julia is in my truck, and we're on our first date since senior year. Blinking, I assume any minute I'll awaken from this dream. My grip tightens because there are so many questions I want answered. I feel like my soul needs them answered, yet I know some things in life are better left locked in the past. Will I like what I find out? What if it was something I did? I wracked my brain for months after Julia left, trying to find the tipping point. Over the years, my memories tried to pull something from my subconscious, but instead, it left me riddled with more questions than answers, along with insomnia.

I swallow thickly as I glance at Julia in my peripheral vision. She looks relaxed in the truck's passenger seat, her hands gently folded over her purse on her lap. The setting sun casts an ethereal glow over her skin making it look golden. She's so fucking gorgeous it makes my stomach clench.

The silence isn't uncomfortable, but the closer we get to our destination, the more awkward I think it'd be to start talking now. Instead, I turn the radio up a little louder and grin sheepishly at Julia when her eyes blink at me in surprise. I wish I had the power to look into her beautiful mind and see what she was thinking about just now.

When I spoke to Trent on the phone earlier today, he suggested I take Julia to Growlers Alley in Topaz Crest. Channing owns the pub, and I've eaten there a few times over the years. The food is good, and the portions are huge. I park the truck on the street, beneath the old-fashioned lamppost on the quiet street in the town center. For a Friday evening, it sure is quiet.

Hopping out of the front seat, I angle my body around the front bumper in time to help Julia open her door. There's a steep drop from the passenger seat, so I reach out and grab her hips, lifting her softly to the ground.

"Where are we?" Julia asks, looking up at the pub curiously.

"This is Growlers Alley. My good friend Channing owns the place. He has a distillery and uses apples from my orchard in his hard cider. He's a good guy, and the food is awesome," I say, placing my palm in the center of her back.

The sign features a beer growler with a slashed label. Four claw marks, like those of a wolf, are visible. When I asked Channing about it one time, he told me it was their way of embracing the wildlife being so close to Glacier National Park. Harleys line the parking space right in front of the heavy oak door. The handle is oversized, with a wooden wolf paw draped over the top.

When I pull the door open, my ears are assaulted by the sound of glasses clinking and country music. Once inside, several patrons pause their conversations to take us in. We're clearly not regulars to the establishment, but I recognize a few faces from my previous visits. This may not be my local stomping ground, but I'm not a complete stranger.

All the stools at the bar are taken by men in either flannel or riding leathers. Luckily, I spy a few empty tables scattered about and breathe a sigh of relief. There isn't a reservation system, so waiting for someone to close out their tab could have kept us waiting all night.

Camille approaches us with a broad smile. She's in her signature uniform for the pub: torn jeans and a black tank. Her thick blonde hair is intricately braided like a Viking warrior, and dark charcoal lines her warm brown eyes.

"Welcome, Dec," she says with a sniff. Turning toward Julia, she extends her hand. "My name is Camille. I'm the manager of Growlers Alley. Are you two dining in or getting an order to go?"

Clearing my throat, I press Julia closer to my side. "It's good to see you, Camille. We'd like to dine in if you have a table."

"I've got one better for you. Follow me. The booth at the back is open," she says, grabbing two menus and striding away.

"Is Channing in tonight?" I ask. "I wondered if he got enough apples for this year's hard cider batch."

Nodding, she glances over her shoulder. "I think it's the perfect amount. However, Channing might order more next year, as our hard cider is one of our most popular drinks. He's in his office. I'll send him out to say hi. We also spent some time discussing your idea of an Octoberfest or Brewfest next October."

We sit at the booth, and I look up at Julia once she leaves. Her eyes are wide and unblinking. "She's kind of intimidating," she whispers.

"Camille?" I ask, feigning shock. She's one of the toughest women I've ever met, and her strength puts me to shame. I grin at Julia's shocked expression. "Yeah, she's tough as nails." I pick up the menu and say, "Their steak salad is delicious here, and so is the flank steak."

Glancing at the options, Julia says, "I think the top sirloin with garlic roasted potatoes sounds good."

A large hand slaps the table, and I smile when Julia jumps. Maybe this place was a little too casual for our first date. I thought it would set her at ease not being fancy, but I forgot she was used to Paris. This is probably like slumming it to her. Wincing, I look up at Channing's amused expression. "What's up, Dec?"

"Wow, your eyes are beautiful," Julia whispers under her breath.

Channing chuckles and extends his hand. "Who is this pretty lady?" I growl when he winks at her. He tips his head back and laughs. "Cool it, pup. I won't put the moves on your woman."

Julia squares her shoulders and extends her hands. "Hello, I'm Julia."

Channing's gaze snaps to mine, and his eyes narrow. Leaning in, he drops his voice near my ear. "Is this your Julia from high school?"

My jaw tightens, and I give a jerky nod. Taking a small step away from the table, Channing crosses his arms over his chest and offers Julia a soft smile. "It's nice to meet you, Julia. Welcome to my pub. Dessert tonight is on me. I hope you both enjoy yourselves. Be sure to let me know if I can get you anything."

Julia grins and reaches for my hand. She squeezes my palm, and the noose around my heart relaxes, some of my fear and reservation waning. I intertwine our fingers before she can pull her hand back, and a peach blush covers her cheeks.

"Thanks, man," I say to Channing. "Julia is an amazing baker, so I hope your kitchen staff can impress her."

Rapping his knuckles against the table, he has a wicked gleam in his eye. "Might I suggest our flourless chocolate lava cake, then?"

Julia squeals, and I chuckle. "Looks like we know what we want for dessert."

Channing leaves with a smirk, waving bye to us as he walks down the hallway to his office at the back of the pub. Camille takes the place where Channing just stood and taps a pen on her notepad. "What can I get you, folks?"

"I'll have the top sirloin with garlic-roasted potatoes," Julia says. "Can I try your Growlers cider?"

Camille smiles and scribbles on her notepad before turning to me. "And for you, Dec?"

"I'll have the flank steak with a twice-baked potato. I'll take an Ambarsan hard cider, too." The corner of my mouth twitches as I return my menu to Camille.

Shaking her head, she says, "Does Channing know you've changed the name of his cider?" When I wink, she chuckles. "These will be right up," she replies and walks to the kitchen.

"So, how have you been?" I ask, feeling stupid at my awkward question.

Nodding, Julia replies, "Good. How about you?"

Sighing, I scrub my hand through the short hair at the back of my neck. "Honestly, with my dad in the hospital and my mom with him, I've been better. I always planned to take over the orchard, but I'm not ready yet. I thought I had another ten years under my parents' supervision. It sounds stupid when I say it out loud. I'm twenty-six years old, for fuck's sake, but I'm not ready."

Julia squeezes my fingers tightly, bringing my attention to her face. "It's okay not to be ready at our age, Declan. You've grown up on the orchard, and although it might be a well-oiled machine, it's still a large operation."

Swallowing thickly, I look up at her. "Yeah. I'm planning to tell my parents once they're back." Camille sets down our drinks and walks away on silent steps. "Are you still planning to leave in three months?" The question tumbles across my lips before I can stop myself.

Slowly nodding, she gulps her cider and winces at the burn of the alcohol. "I've already got an offer on the place. It will set me up with my dream patisserie in Paris. I'll buy my plane ticket in November to head home over Christmas and sign the lease on the new space."

Pressing my lips together, I force a smile on my face. Hopefully, it doesn't look like a pained grimace. If she leaves, I will, too. When it gets closer, I'll tell her I'm coming with her this time. She left me once but won't leave me again, not without me fighting for us.

The food arrives and is as good as I remember it. The portions are so large I can't even finish my dinner. I'm not complaining, though, because it means lunch or dinner tomorrow—one less meal I have to plan.

"This was amazing, but I'm stuffed," Julia says, leaning back against her seat.

Wiggling my eyebrows, I ask, "Do you have room for dessert?"

Julia huffs in mock dismay. "Do I have room for dessert? What kind of question is that? A lady always has room for dessert, especially if it includes chocolate."

Before our dessert arrives, a shadow falls over our table, and I sigh at yet another intrusion. Slowly turning my head, I come nose to nose with the weathered face of Wacky Wayne. His gap-toothed smile looks manic, and the deep lines surrounding his eyes crinkle in delight. His bony elbow jams into my shoulder as he eases his lower body onto the bench beside me. I barely shove myself out of the way before he lands hard on the seat.

"They're everywhere," he whispers, the smell of alcohol heavy on his breath.

"Hey, Wayne. What do you mean?" I ask, suppressing a sigh as I bring my chilled glass to my lips.

"Them. They are all over the surrounding forest. I think I found their lair," he rasps, his eyes darting around the pub. "Don't make eye contact with any of them. You could be entranced, and then when you are under their control, they bite you. Before you know it, you'll be one of them."

Julia's eyes widen in shock. I scramble to redirect the conversation. Wayne is a conspiracy theorist, always looking for Bigfoot, aliens, werewolves, and vampires. He's convinced Glacier National Park is a hub for them, which was his sole purpose for moving to Topaz Falls thirty years ago. As far as I know, he's never found an ounce of proof, but he's always searching, driving his 1970s RV up any road it can handle.

"Wayne, we're on a date, buddy." I motion to Julia. "Do you think we could go over your theories next week?" I ask, trying to get him to leave without downright dismissing the poor guy.

He exhales forcibly. "I saw eye shine while hiking in the forest last night. Are you going to drink that?" he asks, reaching for my half-finished pint of cider.

I slide it out of his reach just before his knobby fingers grasp the handle. "Yeah, there is a lot of wildlife around here, Wayne," I say, trying to hold back my frustration.

"No. Declan, this wasn't normal eye shine. This was intelligent eye shine. The creatures were as smart as me. It wasn't just a pack of wolves. I'm telling ya, they were supernaturals," he rasps. His eyes shoot wildly around the pub.

Before he can spew more nonsense, Channing steps up to the table. With a booming voice, he says, "Hey, Wayne. How about I buy you a beer."

I mouth, "Thank you." Channing leads Wayne toward the bar. His skittish movements make me uncomfortable as his eyes cut from side to side. Channing winks at us before returning to his office, shaking his head.

"He was—different," Julia says, causing me to snort.

Whispering, I raise my glass in front of my face. "Wayne is always looking for the supernatural in this world. He's convinced he'll be the first with undeniable proof of Bigfoot."

Shaking her head, Julia's hair swishes across the top of the table, and a small smile dances on her mouth.

The cake arrives, and we devour it in a few large bites. After paying the bill, I say bye to Camille and direct Julia back to my truck. When we step outside, ominous grey clouds roll toward us. A flash of lightning in the distance is followed by a clap of thunder. We rush to the truck, and after helping Julia into the front seat, I hurry and hoist my frame into the cab.

The ignition turns over as the first fat drop of rain splatters against the windshield. I lean forward and look up at the darkening sky. "Let's hope it holds out a bit longer," I say.

Another bolt of lightning illuminates the sky. Julia reaches for my hand and entwines our fingers, gripping me with a death grip. Her knuckles turn white against my tan skin.

"Hey, it's okay," I say, trying to infuse calm into my voice. With a self-deprecating smile, I say, "I was petrified of thunder as a kid."

Gnawing on her lower lip, Julia tips her head against the headrest. "This is a recent issue. It isn't the thunder. It's the lightning." The next rumble of thunder sounds like it's directly above the truck. The cab rattles as the sound echoes around us. Julia sucks in a sharp breath when the next flash of light illuminates the entire interior.

"Did you get stuck outside in a lightning storm?" I ask. The more I think about it, she loved rainstorms in high school. I remember sitting in the treehouse with her as we cuddled under a blanket and watched the lightning storms travel across the valley to the east.

"No," she whispers, turning her head to look out the window. She'll tell me if or when she's ready. The more I talk to her, the more I think something terrible happened in Paris.

"Are you excited for the baking competition this weekend?" I ask, trying to change the topic.

"Oh shoot!" Sitting upright, she turns in the passenger seat with wide eyes. "I totally forgot. Elin told me she wouldn't be able to be my partner. Would you like to be on the Home Team?" she asks with a chuckle.

"Sure," I reply, surprising myself.

Her gaze searches mine. "Really? You're sure?" I nod, and she says, "Alright. We need to practice before Sunday. Come to the bakery tomorrow after it closes. I need to teach you a few basics."

"I'll be there," I say. Inside I'm pumping my fist like I just set a world record at the Olympics. I bite the inside of my cheek so I don't grin like a loon.

When I pull up to the front of her house, Elin and Britt are standing in the doorway, dancing with glasses in their hands. "Dec. I had such a good time with you tonight. It was nice drinking legally with you."

"I did too, blossom. I do miss the nights at Topaz Peak in the back of my truck, but I don't miss worrying whether the sheriff would show up and bust us. Wait here," I say as I reach into the backseat and grab my oiled canvas jacket. Rushing around the front of the truck, I open her door and hold the coat above our heads. We run to her front porch steps, laughter bubbling from her that's so contagious I can't help but laugh with her.

When was the last time I felt this free?

Britt and Elin sneak back inside before we reach the top of the porch, but I watch the curtain on the side window flit. I assumed we wouldn't have an audience with her living alone. It's like her aunt is home all over again.

Bending down, I press a kiss to her temple. "I had a great time tonight, blossom."

Rotating her head, her lips capture mine, and she melts into my chest. My hand drops the coat as I pull her flush to my body. Her lips taste like chocolate and apples. The taste will stay at the forefront of my mind for the rest of the evening. When she pulls away, her lids are heavy with lust, and I fight the groan threatening to rumble in my chest. Catcalls come from behind the front door and Julia growls. "Why'd they have to stay?" Her fingers play the hem of my shirt, her skin so close to touching mine I can feel the static between us.

"Goodnight, Dec," she whispers against my lips.

Pulling back, I slowly press my mouth against her forehead, breathing her in one last time.

"Night, blossom. I'll see you tomorrow." I pick up my coat and jog down the porch steps. The rain pelts my body feeling like needles prickling any exposed skin. Rivulets of water stream down my face. My body is on fire, and the rain does nothing to cool me down.

Chapter 24

Julia

Saturday, October 12

At 5 p.m., knuckles rap against the door to the back entrance of the bakery. With my dough-covered hands held away from my body, I use my butt to shove open the door. It almost collides with Declan, who quickly steps out of the way. His brilliant smile warms my heart as I take in his jean-clad thighs and narrow waist. The way he's looking at me is anything but innocent, so I take my time perusing him from head to toe.

Clearing his throat, he raises a paper bag. "May I come in out of the rain? I come bearing dinner for us. I also brought the release forms we need to sign for the Baking Network before we can compete. They told me it was fine to give it to them tomorrow."

Shaking my head to clear my thoughts, I head back to the prep counter, taking the last loaf of bread to the proofing tray. With the task completed, I wash up until my skin is pink from scrubbing in the hot water. Grabbing a pen, I walk over and sign where Declan placed yellow sticky notes, then look up at him.

"What'd you bring for dinner?" I ask, curiosity getting the better of me.

Opening the bag, he pulls out two containers and sets them between us. "I went to Mama M's and picked up a chicken pot pie and a shepherd's pie. You choose because I'll eat either."

Without hesitation, I snatch up the chicken pot pie and dig in. When the buttery, flakey crust hits my tongue, my eyes close, and my head falls back. A slight moan slips past my lips as I savor the flavors. "This is amazing."

"Yes, you are," Declan whispers so low, I'm afraid I imagined him saying those sweet words.

My eyes snap open to find Declan staring at me through half-lidded eyes. His pupils are blown so wide, hardly any green is visible in his irises. I twirl the spoon in my mouth, sucking off the crumbs, and his gaze follows my every movement, eyes locked on my mouth.

I quickly inhale the rest of my dinner for fear if we get distracted, we will be the worst team by far tomorrow. "How much baking do you do at home?"

"Do Pop-Tarts count? I can bake four at a time in my toaster, even though we all know they taste better at room temperature," he replies, catching me off guard.

"I was wondering if you still had your Pop-Tarts obsession," I muse.

"If they had a monthly subscription box for Pop-Tarts, I'd be their first member," he says.

"Is frosted strawberry still your favorite flavor?" I ask.

He shrugs. "I don't discriminate. They're all worthy of being my choice for breakfast. If I'm being honest, I'm slightly obsessed with the pumpkin spice one right now. Some people can't wait for the pumpkin spice latte to arrive at Starbucks. I count the days until pumpkin spice Pop-Tarts hit the shelves. I have to ask Gary at the supermarket to order them specially for me."

I gnaw on my lip to keep from smiling. Sometimes, like right now, I swear I can still see the eighteen-year-old boy I was madly in love with. His mannerisms are so familiar to me. He brings with him a sense of stability and home. Even though eating Pop-Tarts like they're their own food group is a little disturbing at twenty-six, I wouldn't change him for the world.

His large palm reaches up and caresses my jawline as his eyes bore into mine. Jolting out of the trance, I clap my hands together and hop out of his addicting touch. "Alright, we need to formulate a plan. The theme is apples. I don't know what we will be required to make, but since I know apples will be required, I want to ensure you know how to peel and chop an apple."

Scoffing, he stands and walks toward me from where he'd been leaning against the countertop.

"Hey, now. Just because I dislike baking doesn't mean I can't peel an apple. My mother had me peeling apples from the time I could safely wield a peeler."

"Makes sense since you grew up on an orchard. Apples were probably in everything your mom made."

He tips his head back and laughs. "One benefit to being the youngest sibling, as Ingrid and Lachlan told me stories of having apples in their breakfast, lunch, and dinner. When I found out, Mom had given up that tradition before I was old enough to eat because Lachlan and Ingrid were sick of apples for every meal. I lucked out."

"Alright, so peeling apples is a skill of yours. What about dicing or slicing?" I ask.

He holds out a tan, callused palm and tips it from side to side. "I doubt the judges will be impressed with my lack of professional technique, but I can make an apple go from whole to many little pieces. I prefer to use the apple slicer." When I raise an eyebrow, he continues, "You know, an apple coring device. You put the tool on top, press it down on the apple, and it slices it into eight equal pieces."

I swallow thickly as I look at his sexy hands. Can hands be sexy? Glancing down at mine, I frown. "Okay. Let's work on measuring. We can make a pan of brownies."

"The only time I made brownies, they came out flat and tasted like buttered popcorn," Declan says, leaning his hip against the island.

"Well, I don't have a response for all that. It probably came out flat because your leavening agent was expired, you didn't use enough, or you forgot it altogether. I have no idea why they tasted like buttered popcorn," I reply as I walk over to the hook of aprons. Pulling one off the hook, I turn and collide with Declan's hard chest, not realizing he was directly behind me.

I splutter, "W—what happened." The fingertips of my empty hand press into the hard muscles of his chest, and I feel him instinctively flex into my touch.

Without breaking eye contact, he reaches out and plucks the apron out of my limp grasp. "Just getting my apron, chef."

His mischievous grin breaks the tension. I'm not sure whether it grates on me or warms me to know he's aware of the effects he has on me. Snorting, I scoot around him back to the safety of my kitchen island.

"First, we will mix the dry ingredients together. Then, we will add the wet ingredients," I say, trying not to sound flustered. Hopefully, my voice won't betray me. The twitch of Declan's lips as he watches my mouth speak has me believing otherwise.

Tamping down my lust, I get to work teaching Declan how to make the batter. "What's the difference between baking powder and baking soda?" Declan asks.

I smile. "Good question. Honestly, not much for brownie batter. If you add baking soda, the brownies take slightly longer to bake and come out puffier. Most of the recipes I've used for brownies use baking powder because it gives them a little lift. I find baking soda gives them a cakier texture."

"Cakier. Is that a technical term they taught in baking school?" he teases.

Nudging him with my elbow, I laugh. "Not exactly."

In no time, I'm pulling the fresh pan of brownies from the oven and turning it off. The moment the oven clicks off, I gasp. A panic attack didn't even cross my mind the entire time we were baking. Declan distracted me with intimate touches and his heated gaze, so I didn't spiral. I was simply on autopilot. I felt like myself in the kitchen for the first time since the fire. Maybe Trent was right; this competition would heal me more than I ever hoped.

Declan returns from the refrigerator with a can of whipped cream. "Can't have brownies without whipped cream."

I arch my brow. "I think a brownie ala mode would taste better," I challenge.

Shaking his head, he replies, "Only because you haven't had whipped cream on your brownies." His voice hints at a double entendre, forcing an electrical impulse to skitter up my spine.

"Open up," he says. Prowling toward me, he vigorously shakes the can.

His pupils dilate as he watches me slowly open my mouth and tilt my head back. He squirts a large dollop of whipped cream into my mouth, and my lips slowly close around it. As I swallow it down, my tongue darts out to capture the small amount left on my lips.

"Hey, that was for me," he rasps, watching my tongue with rapt fascination.

"Sorry," I whisper, closing the distance between us subconsciously.

He smirks at me as he raises the can and drags a thick stream of whipped cream over my exposed chest, from collarbone to collarbone. My traitorous body trembles when his lips descend on my skin. Before my conscience can stop me, my lust detonates like a damn grenade. I want him to consume every inch of me. Dragging my nails through his hair, I pull his face into my chest, where he laps up every drip of whipped cream. He leans back just enough for me to crash my lips into his, attacking his mouth like he's my savior. His fingers deftly undo the buttons of my cotton blouse.

I gasp and break the kiss. Anxiety thrums through my nerves. I yank the shirt closed and take a hesitant step back. Declan matches me pace for pace until my back is pressed into the far wall near the office.

"Blossom, what just happened?" My eyes dart to the ground, unable to make eye contact with him as I swallow thickly. My heartbeat hammers against my sternum, and my ears ring.

Sucking in a deep breath, I whisper, "I can't."

His callused palm gently grips my jaw, bringing my face toward him. When my eyes land on his jaw, he's grinding it with such force that I'm afraid it will break. "Did someone hurt you?" His voice is viciously low. When I don't respond, his voice cracks. "Please tell me what's wrong."

With a shaky breath, I close my eyes, allowing the blouse to fall off my shoulders and down my arms, exposing my skin to the cool air.

"Who did this to you?" Declan rumbles so low it's almost not audible. His hand tenderly grips my neck as his forehead presses into mine. Something wet hits my cheek, and when my eyes open in shock,

I find Declan's water-lined eyes searching mine for information only my voice can give.

"I was in a fire earlier this year. I was working late in my patisserie office. When I jolted awake, I was greeted by the smell of smoke filtering in beneath the door. By the time the firefighters got me out, I had sustained some burns on my right side. I'll always look like this now."

Declan's arms band around me, pressing me into his warm embrace. "You're perfect, Julia. These scars don't make you any less beautiful in my eyes. In fact, they show me how much you endured and fought to survive. Was it arson?"

I bite my lip to keep it from quivering. I've cried over this enough. Chauncy and what he did to me don't deserve another tear. "Yes."

"Did they catch the person?" Declan's fingers tighten against my hips as if he's afraid I'll blow away like smoke in the wind.

"Not yet, but they know who did it," I murmur.

"Who?" His blunt question opens another can of worms I hoped to keep at the back of my mental pantry until it expired and could be thrown away.

Turning my head into his chest, I mutter, "My ex-fiancé."

"Good thing you described him as your ex," he states, pulling me tighter into his broad chest. I yelp in pain when something hard presses against my forehead. Declan immediately releases me, stepping back just enough to look at me.

Before he can ask what happened, one of my hands rubs my forehead while the other climbs his chest. My fingers close around a circle hanging from a chain. Reaching under the collar of his shirt, I pull out the necklace and allow the pendant to swing against his shirt. Only it's not a pendant; it's a ring.

"You kept it?" I say, disbelief lacing my tone.

"Of course I kept it, blossom," he replies, stepping closer to me so he can wrap his arms around my waist. "After you left without an explanation, I wore it as a reminder of why I should never fall in love. Over the years, I realized it was a reminder that you were the only one I could ever promise to love. It has always been a promise ring, but what it promised over the years has changed."

Choking back a sob, I look at the engraving on the inside. My trembling fingers fly to my lips as I read, "JF aime DA."

Slowly, he says, "Did you not keep yours?" The hurt in his tone is hard to miss.

"It's on the dresser in my room at Aunt Rita's house. I still have it. After what I did to you, it was a promise to never hurt you again."

Declan breathes a sigh of relief. "I need you, blossom."

My voice catches when I reply, "I need you, too."

His warm hands capture my face as his lips descend upon mine. My hands quickly untuck his shirt, and he lets go of me for long enough to whip his shirt up over his head. It falls to the floor next to my blouse. My eyes drink in his body. Gone is the eighteen-year-old boy I fell in love with. Before me is a man who, if circumstances were different, I could see loving forever. I'll have to steel my heart so we can take from each other what we need. This will be like a form of closure for us after I left so abruptly last time. This time, he can get the answers and leave me in the past. My heart wants to shatter at the thought of him moving on from us, but he needs to live his life without my tainted shadow hanging over him.

My pants fall to the ground as his erection grinds against my hip. He's hard and ready for me. After seeing the scars, I thought no one would find my body sexy again, but I was clearly wrong. Declan's response is evidence of that.

Picking me up, his hands palm the globes of my ass, causing my hips to cant against his lower abs. His lips suck against the sensitive skin at my pulse point, and I moan as my head tips skyward. He walks us into my new office. Setting me on the edge of my large oak desk, his arm reaches behind me and swipes the notepad and pens I had sitting on top, sending them crashing to the floor.

His lips kiss a burning trail down the center of my chest as he open mouth kisses each nipple through my lace bra, leaving them pebbled in the ambient air. Declan's strong hands spread my thighs wide, and he lowers himself onto his knees. "Oh, you don't have to—" I start to say.

"I want to, blossom. I've been dreaming of what you taste like since the moment I saw you. My memory from when we were teenagers is lacking. All I remember is you were irresistible. Please let me do this." His eyes bore into me, imploring me to allow him access, like I'm a gift.

When I nod, his lips kiss through the sheer lining of my lace underwear, knowing they're soaked. He slides his thumbs up the inside of my thigh. His finger pushes aside my panties and his lips close around my clit. I buck into his face, my back arching off the table. A thick finger swirls around my entrance. In the next breath, he goes knuckles deep. Unable to catch my breath, I grip the edge of my desk and writhe to increase the friction. I can feel my release building in my lower belly, but I need more. He inserts a second finger between one heartbeat and the next, then a third.

"Dec, I'm close," I moan.

"Good," he mumbles against my clit, the vibrations sending me almost over the ledge.

My breath stutters, but before I can let go, he pulls his fingers out and stands up. Opening his jeans, he lets them fall to the floor. His erection strains against his boxers, and I whimper in anticipation. "Get in me now, Dec." Everything tingles, and I'm right on the edge.

His hand rubs my wetness all over his shaft. I watch, mesmerized, as his thumb swipes over the tip, capturing a bead of precum. He leans over me, notching the blunt head of his cock against my opening as he brings his thumb to my lips. My tongue darts out and licks it. Memories flood my system of the first time I went down on him in the back of his truck. The flavor is uniquely him, with a hint of both salty and sweet.

"You ready for me, blossom? I've dreamt of this moment more times than I can count. I have to admit it was never on your aunt's desk, but I don't give a fuck anymore. I just want you." Nodding because words have escaped me, he says, "Nope, sweetheart. I need to hear you say it."

"Yes," I whisper, and in an instant, he glides in, taking me to the hilt. His breaths are shallow as he tries to maintain composure. It makes me happy to see him struggling for control as much as I am.

"Don't move for just a second. This blows every wet dream out of the water," he murmurs into the crook of my neck. When my hips start to push against his pelvis, he begins to move, pounding into me at a relentless pace. My heels dig into his ass as I buck into his every thrust. My nails drag against his smooth back with such strength I'm afraid I might draw blood.

"*Mon autre*," I moan as my walls flutter around him, the orgasm crashing into me with such force I gasp. He follows me over the edge, his knuckles white where he's gripping the desk. With his green apple eyes searing into my soul, he growls my name in a tortured whisper. A whisper that promises more even though, for sanity, we probably shouldn't. This should be a one-and-done, get-it-out-of-our-systems fuck.

His eyes hold mine with reverence that leaves me feeling precious. As he pulls out, he reaches down to take care of the condom and swears, "Shit!"

"What?" I reply, trying to sit up, realizing cum is dripping down my inner thigh.

"Damn it. I was so caught up in the moment I forgot to put on a condom. Please tell me you're on birth control," he pleads. "Shit, I'm so sorry, blossom. I'm clean."

"Don't worry, Dec. I'm clean, too." For the first time in my life, I'm glad I can utter, "Also, I can't really get pregnant." I wince but force myself not to look away.

The look of shock in his expression has me fighting to hide my face. Not only is half my body scarred beyond recognition, but I'm also unlikely to be able to have a baby. I brace myself for the look of disgust, but it never comes.

"What do you mean?" he murmurs, but only curiosity and sadness shine in his eyes.

"It means my body can't hold a pregnancy because my eggs aren't viable. I can't really have kids without medical assistance," I whisper.

"Why?" The question sounds so simple, but the answer is beyond complicated.

Shaking my head because I've had enough emotional talk for the day, I reply, "I'll tell you another day. Don't worry about it, okay?"

He looks at me skeptically but doesn't push me. Instead, he wraps me in a warm embrace and carries me over to the couch, where I spend the next hour being held and cared for beyond my wildest dreams.

Chapter 25

Julia

Sunday, October 13

My skin buzzes with anticipation as I stand beside Declan at our station under the tent. A tall, charismatic man with broad shoulders stands at the front beside two women and another man. I don't watch American television, so I don't know who these people are. Based on the awestruck expression of a few other people in the tent, they must be celebrities.

The camera crew is focused on the four people as a hush falls over the tent. "Welcome to the first round of the Great Harvest Bake-Off hosted by the Baking Network. I'm your host, Brian Ulmer. We are at the Ambarsan Apple Orchard in Topaz Falls, Montana. The theme for this bake-off is apples. Our judges are Pauline Denning, Renea Truman, and Jeff Alderman. Jeff, would you like to tell everyone about the challenges today?"

A man with shoulder-length black hair and intense blue eyes steps forward half a step. "Good afternoon, everyone. As Brian said, I am Jeff Alderman. You might recognize me from my baking show on the Baking Network, where I showcase my specialty of painting cakes with a palette knife. There will be three rounds in today's competition. All seven couples will partake in all three rounds. At the end of the third round, the other two judges and I will choose which two teams will be eliminated, and the remaining five teams will compete in the semi-finals next week. The first bake of the day will be a breakfast favorite. Your second challenge will be a savory dish with the complementary flavor chosen by the judges. Lastly, the final challenge will be a dessert showing each team's kitchen abilities. Remember, this is a team competition. We'd like to see tasks split evenly between the two team members. Pauline Denning is known for her innovative breakfast foods and Renea Truman for her savory meals. Between the three of us, we should be able to determine who will make it to the semi-finals next weekend. Good luck, everyone."

They go over a few more details and rules. Sabotage of another team's creation from either teammate will lead to immediate disqualification from the competition. We are told to begin, and my mind flies with ideas, like flipping a rolodex of recipe cards in my mind's eye.

I hand Declan two apples and tell him to peel and dice them as best he can. "We're going to make bourbon caramel apple popovers," I say, remembering I need to clue him in. "While you chop the apples, I will make the caramel sauce since it's finicky, and if we aren't careful, it can quickly burn. Once the caramel sauce is made, we will fold in the apples. While they soften, we can make the popover dough."

Nodding, Declan replies, "Awesome. What's a popover? Is it like a Pop-Tart?"

Pressing my lips together, I fight the smile because I need to focus on the caramel sauce. This recipe usually takes me forty-five minutes when it's just me. Hopefully, Declan will be a help and not a hindrance.

I make the mistake of glancing at Declan, my body heating from the memory of last night in my office. A shiver thrums through my body, and my mind is mesmerized watching Declan concentrate on chopping the apple. With his flannel shirt rolled up, his corded forearms flex with each movement. My mouth goes dry because, yes, dammit, his hands are sexy. Mine aren't, but his certainly are.

"Is the caramel doing okay?" Declan asks, snapping me back to the present. Oh shoot, it's seconds away from burning. I quickly work on the saucepan, saving my mixture.

We work hard for the rest of the hour, and the popovers look gorgeous. I drizzle the last of the caramel over the top as Declan meticulously wipes up any drips of caramel from the plates.

The judges pass by each station, sampling the creations. I see turnovers, muffins, and what looks like a quiche. When the judges reach our station, my hand grasps Declan's arm with a death grip. I've been so focused so far that the oven isn't worrying me in the slightest. All I can think about is the competition and my desire to win. Now that I think about it, I don't even know what the prize is.

"Well, Julia and Declan. You are our Home Team in this event. Can you tell us what you made?" Renea asks.

Nodding, I step a bit closer to Declan's side. "We made bourbon caramel apple popovers."

"Which are not Pop-Tarts," Declan says conspiratorially, causing the judges to politely laugh.

When they take a bite, the crust flakes beautifully. The apples are semi-translucent, giving them the perfect texture for this pastry.

Pauline hums in approval. "This is wonderful. I love my bourbon more than I care to admit, so this is perfection and something I will definitely make at my next family brunch. Now, how were your duties divided?"

Uh. What? Before I can utter a word, Declan raises his hand. Pauline smirks, nodding for him to speak. "Well, I peeled and diced the apples. I also wiped the plate so no extra caramel sauce was on it to make the plate look unappealing."

Jeff grins. "So, Julia, did you make the caramel sauce, soften the apple mixture, and make the pastry dough?"

Slowly, I nod. "Yes. I am the trained pastry chef of the two of us. Declan informed me yesterday he is a proficient apple peeler."

Declan snorts and wraps an arm around my shoulders. "Teamwork is knowing individual strengths and how to use them appropriately."

With a soft smile, Pauline pats his forearm before moving to the next station. Once they've tasted all the foods, we are dispatched to do the savory dish. Renea clears her throat. "For your savory dish, I want to see how you pair apples with bacon. I want apples to be in the forefront, not a garnish. You have ninety minutes. Good luck, contestants."

Declan turns to me with wide eyes. "What are we making, chef?"

Tapping my finger against my chin, I contemplate the options. "How about an apple bacon grilled cheese sandwich with an apple bacon cheddar soup?"

Clapping his hands together, Declan grins. "Awesome. How do we make those? Do I need to peel apples again?"

Nodding, I look at the pantry at the back of the tent. "Yes. Peel and chop two apples for the soup. For the sandwich, core and thinly slice one apple. The skin can stay on the rings."

Declan spins and rushes to the barrel of apples. I pull out pots and pans and heat them on the burners. I find a flat grill for the sandwiches, which Declan can do.

I work with tunnel vision. Everything comes together perfectly, reminding me of my days as a line chef. When it's time for the sandwiches to go on the griddle, I turn expectantly to Declan. He's leaning against our station, arms folded over his chest, as he watches me with a heated gaze.

Clearing my throat, I ask, "Can you make the sandwiches? Brush butter on one side of the bread and place it face down on the griddle. Then, the order is cheese, apple slice, heirloom tomato, two strips of bacon, and then another slice of cheese. Put the top piece of bread and butter it. Does that make sense?"

His panicked expression is all I get. "I burn grilled sandwiches. I don't think you understand the severity of my incompetence in a kitchen, blossom."

Sucking in a deep breath, I quickly assemble the sandwich. "Alright. You watch the griddle. In three minutes, I want you to use the spatula to look and see if it is golden brown. When it is golden, I want you to gently flip it for another three to five minutes. I have to finish the soup."

Focusing on my pot, I add seasoning and sour cream, folding it in gently. It smells amazing.

Declan taps me on the shoulder with a silicone spatula. "How do I flip it with this?"

Fighting the urge to grumble, I walk over to the utensil drawer, pull out a flat metal spatula, and hand it to him. "Use this, not a scraper spatula."

"Right," he mumbles. With unsure movements, he goes to flip the sandwich, but the execution is too slow, and I watch in horror as the sandwich spills apart. Rushing over, I edge him out of the way with my hip. His hands grasp my sides as he stands just over my shoulder, watching what I do.

With practiced moves, I flip all the sandwiches, taking for granted how simple this recipe seems for me. I swear I could make a grilled cheese sandwich when I was ten years old. I think we are going to need to revisit cooking classes for him. Maybe I can help him learn how to make a few basic food items before I leave.

We plate our food with seconds to spare, and I feel ready to collapse from the adrenaline rush of racing the clock. The judges sample each station. We're last this round, and when Renea takes a bite, she dips her sandwich in the soup. Pointing at the combo, she smiles wide. "This is amazing. It is the perfect autumn lunch. I'd happily eat this on a blustery day. The apple is the main show here. I can taste it clearly in both items."

"Which parts did each of you do?" Jeff asks, lifting an eyebrow.

Declan straightens with excitement. "I peeled and diced the apples for the soup. I also cut the apple rings for the sandwich."

"For the dessert, I'd like to see you share the responsibilities of the dish more evenly. Remember, Julia, this is a team competition. You two are meant to be working together."

Nodding like I'd been reprimanded by my boss, I try to think of a dessert Declan could do.

When it's time to start the third round, I say, "How about we make an apple torte? I'll have you make the entire filling while I make the crust. We will each make half the dessert so the judges can't dock us for your lack of involvement."

He nods with resignation. I think he was hoping to be the official apple peeler for the team. Sighing, I quickly jot down the ingredients for the filling and then hand it over to Declan. "Any questions?"

He shakes his head. "At least I get to peel and slice the apples," he grumbles.

After twenty minutes, I have the dough finished and ready to stick in the oven to pre-bake. Before I can stick it in the oven, Declan tosses a fork on the counter and swears under his breath.

"This is terrible. I've officially met an apple dish I don't like. Of course, it's one made by me," Declan groans from the end of the countertop, where he's taken a bite of the torte mixture.

"How? I've made these a thousand times. I could make them in my sleep. Did you follow the recipe I wrote down?" I ask, shocked as I grab a fresh fork and sample the mixture.

I think I know what happened as soon as it hits my tongue. "Declan? How much salt did you put in the mixture?"

He scratches his head in confusion. "Four teaspoons."

Running my hand through my hair. I stare at the recipe I wrote out. One-quarter teaspoon is clearly written, but he added four teaspoons of salt. I remember how much he struggled with math in high school, but I assumed it was just laziness or being distracted by eighteen-year-old hormones. Swallowing down my unease as it starts to click into place, I formulate a new plan. We'll quickly make up new versions, but personal-sized ones, so they cook faster.

"We can fix this," I say, pointing at it. He raises an eyebrow skeptically. "We can. Well, not this exact one, but we can fix what we turn in. Quickly peel and cut the apples just like we did the first time. I'll prep the frying pan and quickly prepare the dough into different ramekins. We're making individual-sized ones."

We quickly and quietly work side by side.

With under two minutes left and a bead of sweat trickling down my back, I lunge to plate the last two ramekins. Heaving deep breaths, I glance around to ensure I didn't forget anything. Declan's warm palm gently lands on my lower back as he stills me. "I think we're done, blossom."

I look up into his green apple eyes, and time slows around us. He leans in and places a soft kiss on my lips, the taste of caramel present. Narrowing my eyes, I lean back. "Did you sample the caramel?"

"Yeah. I decided to add being the official taste tester to my role on our team along with the apple peeler. I figured it would sway the judges if they saw I did more than peel apples like a potato peeling scullery maid."

"Well, you're on your way up the culinary food chain. Peeling potatoes is literally the first thing they have you do in culinary school," I reply with a wink.

He grins. "Next time, I'm bringing my apple peeler and drill to make this process go faster."

He nudges me with his elbow playfully before pulling me into his side. We silently watch the judges critique the other teams, and my nerves bundle with pent-up energy.

Renea, Pauline, and Jeff step up to our station, and I struggle to maintain my composure. This entire dish was thrown together so quickly that I can only hope the bottom is cooked through and the apples are tender.

"So, Home Team, what did you make us?" Pauline asks, tapping her fork against the flakey crust.

"We made an apple tart," Declan says proudly. "I peeled the apples, chopped them, then made the first batch of filling. It didn't work out, so we—"

I elbow him in the ribs and plaster on a smile. "We made an apple torte. There are individual ones for each judge and the host."

"Well, this is the best dish of the competition today," Jeff says with a wink.

"Wonderful use of spices in this torte," continues Renea.

I stand a little taller, taking the positivity to heart. They love my baking. I'm beaming. All the judges stand at the front of the tent, and the cameras are trained on them.

"Today's winner who will be moving on to the semi-finals is—" Jeff says, holding us all on a knife's edge, waiting in anticipation. "Charlie and Robert."

I instantly deflate since our last dish was named the best of the day.

Renea claps but takes a small step forward, garnering our attention. "Although Julia and Declan made three dishes that left us wanting more, that's exactly what happened. We wanted more. This is a team competition. We need to see the teams working together to create the dish. Not everyone did this," she says, pointedly looking at me. I grit my teeth in frustration.

"Now, for the two teams leaving us today," Pauline says, snapping my attention to hers. I hold my breath, waiting for our name. If we make it through to next week, I will be sure to brainstorm better recipes that are doable for Declan, and we can have a mid-week training session to practice. "Roberta and Douglas, as well as Johnny and Tamra. Thank you for participating. Roberta and Douglas, one of your bakes was not fully cooked. Johnny and Tamra, we struggled to find the apple in all your dishes. The other ingredients you chose overpowered the delicate apple flavor. Thank you for joining us, and we're sorry to see you go."

Brian steps forward. "Thank you for joining us in this week's episode of the Great Harvest Bake-Off. I'm your host, Brian Ulmer. We will see the remaining teams back here next Sunday at the Ambarsan Apple Orchard to see who will be in the finals and in the running to win thirty thousand dollars."

I still. What did he just say? "Did he say thirty thousand dollars if we win?" I whisper to Declan.

Tugging on his neck, he responds, "Yeah. I didn't realize there was a prize of that magnitude. I assumed it was free apples for a month or something."

Split in half, the prize money could set me up for my return to Paris. Losing is no longer an option. Turning, I tap my finger against Declan's chest. "We need to practice. Let me know what day works this week, and I'll teach you as much as I can. We have to win."

He nods, pulling me into a tight hug. "We will, blossom. With you as the heart of this team, no one can beat us. I'll be sure to bring my tools to the next round. I was woefully unprepared."

Chapter 26
Julia
Monday, October 14

The breath of the coming winter whispers across the morning air as I puff out a deep breath and unlock the bakery in the low light before dawn. My key chinks in the lock, the sound echoing around the silent street. River's motorcycle pulls into the space beside my car at the back of the bakery, and I smile, throwing him a jaunty wave. His expression is unreadable under his helmet, but when he pops it off a moment later, a broad smile gleams in the reflection of the streetlamp at the end of the alleyway.

"Morning, River!" I say, pushing the door open with my hip as my arms masterfully balance a box of supplies I picked up last night.

"Ready to bake until we drop?" River asks.

"Always!" I say with a wicked grin. "You're in charge of bread this morning. While it rises, can you make muffins?" I ask, organizing my station and preparing it to make cinnamon rolls.

"You bet, boss. I heard you made it to the next round of the bake-off. I'm sorry I wasn't able to be your partner. I'm glad the guy you found worked, though." River hangs up his coat and shoves a bagged lunch in the fridge before grabbing his apron and wordlessly prepping his station.

"Thank you! It was really stressful but fun at the same time. It was my first time doing a timed baking competition. In the third challenge, I don't know how we pulled off a completed dessert."

River grins. "It's because you're an amazing baker. Simple as that."

"Thanks, River." I dip my head to hide the blush from the compliment. I push my sleeves up, and River grunts. When I look up, he's staring at my bare right arm.

Before he can ask what happened, I confidently hold up my arm. "I was in a fire earlier this year."

He nods in understanding and doesn't push for more information. The confidence in my scarred appearance is getting stronger. Declan gave me that boon of confidence, and I can't thank him enough. This weekend, he taught me to see the scars in a different light.

"I'm going to make a blueberry gluten-free, vegan scone for that one couple this week," I say, trying to break the awkward silence descending on the kitchen.

With a mischievous smirk, the awkwardness fades. "Please don't make me taste test-those scones."

I shake my head and get out the ingredients I need. While we work, River sings beautiful songs of love, heartbreak, and family. Each tune ends, weaving into the next song, never stopping, like a woven chain of music. His voice is entrancing as I shape the last tray of scones. Time bleeds away as River and I work in an unspoken rhythm. A couple hours pass before Maria's blonde bob pops into the kitchen, surprising me.

"Morning, Maria," I say, pulling a pan of cinnamon rolls out of the oven.

My fear of the stove has dissipated like water flowing through coarse grains of sand. I can't even formulate why it scared me to begin with. I know it was mentally connected to the fire in Paris. Baking with Declan allowed my mind to pass right over into acceptance. Maybe I just needed a mind-blowing orgasm in my kitchen's office. It makes me laugh because it's the one thing I hadn't tried or had any therapists recommended to me. You live and learn.

"Hey, Julia. I'm going to open the front door, okay? Do you need help bringing anything else to the display case, or is it ready?"

"We are all set. I've loaded the case as batches cool. I have a set of scones on the cooling rack right now, but I'll bring them out when they are ready. If Oliver and Daniella stop by, the blueberry scones are for them."

About an hour into the morning rush, there is a knock on the doorframe. My head whips up, and River stops mid-song. Tristan stands, leaning against the wall. His top knot is centered at the back of his head, and a short beard covers his sharp jawline. Instead of his running attire this morning, he's sporting blue mechanic overalls. Tattoos cover his knuckles, and the one over his sternum peeks out above his top button.

"Hey, Tristan. How are you?" I ask, looking up from my scones and wiping my forearm over my brow line.

"Good, Jewels. How are you?" I'm not a fan of the nickname, but he's like a wild golden retriever puppy, all smiles and happiness, off-set by the gruff edge he carries with his appearance. When I asked him why he called me Jewels, he told me it was because my cinnamon rolls were gold. Though I hadn't heard that expression before, River told me it was Tristan's way of complimenting my baking. I still think it's because he can't remember Julia.

"Are you making any other flavors of muffins?" he asks with a muffled voice around a mouthful of food.

Placing my hands on my hips, I give him a mock glare. "Did you just steal a chocolate chip muffin?"

"No," he replies. "I liberated it from a harsh life behind a glass display case." I raise a brow as River snickers. I swat him with my towel and turn back to Tristan.

"How many baked goods have you liberated from my kitchen?" I ask.

"Well, I'd say enough that Maria opened a tab for me at the front. I have to write down everything I eat and pay for it at the end of the week." He shrugs.

I need to ask Maria what he's talking about. I guess since his uncle owns the auto body shop in town, we can always bill them if Tristan skips town without closing his account. An open tab system may be a good idea for our frequent customers. I'm not in it to make a load of money. I just need to stay open for three months.

While I'm up front a few hours later, loading the display case with cookies, the door opens and Anders saunters inside. He's wearing a perfectly tailored suit, the navy blue sportscoat complementing his blonde hair and warm brown eyes. He swings a leather briefcase in one hand and a to-go cup of coffee in the other hand.

"Julia," his kind voice vibrates through the bakery, commanding the attention of the people sitting at the tables on each side.

"Hi, Anders. What brings you in today?" I ask, wiping my hands on my apron as I come around the end of the counter to greet him.

"I brought you a coffee since I know what it takes to be up at the crack of dawn to get a morning business open for customers," he says, handing over a coffee. When I sniff the cup to try to see what he gave me, he continues, "It's the same thing you ordered the last time you came to Sleepy Mountain Roasters." He playfully winks before setting his briefcase on a table. "I also brought with me a tentative purchase agreement. I'd like you to look it over and mark up any changes. I put the purchase amount that we discussed the last time we spoke. For the non-compete, I asked for zero miles for zero years. Since you plan to return to Paris, I don't see it being an issue. The closing date is the seventh of January. I did put down a back-out clause. If at any time you decide you want to stay here, I'll make the contract null and void. Does that work?"

I nod as I look over the paperwork, trying to read, but the lines of text swim as I struggle to focus on his spoken words. Less than ninety days from now, this bakery will be his. Would my aunt be disappointed that I'm not putting in more effort? No, I think she'd want me to pursue my dreams. Paris has always been my plan. She knew this from our many conversations at her kitchen table. She wouldn't want me to hold back and live a life I didn't want. I know it.

"When do you want this back?" I ask, trying not to go cross-eyed as I flip through the sixteen-page document.

"How about by the end of the week? I'll have my attorney keep it in escrow, but I'll have him wait until December to draw up the paperwork. Just in case." The meaning is implied. The clause will be there in case I decide to stay. I won't, but I'll let him think he's calling the shots because seven hundred thousand dollars is a life-changing amount of money for me. A business and a flat in Paris will be within my reach. Debt-free.

Nodding, I tap the paperwork on the tabletop. "Can I get you anything to eat?" He moves to pull out his wallet, but I still his hand. "On the house. A trade for the coffee from one local business to another."

With a tight smile, he says, "Alright. Surprise me."

Walking behind the counter, I pull out a chocolate chip cookie. Maria leans in. "What's Mr. McRitchie doing here?"

"Mr. McRitchie? Why do you call him that?" I ask.

Her eyes widen. "He's like the most eligible bachelor in town. He's from Kalispell, but his family is beyond wealthy. I think he owns half the town. Luckily, he wants to preserve it, not tear it down. Also, he's so nice and hotter than a ghost pepper."

"Oh," I say. I know most of this from speaking with Britt and Elin, but it sounds weird coming from Maria. "He's a really nice guy. Yeah, he will buy the bakery when my ninety days are up so I can return to Paris."

Maria's shoulders curl in on her. Frowning, she replies, "You're really going to leave after ninety days?"

"Yeah," I say with a sigh. "Paris is my home."

Biting her lip, her gaze darts around. "I don't think I could abandon my aunt's legacy so easily. I'd want to make this place thrive."

Swallowing the lump at the back of my throat, I reply, "I am. Anders will keep it a bakery, and I'll give him a copy of her recipe book. The only thing that will change is who writes your paychecks."

Maria surprises me by wrapping her arms around my neck and drawing me in for a quick hug. "Regardless, I'll miss you. River will, too."

With a sharp nod, I stroll back to Anders with a plate and a cookie. "Anders? Can we add a clause that you keep the staff as long as they perform well? I don't want these people to be without a job because I returned to Paris."

He smiles broadly. "Of course."

Chapter 27

Declan
Tuesday, October 15

I check my watch. It's already 10 a.m. This morning has flown by. I was up early with the sunrise, pruning the last of the blight. I think we finally have it all contained. Hopefully, it will make my parents proud. During their absence, I will have accomplished something good. At least my dad won't need to get on any ladders for the foreseeable future.

Trudging through the orchard, I realize I need to set up a time to bake again with Julia. Instead of her commercial kitchen, maybe I can get her to come back to my place. Pulling out my phone, I look at the screen. Slapping it against my hand, I decide I'd rather pose the question in person. I was so busy yesterday I didn't get into town to see her like I'd planned.

With an idea brewing, I will swing in and pick up a fresh bouquet of flowers. Julia deserves them for putting up with me and my terrible baking skills. On Sunday, I barely contributed to the team. I was essentially a warm body. Next week, I'll be more prepared.

Cameron emerges from the storage barn just as I get to my truck. "Hey, man! Want anything from the bakery? I'm going to run into town for a little bit."

Lifting his hat off his head, he swipes his brow with the flannel of his shirt sleeve and runs a hand through his crop of messy hair. "You know what? I think I'll join you."

With a smile, I motion for him to hop in the passenger seat. "How's your morning so far?"

He leans back in his seat and replies, "Fine. There's not much to report on at the moment. I think the apple trees to the north are ready for harvest. Do you think we could take them on Thursday or Friday?"

Nodding, I drum my fingers on the door as I contemplate the week. "Let's plan on Friday."

"I'll let Mira know. Without your mom and dad here to help, would Callum, Lachlan, Axel, or Trent be able to join us with their trucks?" he asks.

"I'll contact them today and see if they have some time to spare on Friday afternoon," I reply as we pull into the grocery store.

"I thought you wanted to go to the bakery," Cameron says, looking out the windshield at the grocery store.

Tapping the center console, I say, "Wait here for just a sec. I have to run in and get something real quick, then we can head to the bakery."

Cameron quirks an eyebrow when I come out a few minutes later with a beautiful bouquet in my arms. "Those for me? You shouldn't have."

I move them out of his reach, and he snickers. "No, these are for Julia."

"Oh, Ju-li-a," Cameron repeats, enunciating each syllable like he's ten.

"Yes," I grind out. "Because of her, we almost won the first round of the competition. These are to congratulate her."

Crossing his arms, he wiggles his eyebrows. "And, pray tell, what will be the gift you bestow upon her if you two win the whole thing?"

Sheepishly, I respond, "My half of the winnings. She wants to open a bakery in Paris, so I want all thirty thousand dollars to be hers."

His jaw drops. "You seriously won't keep your half of the winnings? That could really help the orchard or get you a new truck."

Shaking my head, I mutter, "I don't need it. She does. Julia has dreams she wants to pursue, but I don't. Plus, my truck is fine."

"You really like her, don't you," Cameron says, his voice somber.

"I've loved her since I was seventeen. Nothing will change that," I murmur.

We pull into a space in front of the bakery, and I cut the engine. Hopping out, I grab the flowers and stride to the door. Cameron follows me inside, and Maria hollers from behind the cash register to get our attention. Her eyes land on the bouquet of flowers, and she winks. "Those for me, big guy?" She crosses her arms over her chest, and her eyes zero in on Cameron. The blood drains from her face when she takes him in.

"Mariana?" he whispers.

She spins on her heel and runs to the kitchen, almost colliding with Mr. Manbun. Why is he coming out of the kitchen? He grabs onto her upper arms, stabilizing her. Cameron growls a little when they touch, but she rushes past the guy, hardly glancing at him.

"Dexter, good to see you," Mr. Manbun says, sauntering to the display case. He opens a glass dome and plucks a scone out.

"It's Declan," I grind out. "Do you work here now?"

Shoving the scone in his mouth, he shakes his head. "Nope, but I'm addicted to the food here."

He heads over to the cash register. I reach out and grab his shirt. "What the fuck are you doing?"

"Look, Dennis, I'm not here to fight you. I have an open tab. On the honor system, I write down what I eat and then pay the bill at the end of the week. Since I always stop here halfway through my runs, I don't carry a wallet, so I have no money."

"My name is Declan," I enunciate. "What's your name? I can't keep calling you Mr. Manbun." I know Axel told me and his name is burned into my memory, but if he can pretend he doesn't know my name, then I can play that game too.

Reaching out his hand, he says, "Tristan Ballantyne. Nice to meet you. I'm terrible at names. Mr. Manbun is actually perfect. I'd respond to it." He points his thumb toward the kitchen and leans forward. "I can't even remember the bakers' names, so I call the lady Jewels since her baking is like gold, and the bread guy is Kneady. He hates it." Tristan shrugs.

"Alright, I'm Declan, as in I'll deck you if you make a move on Julia." He looks at me confused. "Jewels the baker is Julia." A look of realization dawns on his face, and he scrunches his nose.

"I'm not interested in either baker. I like blondes, end of story. Britt is more my type, but she is a little young for me." He leans over the counter and whispers, "I'm thirty-five."

Yeah. I don't care if he's twenty or sixty. All that matters is that he sees Julia in a completely platonic light. "Well, I have ten miles left in my morning run then it's abs day, so I'm out of here now that I've fueled up at the halfway mark. See you around, Declan. Look at that—I remembered! Go me!"

When I turn around, Cameron is still staring at the kitchen door where Maria snuck off, utterly oblivious to the bizarre exchange Tristan and I just had with each other.

Walking around the edge of the counter, I beeline it for the kitchen. Cameron is hot on my heels, colliding with my back when I stop at the sight of Julia making croissants. Her gorgeous brown hair is pulled up in a high ponytail. A few stray strands hang in her face, blocking my view of her beautiful gray eyes. She's biting on her lip in concentration as she folds a layer in the dough. My gaze flicks to her office door, remembering what happened a few days ago. My blood thrums at the memory, thankful the door is closed.

She must feel the heat of my stare on her, for a moment later, her eyes lock on mine, and the rest of the world fades away. A smile ticks the corner of my lips, and she grins as she pushes her hair out of her face with the back of her hand. It continues to fall across her brow, so I take a couple of steps into her space and reach up to tuck the wayward strands behind her ear. My thumb caresses her cheek, and I warm when she leans into my touch.

"Where'd Mariana go?" Cameron asks, bringing me back to the present.

River chuckles as he focuses back on his bread dough. "Maria stepped out for a minute."

"You know Maria?" Julia asks, stepping around me to see Cameron. "Who are you?"

"Cameron works for me at the orchard. This is Julia and River," I say, making introductions.

Cameron swallows as his eyes dart around the kitchen. His hands twist his hat as he struggles to find words. "She's someone from my past," he murmurs, but there is such sorrow in his voice. Was this what I sounded like when I spoke of Julia prior to her return?

Realizing his discomfort, Julia replies, "It's nice to meet you, Cameron. Welcome to my bakery." Turning to me, her eyes zero in on her favorite flowers. "Are those for me?"

"Only ever for you," I murmur. I want to tell her just like my heart, but I know she isn't ready to hear that level of devotion from me. Not when she intends to leave, regardless of where we stand.

Her eyes brighten, and she quickly washes her hands at the sink before grabbing the flowers from where I'm cradling them in my arm. "These will be perfect at the cash register for everyone to see."

"I wanted you to know how proud I am of your baking this weekend. You were amazing. I'll do better next weekend. Would you like to come over to my place tomorrow night and teach me some more baking skills?"

She nods enthusiastically. "Of course. I can be there around 5 p.m. Should I bring ingredients to make dinner, too?"

"Uh, that would probably be best unless you want to write a list and tell me what to pick up at the grocery store. My kitchen is pretty empty since you said Pop-Tarts and toaster waffles don't count as a meal."

Grinning, Julia wraps her arms around my waist. "Don't worry about it, big guy. I'll bring the supplies. You just ensure no wet towels are on the bathroom floor and the toilet has been cleaned this month."

"I actually have a cleaning company come once a month, so there's no need to worry about contracting E. coli," I mutter into her hair.

She barks out a laugh. "I was more worried about the toilet seat being up. I hate falling in."

"Well, I will check that, but I can guarantee there aren't any hair spiders on the shower wall." I give her a mock glare.

"I don't leave hair spiders in the shower. I may have done that as a teenager, but I don't anymore. Now that I'm an adult, I realize how much work it is to unclog a drain. I avoid it at all costs."

River pipes in, "Hair spiders are way worse than a toilet seat up."

I reach out my hand to fist-bump him. "Damn right."

"Okay, you two. I've got to keep working on this dough. I'll see you tomorrow evening at 5 p.m. with everything we need to work on your baking skills," Julia says, swatting at my chest.

Bending down, I press a firm kiss against her plush lips as a reminder of what's to come.

Chapter 28
Declan
Wednesday, October 16

The toilet seat is down, no dirty clothes are on the floor, and the bathroom is clean. Yesterday, I called my cleaning company and asked them to come and give my place a once-over so it would look presentable tonight. It had been three weeks since they were last here. It was worth the two hundred dollars they charged me. The entire place smells clean, and it may be presumptuous, but I had them put fresh sheets on, too.

On the coffee table in the living room, I set down the two notepads and box of crayons I found in the office. I've seen a social media trend where couples draw each other and then reveal their creations. I can't remember if Julia is a talented artist or not. I have zero talent, but it looked hilarious. Now, I'm dying to try it.

The doorbell rings at 5 p.m. I rush over to the door, quickly rolling up the sleeves of my flannel shirt so I'm ready to bake. I found some ancient oven mitts jammed at the back of a drawer, and I'm even sporting my apron. Lachlan bought it for me when I moved into the house. It's an image of a bare-chested man in nothing but a kilt. He told me it was to honor our Scottish heritage. Oddly, he didn't get himself a matching one, and our genetic makeup is the same. I found him a similar one last year of fat Thor in gym shorts, so I call us even. The best part is, Aislinn makes him wear it for the ranch barbeques.

Pulling open the door, my mouth goes dry when my eyes land on Julia's grey eyes. The light pouring out of the house illuminates them, making her eyes sparkle. Tendrils of mocha hair frame her heart-shaped face, and her lips are covered in a lickable, glossy sheen. Like a magnet, my eyes are drawn to them as I try to imagine the flavor. Cherry? Strawberry?

"Hey, blossom," I say, swooping in for a kiss to test my theory. Surprisingly, her mouth tastes like vanilla sugar cookies. As I pull away, I disentangle Julia's fingers from the bags she's holding and take them from her grasp. "Did you buy out the store? It looks like Gary will need to restock the entire place."

Her fingers swat my back, and my skin tingles beneath her touch. "Just the baking aisle needs to be restocked. I got you all the necessities to make basic baked goods—nothing fancy." Julia's gaze darts to the living room, and her brow furrows. I bet she saw the crayons and construction paper. I fight a chuckle, since they aren't exactly the decor of a bachelor pad. It screams more single dad, which I'm not.

"After we eat dinner and bake, I was thinking we could do a fun couples challenge and then watch a movie," I say.

Her eyebrows lift in amusement. "You have the entire evening all planned out, huh?"

"You have no idea," I murmur. "What's for dinner?"

"Funny you should ask. I'm going to make Alfredo chicken enchiladas if that's okay."

"You had me at Alfredo. What can I do to help?" I ask, looking around the kitchen like I've never been here before. Where do I keep my pans?

"Nice apron," Julia chides. "Did Axel give it to you?"

"Actually, Lachlan gave it to me. I got him a fat Thor one, so we're even." I shrug but can't fight the grin.

"Yeah, I think you won. You're wearing Highlander Thor. The body on your apron looks like a replica of you," she says. A slight shiver flows through her body, causing me to chuckle.

"Are you only sleeping with me for my body?" I tease.

"No, but it's a definite perk," she replies as she unloads the grocery bags and gives me a heated stare across the kitchen island. "How about you set the table while I start dinner?"

It takes me all of five minutes to set the table, so I return to the kitchen island and observe her movements. "Can you walk me through what you're doing?"

She nods as she cuts the chicken into chunks. "Good idea. I guess we don't have to do just baking lessons. Over medium heat, I heated the pan with olive oil. Right now, I'm cutting the chicken into small chunks. I'll add a clove of chopped garlic, half a diced onion, and some seasoning. After cooking the chicken, I'll take a tortilla and smear a spoonful of Alfredo sauce in the center. Then, I'll add a scoop of the chicken mixture and sprinkle cheese. I'll roll each one like a burrito, then place them in a baking dish side by side. Once I've made all the tortillas, I'll pour the rest of the Alfredo sauce over the top and cover them with another layer of cheese. The pan goes in the oven for ten to fifteen minutes until the cheese bubbles."

"Okay, that actually sounds doable. Can I try making the burrito part?" I ask.

With a broad smile, Julia waves me over. "Of course."

We work side by side, and thirty minutes later, I'm pulling a delicious meal out of the oven. I knew we would need oven mitts. The dish feels hot in my hands. Do oven mitts wear out? "These smell incredible. They aren't burned, either."

"I'm impressed, Declan," she says with a teasing lilt to her tone.

After eating, she asks, "Should we bake now and then start a movie or something while the dessert is in the oven?"

I nod. "Sounds good, but we're going to do an art project, not watch a movie. What are we making?"

"Apple upside down cake. You are going to do everything. I will just watch and provide guidance," she says. "Think of me as your baking coach. If given the opportunity, we will make a version of this on Sunday in the dessert round."

I grab a towel off the counter and throw it over my shoulder. "I saw this on TV once. To be a pro baker, I need to look the part."

Julia laughs against the back of her hand and shakes her head. "I think the shirtless Scot makes you look the part," she says.

"Okay, what should I do first?" I ask, reaching for the apples. "I'm guessing you want me to peel and slice the apples?"

She nods. "Peel, then slice in circles. Afterward, you'll cut out the core, so there are no seeds in the cake. We want rings."

Lifting a finger, I open my apple tool drawer because what kind of an apple orchard heir would I be without apple tools? I pull out the apple coring device my dad gave me when I moved in. Most people get dishes, glassware, or silverware when they get their first house. Not my family. I only had paper plates and plastic forks for the first three months, but I had an entire drawer of apple-specific tools. I could core the shit out of an apple but had to eat it off a paper towel—not that I've used them since I usually eat apples straight off the tree. They're all brand new. My mom insisted on removing all the tags and packaging before I shoved them in the drawer, but they are still brand spanking new.

"What is that?" Julia asks, looking at the device that slightly resembles a dandelion puller.

"An apple corer," I say with a grin. "Nifty as shit, huh?"

With a dubious expression, she motions for me to continue. "Let's see it in action, wonder boy."

In one quick motion, I snatch the core from the center of the apple and give her a triumphant smile. Next, I grab my peeler and remove this skin. Then, I slice the apple into rings.

"Perfect," she says, squeezing my forearm. Her fingers linger, and I take a deep breath. We need to practice. We have to bake. Maybe I'll believe myself if I say it a few more times. Now is not the time for my body to have a mind of its own.

Julia walks me through the steps of prepping the pan and laying the apples on the bottom. Next is the dry ingredients. I think this is my favorite part of baking—not the actual measuring, but the act of measuring because Julia steps between my arms allowing me to cage her against the counter. With her fingers gently trapping mine, she shows me how to properly measure each ingredient. I'm struggling to focus because the cinnamon apple scent of her shampoo is dangerously close to my nose, and her ass is snug against my crotch. I don't want to offend her and make it seem like I'm taking these lessons for granted, so I think of everything under the sun to distract my mind from the feel of her soft curves rubbing against me. Unfortunately, the distraction works too well, and I realize I have no idea how we got from an empty bowl to whisking together the wet mixture.

I pour the batter into the pan, covering the apples with the cake mixture. Popping it in the oven, I turn and pretend to dust off my hands. "How long does it bake for?"

Reaching past me, she turns the timer on the stove and rotates into my arms. "Ready to do some arts and crafts while it bakes? We have about thirty minutes."

I place my hands on her hips and walk behind her, guiding her to the couches. Untying my apron, I lift it over my head and drape it on the arm of the sofa. I sit on the loveseat so we're facing each other.

"Okay, so according to the videos I've watched, we will each draw the other person. I'll draw you, and you draw me."

She snickers. "Oh, this is going to be bad. I have zero artistic talent, Dec."

"You don't? I'm sure mine will look like I was trying to draw with my hands on backward."

Julia shakes her head and grabs a pad of paper. With a white crayon, she starts sketching me in earnest. "You realize you picked a white crayon on white paper, right?"

She gives me a withering look before replying, "Yes. I'm getting an outline so I can fill it in once I make sure your facial features are correct. I don't want your eyes to be uneven or your nose not centered."

Not artistic my ass. She's over there talking about dimensions; meanwhile, my mind is at the *PBS Kids* level, and I'm thinking of basic shapes like a five-year-old. Pressing my lips together, I realize her version of sucking at drawing is very different from mine.

I grab the cream color and draw an oval with a point at the bottom for her chin. It looks a bit too severe, so I attempt to round it out. Nodding my approval, I draw two straight lines for her neck and a capital 'c' for each ear. Noses are always so hard. I have a faint memory of a high school art teacher telling me to do a 'u' with a half circle on each side. When I lean back, I bite back a groan. Maybe this was an art lesson on *Sesame Street* because I've never seen a nose look this primitive at an art exhibit. Granted, I can't say I've been to an art gallery, so maybe my nose isn't too far off.

The timer on the oven dings. Julia pops off the couch and runs to take the cake out. I extend my neck to glimpse her work in progress, only to find she put it upside down. When she returns to the couch, I lay my work down because I'm done. If I add any more details, it will look like there should be 3D glasses to view it.

"Are you finished?" I ask. She nods, so I motion toward her. "Alright, ladies, first."

Julia doesn't hesitate. She spins the pad of paper to show a very realistic crayon version of me. You've got to be kidding me. She blushes and says, "I tried my best. I know it doesn't really look like you, but it's the best I can do."

"You're joking, right? If you posted this in your bakery, everyone in town, even those who've never seen my face, would know it was me. That is so damn good. I don't think I can show you mine now. When did you learn to draw?" I ask in disbelief. Did we really try the same challenge? Did time stop for her? It seems like she was magically given hours to complete her drawing and higher-quality art supplies, too.

She chokes on a laugh and says, "I never took any formal courses, but I enjoyed art in school. Now, I need to see yours."

Rolling my eyes, I spin the pad. "Don't say I didn't warn you."

Julia erupts in laughter. Tears stream down her face as she slides off the couch like a limp noodle. "I look like a jaundiced koala with a double chin. Why are my ears so high and my hair so short?"

Clearing my throat, I attempt to defend my piece. "Well, I thought I grabbed peach, but I guess it was a shade of yellow. Also, your hair is in a ponytail, so I can't see any long pieces, only the little ones sticking out. I admit, I screwed up on the nose when I see it side by side with your drawing, but I did a good job on the eyes."

"You clearly have an inflated view of my lips and eyelashes. I look ready to be the main act in the Moulin Rouge." Her peal of laughter strums across my skin, and I can't help but smile. I don't care if it's at my expense. Hearing her happiness is worth it in every aspect.

As her giggles die down, she swipes a tear from her eye. "Should we watch a movie while we eat the cake?"

"Sounds great. Any whipped cream in your shopping bag?" I ask, waggling my eyebrows.

She deflates. "Sorry, Dec, I have to wake up at 4 a.m. tomorrow. Once the movie ends, I need to head home and get some sleep."

"Stay the night? I promise to do nothing but hold you. Just please don't leave," I murmur, giving her my best puppy dog eyes.

Her lips tip up even though she's trying to be stern. "Okay, I'll stay on the couch."

"Like hell, you will. You need the comfort and safety of my bed and my arms," I retort.

"You're right, I do," she whispers.

Now, I just need to make her realize how great life would be if she woke up every morning in my arms. 4 a.m. wouldn't seem so miserable if she slept in the protection of my embrace.

Chapter 29

Julia
Thursday, October 17

The gravel crunches beneath the tires as I approach the barn of Ambarsan Equine Therapy Ranch for my weekly appointment with Trent. I can't wait to tell him about the progress I made over the weekend. I turn off my engine, and before I step out, my phone rings.

"Hello?" I ask, glancing down to see it's Declan. "*Mon autre?*"

"Hey, blossom. I didn't hear you leave this morning. You were so quiet," he says, and it sounds like he's disappointed.

Little does he know, I waited until his breathing evened out and then snuck home. I'm afraid if I allow him to get too close, I'll fall harder than last time. Leaving him eight years ago was like cutting my heart with shards of broken glass. I can't go through that again. I need to keep this casual. It needs to be a fling or friends with benefits. We need to maintain a bit of emotional distance. I should have told him I couldn't stay, but the pleading look was my undoing.

Honestly, I ached to feel his cocooning embrace, even for a short time. I'm sick and tired of trying to be brave and take on this cruel world alone. It felt nice to let him be in charge for a little while. Also, I didn't want to show up to work in the same outfit I wore last night. I'm not ashamed to confess I dressed up a bit for our not-date baking lesson. The sweater wasn't exactly 4 a.m. baking attire. I also couldn't come to work in the oversized t-shirt and gym shorts Declan let me borrow to sleep in. I'm debating whether he'll get those back because they smell like him. I'm not too proud to admit I'd like to snuggle with his well-worn cotton shirt and store it beneath my pillow.

"Yeah, I left really early in the morning. I didn't want to wake you," I reply. I'm struggling to keep my eyes open on three hours of sleep. I'll have to go to bed early to make up for last night; otherwise, River will find me useless in the kitchen tomorrow morning. He already quirked his eyebrows enough this morning to last the entire week. No matter how much I tried to mute my yawns, he made it seem like I was interrupting his ballad.

"Will you join me for pizza at Glacier Crust Co. tonight?" he asks.

My stomach rumbles at the thought. Pizza sounds amazing. "I'd love to. What time?"

"Want to meet me there at 6 p.m.?" he asks.

"Sure. I've got to let you go. I have a meeting in three minutes, and I don't want to be late."

After saying bye, I climb out of my car and rush to the office. I get the feeling Dr. Trent Walsh is one of those people who considers being on time as late. Flinging open the door, I hurry across the threshold, coming face to face with six large men and one woman who could probably take me with her arm tied behind her back. Who am I kidding? She could take me with both arms tied behind her back. They pass me with cursory glances and polite remarks, leaving en masse.

My eyes follow them in disbelief. Do they work here?

A throat clears behind me, causing me to startle. My purse straps slip off my shoulder as I spin toward the sound. Trent stands behind the counter with a bemused expression on his face. I scamper to the front desk, pushing the purse strap back on my shoulder.

"Who were they? Gods from Mount Olympus?" I stammer.

The look on my face must have caught him off guard, for he barks out a laugh, surprising both of us. "They were here for my group therapy session. Each person is a former member of the military."

I open my mouth to ask another question, then think better of it because he's probably bound by patient confidentiality laws and wouldn't be able to tell me much more than that anyway.

He confidently strides past me. Over his shoulder, he says, "Should we meet with Tsunami today?"

Right. I'm here for therapy, too. This isn't a social visit for either of us. Hurriedly, I jog to catch up with his long stride. A file folder is tucked under his arm, and he casually twirls a pen between the pads of his fingers.

"Has anyone ever told you that you look like Michael Fassbender?" I blurt out, then rush to clamp a clammy hand over my mouth.

His gaze cuts to mine, and he slows his pace as we reach the barn door. "Surprisingly, yes. But then again, my grandfather told me I reminded him of a redheaded Spock. So, there you have it. Ms. Fournier, are you nervous about today's session?"

We walk in silence for a few steps before I find the right words to respond. Stopping at Tsunami's stall, I reach out and stroke the gentle giant. I can feel the weight of Trent's gaze on me, though.

"I'm not nervous," I say, taking a deep breath. "Actually, I had a moment of logorrhea because I'm really excited."

"Nice word choice." He chuckles. "How so?" Trent asks, leaning against the stall door and crossing his arms.

"Where do I begin? Oh yes, we almost won the first round of the baking competition this weekend and had no issues using the oven. You were absolutely right. Between the distraction of the judges, the camaraderie of Declan, and the outdoor environment, I had no moments of panic." Well, none related to the oven.

"Wonderful. What about at work this week? Did this translate when working in your commercial kitchen at the bakery?" he asks, tilting his head to study me.

"I'm not sure." I bury my face in my hands. I peek between a few fingers to see his soft gaze on me. "I didn't try. I had River continue to man the ovens this week."

"Is Declan proficient in the kitchen?" Trent's eyes hold no mirth.

Clearing my throat, I reply, "Proficient would be a strong word to describe Declan's baking abilities. He's very good at peeling apples."

I can tell by how Trent glances away from my gaze that he's fighting to remain stoic.

"So, perhaps you didn't have a panic attack because you felt as though you were the captain of the ship. Having a panic attack was not an option when you needed to keep him safe."

"Possibly? I felt like the oven was second nature during the competition. I was so focused on ensuring nothing burned and Declan didn't chop off a finger that I didn't really think about it." My fingers aimlessly move up and down Tsunami's neck. His head shakes as if in agreement, and I chuckle. "Why?"

"I'm wondering if you know your coworker is an excellent baker at the bakery, so you allow yourself to lean on him. It's almost as if River is a mental crutch for you. On the other hand, if you're alone in the bakery, irrational thoughts take over and consume you."

I nod, understanding. "So, you think I should hire incompetent people in the bakery kitchen?"

This time, Trent cracks a smile. "No. I'm saying you are making progress, but continue to take baby steps. You have another competition this weekend, right?"

"Yes. We are in the semi-finals this Sunday," I reply.

"How about you continue letting River man the ovens at the bakery until next Monday. If the competition on Sunday goes smoothly, I want you to try using the oven on your own the next day. River will be there if you decide you can't do it yet. Remember, it's okay to need more time. Perhaps you'll spend next week standing near the oven, observing River's movements. The next week, you can put the trays in, and River can pull them out. Keep making small adjustments. There's no need to dive in head first. Try to continue moving forward. Use the momentum from the competition to roll you into your next feat. Does that make sense?" Trent stands with one hand on the other side of Tsunami's neck, observing me casually.

Swallowing thickly, I nod. "I think I can manage to try this method. Any plan is better than no plan."

"I'm pleased with your progress. I hope you are, too." When I smile in agreement, he continues. "I look forward to seeing how you do in the baking competition this Sunday. Paisley and I will stop by and watch. We'll be cheering for you and Declan from the sidelines."

"Thank you, Dr. Wal—Trent," I reply.

We spend the rest of the session going over other fears, which might be holding me back, but I can't bring myself to talk about my relationship with Declan. I know a large amount of fear stems from my broken heart at eighteen. I don't think I'm ready to share it with Trent, even though I can tell he's aware I'm holding something back.

By the time I leave, I'm pulling away from the ranch with a huge smile. The dense trees blur past me as I pick up speed on the county road. The lights of the town blink into view as the trees become sparse, and the open fields greet asphalt. At the second stop sign, I take a right and pull into a parking space in front of the small pizza place called Glacier Crust Co.

I stride inside and almost collide with a fiery redhead. She has a striking pixie cut that shows off her slender neck. Navy blue eyes blink at me as I stare at the smattering of freckles covering her cheeks and nose. She adjusts her white blouse and walks to stand behind a hostess stand.

"Welcome to Glacier Crust Co. How many are in your party tonight?" she asks.

"I'm meeting someone here. Has a tall guy with brown hair and green eyes arrived yet?"

She arches a manicured eyebrow at me and replies, "Not that I can think of. I think you just described every male lead in my romance novels. What's the guy's name? I know most people in this town."

"Oh, right. His name is Declan Ambarsan," I say, fighting the urge to twist my fingers in my purse straps.

"Well, he definitely fits the description of a perfect book boyfriend. Both the Ambarsan boys should have gone into modeling," she mutters. "Here, follow me. I'll seat you in a booth and tell him you're here when he arrives. My name's Ember."

"Oh, like the flame from *Elemental*," I respond, fighting the urge to wince.

She smiles tightly. "Yeah, well, I was born before the movie was even an idea in the screenwriter's mind."

"Of course. Right. I didn't mean anything by it," I reply.

She slaps the table. "I'm joking with you. My entire family thought it was hilarious when the movie came out, and the main character has a flaming pixie cut and the same name as me. I went as Ember, the character, for Halloween that year."

I smile in relief. I had no desire to insult this woman. Pizza is one of my favorite foods. I'd hate to have to drive to Kalispell because I offended the hostess at the only pizza parlor in Topaz Falls.

"Ember, it's good to see you," Declan's deep voice booms from behind us, causing Ember to drop the menus she was holding. Before she can respond, his gaze finds mine and softens. "Blossom," he murmurs, my name sounding like a prayer on his lips. Leaning in, he drops a gentle kiss on my mouth and tangles his fingers into the hair at the nape of my neck.

"Hi, Dec," I say breathlessly when he pulls away.

"Good to see you, Declan," Ember says, patting his back before casually retreating to the hostess stand.

Declan's large frame effortlessly slides into the booth, his eyes never leaving mine. "You're staring, Dec," I whisper.

"Because I know you need to go home early to get to bed early tonight. I want to get my fill of you while I can. I'll need the memory of you to keep me warm tonight since your body won't." He pouts, and I almost break, telling him to stay at my place.

I'm unsure how to answer, so I ask, "What are your plans for the weekend?"

Waggling his eyebrows, he replies, "Hopefully, spending as much time as I can with you."

I take a sip from my water, then respond, "What did you have in mind besides the competition on Sunday?"

"I thought we could have a picnic at the treehouse on Saturday," he murmurs, his gaze dropping to his water glass.

"Wait, our treehouse is still there?" I ask in disbelief.

Smirking, he wraps his lips around his straw. I watch as his throat contracts with each swallow. "It was a favorite for all three of us Ambarsan kids. My dad would never take it down. Over the years, Lachlan and I have made improvements to the structure. We want our kids to play there one day, too."

My blood runs cold at the flippant mention of kids. The one thing I can't really offer him unless he's willing to adopt. Wait, what am I talking about? At the beginning of January, I'm leaving for Paris and never looking back. Whoever he has kids with will not be my concern. Will I hate her with a passion? Absolutely. But I can't blame him for moving on when I literally push him away at every turn.

"Yeah. I bet that will be amazing. Your parents will be so lucky," I reply. My response sounds stilted even to my own ears. Still, there is no reality in which I would be happy for the woman who can provide him with the family he desperately wants.

Not realizing my sudden change in demeanor, he asks, "So, what do you say? I'd love to reintroduce you to the treehouse?"

"Sure," I reply, trying to sound upbeat. "I can't wait." I know the smile doesn't reach my eyes, but I must stay emotionally detached. If I let my heart get involved this time, I will be wholly destroyed. If I thought heartbreak was bad at eighteen, I can only imagine what it would be like now.

Chapter 30

Declan
Friday, October 18

I slide one last crate into the bed of Trent's truck and smile in triumph. We did it. We have four trucks filled with apples to offload in the storage barn. It rained heavily all night and morning, making the orchard a sloppy mess. Some parts of the outer road looked like a muddy river as sludge slowly churned downhill. Turning toward my brother, Trent, and Callum, I hug them tightly. "Thanks for clearing your afternoon to help us drive this harvest into the barn. I was worried we'd run out of time."

"You know you can always count on me, little brother," Lachlan says, grasping my shoulder briefly.

"I'm always around town, and you're basically my brother. It's only a matter of time before I make it legal," Callum replies, patting my back.

Trent climbs into his truck, but before he closes his door, he says, "Happy to help." He turns over the engine of his electric truck and presses the pedal. The wheels churn unceremoniously in the muddy grass, spinning with no purpose. He guns it a little harder but doesn't have enough traction to get out.

Lachlan slaps his hand on the passenger window. "Hey, you don't have enough traction or torque to pull out of the mud. Don't gun it."

Callum spins toward me. "Do you have any cables so we can tow him out?"

Shaking my head, I hook my thumbs into my belt loops. "No. I bet Lachlan does in his tool trunk."

Jogging over to Lachlan's truck, I hop on the wheel to peer in the truck bed. Lachlan's already bent over, looking through his case. Growling, he grumbles, "I have everything I need if there's an injured animal in here, but nothing to actually tow a vehicle. Aislinn must have organized my trunk with her version of country roadside necessities."

I can't help but laugh because I have no doubt he has a mini-clinic in his truck. The best part is he didn't realize it until now. It's probably been like that for a year.

Unfortunately, I know my truck has nothing but a coat and a blanket. Because I mainly use my vehicle at the orchard, I'm within a ten-minute walk of my place, the barn, or my parents' house. I don't even have a set of jumper cables. As I watch the others scramble around, it might be wise for me to rectify that and add at least an emergency car and medical kit to my cab. That is something future Declan needs to worry about.

Callum turns. "I have nothing in my cab to get the truck out, but I can run back and get something."

Before he can get in the driver's seat, another truck bumps over the well-worn grooves with mud splatter coating the fenders. Jimmy Buffett's "It's Five O'Clock Somewhere" blares from the open window.

Axel.

His truck skids to a stop beside mine, and I thank my lucky stars he didn't take out my tailgate. When his engine cuts, silence surrounds us. Axel's car door creaks open, and he jumps down, the mud squelching beneath his boots.

"Why the long faces, boys?" Axel asks, rounding my truck.

"I thought you told me you couldn't make it today," I reply instead.

"No," he says, drawing the vowel out like a teenager. "I told you I couldn't make it at 5 p.m. with the others." Looking at his wrist, he enunciates, "It's 7 p.m. What do you need me to do?"

Lachlan claps him between the shoulder blades. "Thanks for coming. I know that's what Declan really meant to say. We're all a little frustrated because Trent's truck is stuck in the mud."

Axel's gaze cuts to Trent, who's leaning against the driver's side door. He makes a beckoning motion with his hand and closes his eyes.

A burst of deep laughter erupts from Axel as he bends at his waist. When he stands back up, his head drops to his sternum as he slowly shakes it. "Not enough power in the truck, huh, buddy?" He walks over and pats the hood. "Cold as the six-pack back home in my fridge. Bet you wish you had a Hemi under the hood about now instead of a frunk."

"Anything else?" Trent grinds out. "This is your one chance."

"No can do, Trent. For all I know, you're driving a Decepticon or a Terminator, and it will rage against me," Axel says with an exaggerated sigh.

"Alright. Now, do you have any constructive criticism?" Callum chides. "I have some important things to do."

"Like what? It's Friday night," Lachlan retorts.

"None of your business," Callum groans.

"Ladies," Axel says, garnering our attention. "Give me a minute."

He steadily jogs back to his truck, never slipping in the mud. Dropping his tailgate, he slides something out, and I chuckle at the sight of a pair of two-by-tens in his grip. He lifts them on his shoulder and strides back to the front of Trent's truck. Shoving one under each front wheel, he says, "Alright, Trent. Hop in and turn on your tin can battery."

With an arched brow, Trent drops into the driver's seat and starts the truck.

"How confident are you that this plan will work? Should one of us go get a tow cable just in case?" I ask.

"I'm more confident than an electric truck investor," Axel says with a wink.

"Wait. You just had a pair of two-by-tens in the bed of your truck?" Lachlan asks.

"Those are why I couldn't be here early. After work, I needed to drive into Whitefish and pick up a bunch of lumber. These will be floor joists for the sunroom I'm building off the back of my house." Axel folds his arms across his chest.

"I appreciate you stopping by, but why'd you bother coming here if you have your truck bed filled with lumber? We won't be able to load crates in the back," I say. The whole point was he had a truck.

Narrowing his eyes at me, he slowly flexes. "Because I have a right to bear arms, Dec." A slow smile curves his lips as we all groan in response. "I figured I'd be able to help load or unload from the other trucks."

"I appreciate you coming, Axel," I say because the guy has a heart of gold. "If you want, I can follow you back to your place and help you offload the lumber."

"I'd appreciate the help. Thanks." Axel jogs to the back and puts his hands on the tailgate. "Okay, men. Enough of this chit-chat. Did you guys plan to stand and watch my fine ass single-handedly push this hunk of metal? You realize we probably don't have much time before the battery dies, and it needs to be plugged in for the night."

We hustle over and stand shoulder-to-shoulder with Axel. He bangs his palm on the truck, and Trent presses the accelerator. All of us shove, and the truck rolls right up the wood. Callum catches his toe, and like the rug was pulled out from beneath him, he lands face-first in the mud.

Axel turns around and snorts when Callum's mud-covered face emerges from the sludge. "And that's why you didn't make the summer Olympics team."

"Dammit. I'm supposed to be somewhere in thirty minutes," he grumbles as he looks at his truck filled with apples. Axel reaches down and offers his hand. Callum grips tight, and Axel hauls him to his feet with a fluid yank.

Tossing Callum my house keys, I say, "Head over to my house and get showered and changed. Borrow whatever you need from my closet since we're the same size. We'll take your truck back to the storage barn first and offload it, then I'll drive it to the house so you can leave straight from there. "Shouldn't take us more than ten to fifteen minutes."

"Thanks, man," Callum says, jogging off.

"Where's he off to in a hurry?" I ask Lachlan.

He shrugs, hopping into the driver's seat of Callum's truck. "No clue. I know Ingrid and Aislinn are spending the evening together, since I said I'd be here helping you. I should probably text Aislinn to let her know that after this, I'll be at Axel's helping with his sunroom."

Looks like it's going to be a long night for both of us with getting these apples into storage, followed by lumber. I'd much rather spend time with Julia, but she said Britt and Elin were coming to her place.

Chapter 31

Declan
Saturday, October 19

Julia's sweet ass sways back and forth as she skips ahead of me on light steps, weaving between the trees to the outer orchard. Her red dress floats around her lean calves, showing off her tiny ankles. Ankles I can wrap my thumb and pointer finger around and love to kiss when they're resting on my shoulders. An invisible shiver quivers down my spine at the delicious thought, which will hopefully become a reality within the hour if I play my cards right. I may be crap at poker, but I know her body better than anything.

The sun spent all morning warming the orchard, drying up the ground enough we could stroll out here in regular shoes. As her hair swings across her back, I catch glimpses of her bare shoulders as the sleeves hang from her upper arms. It warms my soul to know she's confident enough around me to show her scars with pride. My stomach still knots when I picture her stunning face twisted in agony when she had to explain what happened and how low her confidence was. I hope my presence and words help her confidence grow in leaps and bounds.

Her light laughter echoes among the trees, lifting my spirits with each step. I have a picnic basket gripped firmly in my hand and a large blanket draped over my shoulder. This morning, I came out and swept the entire treehouse to make sure there were no spiders in sight. I even brought a handheld vacuum to get any debris in the corners. I want her to be comfortable and relaxed in our special spot. The only screams I want to hear are those laced with pleasure.

At the base of the tree, Julia glances over her shoulder and winks. It's not until she begins climbing the new and improved ladder Lachlan and I built last summer that I realize I stopped to watch her. With agile movements, she scales the ladder. The hem of her dress and the soles of her shoes quickly disappear from my view.

With considerable effort, I climb up behind her, lugging the picnic basket in my free hand. My dick hasn't relaxed since Julia kissed me over the center console of my truck before hopping out of the passenger's seat. It makes me wish I hadn't worn jeans and just kept on my sweatpants. Every time I lift my leg to the next rung, I about stumble from the reduced range of motion. You'd think I wore skinny jeans, not my well-worn, relaxed Wranglers.

When my head peeks through the opening at the top, I find Julia slowly wandering around the small space. This tree is old. My dad and grandfather built this tree house when Lachlan was young. It's eight feet by eight feet, which seemed huge when I was five, but now that I'm 6'3", it feels cramped and a tad claustrophobic.

"It's as cozy as I remember it," she says, leaning over to look out the small open window. There is one on each side, but this one looks out over the expanse of orchard for as far as the eye can see. You can make out the edge of our property line in the distance, where the rows of trees stop and the dense forest begins.

"This space seems to shrink each year," I grumble as I shake out the blanket, having to hunch over so as not to brush my head against the roof.

"Either that, or you're getting bigger. First you go up, then you go out, right?" she says with a soft laugh.

"Yeah, yeah. I'm not going out much more than this," I reply, patting my stomach.

Her eyes flash with lust as they follow the movements of my hands and drops momentarily to my crotch. Just when I was finally gaining some room in my jeans, she had to get his attention all over again.

With a huff, I get to my knees and unload the picnic basket.

"What did you make me?" Julia teases, knowing full well I didn't make a thing inside this basket. Wait, that isn't true. I rolled the napkins around plastic silverware I still had in abundance in my cupboards from when I moved into my place.

"Napkin rolls," I say with a grin.

"Are those like egg rolls?" she asks, tilting her head in confusion.

I hold up the rolled napkin with a fork and spoon inside, waving it in front of her face. She takes it from me and swiftly swats my shoulder. A peal of laughter erupts from her, and I smile in triumph.

"Actually, everything in here is from Mama M's, except for the cupcakes. I called River and asked him to make two special cupcakes for me, and he brought them out back when he went on break," I tell her.

Her jaw drops. "I wondered what River was doing with the pastry box. I thought he suddenly wanted a snack at 10 a.m. The sneaky guy." She takes a bit of the BLT and moans.

"I'm not going to be able to concentrate on chewing if you keep distracting me," I mumble looking at my own sandwich.

She covers her mouth and says, "I forgot how good a bacon sandwich is. I can't remember the last time I had one of these. What kind of mayo is this?"

"Chipotle. Do you like it?" I ask and take a large bite, forcing myself to look out the window so I don't accidentally choke. She hums in agreement as we quickly eat.

After we finish our lunch, I go to pull out the cupcakes but still when I see Julia crawling toward me. I blink to make sure I'm not dreaming because this has been my fantasy more than once.

"Do you want your cupcake?" I rasp.

She slowly shakes her head. "Right now, I want something else."

My gaze drops to the exposed skin at the swell of her breast, and I swallow thickly. Her hands reach for my legs, and without conscious thought, my arms reach for her hips, hauling her into my lap. I crush my mouth against hers, searing her lips with mine. The hot brand sparks like electricity down my neck, causing me to groan.

I gently lift her, and she wraps her legs around my waist, crushing her center against my erection. The strain against my zipper is causing enough pressure to make me see stars if I don't figure out how to get some relief soon.

Her delicate fingers slide into the short hair at the nape of my neck, gently tugging at it as she angles my mouth right where she wants me. The taste of her lips is consuming my every thought, distracting me from the position she's in as she slowly rocks against my hard length. My hands roam across her curves, pressing her chest against mine.

My tongue swipes across the seam of her lips, and she opens with a moan. My body is begging her to swallow me whole with each breath. I drag one hand down her leg, finding the hem of her dress. My fingers dance up the outside of her leg with tortuously slow movements. Her skin is smooth beneath my callused touch. All I can do is curse the thick material between us. My fingertips graze against the scrap of lace at the apex of her thighs as she rises up on her knees to give me access.

A rumble leaves my chest as one finger dips into her heated core, beyond wet for me. Swirling my finger at her entrance, I press into her tight channel at an agonizingly slow pace. Her hips buck, trying to urge me deeper. At this angle, she can't lower herself onto my hand because my arm restricts her movement. She growls against my mouth, her teeth nipping my lower lip in protest.

I pull my finger out, and she protests the loss, trying to push me flat on my back. I hold us in place, adding a second finger while she's distracted. Without any notice, I thrust my fingers deep, finding her g-spot as my thumb seeks her clit.

"I need more, Dec," she murmurs, pulling away from my mouth. Leaning back, my other hand gains access to her gorgeous breasts. Tugging down the neckline of her dress, I palm her breast, rolling her nipple with my thumb.

Julia arches, pushing her chest upward toward my face. I take the opportunity to dive down, encasing her nipple in my hot mouth. My tongue flicks against the stiff peak as my hand relentlessly pumps inside her.

Her inner walls flutter before a low moan resonates from her throat. Her eyelids fall closed as her jaw relaxes. I kiss the column of her neck as she rides out wave after wave of pleasure.

This time, when she presses her hand into my pec to push me toward the floor, I don't resist. Her hair drapes around her face as she undoes the button of my jeans with shaking hands. My fingers grip her thighs as I watch enraptured. My zipper sounds like a roar in my ears as she eases it down and frees my aching cock. The cool air shocks my system, but I can only think about her warm heat sinking down around me.

Lifting up on her knees, she positions the blunt head of my erection at her entrance, the view completely blocked by the folds of her dress. The anticipation is killing me. It's taking all my effort not to thrust my hips upward, impaling her on me in one swift motion. As she slowly sinks down, the muscles in my neck strain with my resistance. When my eyes find hers, I see the evil glint in her smirk.

"If you tease me, it's only fair I tease you. How's your restraint holding up?" Julia whispers, the French lilt sounding stronger with her arousal.

I fill her maybe an inch, the head barely in her entrance. Wiggling my hips, I hope she concedes and sinks down quickly, but instead, she tsks me. Lifting back up, the tip no longer sheathed, I grind my jaw to keep from complaining. I will never tease her again. This is torture.

I open my mouth to say something, but only a garbled gasp comes out when she sinks down in one swift movement, taking me to the hilt. My eyes squint shut with the onslaught of pleasure. She stills to catch her breath. She opens her mouth to say something when a deep laugh travels up through the window of the treehouse, and I still. Gripping her hips, I hold her firm to my pelvis.

"Ingrid, it's just a blindfold. You trust me, don't you? Take ten more steps, then I want you to stop and wait. Count to ten, and then you can open your eyes," a masculine voice says. I have no doubt it's Callum. What the hell is he doing here? Why now? Dammit, I was here first. Do I need to post a sign-up sheet at the bottom or leave a sock on the bottom rung? Hopefully, he isn't planning to come up here. I look around, realizing how exposed we would be if he decided to climb up the ladder. I guess I could always chuck the picnic basket down the opening. I'd just feel bad if it hit my sister.

I close my eyes in frustration. I'm balls deep in the woman I want to be my future everything, while my sister is twenty feet below me. Thankfully, the floor isn't made of glass.

Slowly, I sit up, and Julia's eyes go wide. "What are you doing?" she hisses.

With measured movements, I flip us so I'm on top, slowly lowering Julia onto the blanket. With my finger over her lips, I wiggle my eyebrow. "You need to be utterly quiet, blossom. Any noise, and I'll need to stop."

She nods with wide eyes. My hips pick up a slow and steady rhythm. I've been close since we kissed in the truck. I'll have no problem getting there when she's ready. I roll my pelvis, hitting the end with calculated thrusts. Her eyes roll each time I bottom out. Reaching between us, I thumb her clit, tapping and rolling it until her hips cant against mine. We tune out the duo below us, getting lost in each other. When her walls pulse around me, I look down and see her mouth, "I'm close."

Me too, blossom, me too.

I bend down and place open-mouth kisses along her jaw and neck, sucking on her pulse point until I feel her explode. Her pleasure passes on to me, and I fill her as I pump inside her with erratic thrusts.

Breathing hard, I kiss her jaw one last time before quietly lowering myself to her side and tugging one of her legs up over the top of my hips so I don't have to leave her yet.

Her delicate fingers play with the buttons of my flannel shirt as she buries her nose into the crook of my neck. With gulping breaths, my heart beats wildly in my chest as I try to force my pulse to calm down.

"Why is your sister down below, Dec?" Julia whispers in my ear, the gentle caress of her lips tickling my ear lobe.

"I have no idea. It doesn't sound like they're leaving any time soon, though," I reply, fighting the urge to sigh.

I pull out of her and sit up to grab some napkins so she can clean up, but she shakes her head and puts her underwear back into place. Motioning with her hand, she waves me over to the small window. I roll onto my knees and zip my pants before quietly crawling to her side.

She points down to the ground, and when I look out the window, Callum is on one knee, holding a wooden box. Julia pulls out her phone and turns on the camera. I do the same, turning on the video. Pushing record, I sit silently and watch what will play out.

Callum's voice is unwavering and deep as he takes my sister's hand in his outstretched palm. "Ingrid. We've known each other since we could barely walk, but my heart has always been yours. The last ten months have been the happiest of my life. You've supported me since middle school when you'd sit and encourage me to finish my homework. You are my best friend, but don't tell Lachlan, Declan, Axel, or Trent. I almost realized too late that I'd never survive this life without you by my side. Would you please do me the honor of becoming my wife? I want to be your loudest supporter at barrel races. I need to be who you turn to through good times or bad. I will forever love whatever you knit me and wear it with pride. But I can't spend another year without knowing you'll be my mine to love forever, Faline."

My sister is bawling her eyes out as she hides her face in her other hand. When I glance at Julia, tears leak from her eyes as she silently watches the scene unfold.

"With the carving tools you gave me for Christmas and the help of Zane, I carved this ring box. Your grandma painted it with rosemaling. I found this marquise cut alexandrite with diamonds on each side and knew it was for you. When it rotates in the light, the green reminds me of your eyes. Sometimes, light catches a purple color, which I know is your favorite. Will you please marry me?"

"Callum, yes!" Ingrid screams, launching herself into his chest. The position on one knee has him off balance, and I watch in amusement as they tumble to the ground. To my horror, though, the ring box flies out of Callum's hands. "Oh no! I'm so clumsy."

"Faline, you can knock me over or push me down, but I will always keep you in my arms," Callum replies.

Chuckling, she swats his chest and climbs off him, but not before she accidentally knees him in the crotch. He rotates into the fetal position, groaning momentarily while Ingrid obliviously searches for the small wooden box. Scooping up the ring box, she slides the ring out and hands it to him. Callum shakily stands and accepts the ring. Extending her finger, Callum slides it on.

"Perfect fit." His voice rumbles in approval.

Picking her up, Callum swings Ingrid around, whooping in excitement. Setting my sister down, Callum tips his head back and shouts, "She said yes!"

For the next few minutes, they laugh and cheer, enraptured with one another and completely unaware of our existence in the treehouse. A moment later, their laughter ceases, and they passionately kiss. Callum lowers Ingrid onto their blanket, his hands roaming her body with unadulterated abandonment. I click the record button to stop and pull Julia down to the ground.

She fights the urge to giggle when I quietly tackle her to the floor and cover us with the blanket. "If you cover my ears, I'll cover yours," I whisper, causing her eyes to sparkle with mirth.

"Or we could get lost in our own kiss and block out the rest of the world."

She doesn't have to tell me twice. I plan to tune out everything but Julia until we are clear to leave the treehouse.

Chapter 32
Julia

Britt's eyebrows shoot up in surprise. "I want to see!" Her fingers make a grabbing motion as she reaches for my phone.

Shaking my head, I lock my phone. "Not before I ask Ingrid if sharing their private moment is okay. They had no idea Declan and I were hiding in the treehouse."

Wiggling his eyebrows as he plops in the chair beside Britt, Axel asks, "Why were you two spying from the treehouse to begin with?" He tips his beer bottle back, taking a few long gulps. "You realize the treehouse isn't a hunting blind, right?"

My eyes dart to the side. "We think Ingrid and Callum got engaged, but don't say anything! We aren't sure if they are ready to share it with anyone or not."

"You think? Well, is Ingrid wearing an engagement ring?" Axel asks loud enough for the entire table to hear. All our eyes dart to the stage where Ingrid prepares her violin for tonight's live performance. She squats beside her case, partially in the shadows of the stage lighting. Her back is turned to us, neither hand visible.

"I have no idea," Paisley responds, squinting at the stage as she leans across Axel to hear us better. When the song finishes, Axel and Paisley stand up simultaneously. He raises an eyebrow for her to inform us of her plans.

"Wait, I'll find out if they're engaged from Ingrid. I'll be subtle," Paisley says.

"Yeah, like a rockstar at a company picnic," Axel deadpans. He crosses his arms over his chest and looks at her doubtfully.

"Hey! I can be subtle." Paisley grouses, folding her arms across her chest, mirroring his stance. It looks like Thumbelina next to Dwayne Johnson.

"You are as subtle as a fart in church." Paisley goes to reply, but Axel cuts her off by pressing a finger to her lips. "And I'm talking a front row fart, not a leaning against the back wall near the exit fart." She snaps her teeth, threatening to bite him, but Trent pulls her into his lap.

I snort but press my lips together when Paisley's eyes cut to mine.

Axel raises his hands. "The truth hurts gingersnap. I'll go find out and get back to you."

"Paisley, let Axel try," Trent says, rubbing her upper arms as we watch Axel move through the crowd. "Besides, Callum's coming this way, so I think we'll have a better chance of getting the information before Axel."

I snicker as I watch the top of Axel's head approach the stage. Callum sits down with four pitchers of beer in his hands.

"What's the occasion?" Declan asks, arching an eyebrow.

"Well," he pauses for dramatic effect as he looks at each person seated at our table. "Today, I asked Ingrid to marry me." We all smile at him knowingly, and his brow furrows. "What the hell? She told me I could tell you while she prepared to perform."

"Ingrid didn't say a word," Trent says, pouring a glass of beer from the pitcher.

"Wait, why aren't you all surprised? Was I really that obvious?" Callum looks around in panic. "I was trying to be super secretive about it. Last night, after I left the orchard, I stopped by to pick up the ring." He rubs his palms on his thighs as he looks around the table.

Declan raises a finger and Callum huffs. "Actually, Julia and I were in the treehouse today having our own picnic. We saw the whole thing and didn't want to interrupt you when we realized what you were doing. I actually took a video, and Julia snapped a bunch of photos. We weren't sure if you'd want us to share them, so I can send them to you and Ingrid to decide."

Callum scrubs his hand up and down his face in frustration before he takes Declan's phone and watches the video. His eyes get watery, but then he belts out a laugh when Ingrid tackles him. Shaking his head, he hands the phone back to Declan. "Feel free to share. It's the happiest moment of my life, and I don't care who in the hell sees it. I was convinced I wanted our engagement to be completely private, but after watching the video, I'm fucking glad you were there to capture it."

"I got some good photos," I murmur, handing him my phone.

His smile is bright as he flips through the pictures, cradling his jaw in his palm. "These are perfect. Thanks, you two. After Ingrid and I hid during Lachlan and Aislinn's proposal, I told Ingrid I wouldn't return the favor. I guess I didn't clarify that meant for either Ambarsan." Handing my phone back to me, he smirks. "I am glad you got these, though. Ingrid will be thrilled. Especially the one where she's kneeing me in the crotch, followed by the one where I'm rolling around in the fetal position while she's staring at the ground ten feet away. It looks like she thought I was a robber, not her future fiancé."

The whole table laughs before our phones are passed around to the group. A moment later, Axel saunters to the table with a frown marring his handsome face. His ice-chip blue eyes storm with frustration, which is palpable from my spot across the table. "She refused to show me her left hand. She used her right hand for everything I asked her to hand or show me. Subtlety didn't work for us, gang."

We all burst into laughter. Callum clears his throat. "Yeah, she agreed to marry me, man. Grab Declan's phone. He got a video of the entire thing."

Paisley rubs the back of her knuckles down the front of her jean jacket. "Looks like I got the information first, buckeroo." Holding up her fist she opens it toward the floor and mouths, "Mic drop."

Axel heavily sits in his chair, reaching for Declan's phone. "Fine, you win this round due to pure, dumb luck."

Paisley sticks her tongue out at Axel, then says, "It wouldn't kill you to admit I'm better than you."

With a one-arm shrug, he lifts the beer bottle to his lips then says, "We don't know that. For all we know, it just might, and I'd rather not risk my life on your assumption." As he watches the video, he barks out a laugh. "Callum, if I didn't know any better, I'd think Ingrid doesn't want to have kids with you. Isn't it like the tenth time she's kneed the family jewels? The woman doesn't need self-defense training."

"Well, we're all happy for you, Callum," Lachlan says. "I'm dying to know who your best man will be."

After leaning over Paisley's shoulder while they looked at the video and photos, Aislinn plops down on Lachlan's knee and responds, "I'm hoping I get to be the matron of honor. Have you guys picked a date?"

Callum looks at Aislinn like she's grown a second head or developed a mermaid tail. "You realize we got engaged this afternoon, right?"

"Yup," Paisley responds. "We need the details. Will I be building another gazebo somewhere?"

Lowering his beer, Axel says, "I call the bartender role. I'm really good at that job."

The lights blink off and on, causing our group to quiet down. The bar turns silent, the only sound coming from the clinks of glassware behind the bar.

"Welcome to Glaciers. Tonight's band is the Buckshot Rebels!" shouts the guitarist. "Tonight, we'll start with a cover of 'A Bar Song Tipsy' by Shaboozey. Get out on the dance floor and put your hands together. Let's start the song with a strong clapping rhythm that'll rock the roof of this place. Ingrid is filling in for Sylvie while she's out of town visiting family. Rick and I are on the drum and guitar as always."

The lights flicker off for a moment, only to illuminate the entire stage in the next blink. Ingrid stands front and center with her violin poised against the front of her shoulder. With her bow drawn, she pulls a long, soulful note that resonates through the silent bar. The stone in her ring glistens under the bright lights, and her bright smile tells us everything. When I glance at Callum, he's staring at her with a goofy grin.

Rick taps his drumsticks together in a rhythm, and the crowd claps in time with him.

Declan stands at the same time as Lachlan and offers his hand to me. "You heard Mark. He wants us to dance, blossom, and you're my dance partner."

I stumble, trying to stand up because I can't get into Declan's embrace fast enough. He grips my elbow, stabilizing me while I get my feet underneath me. I look up in surprise.

"Don't look like you didn't know teamwork makes the dream work," Declan whispers against the shell of my ear.

"What are we, a beach volleyball duo? You gonna wear a Speedo?" I quip, trying to reduce the adrenaline coursing through my veins after nearly face-planting in a packed bar.

"I will if you will," he teases. I grab his belt loops as he leads me onto the crowded dance floor.

Turning, he grips my hips, pulling me flush against his front, and moves like he was born to dance. My feet follow where he leads, unsure what dance we're even doing. I may have been trained in ballet, but these two times at Glaciers have shown me footwork I can barely keep up with.

He spins me around his back, and I can't help but laugh because my body just goes wherever he directs me. My hair flies around my face, momentarily blinding me.

"I love the sound of your laugh," Declan says, dipping his head near my ear.

Swallowing thickly, I blurt, "When did you learn to dance?"

He stiffens. I want to go back five seconds and not ask that stupid question. He probably comes dancing here with other women all the time.

"I don't want to ruin the moment," he mutters.

"Unless it's because you spend every weekend dancing with a different woman, then I can't see how you could ruin the moment." I lean back just enough to look into the deep green swirls of his eyes, where the stage lights refract off them like a kaleidoscope.

He shakes his head. "No, there has never truly been anyone but you, blossom." His voice is so low I can barely make it out over the sounds from the speaker system. Sighing, he lowers his head beside my ear. "After you left, my eighteen-year-old mind assumed you left because I embarrassed you at prom with my pathetic dance moves and lack of interest in dancing. I bought lessons with the money I made at the orchard." His gaze darts away as his cheeks blush with embarrassment.

"What?" I splutter. "You thought I left after graduation because I was embarrassed by your dance moves at prom." I can barely get the whole sentence out as I numbly move with him, now only swaying from side to side.

He nods, and the uncertainty in his eyes is almost my undoing. There is so much vulnerability sparking through the depth of his gaze. I open my mouth to respond but close it. Taking a deep breath, I murmur, "Prom was the best night of my life, Declan. I loved every moment of it, and your dancing had absolutely nothing to do with why I had to leave Topaz Falls."

Dropping his head back, he groans. Lowering his gaze, he smirks. "Well, dance lessons were a waste of a few hundred dollars."

"I wouldn't say they were a complete waste. Now you can spin circles around me on the dance floor," I reply with a watery grin.

Before I leave this time, maybe I'll finally have the strength to tell him why I left and why I'll need to leave this time, too.

No matter what.

If I'm not careful, I'll get burned, but not by flames, and the damage won't be external scars.

Chapter 33

Declan
Sunday, October 20

Today, I'm going to show the judges my strengths. I may not be a professional baker, but I have some tricks up my sleeve. I didn't realize it until the baking night with Julia, but I can make our team faster and more efficient. Shaking my head, I look down at the bin gripped tightly in my hand as I run toward the large white tent. I'm cutting it close, but I needed to stop at my parents' place for one last item.

As I step through the curtain, all eyes drag toward me. I slowly skirt the edges of the kitchen area until I come to our station, where I drop the bin at the end of the counter and begin to unload it.

I can feel the heat of Julia's touch through my flannel shirt when she grips my arm to get my attention. "Declan," she whispers. "Is everything okay? You were almost late. They're starting in a few minutes."

My gaze cuts to hers, and my breath hitches. Julia looks gorgeous as always, but what leaves me speechless is the sleeveless wrap dress she's wearing. My fingers gently graze the scarred skin as I smile warmly into her eyes. "I'm proud of you, blossom."

A slight blush creeps up her cheeks. "I'm tired of hiding and being ashamed of my scars. You've made me confident enough to ignore them."

Shaking my head, I reply, "Don't ignore them. They're a part of you. Think of them as battle scars to show you're a baking warrior. If anyone asks about them, narrow your eyes and tell them they should see the oven."

Snickering, she pats my forearm. "Thanks, Dec. What's in the box?"

"Well," I say, wiggling my eyebrows. "I brought all my nifty apple tools. Peelers of all shapes and sizes, two different apple corers, a few styles of slicers, and this." I hold up my mom's special pan. It had eight spaces that were shaped like the bottom of an apple.

"What do we do with it?" Julia asks, turning it around in her hands.

"My mom likes to peel and core apples, then fill them with stuff. You can set the apple upright in it and then put it in the oven to bake. I have no idea what you put in it, but that's your job, not mine." I wink at her, but it's true because I know that whatever my mom makes is good. I don't actually know what's in it other than cinnamon. After this is over, I think I'll make a point to arrive early to family brunches and dinners so I can not only help my mom in the kitchen but also learn a thing or two from her that I can pass on to my kids one day.

"Maybe we can use it for the lunch item? I really don't know, but I'll think about it. If we don't use it today, we will in the finals. My plan is to do a cinnamon apple French toast for breakfast and the apple cake we practiced for the dessert round. I won't know what ingredient the judges will choose for the lunch pairing, so we will have to play that round by ear."

Dipping my head beside her ear, I ask, "Do I get promoted from scullery maid to sous chef?"

"Let's see how the rounds pan out, big guy," Julia teases, bumping me with her shoulder.

The host, whose name I think is Bruce or something, lets loose a sharp whistle to get our attention. The chatter in the tent ceases, and everyone faces forward.

I wrap my arm around Julia's upper body, pulling her flush to my side. Leaning over, I press a kiss into her hair and take a moment to breathe her in to settle my sudden spike of nerves.

The camera crew approaches the host and three judges. The only sounds are those of the birds in the apple trees outside the tent. The producer holds up his hand and counts down from five. "Welcome to the second round of the Great Harvest Bake-Off hosted by the Baking Network. My name is Brian Ulmer. I'm excited to be your host for this fun event. I wish the cameras could capture the amazing smells within the tent. We are at the Ambarsan Apple Orchard in Topaz Falls, Montana for round two. Like last week, the theme for this bake-off is apples. Our judges are Pauline Denning, Renea Truman, and Jeff Alderman. Pauline, would you like to tell everyone about the challenges today and what they should expect from the judges?"

Pauline steps forward. Her thick, curly, auburn hair sits twisted on top of her head. She's in a chocolate brown dress and boots with heels that put her eye level with the male judge. Her hazel eyes silently travel to each of the five remaining teams before she takes a deep breath to speak. "Happy Sunday, everyone. My name is Pauline Denning, and I'm honored to be here and excited to see what you have in store for us this round. Like last week, there will be three rounds in today's competition. In the semi-finals, we are down to five couples. At the end of the third round, the other two judges and I will choose which two teams will be eliminated and which three teams will be part of next week's final round, competing for the grand prize of thirty thousand dollars. Like last week, the first bake of the day will be a breakfast favorite. Your second challenge will be a savory dish with the special ingredient chosen by Renea. The final challenge will be a dessert showing each team's kitchen abilities. Now, we will observe to ensure each team evenly splits the tasks. We want equal involvement from each member. Good luck, everyone."

"Ready, set, cook!" Brian shouts, and my pulse spikes for no reason.

I look around wildly, trying to figure out what I'm supposed to do. Julia touches my shoulder and squeezes me for a brief moment. "Deep breath, Dec."

A sharp whistle pierces the air and I hear Paisley shout, "Let's go Home Team!" I grin at her and Trent, who are standing just outside the tent cheering us on. Julia timidly waves to them before tugging on my sleeve.

Pinching my eyes shut, I nod. "Right. But they want us to split the tasks evenly. That will literally kill our chances as a team."

Julia steps in front of me and grabs my jaw in both hands. Her thumbs softly rub against the stubble of my beard. "Have confidence in yourself, Dec. I do. Nothing bad will happen. We're going to rock this round." I nod and take a deep breath. "For the breakfast round, we're making apple French toast, okay?"

Shaking out my hands, I walk to my station. "What do you need me to do?"

"We need to peel, core, and slice three apples. Then, you'll sauté them in butter, lemon juice, salt, and sugar. Let me know when you have the apples ready, and I'll walk you through what to put in the pan."

Without questioning her decision to let me take on a more significant role on the team, I rush to the barrel of apples and grab my favorite variety, the SugarBee. With all three apples in my grip, I head to my side of our station and set up my mom's favorite tool. I place the apple against the frame and crank the handle. The apple rapidly spins, slicing away from the core while peeling simultaneously. I remove the corkscrew of apple from the tool and set it on the cutting board. I cut it in half with a sharp knife, giving me extra thin half circles, which I quickly toss in the pan on the stovetop. I repeat the method four more times until I have a pile of apples ready to sauté.

"I'm ready," I say, picking up a wooden spoon.

With wide eyes, she looks at the pan full of apples and then around at the other competitors. "You did that so fast," she says.

"I brought my A game today. What can I say?" I shrug my shoulder, struggling with the compliment. I was literally born to eat apples; not knowing how to peel and core them would be embarrassing for my family on national television.

"I went ahead and measured out the dry ingredients and cut the cube of butter for you. Add everything into the pan with a teaspoon of lemon juice and stir them around until the apples look soft and the sugar looks like liquid caramel," Julia says, speaking so fast that with her accent, I struggle to make sense of what kind of caramel I'm looking for.

"Like a sauce?" I ask to clarify.

She nods before shoving everything at me. After a brief hesitation, I stir the butter, sugar, salt, cinnamon, and lemon juice into the pan. After about five minutes, nothing happens. The sugar slowly dissolves into the lemon juice; otherwise, it looks about the same.

Clearing my throat, I lean toward Julia, who is plopping thick slices of coated bread onto a flat-top griddle. "Blossom? Nothing's happening over here."

She glances up and narrows her eyes at the stove. Reaching over, she flicks her hand on the nob and turns the stove to medium heat. Biting her lip, she says, "Sorry, I forgot to mention the stove needed to be on."

Her eyes cut back to her French toast, but my cheeks flame. How did it not occur to me that the heat needed to be on? Better yet, how did I not notice the heat was off?

We work in rushed silence. My forearm aches from stirring the apples for twenty minutes.

Julia plates two slices of French toast on each plate while I spoon my apple mixtures over the top. She finishes the entire thing with powdered sugar, and I must admit, it looks good. So good. I wish we'd made an extra dish for us because I'm suddenly starving.

The judges circle the different groups, reaching us last. "What do we have here?" Renea asks.

Julia motions to me, and I momentarily freeze. She didn't mention I'd have to do the speaking. Clearing my throat, I say, "I made the topping. Julia made the bread part."

Jeff raises an unimpressed eyebrow, so Julia picks up where I left off. "We have for you apple pie French toast."

"We used SugarBee apples," I blurt, startling Pauline, who almost chokes on her bite.

She covers her mouth as she finishes chewing then says, "The flavor is wonderful. I'm excited you split the tasks in half. Great job to both of you. This is fabulous."

I can't help the grin spreading from ear to ear. Pride, like I haven't felt before, coats me like armor, making me feel invincible.

Renea catches our attention from the front. "Wonderful job to most of the teams. It seems two groups bit off more than they could chew, and their dishes weren't cooked through or plated in a timely manner. Remember to choose a recipe that fits within the time allotment. This competition is not only based on ability but speed as well. For the next round, the theme is pizza. I love making homemade pizza. You have one hour to make a pizza showcasing apples. Ready, set, and cook!"

I spin and look at Julia, who presses her lips out in thought. "Have you ever had a pizza with apples? I haven't. I need some help with flavor profile ideas."

A slow grin spreads across my lips. "Lachlan makes an amazing pizza. He uses green apples, bacon, goat cheese, red onion, and this thick purple sauce. It's the one you sometimes put on salads but thicker."

"Sounds like he uses a balsamic glaze. Alright. Let's make pizza. It will be a tribute to the other Ambarsan brother," she says with a wink. "I have a dough recipe I love, so why don't you chop up the ingredients we need for the top and get them ready."

The hour flies by. I almost nicked my finger twice while slicing the stupid onion and had more tears streaming down my face than I did when I lost in the pee-wee baseball finals. But the look on the judges' faces when they try our pizza makes it all worth it. All three offer hums of approval.

"Amazing." This one word from Renea was all I needed to hear. My back is straighter, and I'm excited to tell Lachlan how much they enjoyed his pizza recipe. The best part was I didn't mess up once.

"Woot woot!" A deep voice draws our attention to the crowd and I look over, surprised Trent is cheering loudly, only to see Aislinn and Lachlan jumping up and down. Lachlan points at me. "I recognize that pizza, man!" I shoot him a lazy grin with double thumbs up before returning my attention to the front of the tent.

"Last up for today is cupcakes," Jeff states. "Don't forget to make the apples shine."

I frown. "We can't make the cake we practiced."

"Don't pout, big guy. We will make the cake you practiced, just individually sized with a cinnamon apple cream cheese frosting. Everything will work out fine," Julia says, patting my shoulder. "Peel, core, then slice circles for one apple. I'll make the batter. Then you'll make the frosting, and I'll frost the cupcakes."

We break apart like we're on the offensive line, with our sights set on the endzone. Football probably isn't even close to what Julia's thinking about, but the slight distraction makes me grin.

When the cupcakes come out of the flash freezer thirty minutes later, Julia spoons the cream cheese frosting into a piping bag. I steal the mixer blade and slowly lick the frosting like I'm ten years old again. This used to be my favorite part of Mom's baking.

Julia swirls the frosting, making it look like a Dairy Queen ice cream cone, and then she instructs me to drizzle the caramel sauce we made for the filling on top. It glops on in some places, looking less professional than if Julia had done it herself. Still, I am satisfied to know we did these cupcakes as a team. The judges can't complain that I was simply the apple peeler today. I spent more time at the stove this afternoon than in the previous decade combined.

I don't foresee myself getting the baking bug, or making homemade Pop-Tarts, because I'd be cocky to think this little amount of assistant baking would translate to success on my own in the kitchen.

My mind flashes back to elementary school when the pottery teacher instructed us to use the wheel. She let me demonstrate, and while hunching over my back, her hands helped me sculpt a beautiful bowl. When she left, I assumed it meant I was a pottery savant; therefore, she didn't think I needed more help. When the wheel began turning, my small hands quickly converted the clay bowl into a mound of mud. It was the fastest reality check I've ever had.

"Dec?" Julia's voice snags my attention, but her brows furrow in concern when I look at her. "I'd said your name a few times. Are you okay?"

I nod. "Just remembering I'm not a pottery savant."

Her expression is marred with confusion, but she smiles tightly before grabbing my hand. The judges approach our workstation first.

"What did you make for the dessert round?" Jeff asks.

"Cupcakes," I reply, standing up straighter.

"You are a man of many words," Pauline says, taking a large bite.

Julia chuckles. "We made cinnamon apple cupcakes with a caramel filling and a cinnamon apple cream cheese frosting. We then drizzled the caramel sauce over the top."

"Well, you two. It looks like you are the team to beat," Renea whispers with a wink.

I bend down and kiss Julia, only to realize the cameras are rolling. The kiss will be televised on National television. She blushes but doesn't pull away. Instead, she curls her hand into my shirt and stands in my embrace as the judges move back to the front of the room.

"Good job today. Each team really shined in at least one round. Only three teams will make it to next weekend's final round, where they will compete for thirty thousand dollars," Brian says.

I'm confident we aren't going home today. Three teams made obvious errors, and the judges loved what we made in every round. They clearly saw we made them together. I wasn't some sideshow assistant today. I pulled my weight. I mean, I wasn't like an ox, but I was better than a chipmunk.

"The two teams leaving us today are Jeremy and Simone, as well as Tiffany and Scott. Thank you for participating. Today, neither team allowed enough time during the breakfast round to fully plate their finished items. Although the early mistake should have left room for the other three teams to mess up in the second or third round, unfortunately for you, they didn't. Thank you for joining us, and we're sorry to see you go," Jeff says.

Brian smiles at the camera. "Viewers at home, we're glad you could join us in this week's episode of the Great Harvest Bake-Off. I'm your host, Brian Ulmer. We will see the remaining three teams back here for the finals next Sunday at the Ambarsan Apple Orchard to see who will win thirty thousand dollars and be named the Great Harvest Bake-Off Champions."

When the camera cuts, everyone wanders around, and I'm excited to see a few extra cupcakes at our station. Picking one up, I offer it to Julia. I reach for another one and click cupcakes with her like champagne glasses. "To you, blossom. You're the best baker and person I know. I can't wait to stand by your side next Sunday when we win."

She shakes her head but smirks at me. "Win or lose, as long as you're on my team, I'm a winner, Declan."

I beam at her, but before I can take a bite, she jams the cupcake in my face. Her peal of laughter echoes through the tent. She takes off toward the orchard. I open my eyes and take off after her, letting her remain just far enough ahead of me that she thinks I can't catch her. All the while, I'm corralling her where I need her.

My house.

Chapter 34

Declan

Monday, October 21

My body aches from yesterday. I never would've thought standing over a stove and simply stirring apples could use muscles I didn't know existed. I weight train and run. Hell, tonight, I might have to cancel with Tucker because he's expecting me to show up for our guys' night at the ranch. I don't think my quads could do squats if I tried. I'd like to think it was from the workout Julia and I had in the shower after the competition, but I know it's not.

In high school, I considered three hours of intense training on the baseball field and in the gym pain-inducing. I must be getting old if I feel sore after simply standing. I'm honestly too embarrassed to admit it to anyone, so I might just show up at the ranch and be a social butterfly. If I randomly talk to anyone around me, maybe they won't notice me not working out.

I have a long to-do list today. First, I must stop by and talk to Anders about inventory software. Next, I'll take the bouquet of flowers I just bought at the market to Julia. I want her to know how proud I am of all her hard work yesterday. I don't want her to think I've taken her for granted. Finally, I need to get back and check the blight with Cameron. We have a few things to take care of in the storage barn as the next shipment goes out tomorrow. I want to make sure we're ready. Then, there's Tucker and the rest of the guys. They'll know something's up if I'm a no-show. Maybe a hard workout is exactly what I need.

My phone rings, startling me. "Hey, Mom."

"Deckers! It's been a few days since we last spoke. How are you doing?" Mom's voice sounds like home. Just the sound filling the cab of my truck brings me more comfort than she can imagine.

"I'm good, Mom. How're you and Dad?" My voice catches as I think of him lying in the hospital bed. I need to make a trip down to see him, but he claims he doesn't want any of us to waste our time when he'll be home before we know it. Spending a day on the road would be challenging with the harvest and the festival.

"Oh, we're good. I wanted to let you know Dad's gotten stronger. He's using a cane more than his walker now, and the physical therapist and doctor think he might be strong enough to go home next Monday. His bruising is almost completely gone, and he's shuffling around pretty well on his own."

"Seriously?" I ask in disbelief. "Didn't they think he might be there until the second week of November?"

"Yes," she replies. "It appears we'll leave here a little over two weeks early. Dad can't wait to have his bed back. I'll miss the big walk-in shower, but I want my kitchen back."

"Ingrid, Lachlan, and I will help him get settled in at the house. Make sure you tell us what time he's coming so we can be at your place," I say, barely containing my excitement.

The fact Mom will be home when the next round of inventory and ordering needs to take place sends a thrill down my spine. I can't wait to propose the system Anders found, too. Maybe, now would be a good time to mention it.

"Hey, Mom?" I ask. "Have you and Dad ever considered getting an RFID system for the orchard? Anders is helping me research some possible programs, which might really help improve the efficiency of our operation."

"You looked into RFID systems for the orchard?" Mom asks surprised.

"Uh, yeah." Reaching up, I scratch the back of my neck as I fix my baseball hat. "I think it would help organize our inventory."

"It never occurred to me to try, but it makes sense. What a great idea, Declan." Dad's voice is full of pride, as a smile tugs at the corner of my mouth.

"I can't wait to see what you found," Mom replies.

"Now, enough about the orchard," Dad says. "We want to know how you did in the baking competition yesterday?"

"Oh, yes! I keep forgetting you're in a baking competition. Of all my kids, I never would've guessed you, Declan. How did you do?" Mom asks, and I narrow my eyes to the apparent dig. She's right, though. Until two weeks ago, I would've thought the same thing.

"We are in the finals next Sunday. I wish you guys could see us bake. Julia is amazing." My voice takes on a wistful tone. I have no doubt my mom picked up on it.

"We're both proud of you, son, for getting out there and making the Ambarsan family name proud." Dad's words of encouragement only make me want to practice baking more.

It was the same in Little League. Whenever I was told, "Good job!" or "You're doing great!" it made me play even harder. The way I respond to positive encouragement makes me sound like a golden retriever. I'm one of those kids who would do anything to make my parents proud, and luckily for me, they were easily impressed and boisterous with their encouragement.

"Well, good luck, son. The physical therapist is here, so we need to let you go," Dad says.

"Good luck, old man. Show her what you're made of!" I shout to give him the same encouragement he gives me.

"Bye, Deckers. We'll talk to you later in the week," Mom says before hanging up.

I park my truck and hop out. With a smile on my face, I open the door to Sleepy Mountain Roasters. I'm hit by the soothing aroma of coffee beans. I'd sit here for hours if I could.

I've always loved the smell of roasted coffee beans. Dad would be up before sunrise every morning and start a pot of coffee for himself. All three of us kids would wake up and rush downstairs, knowing we could get up. Mom was to never be disturbed before 8 a.m. We learned fast to stay in bed until we could smell coffee, and then it was a race to see who got the milk for cereal first. Until I was in middle school, I lost every morning. It wasn't until my inseam was longer than Ingrid's that I finally made it to the kitchen before her. I think Lachlan beat me until he left for college, and then I won by default.

After I order my coffee, I wait at the end of the counter. At the same time, Anders walks out of his office and approaches me with a big smile. "Hey, Declan. Are you here for just a cup of coffee, or do you have a minute to discuss the inventory programs I found?"

I nod eagerly. "I'd love to hear what you found. I just spoke with my parents, and it looks like they'll be home next week. I want to present them with your recommendations, as I think they'll like the idea of making the orchard more efficient."

"Great. Come back to my office once you get your coffee. I'll leave the door open." He turns and walks back down the hall, disappearing into his office a moment later.

With a coffee in my hand, I knock on the doorjamb. "Knock. Knock."

Anders waves me inside. "Have a seat." He motions to the chairs across from him, and I sit down with a sigh, my thighs and calves burning as I lower myself.

"Hard workout this morning?" he asks.

"Sure, something like that." I wink.

Organizing a stack of papers, he taps them together and adds a paperclip. "Here is all the information I could find on the three inventory software options I found. The one on top is what we use in all my stores, but I wanted to give you a couple of other options. A buddy of mine has a brewery and uses the second one. A restaurant owner I'm friends with uses the third option. Look them over and talk with your parents. I think it would be much easier than the handwritten method you use. It will also be more accurate, because it allows you to track dates with each scan."

I take the stack of documents from Anders and smile. "This is perfect. Thanks for doing this, man. I told my parents about the idea, and they loved it."

Uncertainty flickers in his gaze, and he clears his throat as he sits up straighter in his chair. Anders leans on the desk with his hands clasped, and my eyes struggle to meet his unwavering gaze. His tone is devoid of amusement or lightness when he asks, "Declan, can I ask you something?"

I'm not sure where he's going with this question, and I know I don't like his tone. "Yes." My tone is clipped to match the change in air. I consider Anders one of my friends. Growing up with Lachlan, we always had the same friend group, but I met Anders first.

"Have you ever been tested for dyscalculia?" he asks.

My gaze cut to his, and I narrow my eyes. "Excuse me?"

Putting his hands up in surrender, he leans back in his chair. "I'm not accusing you of anything. I noticed you really struggle with numbers and time. A couple of the figures you wrote in the margins had flipped numbers. My little sister was diagnosed with dyscalculia in the fourth grade for the same reason. Has math always been a struggle for you?"

I bristle, and my first thought is to get defensive. But I force my anger to the bottom of my stomach because this is Anders. He's not some bully outside my locker, ready to tease me for the incorrect answer I wrote on the whiteboard in Mr. Horton's math class.

Sighing, I pinch the bridge of my nose. "Yeah. Point blank, I suck at math." I took the bare minimum to graduate from high school, and even then, I barely passed. My parents just assumed I wasn't interested or was bored in class. It's the whole reason they didn't push for me to attend college like Lachlan and Ingrid. "What is dyscalculia?"

With a soft smile, which makes me want to tense again for fear he'll turn condescending, I hold my breath. "Dyscalculia is a learning disorder, like dyslexia, but it makes your ability to do math challenging instead of reading. It affects the areas of the brain, which handles math and number abilities. This can make learning and understanding mathematical concepts difficult. The doctors told my parents symptoms often appear in childhood. Still, many adults have it without realizing they do because, as children, they found coping mechanisms or ways to get out of doing math. Some people also struggle with time and money."

"What should I do?" I ask. "Is there a medication for it, which will reverse the issue like people who have anxiety or ADHD?"

"I'm not a doctor, Dec. It might be a good idea to see a neuropsych person. My sister saw a neuropsychologist as a child, but I don't know who adults should see. You could start by asking your primary doctor. Do you go to Dr. Duffy?"

I nod. "I've seen him since I was born. Honestly, I can't believe he hasn't retired yet." I stand up. "Thanks for letting me know your thoughts. I trust your opinion, and like I said, math has always been a struggle for me. This is nothing new. My workaround has always been to avoid it, but with my parents unable to do the administrative side of the orchard that hasn't been an option. After years of living in the back recesses of my mind, my math issues are glaring me in the face."

He stands up and grabs another folder off his desk. "Let me know if I can help any more. I wasn't sure how to bring it up with you, but the similarities to my younger sister were too much of a coincidence for me not to mention it. I hate to run, but I need to stop at the bakery before heading to my shop in Kalispell."

My gaze whips to his. "I'll walk with you. I'm heading to the bakery next. Julia and I made it to the finals of the baking competition at the orchard this weekend, so I'm taking her some flowers to congratulate her."

Nodding, Anders follows me out to my truck. I reach in and grab the bouquet, and we walk a couple blocks to the bakery. I take the time to pick his brain about the system he uses, even though many of the technical concepts go over my head.

When the chime over the bakery door announces our arrival, Maria shouts, "Hello! Julia, Anders and Declan just arrived!" When we get to the counter, she beams at me. "You brought her another bouquet."

Julia strides out of the back room with her frilly apron on and a smile spread across her face. She looks gorgeous. The deep red on her cheeks from working in the warm kitchen reminds me of other ways she gets the flushed look, and I tighten my grip on the flowers at the memory of last night before she left my place.

"Anders. Dec. What are you two doing here?" Julia asks, wrapping me in a hug. I press a kiss on her cheek and pass off the flowers.

"These are for you, blossom. Congratulations on your amazing baking yesterday. We're almost the bake-off winners," I say into her hair.

She beams at me. "I can't wait to put it on the front counter for everyone to see. So many people were watching yesterday, and I didn't even notice. Dozens of people have come in this morning to tell us great job. It's exhilarating, but I'm struggling to keep up with the demand for baked goods. River is cranking out bread like he's a bread factory."

When she turns to Anders, he hands her the folder he brought from his office. "I came over to see if you had a chance to look over the agreement. My attorney wanted to know if there were any changes you wanted to add."

Her eyes widen. "Yes, it looks perfect. I didn't see anything that looked wrong, and I had two other people read over the agreement. Elin told me it was a standard broker form and overall appeared to be very neutral. I guess she worked at a Real Estate office for a few years." A dark cloud passes over Anders causing him to frown.

I'm lost. "What agreement?" I ask.

Anders motions to Julia, who swallows thickly. "The purchase agreement for the bakery. Anders plans to buy it at the beginning of the year at the ninety-day mark."

No. I didn't think it would really happen. At least, not yet. I was under the impression he was still discussing terms with her. How do they already have an approved agreement?

An almost inhumane sound leaves my chest. She's really planning to sell and leave me again. It looks like I'll have to get my affairs in order. I'll let my parents know when they return that I'm moving to France next year. I've lost her once. I can't lose her again. I'll tell her once I have everything figured out on my end.

My mind swarms with all I need to do. I drop a soft kiss on the top of Julia's head and mumble, "Bye, blossom. I'll talk to you later."

I stumble out of the bakery and return to the orchard on autopilot.

Shit just got real, and the happy bubble I've been living in just burst.

Chapter 35
Julia

What just happened? "Was Declan's behavior a little odd?" Anders nods as he watches Declan's broad shoulders march down the sidewalk until he's out of view.

"Did he know you were planning to sell? It seemed to catch him off guard. I believe I even mentioned I was planning to make you an offer a couple weeks ago."

"I've been straightforward with him since we first spoke. I always intended to leave after ninety days. Nothing has changed," I say evenly.

I square my shoulders, but do I really mean it? Am I only saying it out loud to convince myself? Topaz Falls isn't for me. I want to live in a big city where tourist attractions are everywhere, and swarms of people bustle down the busy sidewalk, walking from one place to the next. Will I miss my aunt's Victorian house? Absolutely. The downside to living in the city is the studio flat I'll rent or buy in Paris. I won't be able to afford even one bedroom unless I can get the shop location at a bargain.

"Thank you for stopping by. Let me just grab the signed agreement for you. It's in my purse. I was planning to take it to Sleepy

Mountain Roasters later today after I finished for the afternoon," I tell him as I stride into the kitchen.

Digging the document out of my oversized purse, I walk back to the front and hand it to him with shaking hands. This doesn't feel right, but neither does staying. I can't be in two places at once.

He flips through the agreement. "The only thing missing is Exhibit A, which is an equipment list. I know you can only take so much back to Paris. I figured we could write an umbrella statement for all items inside the bakery on the transfer day?"

I nod and extend my hand. "Thank you for making this such an easy process. I was honestly dreading it."

"No big deal. Like I told you before, I love this community and want to keep it running as a small town. I want to prevent any large corporations from plowing down historical buildings. If that means owning the entire town, then I consider it money well spent." His reasoning makes sense, but I can't imagine having that much money to burn. I want to ask him why he cares so much, but we aren't close friends. It's not really any of my business.

What would I buy with that amount of money constantly at my fingertips? Definitely a closet of shoes. Call me shallow, but I don't care. Shoes are the best accessory; I will argue with anyone who thinks otherwise. Would I buy historical buildings to restore and keep in business? Probably not. I'd definitely buy a Belshaw donut maker for the bakery.

Anders leaves a moment later with our agreement in his hands. I rub away the goosebumps prickling my arms and return to the kitchen.

Maria follows me to the kitchen island, where she watches River shape dinner rolls. He's experimenting with different loaf sizes to see what sells the best. River is convinced people will buy six packs of dinner rolls. I didn't hate the idea, so I told him to give it a shot.

"So, if Anders buys the bakery, will River and I be without a job in January?" Maria asks, her eyes locked on the toe of her pink patent leather pump.

"Actually, Anders had an employment clause put into the agreement, which basically states all employees at the time of the transition are welcome to stay on board as long as they remain good employees. In other words, don't slack off just because I'm not here to crack the whip," I reply with a wink.

River shakes his dough-covered hands in the air and bites his lip like he's scared. "You're the most terrifying boss I've ever had. You make the other inmates seem tame and amiable."

I tip my head back and laugh. My stomach rolls, catching me off guard. Pressing my hand to my mouth, I rush to the bathroom. Maria's shoes rapidly click behind me as she follows me into the bathroom before I can shut the door.

For a few minutes, I dry heave over the toilet until the wave of nausea subsides. Maria's hand rubs small circles between my shoulder blades, offering me much-needed comfort.

"Are you okay?" she murmurs.

Nodding, I push hair from my face with the back of my hand. "I don't know what happened. I feel fine otherwise. I forgot to eat breakfast, and I'm due to start my period today. Sometimes, the hormone changes and PMS cramps cause nausea. I don't do well with pain. I'm kind of a wimp."

Maria furrows her brow skeptically and places her palm on my forehead. "You aren't warm, so I don't think you have a fever. You feel almost clammy. Is it from the stress of everything that's happened in the last few weeks? You're burning the candle at both ends and then some."

"I'm fine. Really. I'll just take some Tylenol and call it good. A special client is coming in today, so I want to be here for her. Once she leaves, if I'm still tired, I'll duck out early. You wouldn't mind closing up today, would you?" I ask.

Maria's gaze darts around the cramped bathroom as she presses her lips together. "Okay. But, if you feel worse, then you need to leave. You aren't contagious, are you?"

"I don't feel like I have a fever. I'm not coughing or sneezing. Seriously, my lower back has been sore, and the pain makes me nauseous. I'll try to take it a little easier today, but I must finish the cake I'm decorating within the hour." After washing my hands twice, I turn the doorknob and walk into the kitchen to find River frowning.

"Are you okay?" he asks.

I nod, and he gives me a tight smile in return. "After you finish the cake, head home. Maria and I can hold down the fort for the last few hours of the day."

"Thanks," I murmur. "I feel fine. It's not a big deal. The Tylenol should kick in fast."

Maria and River share a silent stare before she spins on her heel and goes back out front. I focus on the two-tier cake at my station and pick up the orange piping bag. For the next thirty minutes, I lose myself in my work. I swirl the last ribbon and step back. With gold frosting, I scrawl, 'Congrats, Elia.'

"It looks great, Julia," River compliments me with a smile. I feel flushed under his scrutiny. Cake decorating was never my strength in the kitchen, but this cake was very important for me to get right.

Maria peeks in the kitchen and hisses, "Julia. A family is asking for you."

I smile. "Tell them I'll be right out. I only need to box it up." I motion to the finished cake and Maria gives me two thumbs up and an encouraging smile.

I have the oversized pink bakery box in my hands a few moments later. Walking out to the front, I spot a family sitting off to the side. The little girl is dressed in a unicorn dress with a tube bandana covering her head.

"McPhearson family?" I ask.

The parents look up, but I'm intently focused on the little girl. Her spindly legs swing in the chair, her toes barely grazing the linoleum floor. The dark circles under her sky-blue eyes highlight her slightly sunken cheeks. Even though she looks unwell, her bright smile makes her eyes sparkle.

"Are you Elia?" I ask, gently setting the cake box in the center of the table.

The little girl nods and points to the box. "Is that my cake?" Her voice sounds thready but full of excitement.

I smile. "It sure is, sweetie. Just as you requested on the intake form, which I received from Frosting On Smiles. You requested a bright blue cake with orange chemotherapy ribbons all over, right?"

Elia nods excitedly. "I did. I start maintenance this week. Do you know what that is?"

Tears prick my eyes. I know all too well. "Elia, I know exactly what maintenance is because I went through it about twenty years ago when I was your age."

"And now you're a baker?" she asks wide-eyed.

"I am. I always wanted to bake. I underwent treatment in France, but there was a small bakery in Paris that made cakes for cancer kids like me. I knew I wanted to do the same thing when I was a grown-up," I tell her. "Maybe one day, you will bake desserts for kids undergoing cancer treatment, too."

"Did you have leukemia, like me?" she asks.

"I did, and I fought it just like you," I reply as tightness tickles my throat. "Ready to see your cake?" I rasp.

When she nods, I lift the top box off and reveal the two-tier cake I made this morning.

"It's my favorite shade of blue," Elia whispers. "The ribbons are perfect. Orange represents leukemia."

I smile softly at the little girl who reminds me so much of myself at seven. I want to tell her the hard part is behind her, but with the risk of relapse, those are words I would never utter, just in case.

"Thank you for this beautiful cake," Elia's parents say in unison. Her dad sniffs as her mom pulls her sunglasses over her eyes.

"You're welcome," I reply. Turning toward Elia, I squat down to be at eye level with her. "Keep fighting, okay?"

Her eyes search mine, and she whispers, "You too."

I watch in silence, swallowing down the tears I refuse to let fall. Whether they were happy tears or not, I no longer want to spill any. I've cried enough this year. I'd rather end the day with a smile. It'll help guarantee a happier day tomorrow.

Chapter 36

Declan
Wednesday, October 23

In the kitchen of Axel's clubhouse, I help open the bags of chips and pretzels he picked up for tonight's poker game. I brought two six-packs of the beer he likes to make up for my crappy choice of money for the last game.

"Who's in charge of choosing the poker currency tonight?" I ask.

"Callum. He better have brought something better than trail mix. I have a bag of Halloween candy, but there are only about twenty-five pieces because I buy full-sized bars. I don't get many trick-or-treaters at my place. Frida's my neighbor, so she and I usually sit outside our front gates together and keep each other company. I'm crossing my fingers we won't get any rain. I had to put a tent up one year to keep us dry. Frida's always a good sport. She dresses in an inflatable chicken outfit," Axel says.

"Why is your Halloween candy here?" I look at him, confused. "Shouldn't it be at your place?"

"If I keep it here, I don't eat it all." Axel shrugs.

I guess that makes logical sense. I'd just buy the types I don't like.

We head back into the other room where the green felt poker table sits, surrounded by our friends.

Axel deals the first round, and I don't hesitate to pick up my hand.

My shoulders hunch in frustration. For the first round, I have nothing good. A pair of tens is nothing to write home about.

"Alright, men. I wanted to let you know the official name of our man cave is Command Center. Thank you, Trent. There were some good recommendations. I also like The Pecker Fortress and Mission Control. You'll find the Command Center rules on the wall near the front door. We have a new inductee tonight. Please give a warm welcome to Tristan Ballantyne. He's leaving this weekend but will be back full-time at the beginning of the year when he takes over his uncle's auto shop," Axel says.

The guy sure knows how to command everyone's attention. There is a chorus of hellos as Tristan rises from his seat and gives a little wave. It's the largest group for poker we've had in weeks.

"Welcome, Tristan," Trent says, dipping his head toward the newcomer. "Have you played much poker?"

Tristan sits back down and picks up his cards. Shaking his head, he replies, "Nope. I played some Blackjack in high school, but that didn't go very well for me." He furrows his brows as he looks at his cards. "I mean, I know how to play poker. It just isn't something I do regularly." Looking around at each person seated around the table, he says, "I look forward to joining you guys more frequently next year."

"Callum was in charge of the money tonight since we never play with real cash. But based on the fact Declan brought trail mix with raisins last week and Callum thought toothpicks were a good idea this week, I may amend the rules and change it to pennies or something nominal." Axel shakes his head, trying not to laugh. "Toothpicks," he mouths, and Lachlan barks out a laugh.

Looking at Axel, he says, "I forgot I was in charge of bringing currency this week. I couldn't find anything better to bring, and I didn't have time to stop at the store."

"You couldn't think of anything better? Nothing. You didn't have pretzels? Hell, Chex cereal or Rice Crispies would've been better. You can't even eat the toothpicks if you get bored," Axel states with a huff.

"Does Ingrid know you took the toothpicks?" Lachlan asks.

Callum smirks. "Not really, but I'll remember to replace them before next summer. I doubt she'll need them before then."

Axel narrows his eyes. "Are toothpicks seasonal? What does she use them for in the summer?"

"I'm pretty sure they're year round, but as far as I'm aware she only uses them in the summer for the ranch BBQs. The little appetizers she makes always have a toothpick in them or on the side." Callum shrugs and grabs his drink to take a drink.

"Cal, she uses them to check and see if her muffins and cupcakes are fully cooked. Haven't you paid attention when she bakes? You better replace them before the weekend in case she gets the baking bug," Lachlan says with amusement. "She'll be pissed if she goes to grab one from the cabinet and can't find any."

"Huh. Okay." Shaking his head, Axel taps the deck of cards on the table. He deals us in and we ante up. After the first turn of cards, I wrinkle my nose at my pathetic hand. "Alright, first round of bets, men," Axel says from his place as the dealer. "Trent, you're up first."

"Two toothpicks," Trent says, tossing them into the center. Huffing out a laugh, he mutters, "M&Ms would've been better. Is it sad I miss the trail mix?"

"Tristan, what would you like to do? Fold or match the bet?" Axel asks, tapping his cards on the felt tabletop.

Tristan smiles wide and pushes all his toothpicks into the center. "I'm all in!" He sits back in his seat with a stupid grin on his face.

Lachlan arches a brow but pushes his cards face-first into the pile. Callum follows Lachlan's lead and pushes his cards into the center, leaning back into his chair with his arms crossed. We finish going around until it gets to me.

"Why not. It's only toothpicks." I push them to the center and stare at the new guy. What's he got up his sleeve?

We finish the round, and Axel calls us to show. Only Tristan and I are finishing out the round. I flip over my pair of tens. It's a pathetic hand to go all in, but I'm calling Tristan's bluff.

He smiles smugly. "Well, I have an ace." He flips his cards over, and at first, I think he means a pair of aces, which would beat my tens, but there is only one ace.

Axel burst into laughter. "No way, man. You have a low ace flush." I look closer at the cards as Axel reaches over the table to rearrange Tristan's cards numerically. "Ace, two, three, four, and five, all spades."

"Oh, look at that. They're all with the shovel symbol, too." He leans over and scoops the pile of toothpicks toward his spot.

I lean back and observe the next couple of rounds. Tristan is wiping the guys clean. Either he has dumb luck, or he's a card shark pretending to be an idiot. I'm going with dumb luck, mainly because I still have reservations about the guy.

"Dec, congrats to you and Julia for making it to the baking finals! You two were awesome last Sunday," Axel says as he deals the next round.

"You came and watched?" I ask in surprise. "I didn't see you there. Who were you there with? I must've been really focused. I actually made the sauce and filling for a couple of things we baked. I didn't only peel apples this time."

"Well, I wasn't there physically, but you were the talk of the town at Mama M's. People can't stop talking about Julia." Trent and Tristan are the only two remaining in the game. Axel keeps his eyes trained on their movements as he talks to me. "I'm sure I'd have recognized your baking prowess if I'd been there, though. If it makes you feel any better, the ladies thought that you looked great in your flannel and were a dead ringer for Liam Hemsworth. I don't really see it though. You have different noses, and your eyes are green."

Ignoring his random commentary, I nod and reply, "Yeah. The finals are on Sunday, but the Apple Harvest Festival is all weekend. Will you guys stop by? Who all is doing the 5k run?"

Everyone raises their hands except Tristan. "I fly out Friday," he says.

Ah, shucks, what a bummer.

"I signed Daniella up for the race, too," Oliver says. "She hates to run, but I promised to carry her over my shoulder if she can't make it the entire way."

"Last year, Aislinn and I ran back to walk beside her the last mile. I can't imagine trying to run any distance with such short legs," Lachlan teases.

Oliver reaches over, picks a toothpick out of Trent's pile, and flicks it at Lachlan. "Watch it, buddy. That's my wife you're talking about." He winks. "Yeah, me neither. But don't tell her I said that out loud."

"I love distance running. I wish I was staying around for it. I'll be sure to sign up for the race next year," Tristan says, pushing all his toothpicks into the center again.

This time, Trent matches his bet. This hand will finish the game. Tristan flips over a full house with queens as his three, while Trent shows three of a kind in twos.

"Who wins?" Tristan asks.

Trent grumbles, "You. Good game."

Turning toward Tristan, Axel says, "You are the proud winner of Command Center poker night and get to take home all two hundred and fifty toothpicks." Axel claps his hands and stands up from the table to stretch. "Anyone want another beer while I'm up?"

I raise a finger in the air, and Axel nods. "Blonde or brunette?"

"I like my women brunette and ale blonde," I reply with a wink.

"Yeah, I didn't need to know how you take your women," Axel deadpans.

Shrugging, I turn back to the table. "What are we playing now?"

"Axel has a pinball machine," Callum states.

"No! That is off-limits. Remember, no one is allowed in my office," Axel shouts from the kitchen.

Lachlan snickers. "It's his 007 vintage pinball machine. He sucks at it, so I think he's afraid one of us will take his high score spots."

"Not true," Axel replies, cuffing Lachlan upside the back of the head. "How about a round of darts? The first one to two hundred points wins."

"Wins what?" I ask.

"M&Ms," Axel says with a shrug, pointing to a large candy bowl in the center of the coffee table.

"That's what I'm talking about," Trent says, more animated than I've seen him all night. "Why didn't we use those for the poker game?"

"Tristan, are you any good at darts?" Oliver asks, standing up to head into the living room.

"I guess we'll find out," Tristan says, hopping up from his place and following Oliver.

"I think I'm going to head home. I want to stop by Julia's on my way back. She texted me that she wasn't feeling great today," I say, scratching my stomach as I stretch the kinks out of my back. "It was good to see you guys."

To a chorus of goodbyes, I head out the door. The drive to Julia's house is silent. I kept the radio off so I could think. Should I see if River or Maria would bake with me if she is too sick to compete on Sunday? I want to win the prize money for her so badly.

When I pull up to her aunt's Victorian house, I put the car in park but don't cut the ignition. Rotating my wrist, I see the time is just after 10 p.m. All the lights are off, even the porch light. She must've gone to bed early. Since she wakes up at 4 a.m. every morning, I guess this isn't an early bedtime for her.

I'll stop by tomorrow morning to see how she's doing. If she isn't at work, I'll return to the house to check on her. When I look at my phone, my last text from an hour ago is still unread.

Chapter 37

Julia

Thursday, October 24

Leaning over the cold toilet bowl, I retch another few times. The unforgiving porcelain is making my forearms go numb. As soon as my alarm went off this morning and I opened my eyes, the nausea rolled through me. Even though my stomach was empty, I barely reached the bathroom.

I feel like death warmed over. I still don't have a fever, but I feel awful. Dark shadows sprawl against the wall as moonlight silhouettes the old oak tree in my aunt's backyard. I watch the secondhand slowly move around my watch face as the clock ticks closer to 4:10 a.m. I don't know what to do. Should I try to make it into the shower and see if the warm water will snap me out of it as it did on Tuesday and Wednesday?

I'm not sure I can put on a brave face and bake through this discomfort again. My lower back and boobs ache. Trying to think positively, I keep repeating, "Everything will be fine once I soak in hot water and relax my back muscles."

I know River noticed my discomfort the last two days, but he kindly said nothing other than to tell me he had the afternoon handled and to head home to rest. I feel bad I've been slacking off this week.

I'm glad the baking competition is over this weekend. I need rest. Maria was right. I am burning the candle at both ends, and this is my body's way of telling me to slow down. I can't let Declan or the community down. Everyone depends on me to make the town look good on national television.

Groaning, I basically slide to the floor as my stomach threatens to roll again. Crawling into the shower, I reach up and flip the water on, huddling against the wall so the cold water doesn't touch me. The old house is chilly enough that I don't need to catch a cold from taking a cool shower in the brisk autumn weather.

Shivering, I anxiously wait for the water to warm up. I extend my toes so they can monitor the temperature. Leaning my head back against the cool tile, I fight the urge to nod off.

My eyes snap open when it hits me. I'd told Maria I get nauseous when I PMS, which is true. Only I was supposed to start on Monday. With the birth control I've taken for the last five years, I've been like clockwork. Monday morning at 10 a.m. Now, it's Thursday. This is like senior year all over again. Why didn't I make the connection earlier? Maybe because I didn't have my aunt here to point it out to me this time. I've tried desperately to block that entire situation out of my memory. The pain is still too raw if I allow myself to focus on it.

I have the same plans and dreams, which revolve around a bakery in Paris. Nothing has changed except my age.

I missed my period. So what? Three days isn't very late. I need to remember that I've been highly stressed, and stress is known to delay periods in women all over the world. Maybe I should try some yoga or meditation.

Breathe in and out. I force myself to take ten measured breaths. Getting to my knees, I use the wall to brace my weight. I feel exactly like I did the last time this happened, on the day after graduation. After speaking with my parents, my aunt bought me a plane ticket for the next day. They told me it was for the best. All the doctor appointments that followed were awful to endure alone at eighteen.

The symptoms are too familiar. No, I can't let my mind get carried away. These are the same symptoms I get from PMS. Maybe they aren't usually this severe, but they are the same nonetheless.

After showering off, I feel marginally better. I throw on an old t-shirt and sweats. I don't intend to dress up to bake when I feel this awful. I force down some plain yogurt with granola and a cup of coffee. My stomach felt like it was eating itself. It was getting to the point where I couldn't tell if I was feeling hunger pains or stomach cramps. Maybe I haven't eaten frequently enough. I've always struggled with low blood sugar, so perhaps I'm simply hungry. I take a dose of Tylenol and cross my fingers that it will kick in soon.

I slowly walk out the door and slide into my car on unsteady legs. I'm out of breath from the exertion it took to climb down the back porch stairs. This isn't good. Maybe something else is seriously wrong with me, and I need to go to urgent care. I knock my head into the headrest while I contemplate my options.

Either drive to urgent care now or go in and quietly get my work done. Option two lets me see if the fog clears, and I bounce back. It would be really embarrassing if I got to the urgent care and started my period. It would also be a waste of money since I don't have good health insurance.

Well, that settles it. I have no desire to embarrass myself, and the kitchen is supposed to be busy with orders today. Placing my hands on my lower belly, I whisper, "Please start, period." It's not like my body will listen to me, but it's worth a shot.

I pull into the bakery, and River shuts off his Harley as if he were waiting for me to arrive. Still feeling weak from lack of sleep and calories, I slip out of the car and steady myself on the door frame.

"Julia, you don't look very good. Are you sure you aren't sick?" River asks, striding toward me confidently. He gently slides one arm around my waist and helps me to the back door of the store.

With a soft smile, I reply, "I'm fine. I didn't get much sleep last night, and my back pain is still making me nauseous."

Frowning, he says, "Maybe you should take the next two days off and drop out of the competition. Your body sounds like it's demanding you should rest. Your health is more important than some competition."

Shaking my head, I respond, "No. I need the prize money. The town and Declan are counting on me to compete for the community. I want to make everyone proud."

With a raised brow, River pushes open the door and ushers me inside. He leads me to my workstation. Before he turns away, he places a hand on my forehead. "At least you don't feel warm. Any other symptoms?"

"No. Just lower back pain," I murmur because I don't want to tell him my boobs are tender or my uterus is cramping. He doesn't need that tidbit of information to assess my overall health.

"Okay, then." He claps and strides to the coat rack to hang up his leather jacket. Grabbing two aprons, he tosses one to me and walks to his workstation. "What would you prefer to make first? I'll get you all the ingredients. Muffins would be the easiest on your body, with no rolling or kneading. Today, we planned on making chocolate chip banana, blueberry, and pumpkin muffins. Is that still okay?"

Pressing my lips together, I nod in silent agreement. Muffins. I can make muffin batter. River sets all the ingredients on the table before me to make chocolate chip banana muffins first. The moment I peel the first banana, the stench of an overly ripe banana hits my senses, and I swear I turn three shades of green. I suck in a deep breath and hold it while I quickly peel the rest. Turning, I toss the peels in the garbage and lift my shirt to take another breath against the smell of laundry detergent.

I quickly add the rest of the wet ingredients, the vanilla quickly overpowers the banana smell. I sigh shakily when the nausea temporarily subsides. You can do this, Julia.

For the next few hours, I push through and lose myself in the soothing repetition of baking. Maria arrives and frowns at my appearance. "Boss lady, you aren't looking better today." Leaning in, she whispers, "Did you start your period yet?"

I shake my head and look away so she doesn't see the lie falling from my lips. "I'm due to start any day." Monday. I was due to start Monday, but if I tell her this, her hyperactive thoughts will spiral faster than Britt's. She may not have loose lips like Britt, but her rapid-fire responses are sure to alight my anxiety, which is already pumping double time. This is the most stressed I've been in a long time.

Maria wraps her arms around my neck and whispers into my hair. "Have you been? You know? Active?"

I lean back and narrow my eyes at her. "What are you trying to imply?"

Gnawing on her lower lip, she looks at River, who's ignoring our hushed conversation. "You should maybe take a test. Just to rule it out."

My cheeks flame because Declan and I haven't broadcasted our romantic activities together. In public, we look like we're dancing around each other. Just a couple of old flames, checking to see if there's still a spark. Little does Maria know, there's more than a spark, it's a raging bonfire, which I'll need to douse with ice water before I travel halfway around the world.

Britt and Elin come into the kitchen during their lunch break at noon. Britt sits on the stool I'd pulled up to perch on as my energy quickly faded throughout the morning. Popping a bite of muffin in her mouth, she narrows her eyes at me. "You don't look so hot."

Grumbling, I swipe my hair out of my face. "I felt awful earlier, but whatever the problem was passed by mid-morning. I feel okay, right now. I'm just worn out. Do you like the muffin, Britt?"

Elin tilts her head and takes a long look at me. Her eyes widen, but she presses her lips together when I shake my head. Britt needs to stay utterly oblivious to my potential issue. I don't need the entire town to know what might be happening to my body.

"It's amazing! I need another one of these," Britt remarks before striding back to the front counter.

"Grab one for me, Britt!" Elin hollers before rushing to my side. "Are you okay?"

I grab her shoulders and pull her face close to mine. "Elin, I need your help. After work, can you stop by my house and bring me a test?"

"What kind of test? I thought you had a valid driver's license," she hisses.

"No. No." Leaning so my lips are beside her ear, I murmur, "A pregnancy test."

She leaps away from me, almost knocking me on my butt as her eyes go wide. Her eyes dart from River to me and back to River. "You?"

I quickly shake my head. "Declan," I hiss.

She blows out a sigh of relief and gives me a thumbs-up. Hitching her thumb over her shoulder in the direction Britt went, she makes the motion of zipping her lips. I close my eyes and nod. My lips mouth the words, "Thank you."

"I'll see you after work," she says, squeezing my shoulder gently. "Hang in there for a few more hours."

After I tell them goodbye, I call Trent. The phone rings twice before he picks up. "Hello?" he says.

"Hi, Dr. Walsh. This is Julia Fournier. I just wanted to let you know I've been under the weather and won't be able to make our appointment this afternoon."

"Take care of yourself, Julia. Let's touch base next week. Be sure to call me if you need any help, okay?"

"Thank you. I really appreciate it. Maybe I'll see you this weekend at the Apple Harvest Festival if I'm feeling better."

"Sounds great. Paisley and I will be there Saturday and Sunday. We're coming to cheer you on in the baking finals. I hope you're back to normal tomorrow. Get some rest and stay hydrated."

"Thank you. Bye!" I click off the phone when I hear his mumbled bye and wince. Everyone is counting on me to compete and win. I can't let the community down.

Chapter 38
Julia

The grandfather clock in the hallway sounds louder by the minute. The ticking, which once sounded soothing, is wearing on my last nerve as it seems to match my rapidly increasing heartbeat.

I'm standing in the entryway, looking through the front window like the busybody on the block. At least I don't have a pair of binoculars around my neck. Slap a white curly perm, and I'm basically Sophia from *The Golden Girls.* My behavior made me think about *101 Dalmatians* because each dog who passed resembled their owner. I saw three different people walking their dogs. My favorite was the bulldog. The guy holding its leash could probably bench press twice his weight.

I'd only left my observation perch to use the bathroom and eat. Luckily, I could eat a regular lunch and a big dinner. I'm no longer shaky or suffering from hunger pangs. Maybe whatever plagued me the last few days has subsided. A girl can dream.

Sighing, my eyes drift as far down my street as I can see. Going up on my tiptoes doesn't gain me much. My fingers went numb about thirty minutes ago as I clung to the curtain with a death grip. Elin's car pulls up, and I let the curtain flutter shut so she doesn't see me watching my driveway like a crazy person. What would she think if she knew I'd been standing in my entryway since 4 p.m.? It was now 7 p.m.

The doorbell rings, and I force myself to count to ten before answering the door. As I tug it open, Elin smiles, then glances over her shoulder and hands me the paper bag in her grasp.

"Sorry I'm so late. I drove to Whitefish to buy the tests so no one here would question me," she says, rushing past me into the living room. Plopping into a wingback chair, she takes a deep breath. "The pharmacist walked me through the process. Have a seat."

I fight the urge to tell her I've taken a pregnancy test before. I try to act oblivious to avoid any questions. My eyes roam over the mantle above the fireplace. It's still lined with photos of me at various ages. The last two are photos from my senior year when I stayed here. Picking up the embroidered pillow my aunt made, I climb onto the couch and hug it to my chest, hoping it will provide me strength and comfort.

Grabbing the paper bag off the coffee table, where I placed it when I entered the room, Elin pulls two boxes out. "Why are there two?" I ask.

"Just to be sure we don't get a bad test. False positives are always possible, but you aren't likely to have four false positives," she sighs. "Actually, I'm not a doctor, so maybe you can get four false positives, but that seems like a stretch to me."

"Alright. I see your point. Go on," I reply, motioning for her to continue. I push myself further into the corner of the couch and cross my legs.

Reaching into the paper bag again, she pulls out a stack of cups. "I also bought these paper cups. I wasn't sure if you had any or not."

I shake my head. "I don't think my aunt has cups in her cupboards like those. At least, I haven't come across any."

Elin tears open the package and pulls out a cup, handing it to me. "Take this to the bathroom and pee in it. Then, once you have about an inch of pee in the cup, take three tests and stick them in the cup. After five minutes, we'll check to see what they say. The best-case scenario is they're all negative, right? Or are we hoping for all positive?"

My eyes widen. "Definitely hope for all negative. I have too much going on, among other things, to deal with a positive pregnancy test."

"Okay." Crossing her fingers, she closes her eyes, and her lips move silently. When her eyes pop open, she smiles widely. "Wish made."

"What about the fourth?" I ask, slowly pushing myself off the couch.

"Well, the pharmacists said the best results occur when your urine is concentrated first thing in the morning. If you get a mix of positive and negative, it would be worth trying again when you wake up. I didn't think you'd want to wait until morning, so it's worth a shot," she says, tucking her legs up underneath her.

Exhaling a deep breath, I grab three tests and head to the bathroom to pee in a paper cup.

I avoid peeing on my hand like a champ and plop the three tests inside. At first, I pace back and forth until I look at my watch and realize only thirty seconds have passed. I throw open the bathroom door, and Elin falls backward, tumbling into the room.

"Sorry," I mumble. "I didn't realize you were there."

"I was trying to offer some moral support without actually being in the bathroom and holding your free hand," she grumbles, getting on her hands and knees. Standing up, she looks me up and down. "How many more minutes until we know?"

"Four minutes left," I reply. Walking out to the kitchen, I fill up the electric kettle to make some tea. My fingers nervously drum the counter as I stare at my watch.

"Do you want me to bring you your bunny to cuddle?" she asks, looking over her shoulder toward the living room where Madeleine's cage sits.

Shaking my head, I murmur, "No. I was cuddling her while I waited for you. I put her back right before you arrived."

"How about a game called *Would You Rather*?" I nod, figuring the distraction couldn't hurt. She smiles, leaning on the kitchen island. "Would you rather have a picnic on a hillside at sunset or dinner on the top floor of a skyscraper?"

"I'd rather have the picnic. I'm not a huge fan of eating in front of people. What about you?" I ask.

"I've never dated anyone who could afford to take me to dinner in a skyscraper, so I'm picking the picnic. I'm too broke to pay half a fancy restaurant bill. I don't want to set my sights too high. You know?" she replies, pouring the hot water into two mugs and dropping in chamomile tea bags.

"Would you rather live in a small cottage surrounded by a forest or in an apartment within walking distance of everything?" I ask.

I close my eyes and try to picture a small flat within walking distance of the Eiffel Tower, the Louvre, Notre Dame, and the Arc de Triomphe, but nothing happens. My mind brings up pictures of Declan in the orchard, following him into the treehouse, and hiking in the forest at the edge of his property. I shake my head to clear my thoughts.

"Oh, a cottage for sure. But I'd rather it was a log cabin than an Irish cottage. I prefer mountains to the ocean. What about you?"

Elin cups her mug between her hands and taps her index finger against the outside as she waits for my response.

"Actually, a cottage. The one thing I dread about moving back to Paris is the tiny flat I'll be living in since anything with multiple bedrooms and bathrooms would be out of my price range," I say, dunking my tea bag.

"Do you prefer driving on wide open roads where you may not see a car for miles or be able to catch a taxi by just raising your hand?" Elin is watching me curiously.

"I enjoy driving. When I'm in Paris, I rarely use my car. I think I'll go with wide-open roads," I reply.

"Me, too." She smirks, lifting her mug to hide her expression. "What about, would you rather have a tight-knit community or anonymity?"

Raising an eyebrow, I grumble, "I see where you're going with these questions. Why can't we have chocolate or vanilla ice cream?" When she shrugs, I reply, "Tight-knit community is more my style.'"

"Same. Alright, last one. Would you rather walk around at night and look at city lights or a starry sky?" Elin plops down on the kitchen stool and lifts the mug to her lips, softly blowing across the surface.

"A starry sky," I reply wistfully. "I love how there's no light pollution here, and the stars explode across the sky on a clear night."

Her brow furrows. "Me, too. So, why do you want to live in Paris if you prefer living in the middle of nowhere?"

I push my lips out. "Because I've dreamt of owning a patisserie since I was little."

Opening her arms wide, she replies, "Can't you say you've already opened one in Topaz Falls? It seems extremely successful and will be mentioned on national television when the baking competition show airs. I mean, right?" She shrugs, then says, "I'll really miss you if you return to Paris. Also, what will you do if the test is positive? Will you tell Declan?" I can't answer those questions. Not right now. Glancing at my watch, I see it's been six minutes. I turn on the ball of my foot and race to the bathroom with Elin right on my heels. At the bathroom door, I stop, bracing myself against the doorjamb.

"I can't do it, Elin. Have you ever taken a pregnancy test before?" I murmur.

"No," Elin squeaks. When I look over my shoulder, she looks everywhere but at me, and her face is bright red.

"Would you mind checking for me? I think if I look, I might throw up," I grumble.

She mashes her lips together. "They've been sitting in your pee. I think I'll throw up if I have to touch them."

Hanging my head in defeat, I trudge into the bathroom. My feet feel like they're stuck in a slab of wet concrete as I shuffle to the cup. Closing my eyes, I take a deep breath. "What symbol means positive?"

Chuckling, she responds, "I bought you the ones that have the word pregnant written out. No symbols to try to decipher."

When I look down at the cup, I gasp. "Two of them say pregnant, and one does not. What does that mean?"

Elin makes a weird gurgling noise behind me. When I turn around, Declan's broad shoulders are standing behind her. His wide eyes show his shock at what he just walked in on. "Elin is pregnant?" he asks.

"No!" she shouts as the world goes black around me.

Chapter 39

Declan

What did I just walk in on? In slow motion, Julia's eyes roll back, and her body goes limp. Elin lunges for her, catching Julia before her head hits the tile floor. Blood sluices in my ears as time suddenly snaps back to normal speed.

"Declan!" Elin shouts. "Help me. I can't hold her. She's slipping out of my grip."

I rush into the small bathroom and scoop Julia into my arms. With her cradled against my chest, I stride to the living room and lay her on the couch. Reaching for a pillow, I stuff it behind her head, then gently move her hair out of her face.

"What's going on?" my voice rumbles, uncertainty in my tone.

"That's not my story to tell," Elin mumbles as she walks past me into the kitchen.

I take a moment to look over Julia's unconscious form. "Do we need to go to the doctor?" I yell.

"No. No. Well, yes, but not right now. Julia was just overwhelmed, and with all the vomiting she's been doing, I think she just fainted. She was weak. I'm getting her something to drink and eat," Elin says so quickly that I have to strain to understand her.

"Is she sick?" I ask.

I know she wasn't feeling great on Monday, but I assumed it was just fatigue from the competition and then waking up before dawn to bake at the bakery. I push my fingers into my hair. Did I cause this? Am I pushing her too hard? I shouldn't have pressed her to be in the baking competition when she was reopening her aunt's bakery.

Elin makes a weird sound, causing my eyes to shoot to hers. She winces. "Well, not in the sense you're thinking?"

My eyes narrow. "So, if you aren't pregnant, then who—" For the first time in my life, I gasp like Aislinn. It hits me like a ton of bricks right in the gut.

Julia's pregnant.

"There you go, big guy. Now you're getting it," she murmurs, widening her eyes for me to connect the dots faster.

"Is it mine?" I whisper, my eyes suddenly struggling to focus on the various colors of woven thread in the carpet at my feet. Where did the rug come from?

"Breathe, Declan. Keep your head between your knees and breathe. Dammit, I do not need both of you passing out on me. You guys are like those fainting goats. I can just imagine you as parents. 'Hey, Mom and Dad, I got my nose pierced.' Splat, you both go down like a sack of potatoes." Elin is mumbling about goats and piercings. I'm so lost as my head spins. Her voice sounds garbled like she's talking to me through bubble wrap.

"Elin? Declan? What happened? Oh my goodness, what's wrong with Declan? Did he spill something on the floor?" Julia shouts, but it sounds like she is three rooms away.

"What the heck is wrong with you two? You! Lie down. No moving, Mama. Declan? Are you still with us?" Elin pats my back, and I suck in a sharp breath. Her fingers snap beside my ears causing me to flinch.

The bubble around my head pops, and sounds flood my system all at once. I sit up, and the world momentarily spins. "I have to pee," I blurt and rush to the bathroom. I shake out my arms. My legs misstep beneath me like I just got off a ship.

I don't need to pee. But I need to see those tests for myself. I stumble into the bathroom and lock the door. Pressing my back against the door, I close my eyes and take a deep breath. Why the hell does it smell like piss in here? I crack open one eye and look around. The bathroom is just how I remember it from when I'd used it in high school. Only the towels are different. The royal blue stands out nicely against the white cabinets.

My sight lands on a paper cup with three sticks poking out the top. I take a tentative step toward it, then screw my eyes shut. Taking a deep breath, my gut churns. I hate the smell of urine. Is there a litter box in here?

When I open my eyes, I stare into the cup. Two of the sticks say pregnant, and the other says not pregnant. Does that mean there are two babies? It's then that I notice the cup is full of piss. My stomach revolts, and I dive for the door.

I don't do well with seeing bodily fluids. When we did the Presidential Fitness Testing in elementary school, any time a kid threw up from running the mile, I threw up, too. It was incredibly annoying.

"Dec?" Julia calls from the living room. My feet carry me there on autopilot as I try to wrap my mind around what I saw.

Am I going to be a dad? She said she couldn't have a baby.

When I enter the living room, I lean against the wall. "Twins?" I rasp. "You're pregnant with twins?" I hold up two fingers and stare at them in disbelief.

"What?" Elin says. "As far as I'm aware, there's no way of knowing until the ultrasound. I can't say I know from experience."

Julia meets my gaze with wide eyes. "I took three tests; two were positive, and one was negative. It doesn't mean a positive for each baby."

I breathe a sigh of relief. "This might be an offensive question, but is it mine? I know we never spoke about being exclusive. Hell, we just got back together."

Julia smiles softly. "Yes, Declan. You're the only guy I've ever slept with in Topaz Falls."

"It would sound better if we widened the range to the United States," I say with false bravado.

Mashing her lips together, she replies, "Alright. You are the only guy I've ever slept with in the United States. I mean, we could even go as far as, say, in all of North and South America. Technically, the only person outside of France."

Smiling smugly, I respond, "Much better. So, what's the plan?"

Both Julia and Elin sober, sharing a silent exchange. "That's a good question. So, Declan, I was hoping to leave the past in the past when I came back, but it looks like history was hell-bent on repeating itself."

I look at her, confused. "What are you talking about?"

Taking a deep breath, Julia says, "The reason I left so abruptly after graduation senior year was because that week, I'd discovered I was pregnant. Due to a health condition I was born with, my aunt thought it would be best to immediately fly me home to be assessed by my specialists."

"You were pregnant with our child, and you didn't tell me?" I stand up and pace in disbelief. "So, we have a seven-year-old, and you never told me?" My voice cracks, and I squat down as the pain splinters my chest. I've always wanted to be a father, like my dad. Hands-on and affectionate. Always willing to throw a baseball on a Saturday night or look for bugs at dawn. Tears blur my vision as I fight back the sob locked deep in my chest. "Is it a boy or a girl? Why did you leave me out of it? You knew how much I wanted a family. It was all I ever talked about. I never spoke of college. For me, it was always a family and the orchard."

Julia's small hand grips my shoulder. "No, Dec. I miscarried at seven weeks. The condition I was born with makes it almost impossible for me to carry a healthy pregnancy to term. This is the reason why I never came back. It's why I couldn't face you. Knowing what you wanted most in the world, I could never give you."

"What?" I whisper in disbelief. "Having a family doesn't mean the child has to biologically be mine. We could adopt or foster. I would have run a doggy daycare if it meant spending every day with you," I murmur.

Standing up, I fold Julia into my arms and press her into my chest. She quietly sobs, and I startle when I hear the front door click shut. My gaze follows Elin's lithe form as she rushes to her car, wiping her cheeks with the back of her hand.

"What if I miscarry again, Dec? My doctor told me that without medical intervention, most of my eggs weren't viable, and I'd miscarry in the first trimester. He immediately put me on birth control to prevent an accidental pregnancy from happening. Obviously, it wasn't one hundred percent effective." Julia intertwines her fingers against my lower back, and I rock us back and forth as I think of what to say.

"First, we need to get you a doctor's appointment to make sure you're healthy and get you on vitamins and stuff," I say. "Tomorrow morning, I'll call Dr. Duffy and see if he can squeeze us in for an emergency consultation or something. Can we video chat with your French specialist doctor?"

"Thanks, Dec. You'd be okay with this either way? I mean, there's always a chance it was a false positive, and I'll start my period any minute," she grumbles.

Kissing her hair, I murmur, "I'll support you any way I can, but remember, I just want you. Kids, dogs, or bunnies are all an added bonus of spending my life by your side."

"By the way, why are you here? Don't get me wrong. I'm glad you came so we could get this conversation behind us," she says, tilting her head back to look at me through red-rimmed eyes. The grey seems a little duller, but an unmistakable spark still draws me to her like a moth to a flame.

Oh, right. Dropping my arms, I walk back to the entryway and grab the paper bag I brought. I walk back into the living room with a big smile. I pull out a container of chicken noodle soup, a roll, and a slice of pumpkin cake and set it on the table in front of the couch. "I wanted to check on you and bring you some food from Mama M's. I went down there for dinner and saw chicken noodle soup on the menu. I remember Aunt Rita making it for you when you were sick during senior year."

Tears prick the corner of Julia's eyes as she sniffs. "That's really sweet, Dec. Can you grab me a spoon?"

I return from the kitchen a moment later with a spoon and napkin.

"I also wanted to ask you about your agreement with Anders. Are you serious about selling the bakery? Even if you're pregnant with our baby?" I ask, my voice sounding steadier than I feel. This could blow up in my face. She could tell me to forget it.

She nods hesitantly. "I'd like to. Paris is my dream. I almost made it before my dreams burned down earlier this year. I want to prove to the world and myself that I could operate a successful patisserie in Paris."

I press my lips together and clap my hands. "Then, I'm coming with you. I'll let my parents know when they get home from the rehabilitation center next week. They won't officially retire for another ten to fifteen years. Maybe by then, we'll be ready for a change of pace. If we aren't, then so be it. I just need you."

Julia stands and cups my jaw. Blinking back tears, she murmurs, "Oh, Declan. My sweet, sweet, Declan." Leaning in, she presses her mouth to mine. The salty taste of her tears coats her lips, and I pull her body flush against me. Leaning my forehead against hers, she says, "Let's take one step at a time."

"Regardless, I'm fighting for us." My tone leaves no doubt in my words.

Chapter 40

Declan
Friday, October 25

I sit beside Julia in the outdated reception area of Dr. Duffy's office. I don't think this place has been redecorated since Nixon was in office. I'm almost positive Dr. Duffy was practicing back then. Doc is a legend in town. I think he delivered every child from the 1970s to 2000s, but that may be an over-exaggeration. My mom always likes to remind him that he was the first person to ever make her kids cry.

I've looked at every magazine, photo, and fish about twenty times, struggling not to yawn from boredom. If I look carefully at the vinyl chair by the fish tank, I bet I could see the first letter of my name written with the blue pen I'd found in my mom's purse when I was six.

My knee bounces uncontrollably. I can hardly sit still. I'm thankful Dr. Duffy could see us today, but when the receptionist told me to show up, and he'd fit us in when he could, I didn't think we'd be waiting for over an hour. Families have come and gone. Little kids have received their token lollipop for getting a vaccine. Growing up, they were the good suckers; now, they're special lollipops meant to prevent cavities. Is that even possible? It reminds me of fat-free mayo or sugar-free chocolate milk.

Julia's small hand lands on my knee, stilling it. When I look up, she smiles with an arched brow. "Are you doing okay, Dec?"

Furrowing my brow, I whisper, "Yes. I just want you seen by a doctor so they can tell me you and the baby are going to be alright."

She smiles tightly, and I know her thoughts are verging toward negativity. I can see it in her eyes. She's convinced herself it will lead to a miscarriage like last time, but we won't know until we meet with the doctor. I've chosen to stay positive. Worried and nervous, but still positive.

"Julia Fournier?" Lynn, the nurse I've known for two decades, shouts from the door leading to the exam rooms.

Julia stands and grabs my hand. We walk to the door, and as it closes behind us, Nurse Lynn says, "This is an OB appointment, right?"

I nod. "Yes, we are here for an Oh Baby appointment," I clarify.

Nurse Lynn cackles and shakes her head. Julia leans in and whispers, "OB stands for Obstetrics, which covers pregnancy and delivery." She pats my forearm, and I fight the urge to groan. I like my version better.

Julia stands and gets her weight and height measured. "Did you grow? You weren't 5'5" in high school, were you?"

She giggles. "I wasn't the one who grew. You were only 6'1" in high school. Now, you're easily 6'3" without shoes on. When you wear your boots, you're huge."

"That's what she said," I whisper, and Julia rolls her eyes. Grumbling, I say, "I'm still shorter than Lachlan, though."

She makes a pouty face and mouths, "Poor Declan, he's a whole inch shorter than his big brother."

I wink at her and rub her back. "Yeah, yeah. Just think. The little peanut in your stomach could be itching to reach 6'5" or taller."

Julia pales. "How did your mom deliver two mega babies?"

"We were both about ten pounds, I believe," I squint, trying to remember. "Ingrid was smaller. She was only nine pounds, I think."

Sitting down, Nurse Lynn puts a blood pressure cuff on Julia's arm, then clamps something on her pointer finger. "Blood pressure and heart rate are normal. You don't have a fever. How has your morning sickness been?" she asks.

"Terrible," Julia murmurs. "I'm a baker, so I wake up at 4 a.m. Mornings are the worst time for me to deal with nausea."

"Alright, dear. Let's get you both to an exam room. Dr. Duffy will be here to see you shortly. He should have some homeopathic or prescription options for the nausea." Nurse Lynn ushers us through an oak door covered in scuff marks and remnants of stickers. "He will be in soon." She closes the door, leaving us to wait in the confined space.

We sit on a double-wide chair in the exam room. My arm drapes along the back, cradling Julia into my side. The walls are mint green with pictures of hot air balloons flying over different parts of the United States, looking like a sea of color floating in the sky. I've been in this room a few times over the years, and I notice something unique in the photos every time. The one on the far wall has a dog in one of the hot air balloon baskets with its front paws propped up on the edge. A woman with long white hair has a hand on the dog's head as she looks down at the ground below.

Glancing at my watch, I notice we've been in the room for almost forty-five minutes. Knuckles rap against the door three times before the handle turns. The bushy silver curls of Dr. Duffy poke through the door, his stooped, lean frame following. He immediately starts talking like Daffy Duck, an act he's done since I was a toddler.

He does it for every pediatric patient as a way to ease the tension, and for me, it always works.

Julia's face is priceless as she stares at Dr. Duffy. He laughs at her expression. "Sorry, young lady. My name is Dr. Duffy, and talking like Daffy Duck has always been my thing with young patients. In my eyes, Declan is still five years old."

Pressing her lips together as a smile tugs at the corner of her lips, Julia nods. "It's a lovely accent you have, doctor."

He chuckles as he shakes a finger at her. He walks over to the round spinning stool in front of the computer system and sits down with a sigh. The pleather groans beneath his weight as it slowly depresses. It took all my strength not to sit and spin on it while we waited.

Adjusting his green-rimmed glasses, he opens the chart in his hands. "I want to apologize for making you wait so long." He sniffs and looks up, meeting my eyes. His gaze cuts to Julia, and he speaks directly to her. "With the digital form you signed on our patient portal after Declan made the appointment, I contacted your doctor in Paris. After receiving your medical history, I reached out to a colleague who does genetic oncology research."

I furrow my brow. Does Julia have cancer? My eyes cut to hers, but she's staring unblinkingly at Dr. Duffy.

Swallowing thickly, Julia rotates her body toward mine. With her hands folded in her lap, she takes a deep breath. "Dec. When I was seven, I was diagnosed with leukemia. I underwent two and a half years of treatment, which is longer than the standard protocol because it turned out I had a genetic mutation. It's called a Robertsonian translocation 15;21. My parents were both tested, and neither of them tested positive, but it's the main reason I'm an only child. They didn't want to risk having another child with this issue."

Dr. Duffy continues when he sees Julia struggling. "My colleague informed me the Robertsonian translocations of chromosomes fifteen and twenty-one increase the risk of leukemia astronomically."

"I don't understand what you're talking about," I reply, scratching my ear.

With a soft smile, Dr. Duffy straightens his back and sets the folder on the counter beside the computer screen. Holding up both hands, he starts to speak. "Alright, when parents make a baby, half the DNA comes from the father and the other from the mother." He pauses, so I nod for him to continue. "When their halves combine, there is an even split in a healthy baby. The chromosomes match up and create a new individualized set for the baby. In a translocation case, the chromosomes don't match up properly. In Julia's situation, the long arms of fifteen and twenty-one combine to make a unique chromosome, leaving her one short chromosome."

I picture the little x diagram from high school science, where all the chromosomes look like worms. Nodding, I smile tightly. "I think I understand, but what does this have to do with Julia?"

"Well, because she had a positive pregnancy test, we can assume the halves of your DNA successfully split and combined with the halves of her DNA. Now, the struggle for people with this translocation is if the egg also contains the translocation, then it can't equally split and successfully bind to your DNA. In this instance, one of two things occurs. It's possible the body miscarries the pregnancy within the first twelve weeks. The other possibility is Julia's body will carry your baby to term, but then your child may be at a higher risk for a chromosomal imbalance." Dr. Duffy allows that all to sink in.

"Is this why you miscarried in high school?" I whisper.

She sniffs and nods. "The doctors believe so, yes."

"Now, not all of Julia's eggs contain translocation DNA. She will have some healthy eggs. For all we know, that's what happened this time," he states, shrugging both shoulders.

"How do we find out what to expect?" I ask because I think Julia is mentally shutting down. I tug her into my arms and gently run my fingers through her hair.

"My colleague suggests you undergo genetic testing to ensure you and the baby are healthy. This is above my pay grade. With retirement around the corner, I've become a Daffy Duck prescription pad for Topaz Falls. I'm not up to date with the current treatments and interventions. The first question is, do you intend to keep the baby?" Dr. Duffy isn't looking at me, even though I nod like a fool.

Gnawing on her bottom lip, Julia looks from me to Dr. Duffy. A watery smile graces her gorgeous face, and I reach out to grasp her delicate hand in mine. "I'll follow you anywhere, Julia."

She slowly nods. "I'd like to proceed with genetic testing. Even if I miscarry in the next couple of weeks, I'd like to learn more about my options for future pregnancies." Turning toward me, she murmurs, "I'd like to keep this knowledge between the three of us until we are sure the baby is healthy enough to be carried to term. I can't bear to explain a miscarriage to the entire town."

Pressing my lips together, I whisper, "You might want to text Elin since she was there for the entire reveal yesterday."

"Goodness, was that only yesterday?" she mutters, causing all of us to chuckle.

"Now, the notes from Nurse Lynn state you're struggling with morning sickness. I'm going to put in a prescription for a multivitamin and anti-nausea drug. I'll also include our homeopathic list if you want to avoid taking any medication. In our new mother packet, you'll find a list of foods and activities to avoid or limit. If you have any questions, please call or log in to the portal and message us. I try to respond during lunch or at the end of the day."

We both nod as he goes through more items in the packet. I desperately try to think of what else to ask, but my mind becomes blank.

Clapping his thighs, Dr. Duffy stands and extends his hand, which I shake enthusiastically. "Thanks for squeezing us in on such short notice. It means the world to me—to us."

"No problem," he replies in his Daffy Duck voice, winking at us before he opens the door. "On the table, you'll find a gown. Go ahead and get changed so I can do a quick physical exam. I'd also like to do a blood test to check your hCG levels, blood type, Rh factor, and hemoglobin. We'll also need a urine sample. These tests will help us confirm what you found on the at-home pregnancy tests. Nurse Lynn will bring you the paperwork for the referral. You'll have to go to Missoula to meet with Dr. Johannson, but she's brilliant in this field. Her clinic will be able to help you much more than my little practice."

"Thank you," Julia replies before rushing over and quickly hugging him. He blushes three shades of pink before patting her head and leaving without another word.

"Should I call and make an appointment in Missoula?" I ask, wrapping my arms around Julia's waist. As I rock us back and forth, my fingers snag in her belt loops.

"I think it's for the best. I'm sorry I've kept all this from you, Dec. Leukemia was two years of my childhood that I tried to block out. The entire process was extensive. I spent a total of seventy-six days in the hospital during the first year of treatment. All the port accesses and arm pokes are traumatic for me. I get terrible nightmares when I think about that time too much." She tugs down the collar of her shirt and slides her bra strap to the side. Just below her right clavicle is a faint white scar about an inch in length. "This is the scar from where my port was placed. As soon as I completed the twenty-eight months of treatment, it was removed, and although the scar has faded, not all my memories have."

Dropping a kiss on her forehead, I murmur, "I'm here with you through all this. We're going to get through this together. I'm going to stay positive for the both of us, okay?" When Julia nods, I whisper, "Let's go to Whitefish and pick up the medications. If you're feeling up to it, we can stop for dinner, too."

"Thank you, Dec. I—I," she stammers into my chest.

"I love you, blossom," I murmur against her hair.

"I love you, too. I wish I'd told you everything sooner," she sobs against my shirt, her fingers clinging to my flannel. "I thought you'd hate me if you knew I was broken."

"You've never been broken. It will all work out this time. Everything will be fine. Let's take it one day at a time," I whisper.

"One day at a time," she repeats, and I struggle not to hold her tighter. "I think I should probably get into the gown before Dr. Duffy returns." Reluctantly, I release her from my embrace.

"The sooner we can get this confirmed, the quicker we can go get you vitamins and other supplies to make you more comfortable," I say, trying not to get hard as she slowly undresses beside me. There are some things Dr. Duffy doesn't need to see.

An hour later, the exam and tests are done, and Dr. Duffy walks back into the room. "According to the preliminary test results, we can confirm you are pregnant. Congratulations, you two."

The words hit me as the confirmation of our situation envelops me. There is a very good chance that next year, I'll be a dad. I'm going to stay positive for both of us.

Chapter 41

Julia

Saturday, October 26

Declan picked me up a few minutes ago, and we're driving along the open roads further into the countryside. The fields blur past us, a sea of gold against the mountain backdrop of Glacier National Park. Utility poles flash by in a hypnotic rhythm, offset by the occasional tree. Thankfully, the anti-nausea medication worked wonders this morning. I almost feel back to normal.

The questions Elin asked me the other night while we waited for the results of the pregnancy tests have played on repeat every waking moment. My responses are haunting me because she made me question everything. I still haven't started my period, which means Declan and I are one day closer to potentially being parents. Together.

This morning, I placed my promise ring on my right ring finger, and I can't help but rotate it nervously. Declan's gaze lands on my hands, and a grin takes over his face. "Is that the ring I gave you? It still fits?"

Nodding, I return his smile, relieved he recognized it. "Yeah. I hope you don't mind. I missed wearing it."

Arching a brow, he reaches up and quickly lifts the chain over his head where his ring resides. He hands it to me and says, "Can you take the ring off the chain?"

I quickly unlatch the chain and slide the ring off. It lands solidly in the center of my palm. Rotating it in my fingers, I find the initials engraved on the inside and then offer it to him.

He goes to slide it on his right ring finger like mine, but it won't go past the second knuckle. Frowning, he slides it on his pinky. It's a little loose, but at least it goes on. "Looks like my hands have gotten a little larger since I was eighteen," he grumbles.

"Well, I have a feeling you'll have a new band for the left hand in the near future," I whisper.

He wiggles his eyebrows. "Do you, now?" When I nod, he lifts my left hand to his lips and gently kisses each finger. "I like the sound of that. So, are you okay with me coming to Paris with you? I'll let my parents know when they return on Monday."

Rolling my head to look at Declan's strong profile, I murmur, "Can I ask you a few questions?"

His grip tightens on the steering wheel, and he swallows forcibly. "Yeah," he rasps. "Blossom, you can ask me anything. I'm an open book for you."

"Would you rather lie on a blanket and look at stars or go for a walk on a boardwalk under twinkling city lights," I say.

He furrows his brow and opens his mouth before snapping it shut. Clearing his throat, he replies, "I wasn't expecting that to be your question. But, stargazing, without a question."

With a smirk, I continue. "Would you rather live in a cottage on lots of property backing up to a dense forest or a penthouse apartment overlooking a bustling city?"

Narrowing his eyes, he briefly darts his gaze to mine before returning it to the road. "A cottage in the woods. Where are you going with this?"

"Last one, I promise. Would you rather float down a river or go see historical sites?" I ask. Folding my hands in my lap, I stare at my thumbs because I'm ninety-nine percent sure I know the answer.

"This seems like a trick question." When I glance up, he's cutting his gaze to mine. I shake my head, so he replies, "Floating down the river then. Look, if you're trying to show me how I won't fit in with you in Paris, believe me, I know. But I will make it work. If it means clearing and washing dishes or sweeping and hauling out the garbage so you can follow your dreams, then I'm your guy. I don't need a fancy home; I just need you and our baby."

"Declan, that isn't where I was going with those questions," I say, but he reaches out and grasps one of my hands.

Sighing, he replies, "I know I'm not the brightest guy. Anders is pretty sure I have a learning disability called dyscalculia, but I'm smart enough to know I can't live without you. I won't be a doctor or have a high-paying white-collar job, but I don't need that to be the best supporter you've ever known."

"Don't do that, Dec," I say a little louder. "I've never thought you weren't smart just because you didn't go to college or get a corporate job. Hell, I didn't go to a traditional college. Does that make me an unintelligent drop-out?"

He glowers at me and shakes his head, "Of course not. I think you were admirable in following your dream, and the program you were in was rigorous and selective. I'm damn proud of you."

I smirk and respond, "Thank you. I was asking you those questions because I answered them the same way." When he looks at me in confusion, I continue, "The other night, Elin asked me similar questions, and I answered country for every single one. She wondered why I wanted to live in a city if I preferred small-town life."

"Why do you, then?" he asks. His voice is soft as he pulls the truck over so he can give me his undivided attention.

My fingers pick at the frayed seat seam on the right side of my knee. Sucking in a deep breath, I reply, "Because I wanted to run a successful bakery. Elin pointed out I already do. Hop Along Bakery is struggling to keep up with the demand, and soon, I'll need to hire more staff. It's exactly what I dreamed of opening, just in a different town. The more time I'm here, the harder it is for me to remember why, though."

Declan's eyes bore into my temple, so I slowly drag my gaze to meet his. "What are you saying? I need you to spell it out for me."

"I don't want to leave anymore," I whisper as my eyes search his.

A beautiful smile blooms across his face as he wraps both of his hands around mine. "You want to stay?" He hesitates before he clarifies, "You want to stay in Topaz Falls with me?"

I nod and bite my lip. "Yeah, I do. If you still want me."

His hand climbs up my arm, and while gripping the back of my neck, his long fingers tangle in my hair. "Julia, I have wanted you every minute of every day since I first gazed into your flint grey eyes during first period senior year. My desire for you will never change, and over the last eight years, it's only gotten stronger."

With his other hand, he unbuckles my seatbelt, then sinks his fingers into my hip and drags me onto his lap. The steering wheel gently digs into my back, so I press my torso harder against his. My upper body is on fire, and my splayed fingers press up his broad chest, rounding his shoulders. I roll my hips against the ridge below me, eliciting a deep groan from the back of his throat, which I hungrily swallow.

This was the response I was craving from him, and he didn't disappoint. I had hoped he was serious about his declaration to follow me so he'd be thrilled when I told him I'd rather stay with him. The way his hands command my movements and demand more, I can tell he wants this as much as I do.

My thoughts stray to the potential baby in me, and I shiver to think we may have made something great. I refuse to think of the negative possibilities attached to this pregnancy. As Declan promised, we'll take one day at a time and stay positive. I'm calling the specialty clinic on Monday morning to set up our first appointment. The sooner, the better.

I draw my fingers down his chest, causing his body to deliciously quiver beneath my touch. Reaching between us, I unfasten his belt buckle and unclip the button of his jeans. As the zipper lowers, he lifts his hips to ease the pants down. Just as I pull them under his butt, there is a loud rap against his window.

Screaming, I bury my face in his neck. His heart feels like it will leap from his chest as it pounds in rapid thuds against mine. I suck in deep breaths, trying to calm my racing heart. Declan reaches for the door and lowers the driver's side window.

"Edwin. What can I do for you, sheriff?" Declan says a little breathlessly.

With a chuckle, he says, "Well, I'll be damned. I never thought I'd follow this closely in my father's footsteps and bust you two for making out on the side of the highway. In thirty years, will my future kids get the pleasure of busting you two as well?"

"Ha ha," Declan deadpans. "We were just celebrating."

I slowly turn my head and peek under Declan's chin to find Sheriff Edwin Toker staring at us with a stupid grin on his handsome face. It was his first year as a deputy my senior year, and he isn't joking when he reminds us of all the times his dad found us, which is more times than I care to admit. If we couldn't sneak away to the treehouse, Declan's truck was the only other place we could get privacy. Between my aunt operating on baker's hours and his parents up with the sunrise every morning, it made it hard to be alone at either of our houses.

"What kind of news?" Edwin asks.

"The kind where the woman I've loved since I was a teenager is going to stay and be mine forever," Declan says, and a slight shiver skitters down my spine. A smile spreads on my lips. I press my mouth against his stubbled jaw and snuggle into his chest.

Looking off into the distance, Edwin replies, "That is celebratory news. Congratulations, you two." Patting the door, he says, "Well, I don't see the need to bust you, but at our age, you might be more comfortable in a bed." With a wink that makes me blush with embarrassment, he strides back to his cruiser. I lift my head to watch him climb into his vehicle and smile when he chirps his car a few times before flipping around and heading back toward town.

Climbing off Declan's lap, I adjust my shirt and sweep my fingers through my hair. I clear my throat and pull out my phone. Flipping through my contacts, I find the name I want to call and wait for it to ring while I flip it to speakerphone so Declan can hear the conversation.

"Who are you calling?" Declan whispers, but I hold up a finger to quiet him.

"Hello?" Anders says on the other end of the line.

"Anders? It's Julia. Do you have a minute?" I ask, wiping imaginary dust off the dashboard.

Clearing his throat, he says, "Hi, Julia. What can I do for you?"

"Actually, I was calling to see if you'd still honor the cancellation clause you had added to our Sale and Purchase Agreement," I ask, suddenly feeling nervous that there were no loopholes or hidden outs and it was all a trick.

"Of course," he chuckles. "I told you the town has a way of keeping those meant to stay here."

Smiling, I glance at Declan. "It isn't just the town encouraging me to stay. I have quite a few good reasons."

"I'm glad to hear it. Should I let my attorney know Hop Along Bakery will stay under the ownership of Julia Fournier?" he asks with happiness in his voice. "If you haven't told Declan, I'm sure he'll be glad to know you plan to stay," Anders says, and my eyes find the man in question grinning at me.

"Anders, I believe I am one of the many reasons she wants to stay in town," Declan says, and Anders barks out a deep laugh.

"Is that true, Julia?" Anders teases.

"Of course," I reply without hesitation. "The biggest reason."

"Alright, you two love birds. I'll see you at the festival in a little bit. Bye!" Anders hangs up before we can respond.

"One last thing," I murmur as I frantically type on my phone.

"What are you doing?" Declan asks, fighting the urge to crane his neck to see my screen.

With a wink, I lock my phone and jam it in her purse. "Just letting my parents know we'd call them later. I have some exciting news to share with them."

Swallowing thickly, he sucks in a deep breath. "Are you going to tell them about the pregnancy?"

Quirking my lips to the side, I shake my head. "I want it to stay between us for now. Once we meet with the specialist and confirm everything will be okay, I was hoping you'd fly back to Paris with me over Christmas to tell them in person."

"I've never been outside the US," he mutters, picking at the steering wheel.

Grasping his hand, I bring it to my heart. "Then let me show you the world, Dec."

I rotate toward Declan, and he grips the wheel tighter. "I can't wait to meet your parents, blossom. Even though I'd love to take the next right into the back entrance to my place, I know we need to get to the orchard. The festival is due to start in an hour, and without my parents there, I need to make sure it goes off without a hitch. Cameron and Mira are waiting for us. I don't want you to stress your body today. Promise me if you're tired, you'll sit down and rest. Also, Dr. Duffy recommended lots of water and small snacks."

Grinning, I grab Declan's hand. "I promise." This time, the promise seems all-encompassing. I'm promising everything I tried to run away from the first time. I refuse to sacrifice our future this time around.

Chapter 42

Declan

Julia and I hop out of the truck as members of the community race around to set up their booths and activity stations. We have a lot planned today. I pull an extra chair from the stack beside the barn and set it by Mama M's booth.

"Oh, sweet boy. Is this for me? These swollen ankles will be thanking you by noon," Mama M says, plopping into the chair with a groan.

Pressing my lips together, I offer her a tight nod because the chair was actually meant for Julia. I was going to let her rest with Mama M while I ran around like a chicken with my head cut off for an hour. Instead of saying anything, I hurry back to the stack of chairs and grab two more to place at her station in case her husband, Carl, shows up and needs to take a load off.

"Here is an extra chair in case Carl stops by and one for Julia. I figured she could keep you company for a little bit," I say, and Julia subtly rolls her eyes.

"Dec? Hop Along Bakery has its own booth. Why don't we go see how Celeste and Vincent are doing? I told them I'd stop by and help for a little while," Julia says, motioning to the chair. "I'd appreciate the chair, though. Thank you," she whispers as she leans into me and kisses the corner of my mouth.

I pick up the chair and feel like an idiot for forgetting she had her own booth. Now it seems like I'm giving this stupid chair a tour of the festival as I lug it around under my arm. Hop Along Bakery is on the other side of the open field. Julia's weekend workers are scurrying around when we arrive.

When Julia steps up to the tables, they look up and smile. "You two did a great job. This is a beautiful display."

Vincent tugs at the back of his neck. "Actually, we can't take credit for it."

Julia furrows her brows. "Then who did it?" She looks up at me, but I shrug my shoulder. We don't have enough staff to assign decorators to each booth. Everyone who wants to participate is supposed to be in charge of their own station.

A familiar laugh has me turning around. Britt and Elin stride toward us with wicker baskets and old-fashioned crates. "Oh no! You got here too early, Julia!" Britt shouts. "This was supposed to be a surprise. We aren't done yet."

Elin holds up the crates in her hand. "We're lining up cookies and brownies in these."

"Muffins will go in these baskets," Britt says, heaving them onto the corners of the tables, which they have set up in the shape of a horseshoe.

Julia wraps her arms around both women and replies, "Thank you so much for doing this."

"Of course!" Elin says. "Maria, Poppy, and River are almost here with all the baked goods. Poppy and River have been going nonstop since sunrise. They know you haven't felt perfect this week, and with the finals of the baking competition tomorrow, they wanted this to be a stress-free event for you."

"I have the best team. When Poppy, River, and Maria arrive, I have something important to tell all of you," Julia says.

Elin gets my attention and widens her eyes before glancing at Julia's stomach. I shake my head and press my lips together. I mouth, "Later." She smirks as she arranges the fall leaf décor around the crates.

"Are any of you running the 5 km race with me? It's a large loop around area." I ask, attempting to change the topic in case anyone saw Elin's knowing look. Everyone's gaze darts around as they divert their eyes. Not even Julia looks at me. I know she hates running. I grin and whisper in her ear, "I'll carry you the entire way."

Tipping her head back, she laughs. "No, I think I will stay here and help my team. Prop my feet up for a little bit. After the race, come pick me up, and we can walk around together and check out the other booths."

Pressing a kiss to her soft lips, I turn to leave but see River, Maria, and Poppy striding this way, hands laden with trays of baked goods. I rush over and take a few things from Maria and Poppy, who thank me profusely. When we arrive at the tent, Julia claps her hands.

"Team Hop Along, I can't begin to thank you enough for helping me in our first appearance at the Apple Harvest Festival. Your being here means more than you can imagine. I have two announcements I'd like to make. First, I'll hire an additional baker for Wednesday through Sunday because of our success this month. I'm also looking for two more people to work the front. If you have any friends or family members you think would be a good fit, please give them my number so I can meet with them." Julia is smiling so big that I can feel the happiness radiating off her. I step in closer so I can rest my palm at the base of her spine. She leans into my touch as she gazes up at me. "The second announcement is I won't leave at the ninety-day mark. Hop Along Bakery is officially off the market. I hope you all are in it for the long haul with me because I can't imagine a better team to work with each day."

Claps and whistles fill the air as each team member hugs her. I can feel the smile tugging my cheeks. My face will be sore from smiling so much. I can't remember the last time I was this happy. I kiss her lips and murmur, "Good job, blossom. I'm beyond proud of you. Your team loves you and Hop Along Bakery is the best thing to happen to Topaz Falls. I'm going to head over to the race, okay?"

She nods, giving me one last hug. Winking, I jog toward the barn, where I saw Tucker and Emma setting up for the race. Since Tucker is the personal trainer at Lachlan's therapy ranch, he offered to host the race this year. He even ordered participation medals with an apple pie. The entry t-shirt says, "Why did the apple need a trainer" on the front and "To work on their core" on the back.

"Hey, Dec," Tucker says, throwing me a t-shirt. "Put this on. The race will start in fifteen minutes. Emma and Amelia are going to stand at the finish line and hand out the medals. I brought an air horn to start the race. People are starting to line up. Why don't you go find the rest of the gang?"

While pulling the t-shirt over my head, I walk blindly toward the runners lining up near the balloon arch. "Lachlan, are you and Aislinn going to win it two years in a row?"

Aislinn jumps up and down, pretending to bob and weave around me. "You know it, brother," Lachlan says, chuckling. Shaking his head, he whispers, "The new girl at the coffee shop accidentally gave Aislinn caffeine. She's going to speed out of here like the Road Runner. I think I'll have to sprint to catch her this year."

"Now I understand why she never drinks caffeine," I reply as Aislinn animatedly talks to Paisley and Daniella. "Why does Daniella look like she's going to be sick?"

Lachlan laughs. "She hates running. Remember last year?" I shake my head with no memory of Daniella even running it last year. "The knitting ladies passed her at the two-mile mark. When Aislinn and I finished, we backtracked and walked the rest of the way with her. Oliver said they've been working on her stamina over the summer, so she's excited but still nervous."

Axel does a double eyebrow raise as a smile tips the corners of his mouth. Clapping Lachlan on the back he says, "This year, I'm in the race. Aislinn better watch her back because I'm gunning for her title." With a wink, he shadowboxes Aislinn, who I'm afraid might crash before the race even begins. Tucker better blow the horn early. I bet she passes out under a table within the hour.

"Good morning, everyone!" Tucker announces with a megaphone. "Thank you for attending the Ambarsan Apple Orchard's 2nd Annual 5 km race. We have seventy-five participants this year, give or take. I have a feeling a few only registered for the awesome t-shirt, but to get the medal, you have to cross the finish line. Without further ado, on your marks, get set." The air horn blows, and we all take off.

Axel and Aislinn take off like racehorses out of the starting gate. Lachlan groans beside me before he picks up his pace and races after them. I sidle up beside Oliver and Daniella, but he is clearly coaching her, and I don't want to disturb them. My mind wanders, and before I know it, the finish line is in sight, and my muscles are starting to pleasantly burn. A squeal comes from behind me, and when I glance back, I find Oliver has Daniella hoisted over his shoulder in a fireman's hold. I run beside him and grin. "Are you doing this for your finishing photo or is Daniella injured?"

"Definitely the photo. I need to add it to the collage. It's better than any medal," Oliver says with a sly smile.

Daniella grumbles. "One of these days, I'm going to be such a great runner that you'll struggle to catch me."

"I like your optimism, honey," Oliver replies as we cross the finish line together.

Little Amelia runs up to me. While catching my breath, I squat down so she can loop the medal around my neck. "Good job, Uncle Declan. You did great. Uncle Lachlan beat you, though. He told me to remind you."

"I won, and you know it," Aislinn teases Axel off to the side as she sips from a bottle of water.

"You wish, sweetheart," Axel replies, grabbing her water bottle and squirting some into his open mouth.

"It doesn't count when you physically lift me and carry us backward over the finish line, so your ass crosses first!" Aislinn shouts through laughter.

"A win's a win," he replies. "Looks like I'm the one to beat next year."

"Oh, you're going down, even if I have to pay Declan and Lachlan to hold you back," Aislinn teases.

"I'll do it for free, hurricane," Lachlan says, bending down to claim her mouth before she can make any more harmless threats.

"Axel, are you going to bob for apples?" I ask, stepping up beside him.

"Hell, yeah. Let's head over there. It will feel refreshing," he says, clapping me on the shoulder.

"I'll meet you over there. I told Julia I would come get her after the race." I reply as I walk backward away from him.

I run to Julia's booth and see a long line waiting for her baked goods. "Do you want to walk around for a bit?"

She grins and grabs my hand. "You guys, I'll be back in thirty minutes, okay?" I nod and wave, so Julia takes off, pulling me behind her.

We arrive at the apple bobbing booth just as Cameron is tying Axel's hands behind his back. "Alright, the goal is to get an apple in your mouth and pull it out."

"Easy," Axel scoffs as he widens his stance. The moment his head touches the water, Callum and Trent race up and shove him into the water up to his shoulders. "What the hell?" he splutters, wildly shaking the water out of his hair and eyes.

Callum and Trent high-five. "Paybacks as sweet as revenge, Axel. That's what you get for yanking us into the river during Lachlan's brodal shower!"

Tipping his head back, he laughs. "Seriously? Okay, classic. Are we even, or does this mean war?"

Callum shouts, "War!"

At the same time, Trent holds his hands up in surrender and backs away, saying, "We're even."

Ignoring Trent, Axel looks at Callum and says, "You're on, my man. Now, I need to win." He dives back into the barrel and within seconds comes out with two apples. The whistle blows as he drops the second apple in the bucket. If Trent and Callum hadn't sabotaged his attempt, he could have retrieved five.

We watch a few more people attempt to get an apple, but only half are successful in the one-minute time allotment.

"Can we watch the pumpkin carving?" Julia asks. I guide her in the direction Callum and Axel are walking.

Callum and Ingrid are seated beside Oliver and Daniella when we get to the booth.

"Oh, seriously?" Oliver asks. "Callum carves wood. We don't stand a chance. Remember how terrible my Bigfoot carving came out?"

Daniella pats his forearm. "Oliver, you have me as a partner this time, not your brothers." Leaning over, she asks Ingrid, "What are you two planning to carve?"

My sister smiles at Callum and says, "I asked him to carve our dogs' faces, Missy and Nicholas." She leans into his shoulder, and he kisses the top of her head.

"Yeah, Oliver. We can't compete with them. How about we do a happy face?" Daniella asks.

"This is a jack-o-lantern, honey," Oliver says confused. "Shouldn't we do a scary face?"

She shrugs. "I'd rather have a happy face for when the kids come to trick-or-treat at our house."

"You got it," he murmurs, kissing her cheek.

"Am I too late?" Axel asks, running up with a tool belt on, his upper body still drenched in water.

"No," Mira states, handing him a large pumpkin. He sits beside Callum and pulls out an electric drill with about five drill bits in different sizes and shapes.

"Phew. I had to run back to my truck to towel off and grab my drill for carving. I'll have this baby gutted and carved in under five minutes," Axel says, lining up his supplies on the crate beside his pumpkin.

"Man, it isn't a race," Callum says.

"Of course it is," Axel scoffs. "I know I'm shit at art, so I know I won't win for the prettiest pumpkin. I'm going for speed, man."

Mira calls, "Alright, everyone. Two hours are on the clock. Ready, set, carve!"

I watch enthralled, but it's like watching a car crash as Axel pulls out his large hunting knife and cuts an eight-inch circle around the stem. He has his pumpkin cleaned out in under a minute with a half-inch spade drill bit. Next, he positions a two-inch Forstner drill bit against the outside of his pumpkin and drills two perfect holes for eyes. With a traditional Brad-Point, he carves out a toothy smile and nose. The moment his final piece is cut, he lays his drill down and raises his hands in the air. "Done!" he shouts.

When he looks around, Oliver and Callum are still scraping the insides out of their pumpkins. "Three minutes and twenty-eight seconds," Mira says in disbelief.

Axel sits back in his chair and props his feet on his crate. "And that, gentlemen, is how it's done."

Julia chuckles beside me as I shake my head, but I can't hide the smile as Axel grins with pride. "Where are Paisley and Trent?" Axel asks. "I figured this is something Paisley would have done. She and I could have had a drill carving competition."

Julia points toward Mama M's tent. "Trent and Paisley are at Mama M's getting chili with Trent's family. They all surprised him and flew in yesterday. Even his sister came for the weekend from college."

"Come on," I say to Julia. "Should we go get some kettle corn?"

"What's kettle corn?" Julia asks, narrowing her eyes.

"It's like caramel corn, kind of," I reply. "Here, I'll show you!"

I'll show her anything and everything this world has to offer.

Chapter 43

Julia
Sunday, October 27

My nerves begin to settle as the judges enter the tent. I almost forgot to be nervous today after yesterday's fun and exciting day at the Apple Harvest Festival. Hop Along Bakery had a successful day of sales, selling out of everything by 2 p.m. River offered to go back and bake more, but I could tell by the strain across his shoulders that, like me, he was dead tired. I knew he and Poppy would return to bake more for today at dawn. Luckily, we closed the bakery, so we aren't trying to run both locations. It will be another day of all hands on deck, and I feel terrible that I'm in the baking tent for a few hours and unable to help.

A hush falls over the tent, and I realize I wasn't paying attention. Blinking, I look around and find everyone focused on the judges and host. Even Declan is paying attention but is incredibly distracting in his hunter-green flannel shirt and snug-fitting denim. I bite my lip as my eyes traverse the muscles rippling under his sleeves as he slowly rolls them up, revealing his corded forearms.

Declan's gaze darts to mine, and he narrows his eyes before motioning to the front of the tent. I am insanely distracted, and I don't know how to refocus on the tasks at hand. When I take a deep breath, noises rush in, and I realize the host is mid-sentence. "The breakfast round will consist of apples, but you need to create two different toppings. Ready, set, cook!"

My eyes widen. Whipping my head to Declan, I gasp. "What did I miss?"

He looks confused. "Nothing. You were here with me the whole time." He glances around behind him like he's afraid I'll do a vanishing act. "Weren't you?"

I eye him suspiciously as my gaze lands on his exposed forearms, and my mouth goes dry again. "I was distracted," I say as I slowly drag my gaze to his face.

Smirking, he pulls me in and kisses the tip of my nose. "And now we're losing time. They said we needed to make two dozen breakfast pastries with two different toppings. I vote for donuts."

Right. This is a timed competition. "How much time are they giving us?"

Looking at the front of the room, where a giant clock sits counting down the time, he murmurs, "Forty-two minutes."

I frantically look around. "We can make donuts. There isn't a deep fryer, but we can do baked donuts. Mom made them all the time at home."

Holding up his fingers, he ticks off two and says, "Maple frosting for one topping and cinnamon with sugar for the other."

Smiling, I rush around, grabbing the ingredients we'll need. At our station, I grab Declan's hands and say, "Peel two apples and grate them. I'll work on the batter."

Declan rushes over to the barrel of apples, and I see he's coming past the shelves of baking pans. "Dec, grab a few donut pans on the middle shelf."

I begin throwing ingredients in the mixing bowl, eyeballing the measurements because my moment of distraction left me severely behind on time. 'Don't think, just bake' is my motto. As I whisk together the dry ingredients, my mind quickly runs through the wet ingredients I need, and I fly around the kitchen as if I have wings guiding me. On autopilot, I mix the batter to a perfect consistency and quickly prep a piping bag. With a stick of butter, I grease the pans, and then I notice the mound of grated apples on the cutting board in front of Declan. I quickly fold the apple in and close my eyes, thankful we didn't forget the key ingredient. I would've felt like an idiot.

While the donuts bake, I task Declan with measuring the sugar and cinnamon on a deep plate. I decide to make the maple frosting. I wish I had an old-fashioned donut to dip in and try it out.

Declan and I set the last of our donuts on their respective trays as the timer dings, notifying the round is over.

When the judges come over, they look at us in confusion, glancing along our workspace. A chill courses through my veins as I realize we got something wrong, but I have no idea what it is.

Pauline Denning steps up, and I square my shoulders. "What do we have here, Declan and Julia?"

Pressing my lips together, I try to compose myself. "We've made two dozen apple donuts with two different toppings. One is sugar and cinnamon, and the other is maple frosting."

I look at them nervously as they take tentative bites. Jeff speaks first. "The flavor is good, but I think if you'd added apple cider, the flavor would've popped more. Also, I know we don't have a deep fryer in the tent, but I am not a fan of a baked donut. They are too doughy for my taste. The texture reminds me of a cake donut, and I prefer yeast donuts."

Renea smiles tightly. "I have the same criticism. I'm glad to see you finished your bake, but I think you misunderstood the instructions. When Brian introduced today's event, he said the goal was to share with all the viewers watching this event from behind the rope. We'd asked each team to bake two dozen of each topping for a total of four dozen. Unfortunately, you gave us only a dozen of each flavor. The maple frosting is good, though."

"Damn it," Declan grumbles under his breath as he lowers down on his haunches and grips the back of his neck.

I kneel down behind him as my face flames with embarrassment. "It's okay, Dec. I'm sorry I didn't pay attention. I promise I'll focus. We can still win the second and third rounds. The prize money will be ours."

"Blossom, it's never been about the money for me. I just want to be by your side and make you proud of me. Instead, I've humiliated us." Declan groans, and he lowers his head to his knees.

"You could never embarrass me, Dec," I reply, my heart aching for him. "I'm proud of you for being here and partaking in something you aren't passionate about just so I can." Wrapping my arms around his shoulders, I press a kiss to his neck and breathe in his woodsy scent. "We've got this. I don't care about the money. I care about you. I love you, Dec."

"I love you, too, blossom," he says, his eyes boring into me. "Let's do this!"

Standing, he extends his hand to me and pulls me to my feet.

Brian stands beside the three judges, rubbing his hands together. With a big smile, he says, "Next up is lunch items. Renea, what is your request?"

"Thanks, Brian. Hi, teams. The first round was rough for all three teams, but for very different reasons. For this round, we want you to make a lunch item where the apples are within a wrap of some kind. We look forward to seeing what you come up with," she says with a warm smile. I raise my hand, and she raises her eyebrows in surprise. "Yes, Julia. What's your question, dear?"

Clearing my throat, I ask, "How many would you like us to make for this round."

With a knowing look, she replies, "Four." With a wink, she says, "Ready, set, cook!"

I twirl around. "Crepes. I'm French. This is the perfect round to make crepes!" Gripping his forearms, I jump up and down, and his eyes soften as he watches me explode with excitement. "Your job is to slice and soften apples with a bit of butter and half a diced sweet onion."

"Right, a sweet onion. I didn't realize there were different types of onion other than yellow and purple," Declan whispers.

"Grab the yellow one," I say, pointing to the basket against the back of the tent. "Pick the one next to the cucumbers."

Nodding, he sets off on his mission. I head to the cooking shelves and find the round flat-top griddle, a wooden spreader, and a spatula. I quickly whip together the batter. When the griddle snaps the water droplets I flick at it, I begin pouring and spreading the batter into large circles. The crepes come off hot and perfectly golden. I line them up on individual plates and place a slice of provolone on each one, slices of thick carved turkey, and sliced golden tomatoes. With a drizzle of poppyseed dressing, I add the apples and onions Declan finished softening, then close them up into a burrito.

The timer dings, and Declan steps up behind me and rubs my shoulders. "Are you feeling okay? You don't need to sit down or rest, do you? Do you need water?"

I shake my head but lean into his touch. "I'm okay."

When the judges get to our station, they each take a bite of their crepe. With a tight smile, Pauline says, "This is delicious, but we were watching each of the three teams closely, and unlike last week, the duties weren't evenly split this round. Julia, you did about seventy-five percent of the work. Remember you work as a team. Make sure Declan does more than simply chop apples in the final round."

My shoulders slump. I completely forgot to delegate our tasks. Closing my eyes, I take a deep breath. "Declan, for the final round, I want to make French macarons. I'd like to make the cookie bases apple-flavored with caramel filling. Do you feel confident enough to create the filling if I write down the instructions?"

"Yeah," he rasps. "You can count on me. I promise to ask if I get stuck."

"For the dessert round, we are going to do four dozen of whatever dessert you choose to make. Obviously, it needs to have apples, but I also want to see caramel in this flavor profile," Jeff says. "After we do the final judging, the treats will be passed around to everyone watching."

"Ready, set, cook!" Brian shouts, and the timer begins counting down the ninety minutes of the allotted time.

Cheers from the crowd on our side of the tent catch my attention. When I look up, I nudge Declan. "Look, all our friends are in the crowd."

Declan blushes when he sees his brother and sister cheering for him alongside every person I've come to know over the last month. Britt's blonde curls bounce with each jump as she tugs on Axel's arm.

"Time to impress our friends. Let's show 'em what we're made of, blossom!" Declan says, tugging gently on my braid.

Declan follows my instructions. Once the filling is ready to pipe, I fill the center, and Declan gently puts the tops on each one. When the timer goes off, we have forty-eight gorgeous macarons. I'm proud of our final product, and I leap into Declan's waiting arms with excitement. The competition is over, and now the cards will fall where they will. We either win or we don't, but at least we have each other and more friends than I ever imagined calling mine. I've discovered one of my favorite parts of being a small-town bakery owner is knowing every patron. The anonymity of a patisserie in Paris no longer sounds enjoyable. I love knowing everyone when they walk through the door.

"These are fabulous," Renea says. "I was pleased to see you evenly split the tasks, and the final product is wonderful."

Callum whistles loudly, and I can't help but laugh. "Home Team! Home Team!" They all cheer, and my cheeks warm from their attention.

"Well, we had a fabulous day of baking. Unfortunately, there is only one winner. Lucille and Terri, you both worked hard and created an apple croquembouche with caramel threads. I've never seen this flavor combination with pate a choux dough. I'm extremely impressed. You were also the only team who didn't stumble in any round. It's with great pleasure that we award you as the winner of the Great Harvest Bake-Off," Pauline announces. I can't help but be happy for everyone who participated today.

Hugging Declan, I look up into his eyes, and he says, "I don't care who won this competition because I already won your heart and now I've won a future by your side."

"Dec, please tell me that line didn't come from an inspirational greeting card." I grin.

He presses his lips to mine and whispers, "Did it work?"

"Yeah, it did. You won my heart eight years ago, and it will continue to be yours for the rest of our lives," I murmur.

"That's what I like to hear," Declan whispers against my mouth. "Ready to try the apple slingshot and party with our friends and family?"

"As long as we are together, I'll try anything," I reply, intertwining our fingers as he pulls us toward the group cheering for us.

I'm thankful I returned to Topaz Falls and glad the town welcomed me back. Aunt Rita must be looking down on me with a huge smile on her face to see I had the courage to stay.

Epilogue

Elin

Thursday, December 19

I hate him. I hate him. I hate him. At least there's no way for him to mess with my job, my mom, and my non-existent love life. Those are the only consistencies in my life. I glare across the room, at the source of all my problems. Anders Tollefson may look like a demi-god, but he's more like a golden demon.

I lower my gaze as I think of all the strife he's brought into my life. Over eighteen years of conflict have led to a week from hell. I pick at the threads of the rough textured blanket draped over my lap as I lie on the emergency room hospital bed in Whitefish, Montana. My left arm currently rests in a cast at a ninety-degree angle. The doctor said my X-rays showed a fractured ulna near the elbow. The nurse kindly placed a red and green striped cast on my arm, perfectly timed for Christmas. Awesome. Just what every thirty-six-year-old hopes for at Christmas.

My mind runs through the events that led me here, like fuzzy still frames. The pain meds are already kicking in and I find my concentration struggling to keep up. A pipe burst in my apartment, flooding it and making it unlivable. I safely made it out of my apartment and down the stairs, only to slip on the ice-covered parking lot. Anders drove up a minute later to salt said parking lot, only to find me sprawled on the frozen asphalt and moaning in agony. If he'd de-iced it when I texted him on my way to work, this wouldn't have been an issue. Does he listen to me? Never. Due to the holidays, the soonest my apartment can be fixed and cleaned up is after New Year's. My jerk of a landlord informed me I needed to find another place to live for the next two weeks.

Over the holidays, you'd think this would be an easy task, but with my luck it won't. I already know I can't lean on my best friend Julia because she is flying home to Paris with her fiancé, Declan. I'm the only person in Topaz Falls who knows she has a bun in the oven, and it isn't the kind in her commercial kitchen. She told me they wanted to announce it to her parents in person, so I've kept my lips sealed. Luckily, her pregnancy is finally going smoothly. All the tests have been run, and it looks like a healthy baby will be here in the summer. Now that her first trimester is almost over, they want to announce on Christmas morning that they are expecting. It's been harder than I imagined keeping this kind of a secret from the rest of this small town.

Shaking my head, I try to focus. The doctor said I shouldn't be alone for the first week, as the pain meds will make me drowsy, and I might need help showering, dressing, or basically anything else that requires the use of my dominant hand. It's days like today when I wish I was ambidextrous. Based on the fact I can barely cut food with my right hand; I don't believe my wish will be granted.

"Elin, you need to make some calls so I know where to leave you once you're discharged," Anders, my landlord from hell, says from the shadowed corner of the room.

"Shut up," I growl, causing his gaze to darken. My head is pounding from the stress threatening to consume me.

It wasn't enough for him to raise my rent at the beginning of the year. Like money bucks over there needs the extra cash. He owns half the darn town but seems determined to squeeze every cent out of this little veterinary assistant. It was already a stretch for me to pay rent on top of all my mom's bills, but it's going up two hundred dollars a month. That's more than a week's worth of groceries for me. I can only hope the veterinary clinic where I work will give us a Christmas bonus and I'll get a raise. I highly doubt I will since this is a small-town clinic, but I can stay positive. If I had to guess, he wants to run me out of town. I'll search the area to see if I can find a cheaper place to rent.

Unlocking my phone takes about three tries because my fingers are too swollen on my left hand, and I can't draw a straight line with my right hand to save my life.

Holding out my phone, I grind through clenched teeth, "Can you please help me?"

Anders stalks over, and his jaw flexes as he stares at me. "What?" It doesn't sound compassionate; it sounds like barely contained hostility.

I bristle. "Can you draw a zigzag from top to bottom, right to left? It isn't accepting my face."

He arches a brow but quietly complies. The screen unlocks, and he turns without another word, retreating to his corner.

Dialing Aislinn, I know the answer before we speak, but I still need to ask. The phone rings twice before Aislinn's rushed voice fills the line. "Elin, how are you?"

"I've been better. I was wondering what day you and Lachlan flew out for your cruise?" I ask, tugging on a frayed string as I gently wrap it around my knuckle.

"Ingrid, Callum, Lachlan, and I are meeting their parents and my brothers at the airport in two hours. Did you need something before we leave?" she asks, and my heart melts at her kindness. I refuse to be jealous that she and her husband will be on a cruise in the Caribbean in twenty-four hours, while I look like an elf wrapped me in crepe paper.

"No, I was in a small accident, but I'm going to try Britt. Have a great time," I say and hang up before she can question me further.

I dial Britt before Aislinn can call me back, and the phone rings once before Britt answers. "Hey, Elin! Do you want to meet for drinks before I leave for Whistler?"

I wrinkle my nose. How did I forget she was leaving for Whistler tomorrow? The pain meds they gave me are doing a number on my brain. I feel like I'm treading through a thick fog.

"No, I just wanted to tell you to have a great time," I say wistfully as I glare at my candy cane vibing cast with the red and green swirling around my arm.

"Thanks, girl. Tell your mom I say hello and give her a hug for me when you see her on Sunday," Britt says, hanging up after I promise her I will. Damn, I forgot I have to drive down to my mom's place on Sunday. I need my mind to clear up. I can understand why they suggest you have someone to help you when on these meds.

I thump my head against my pillow, frustrated at my predicament. Next, I dial Oliver and Daniella. They were quiet at work this week, so I don't remember what their plans are for the holidays.

"Hello?" Daniella's soft voice says. "Elin? How are you?"

"Hey, Daniella. I was wondering if you and Oliver had any plans this weekend?" I keep my tone casual because Daniella is the type who will go out of her way to accommodate me, and the last thing I want to be is a burden to her.

"Oliver and I are going to go skiing in Vale for the holidays. Our families are meeting us there, so we will be back on January 2nd. I hope you have a great Christmas. Sorry, we can't meet up tonight. It would've been fun to get drinks at Glaciers or something."

"Right, well, have a great time," I say, trying to hide my frustration.

Next on my list is Paisley. "Hello?" Paisley's bright voice makes me smile even though I'm fighting back tears.

"Pais? Are you and Trent going to be home this week?" I ask nonchalantly.

"No," she says. "Did you need something? We're going to spend Christmas with Trent's family this year. My parents are going to meet us in Colorado. Then, for New Year's, we're going to go see his grandparents in North Dakota."

"I hope you all have fun." I hang up the moment she says bye before I can hear more platitudes.

I know Frida is going to be with her grandparents as her grandfather recently had knee replacement surgery. I stare at my phone, thinking of who else I could call. All my coworkers are out of town, and my other friends are busy with their families. Sighing, I wish I had a normal family to fall back on, but that isn't the case for me. I barely can remember when it was.

Anders shifts his position, leaning against the wall, and I glare at him, daring him to say something. After a moment, he says nothing, so I pull up Axel's phone number. He is my last chance.

"Axel? Oh, thank goodness you answered. I'm at my wit's end." I let out an exasperated sigh as Anders stands with his hands stuffed in his expensive pant pockets at the end of my hospital bed, slowly inching out of the shadows like some creature straight from hell. A blonde Lucifer hiding in plain sight.

"Elin? What happened? Are you okay?" The concern in his voice is sweet. He's always unflappable.

"Actually, I was wondering if you'd be willing to have a gimp for a roommate through the new year." I say in a voice so small that I'm not sure he can even properly hear me.

"Two things to unpack there. Gimp and roommate. What do you need sweet cheeks?" he asks, and a small growl comes from Anders as he turns and sits in a chair on the far side of the room, returning to his shadowed existence. Now I can go back to pretending he doesn't exist.

"Well, my apartment flooded, I slipped and broke my arm, and the earliest I can get back into my apartment is sometime in January. I've literally tried everyone I know. The Ambarsans and Hewsons are all going on a cruise. Trent and Paisley are visiting family between Colorado and North Dakota. Frida is going to see her grandparents. Daniella and Oliver are going skiing in Vale. Britt is going to Whistler. I am literally out of options." Tossing my head back into the pillow, I groan.

"Are you telling me I was plan Z?" he asks. That's what he got out of this conversation?

"More like X?" My voice wobbles as I fight back tears.

"Yeah, for the extremely awesome plan," he chides, and I bite back a watery smile.

"More along the lines of extreme measures," I mutter.

He barks out a laugh and then sobers. "I'd love to help, but I'm going to Vegas with some of the guys. You are welcome to join us? I don't mind sharing a bed." I know he just winked, even though I can't see his smug face.

"You can stay at my place," Anders grinds out in such a low growl it makes my eyes widen. Like hell, I will. That would be like living with Hades in disguise. I'd be an idiot to cross into enemy territory.

Narrowing my eyes at Anders, I ask Axel, "When do you fly out?"

"Uh, well, that's the downside to this fun plan. We're at the airport. Our flight leaves in about an hour. If you get a plane ticket, you're more than welcome to fly down."

Anders marches over and yanks the phone from my grasp and puts it on speakerphone. "I'll take care of the problem," he says in a loathing tone.

I look down at the ugly cast I'm outfitted with and wish I was standing so I could stomp my feet. My eyes cut to Anders, whose steely gaze is boring into me. "Well Axel, it appears Anders just offered me a place to stay at his house."

"Alright, if you're sure. The offer still stands. If you get bored, you can always fly down. We got king-sized beds," Axel says a little louder than necessary, causing me to lean away from the phone and wince.

"Well, alrighty then. You two have a good Christmas. See you in ten days!" Axel clicks off before Anders can reply. For a few moments, Anders grumbles under his breath then tosses my phone to the end of my bed. Just out of my reach. Jerk. He storms out of my room, and as the door slams, I'm left in blissful silence, wondering what the hell I'm going to do and, more importantly, how I'm going to see Mom each Sunday. I can't miss our scheduled time. It would devastate us both, especially around the holidays.

When Anders returns half an hour later, it takes all my strength not to say, "I hate you." Those are the words I've uttered in my head for as long as I can remember. I've hated Anders Tollefson for almost two decades, and now I'll need to rely on him to survive the next two weeks.

Hey, Santa? Please don't let us kill each other before the year ends. My mom needs me too much.

Declan's Apple Pizza

Ingredients (12-14 inch pizza):
Dough –
1.5 cups of warm water to activate yeast
2 tsp of quick rise yeast
1 Tbsp of sugar
3-3.5 cups of flour
3 Tbsp of olive oil
1 tsp of garlic salt

Toppings –
1 green apple, thinly sliced and cored
1 Tbsp of brown sugar
4-6 oz of fresh mozzarella, thinly sliced
.5 lbs bacon, cooked and chopped
½ red onion, thinly sliced
Dried oregano to taste
.5 cup of crumbled goat cheese
1 cup of baby spinach, washed and dried
Balsamic glaze
1 Tbsp of olive oil to brush on crust

Directions:

1. In a bowl add warm water, yeast, and sugar. Stir and let sit for approximately five minutes until a nice froth forms on the top.
2. Preheat oven to 450 degrees F.
3. In a mixer, add activated yeast mixture, olive oil, and garlic salt.
4. Once incorporated, slowly add flour until a dough ball forms and dough is no longer sticking to the sides.
5. Cover and let rest while you cook the bacon.

6. In a pan over medium heat, cut the bacon into one inch chunks and cook until brown.
7. Remove bacon to cool.
8. In the pan, add onions, apples, and brown sugar. Cook over low heat until softened.
9. On an olive oil coated pan, press dough into pizza shape.
10. Drizzle with olive oil then add mozzarella cheese, apple, onion, and bacon.
11. Cook for ten to fifteen minutes until crust is golden brown.
12. While pizza is resting, top with goat cheese and baby spinach.
13. Drizzle balsamic glaze.
14. Cut and serve warm.

Julia's Apple Grilled Cheese

Ingredients (1 serving):

3 slices of thin bacon

¼ sweet onion, sliced

2 slices of French bread

2 slices of smoked gouda cheese

½ green apple, sliced and cored

½ tomato, sliced

1 tsp of mustard

Butter for outside of bread.

Directions:

1. Cook bacon in strips over medium heat.
2. Once cooked, remove from heat and add onion and apple. Cook until softened.
3. Preheat griddle, panini press, or pan.
4. To build the sandwich, begin by buttering the outside of one slice.
5. Place cheese, bacon, apples, onions, and tomato on top of the first slice.
6. Butter the outside of the second slice and put mustard on the inside, facing the tomato.
7. Place sandwich on griddle or panini press.
8. Cook until golden.
9. Remove and eat.

Acknowledgments

Thank you for reading the fifth book in the Topaz Falls series. I truly appreciate each reader who has taken a chance on this small, indie author. I had so much fun writing Declan and Julia's second chance romance. Books one through four contained main characters we'd met in previous books, but this book was fun to write because we'd never met Julia before. There were hints of her existence, but nothing more. The translocation and childhood cancer Julia battled when she was seven was written on behalf of my youngest child. She ended her two and a half years of treatment on August 31st of this year, which was the same week I finished this book.

As always, many of the scenes that happened in this book have happened to me or were brainstormed with my kids. Their favorite character is Axel, so he makes a lot of appearances in this book. They hope I will skip the next three books in the series and just write Axel's book, but I'm saving the best for last, I hope.

Thank you to L.A.A., my line editor, Paige Kraft, my copy editor, and T.J.A., my proofreader, for helping me polish this book and get it ready for the public to read. I appreciate my ARC readers who took the time to read this book before it was released to the public and give me positive encouragement. One of the hardest parts of writing is marketing, so this book wouldn't be as widely spread without the help of my ARC readers and Instagram followers. I appreciate every like, share, and comment. It makes my day when I get to read a review or see how my book positively moved someone.

If you and your significant other do the drawing challenge, please tag me or let me know how it went. I'm dying to try this with my husband, because the videos I've seen on social media are hilarious. This seemed like the perfect activity for Declan and Julia, mainly because I wanted to live vicariously through them.

I hope you will continue to join me on this writing adventure. Topaz Falls has four more planned books. When I finish Axel's book, I may continue because there are so many characters I'd like to offer a happy ending. I have a lot more ideas running through my mind, and it will be hard to choose. I promised my sister I wouldn't take a writing detour or get distracted until Axel's book was finished, so I hope you'll stick with me. As always, if there is a character you think deserves their own book, please let me know! I am always open to suggestions.

Thank you again for reading Counting On Forever!

About the Author

I am from the Pacific Northwest, where my family loves to have our own adventures. My youngest child has been undergoing chemotherapy since May, 2022. To help distract her during appointments I would tell her stories of an imaginary town called Topaz Falls. We would brainstorm the names of people and farm animals. Topaz Falls started as an imaginative brainstorming session with my kids, as a means to distract and bring smiles during stressful appointments. Since then, it has turned into an entire series. My kids loved my stories so much, they challenged me to turn them into adult novels. Now, I feel it needs to be told. I hope you will join me and meet the characters who have worked their way into my soul. If I don't have my nose in a story, then I'm busy creating art. My favorite genre is any form of fiction. I strongly believes that reading books and collecting books are two different hobbies.

Topaz Falls Series
Publication List

Eyes Like A Hurricane (Lachlan & Aislinn)
Published February 9, 2024

Skye Full Of Stars (Callum & Ingrid)
Published April 26, 2024

A Tsunami Of Sunshine (Trent & Paisley)
Published June 28, 2024

Faking A Whirlwind (Oliver & Daniella)
Published August 23, 2024

Counting On Forever (Declan & Julia)
Published November 12, 2024

Steeping With The Enemy (Anders & Elin)
2025

Changing Their Tune (Tristan & Sylvie)
2025

To learn more about future books, please visit:
www.tarynnikolic.com

Synopsis

First is the worst.
Second is supposed to be the best.
I'm counting on this truth, as our first try ended miserably.

Julia. In the span of six months, I've lost my Paris patisserie, my fiancé, and my self-confidence. My only choice is to return to Topaz Falls, Montana and fulfill the requirements of my aunt's will. After ninety days, I can return to Paris and never look back. This year will become a bad and distant memory. One thing I didn't take into account was the tight-knit community and how often I'd run into my first love, Declan Ambarsan. I forced myself to leave him when we were eighteen. It was the hardest thing I've ever done, but it was necessary for him to have what mattered the most. I'll keep my heart locked up tight because although some people were meant to have second chances—I'm not one of them. I did what needed to be done, and I'll do it again when the ninety days are up.

Declan. Eight years ago, the only woman I've ever loved left without saying goodbye. I wear her promise ring on a chain around my neck as a reminder to never let my heart fall in love again. That is until Julia Fournier returns to my small hometown and turns my world upside down. It takes one touch, a single whispered breath, and her smile to remind me why I fell in love with her. This time around, it doesn't matter where she goes. When she leaves Topaz Falls this time, I'll be by her side. I might be the only Ambarsan sibling who wants to continue the family orchard, but my heart belongs to Julia. In my parents' absence, running the orchard and preparing for the Apple Harvest Festival falls on my shoulders. I'll try my best until my parents can return, then I'll put in my notice. This time around, I'm choosing us above all else. This is the second chance I've always wanted.